M000276478

"*Answering Liberty's Call* proves the American Revolution wasn't a 'men only' war. Anna, the protagonist in this great read, is a fictionalized character, but she exemplifies many of the real, courageous women to whom we owe a debt of gratitude—right alongside our male Founders. This is a superbly written book you'll find hard to put down."
— LtCol Oliver L. North USMC (Ret), best-selling author
   of *The Rifleman* and host of the *Real American Heroes* podcast

"Tracy Lawson's newest book, *Answering Liberty's Call: Anna Stone's Daring Ride to Valley Forge*, is a powerful story of a woman's bravery on an anguishing journey, racing by horseback to bring vital supplies to her husband and brothers who were facing extreme hunger and disease at Valley Forge in the midst of the Revolutionary War. Anna's mission turns from rescuing her loved ones from want to protecting the nation they were fighting to create. America's history almost certainly includes many Anna Stones whose adventures and deeds were not recorded, so Lawson's book serves the dual purpose of providing truly enjoyable fast-paced entertainment as well as honoring the strong women whose roles in forming and protecting America will never be known but should nonetheless be remembered."
— Debbie Georgatos, host of *AmericaCanWeTalk*

"With Tracy Lawson's extensively researched new book in hand, readers who love historical fiction will gallop into Valley Forge on a journey through some of the lesser-known aspects of the Revolutionary War. In *Answering Liberty's Call*, we're reminded of the many pressures on Washington as he molded state units into the United States Army and defeated the world's most powerful military force. And as readers will discover, it could have turned out very differently had some disgruntled officers had their way."
— Lee Wright, founder, History Camp and The Pursuit of History

"A riveting portrait of a young woman risking her life for family and country, this historical novel by Tracy Lawson takes us on the adventure of a fiercely independent patriot devoted to freedom. *Liberty* defines the heroine of this book, both in her role as a disguised messenger galloping toward Valley Forge and General Washington and in her equal partnership with her husband, a soldier in the Third Virginia. *Answering Liberty's Call* captures the spirit of the young nation, while taking the time to carefully detail the materials and habits of family life as it meets the realities of the battlefield: from the loving letters between husband and wife, to field hospital nurses struggling to treat pox, to the value in a simple package of salt. The heroine's determination and grit give this novel a voice of ambition at once unique to her and wholly American."

— Jill Phillips Ingram, associate professor,
Department of English, Ohio University

"The beautiful landscape of Revolutionary-era Fauquier County, Virginia, comes into vivid focus in *Answering Liberty's Call: Anna Stone's Daring Ride to Valley Forge.* Coupled with a fresh perspective on the challenges women faced as the colonies went to war, this novel will bring readers right into a thrilling time period for our nation with the deftness and skill of Tracy Lawson's writing. A must-read for history buffs, Virginia lovers, and fans of historical fiction."

— Sean Redmiles, executive director,
Fauquier History Museum at the Old Jail

TRACY LAWSON

Answering Liberty's Call

Anna Stone's Daring Ride to Valley Forge

BOOKS

Columbus OH • Dallas TX
graylionbooks.com

ISBN 978-1-735428-51-2 (paperback)
ISBN 978-1-647045-19-7 (ebook)

Copyright © 2022 by Tracy Lawson

All rights reserved.

Reproduction or translation of any part of this work, except for short excerpts used for reviews, without the written permission of the copyright owner is unlawful. Requests for permission to reproduce parts of this work, or for additional information, should be addressed to the publisher.

This book is a work of fiction. Names, characters, places, and incidents are either products of the author's imagination or are used fictitiously. Any resemblance to actual events or locales or persons, living or dead, is entirely coincidental other than those in historical records.

All Scripture quoted herein is from (KJV) King James Version in the public domain.

Available for wholesale and bulk purchase via Ingram.

Author photo by Owen Jones
Interior layout by LParnell Book Services
Cover models: Michaela Lukowich and Scout
Cover photo by Brad Barton
Cover design by EbookLaunch.com

Manufactured in the United States of America

Contents

VALLEY FORGE

1

None of a Woman's Business

The man following me on this lonely road is nowhere in sight—but that doesn't mean he has given up. He can wait for me to ride Nelly to exhaustion and overtake us at his leisure. Though I want to gallop her, the mare is carrying a full load of provisions. She cannot do more than pick her way through the churned-up, frozen mud without the risk of coming up lame.

Despite the cold, a bead of sweat rolls down my cheek. My tortured imagination conjures the rush of oncoming hoofbeats and the swish of a quirt. As I look back, the weak winter sunset flares along the edge of the ridge and I shade my eyes as I scan the shadows to make certain we are still alone.

His mission must have sounded like a lark—for how difficult could it be to waylay a lone woman and steal the message she carries? A strangled sob escapes my lips and I clap a gloved hand to my mouth. This is no time for weakness. I've eluded him for two days and kept my wits every time my capture seemed certain. The trick I pulled to make my escape just before dawn surely raised his ire and I reckon he'll show no mercy if he overtakes me before I reach Valley Forge. I square my shoulders inside my husband's jacket and trace the outline of the letter concealed in my stays—the only feminine garment I'm wearing at the moment.

Eyes gritty with exhaustion, I stand in the stirrups and peer into the darkness ahead. Before I left home, my brother-in-law sketched a crude map to guide me from Virginia to Pennsylvania and marked this stretch with the name of an ordinary he frequented before he deserted from the Sharpshooters last month. When I come upon the Seven Stars Inn, I'll know I'm nearing the Continental Army's camp.

Nelly shies as something scuttles across the path and rustles into the brush, and I struggle to keep my seat as I rein her down. It's likely naught but a possum or raccoon, but telling myself so fails to calm my racing heart. As we carry on, I cast wary glances into shadowy clumps of trees lining the sides of the road. My pursuer may not be the only threat I encounter before I reach the picket line.

When I spot the warm glow of candlelight in a building's windows ahead, I lean forward in the saddle in anticipation, and the wooden sign out front, emblazoned with seven stars, bolsters my spirits. Nelly jerks her head toward the inn's fenced paddock as if to suggest she wouldn't mind stopping to rest and eat, but succor cannot be ours until our task is complete.

"What's a few more miles when we've already come so far? We can do it, girl!" Never one to disappoint, my weary horse minces onward. Minutes tick by and when we pass a mile marker at a crossroads, it has grown too dark to read the sign, but I remind myself it is just a few miles more. Further on, my scalp crinkles when a wolf howls somewhere in the hills to the north. Now my ears are attuned to every sound, but after that solitary cry, I discern only the creak of leather, the rasp of the rough fabric of my borrowed breeches, and the *clop clop* of Nelly's hooves.

As we round a bend in the road, pinpoints of light flit through the darkness ahead the way fireflies dot the hills at home on summer nights. Is this my destination—or an obstacle in my path?

Someone raises a light in greeting. Words in the German tongue drift from up ahead and my breath snags in my chest. Could they be Hessians? This far west? My mother tried to dissuade me from making this journey with whispered suppositions of what enemy soldiers will do to a defenseless woman. Though my first instinct is to wheel, I must complete my mission—and retreat will drive me into the clutches of the man who lurks somewhere behind me.

I settle my cocked hat more firmly on my head and turn up the coat collar. In this disguise I could be mistaken for a lad of thirteen or fourteen, instead of a twenty-nine-year-old mother of three but my voice will betray me.

Shadowy forms and a horse-drawn cart block the road. Perhaps they're a foraging detail. Hoping it's just these few, without a saddle horse to give chase, I bark, "*Was geht hier vor?*" It's the only phrase I know in their language that makes sense under the circumstances, and I wonder, just as I have asked, what goes on here.

One man responds in a rapid stream of German. Lantern light falls across his face as he comes closer, showing leathery skin and bags beneath rheumy eyes. He is unarmed, his rough coat and breeches those of a farmer, not a soldier.

Reverting to my normal voice, yet poised for flight, I call, "I beg your pardon, do you speak English?"

A boy steps up beside the old man and answers, "I do, missus."

"Please, how far to Valley Forge?"

"Near ten miles."

Every weary bone in my body seems to cry out in disappointment. I've pushed the limits of Nelly's endurance today to put thirty miles behind us and it isn't enough. "Then I must make haste. Do I stay on this road?"

"*Ja.* Bear to the right at the fork ahead."

In the flickering light, two sets of dirty, bare feet protrude from under a ragged blanket on the cart. "What's going on here?"

"There's soldiers with fever in the church up yon. I'm Jacob Hippel." He jerks his thumb toward the older man. "This is my grandfather, Lorenz. He offered land to lay the dead to rest. We're taking bodies to the icehouse until we get a thaw."

"These soldiers—where are they from?"

"Pennsylvania, mostly, but there were some from Virginia."

Dread chills my blood. "Do you know their names?"

"Sorry, missus. You could ask Herr Doctor, at the church." The boy swings his lantern toward a whitewashed log building a short distance down the road.

"My brothers are with the Third Virginia. I received word that they were ill. May I see those men's faces?" I urge Nelly up beside the cart and steel myself as Jacob relays my request and old Lorenz turns back the blanket.

My two errands, both urgent and of near equal importance to me, lead to the same destination—Valley Forge. I haven't considered what I'll do if Henry and Jeremiah are in hospital elsewhere. Jacob holds his lantern up over the wagon bed and the letter's corner presses against my bosom as I lean forward and study the slack, hairy faces. I breathe a sigh of relief. "These are not my brothers. Why is the hospital so far from the Continentals' camp?"

"There are field hospitals all over the county, in churches, barns, and houses."

My heart plummets at this news. My brothers could be languishing anywhere. "Most obliged." As I dig my heels into Nelly's ribs, the mare, caught dozing, surges forward in alarm. She carries me to the church, where, unable to suppress a groan as my feet hit the ground, I loop the reins over the handrail and hurry up the wooden steps. It's a risk to stop, but I can't take the chance of riding right past my brothers.

A tired-looking man with hair as fluffy as carded wool meets me at the door, candle in hand. "See here, boy . . ."

Removing the hat reveals my face and my long hair straggling loose from its tail.

He squints and raises his candle higher. "Beg your pardon, madam."

"Doctor, please, I've come from Virginia seeking my brothers, soldiers who have taken ill. May I see if they are among your patients?"

He gestures me into the sanctuary where rough benches, pushed against the walls, make room for two rows of men laid out on cots and pallets. In my haste, I forget to take shallow breaths, and gag as the stench of sickness, unwashed bodies, and human waste assaults my nostrils.

"If they're not here, you might try Captain Francis's barn, off Pawlings Road."

Candlelight falls on the drawn faces of the men. Their beards crawl with lice and fleas, but they're so far gone with fever they don't seem to notice. At the end of the row, I stoop to lift the blankets covering four corpses on the floor. As I start down the second row, hope surges in my chest. Perhaps my brothers have recovered since my husband posted his letter and they'll be on picket duty when I arrive at Valley Forge. My vision of a happy reunion melts when at the last cot, a young soldier clutches my coat sleeve, staring up at me with glassy eyes. "Ma?"

"Shh. Everything will be all right." As I smooth the hair off his clammy forehead, he relaxes at my touch. His skin looks waxy, bloodless.

"Don't go, Ma. Please. I'm afeared."

"Shh, shh, now. I'm here. Don't fret." In my experience, all sick children cry out for their mothers. "The Lord is my shepherd—I shall not want . . ." As I add my silent prayer that a kind woman has been there to console my brothers, Henry and Jeremiah, the young soldier closes his eyes, and a rasping breath escapes his lips. His hand falls to his side.

The doctor hovers nearby. "Was that your brother, madam?"

"No." I blink back tears.

"I fear the rest will soon follow, for I have exhausted my supply of medicines."

"I have tea in my saddlebag that brings down fever. I'll fetch some." Knowing I can help quickens my steps. My first lungful of fresh air should be a relief, but it turns into a gasp. The jingle of a horse's bit carries on the still night air and my skin prickles as intuition warns me of danger.

One of the men on the road motions toward the church with a lantern and I hear hoofbeats on the frozen ground. When the old doctor joins me, I take him into my confidence. "I'm in danger. I carry an urgent message for General Washington. The rider approaching has been trying to steal it from me since I left York."

He raises an eyebrow. "A lady spy, racketing around the countryside dressed as a boy, carrying secret dispatches and medicinal teas?"

"No sir, not a spy. A patriot. Everything I have told you is true."

"Remain inside, out of sight."

"What of my horse? And my bundles? He cannot fail to notice . . ."

"Leave it to me." He extinguishes the candle, leaving the sanctuary lit only by the glowing embers in the fireplace. As I duck inside, he hurries out and clucks to Nelly. Then there's a thud which must be the provisions, cut loose from behind my saddle and dropping to the ground. My knife slips from its sheath with a hiss as the approaching hoofbeats slow to a walk.

"Where is she?" My pursuer's voice cuts the air like the blade I hold clutched to my chest.

"You mean the woman who swapped this winded animal for mine?" Water sloshes as the doctor sets a bucket in front of Nelly, who submerges her muzzle, drinking noisily. "What's your business with her?"

"That's none of your concern. Which road did she take?"

"Doubled back to the Seven Stars. Said she'd return my horse tomorrow."

Leather creaks as my pursuer dismounts. At the thud of his heavy boot on the stairs, I shrink away from the door.

"When I called at the tavern, she was not within. That boy said she was here."

The doctor, brought up short, hems and haws before he speaks. "She must have taken the south road."

He gives a disbelieving snort. "I'll have a look inside to make sure."

There is no other door through which to escape. My eyes dart around for a place to hide.

The doctor's voice rings out. "There's sickness within. You've had the pox, sir?"

He will spot me beneath a cot, and the reeking pile of dirty laundry in the corner is too small to burrow into.

The man scoffs as he continues up the steps. "I won't be long."

The doctor tries again. "That's a nasty gash you have there. Shall I clean and stitch it up for you?"

"No. It's but a trifle."

In desperation, I grab the topmost soiled sheet, take off my hat, and lie on the floor beside the dead soldiers. The stink of disease and decay surrounds me as the sheet comes to rest against my face. Though I am immune to the pox, only God knows what other diseases afflict these men. I cannot dwell on what I may contract from this filthy covering, but I tuck my chin, so the sheet does not brush against my mouth.

No sooner am I settled than the door creaks. As I await my fate, my thoughts run first to my children. Rhoda. Elijah. William. If I die in the service of the Cause, will they ever know what became of me?

And what of my husband, Benjamin, and my brothers? Failure to deliver the message puts them—and everyone in the army—in even greater jeopardy.

The man swears and retches, and his vomit hits the floor with a splat. "You call this a hospital? It's naught but a pest house."

"I warned you." The doctor doesn't sound sorry at all.

The floorboards tremble beneath the man's tread and as he draws near. I exhale slowly and breathe through my mouth. I cannot expect the old doctor to overpower him. On my vow, an unmarked grave will not be my final resting place. Every muscle in my body tenses as I prepare to defend myself.

Candlelight glows through the threadbare sheet as he bends closer. I manage not to flinch as he pulls back the blankets on the corpses, one by one. My hand clenches the knife's handle.

The doctor's voice is gruff. "Are you an utter fool? Don't you know those blankets carry disease? Do you want to end up in the icehouse with the dead?"

The man retches again, and the candlelight grows fainter as he backs away from my hiding place. "She took the south road, did you say?"

"Yes. If you'd heeded me the first time, you'd have caught up to her by now."

"My new bride is headstrong and unused to a firm hand. In time, I will school her."

Grim pride surges past my ebbing terror. It is I who has been schooling—and besting—him for the past two days. When his mount's hoofbeats fade, I creep out to where the doctor loads my bundles back on behind Nelly's saddle. He has acquitted himself admirably in my defense. "I never would have married such a man. My husband is a sergeant—and a chaplain—in the Third Virginia."

"Indeed, madam. I did not believe a word that blackguard said. Do you know the way to Valley Forge?" He pulls the rope taut.

"No, but I must get there tonight. Will the south road bring him into my path?"

"They do not intersect, but once he reaches that road's end, he's sure to double back. It doesn't give you much of a start."

Deep in the saddlebag, my fingers close around one of the tins of peppermint and yarrow tea. "Thank you for putting him off my trail. This will help bring those lads' fevers down."

He nods. "Now mark me, stay on this road past Gordon's Ford and the White Horse Inn, and then take the right-hand fork. From there it's naught but a mile to the picket line."

Back in the saddle, I clap my heels against Nelly's ribs. The mare, refreshed, churns up dirt and gravel as she takes off.

Under the waning moon's illumination, I can see well enough to avoid patches of ice and the stumps and boulders protruding from the road's scarred surface. The state of the road and the substantial stone houses and barns looming in the darkness every quarter mile or so lead me to believe this is a well-traveled highway during the day.

Two hours gone we pass the village of Gordon's Ford, and soon after, a flickering fire in an iron brazier illuminates the painted sign for the White Horse Inn. Subtle pressure from my left knee is all that's needed to guide Nelly toward the curving, downhill fork, and I turn her at an angle to help her negotiate the icy slope.

The road leads into the deep shadow of a grove of trees and we continue slowly while I wait in vain for my eyes to adjust. When minutes pass with no relief to the darkness, I murmur to cheer her and keep my worries at bay. "I'll make sure the soldiers give you a nice, soft bed of hay when we arrive. You've done all I could ask and more. What a good girl you are!" No sooner are the words out of my mouth than Nelly shies and rears. Launched from the saddle as though I've been shot out of a cannon, I land in a graceless sprawl in the road. She snorts and clatters off.

Everything hurts. Biting back tears, I sit up and press both hands over the torn knee of my breeches. Blood seeps into the fabric, but the cut doesn't seem serious enough to bind. Rubbing my hands clean on the breeches, I feel around for the hat and put it back on over my tumbled hair. Staggering to my feet, I call out, "Nelly? Come back. Where are you?" As I take a tentative step, the toe of my boot catches on the rutted road, sending me headlong onto the frozen ground.

I might be steps from shelter or from some unseen hazard. Only one thing is certain: I cannot lie here in the road when every second counts. I want to, though. I want to kick my heels and curse the circumstances that brought me to this point. Over and over, I've been told the war with the British is none of women's affairs. So why is it me and not some man, out in the cold night without my mount, desperate to deliver a message that could change the war's outcome?

Oh, bloody hell. I would never utter such an oath aloud, but in my thoughts, perhaps it doesn't count. I made this journey for Benjamin and our children—and their children's children, down through the ages to come. Benjamin is willing to fight and die for the cause of liberty. My cause is keeping him alive to witness that freedom come to pass.

Nothing deters my first halting steps. Hoofbeats, punctuated by the sound of metal on metal, grow louder. The animal is not moving fast, but my disorientation is so profound I can't seem to get out of the way. As it bears down on me, a muzzle and trailing reins brush across my upraised hand. "Nelly?" This time the horse's nose bumps against my face, and I grab for the reins. Skittish, she rears again, and fear of her metal-shod hooves makes me stumble back.

Time slips past me. Has my pursuer come on the right road? I grit my teeth, compose myself, and speak in a crooning voice. "I will get to Valley Forge tonight and tend to my brothers. I will deliver that letter to the general, have a cup of coffee before the fire, and take a bath. Won't it be—oh, honestly, Nelly!"

The mare tosses her head and refuses to be still. I've lost my riding crop somewhere in the dark, but I could never bear to beat my exhausted, frightened pet. With effort, I set aside my anxiety and frustration, put my hand behind my back as if I might produce a treat, and sink into a curtsey.

"Your Majesty." Perhaps Nelly will respond to the trick she learned long ago. She paws the ground, and I visualize her as she kneels, bowing her head along her extended right leg.

"Good girl. Steady now." My hand closes around the reins, a lifeline in the darkness, and I run my other hand down her side to find the stirrup. Then I sing out, "Charmed, I'm sure!" and Nelly rises. Knee shaking with fatigue as my weight leaves the ground, I feel all my fresh bumps and bruises as I land in the saddle.

Every minute seems like an hour as Nelly picks her way through the darkness. Some of my tension ebbs away as we emerge from the forest, and I can see the road ahead curve uphill toward a large house. Then a whinny draws my attention to a horse and rider halted near the brazier burning at the house's front door. Stifling a scream, I recognize both the White Horse Inn—and the man who pursues me.

I've been traveling the wrong way.

TWO WEEKS EARLIER

2

Home for the Holidays

Asbury Manor, Fauquier County, Virginia
January 5, 1778

My cousins Mollie and Nancy gathered around my aunt Jean at the pianoforte, and as the opening chords of the ballad "Turtle Dove" tore at my heart, I picked up baby William and dodged my mother's restraining hand.

"Anna, stay and listen to the music."

"He needs his napkin changed."

"Do you forget we have servants for that?"

"Don't trouble Phillis or Lynn, Mother. I'll do it." My cousins' voices drifted after me as I hurried from the room.

Fare you well, my dear, I must be gone, and leave you for a while; if I roam far away, I'll come back again, though I roam ten thousand miles, my love . . .

Upstairs, I shut my chamber door to muffle the rest of the song, hugged William close, and fought back tears. No letters, no word from Benjamin in two months. Most of the time I could bear his absence, but tonight I missed him so keenly I was terrible company. Time spent changing little William's napkin would grant me a short respite from my family's Twelfth Night celebration.

Our son's dark hair and bright brown eyes echoed his father's, and when he smiled, my warring feelings of joy and sadness threatened to overwhelm me. How I would have preferred to be at home, with just Benjamin and our children. Instead, he was somewhere in Pennsylvania with the army, and the children and I were in exile at my uncle's house. Our young ones had no memory of fat turkeys, mistletoe, and simple, cozy holidays spent at our dear little home near the apple orchard. The house stood empty and forlorn for a second winter. My own memories were fading.

The baby chortled as I kissed his feet in their knitted booties. "Your father will be so excited to meet you when he comes home, my sweet boy." When that would be, I could not say. Though it was like picking a wound that wouldn't heal, my eyes strayed to the ribbon-bound packet of letters on the escritoire. Better to stay in my chamber, where it was quiet, and re-read every one of Benjamin's letters.

I had long been under the spell of my husband's words. Most of our courtship was conducted by correspondence, and even now, after ten years of marriage, his writing and oratory skills kept their hold on me. In the pulpit, he had the power to lift a congregation. In an ordinary, he could raise a mug of ale and inflame the passions that drove men to seek political change. I often faded into the background of his public life, just as he let me tend to mine without interference. But at home, we treasured our intellectual discourse. It was one of the many facets of our marriage that bound us, one to the other. At home, we were equals.

I suppose that was why his decision not to consult me before arranging for me to live here, at Uncle's, still hurt.

Stone Orchards and Farm, Carters Run, Virginia
October 1776

I didn't protest when Benjamin joined the Culpeper Minutemen in the fall of 1775, for it was every able-bodied man's duty to serve in the militia. He was delighted—far more than I, to be honest—when the Virginia Assembly called the Minutemen to defend the arsenal at Williamsburg just before Christmastide. When he returned three months later, he was restless, and a chasm formed between us that had not existed before. Even though Governor Dunmore's expulsion from the colony restored peace to Virginia, Benjamin would not be content until the unrest in all the colonies was resolved.

The following spring, I quailed with fear when the main army attached our local militia to one of the Virginia regiments. But months passed, and despite the escalating conflict, Benjamin was not called to do anything more dangerous than take a turn guarding disaffected Loyalists from Virginia's tidewater coast who were brought inland to Fauquier County.

Though he spent long days in the fields or the orchards, he often rode off after supper to spend a few hours at Edwards' Ordinary in nearby Fauquier Court House. There, he and his fellows followed the news of the continuing rebellion in the north and rejoiced in the daring exploits of the Sons of Liberty.

Unsure how to make him understand my worry, I settled for pointing out it did not look well when a preacher spent more time in the ordinary than in church.

One October evening, Benjamin was unusually quiet as he cleaned his rifle. Even after the children were in bed, he continued to polish the barrel in silence. This was our time for conversation, and I waited for him to speak his mind. When he rose and hung the rifle on its pegs over the door, I could hold my tongue no longer. "What troubles you?"

"I'm not troubled—just trying to decide how to tell you."

As it happened, I had news for him too. At the children's bedroom door, my keen mother's ear discerned Rhoda and Elijah breathing in unison. I took my shawl off its peg. "Come for a walk with me."

Outside, our shadows melted into the darkness between the rows of gnarled apple trees that seemed to march across our orchard's hills. When the climb grew steep, he took my hand, steadying me until we stood together on high ground. Here the Blue Ridge Mountains rolled away to the east, the north, and the south. To the west, the last rays of the setting sun turned the horizon orange and pink. Silhouetted against the fading light, his profile put me in mind of a Roman emperor I once saw in a book and it tinged my surge of affection with foreboding. I married a farmer. A preacher. I had not expected him to become a warrior. "Do you remember the day you asked Uncle for my hand?"

He chuckled. "If I recall, you tried to put me off. You said that you had but a small measure of liberty, which you'd lose as soon as you expressed tender feelings for someone."

"You argued I needn't fear losing my liberty and promised our marriage would be an equal partnership."

"I was so smitten I'd have promised you anything. But have I not kept my word?"

"Yes. Since we wed, I've wanted for nothing and feared nothing as long as you were beside me."

"And have I not encouraged you to use your skills as a healer?"

"It has been a blessing to be able to tend to the spiritual and physical health of our community together."

He paused and sighed before he continued. "The Department of Safety has dissolved my unit out of the Continental Line and back into the militia."

My heart leapt at this turn of fate. "So you'll be—"

He cut me off, speaking in a rush. "I enlisted as a regular."

"No!" Just as quickly, my heart plummeted like a bird shot out of the air.

"It would mean payment and a pension, not just volunteering."

"How could you make such a decision without asking me?"

"The army needs men skilled with rifles and artillery. Many of my fellows from the Minutemen have also joined the Line."

"Then let them go. You're needed here, at home." Swallowing did nothing to force down the lump in my throat. "I didn't object when you joined the Minutemen, but now I cannot help but believe you prefer soldiering above everything else—including me and the children. Do you prefer it above your calling too?"

He put his hands on my shoulders, holding me at arm's length. Though I couldn't see his face in the darkness, the hurt in his voice was clear. "I soldier to win liberty and the freedom to worship as we choose. I can't ask the men of my flock to do what I refuse to do myself. How can I abandon a course of action that will make it possible to realize all my other dreams? When I promised I wouldn't seek to own you or hobble you, I believed you'd grant me the same concession."

"I do, but I am still a wife who fears losing her husband."

He pulled me against his chest, and his lips brushed my hair as he spoke. "I vow you shan't lose me, Anna."

"You cannot make such a vow, for you can't know what comes on the morrow."

"I daresay I do. We've been assigned to Stirling's Brigade in the Third Virginia Regiment. They'll be calling us up in a few days."

A sob escaped my lips. "The last time, you left when Elijah was a babe. This time, you'll leave while I'm with child—and you'll be gone for a year or more."

His hand sought my still-flat stomach. "Really? When do you expect?"

"In the spring. April or May."

His whoop rang out across the hills. He swung me around and smothered me with kisses until I forgot everything I'd planned to say. When he took me to bed later, it was with passion that recalled a night in August after he read the newly signed Declaration of Independence aloud to his congregation. That, I suspected, was the night he'd gotten this child on me. No doubt he was as well pleased about the pregnancy as I, but it soon became clear I was foolish to hope the news would alter his course.

I'd assumed we'd take the matter up again the next day, but Benjamin left early. When he returned in the afternoon, he was driving a borrowed wagon. I came out on the porch, Elijah on my hip.

"What's this about?"

He jumped down. "I paid a visit to your uncle and expressed my worry about leaving you alone with two little ones while you expect. He offered to have you return to live with them while I'm away. We can move your things and the stock over tomorrow."

I put my hand over my belly, my trembling voice conveying my hurt. "You didn't think to discuss this with me either? We decide about the children—and our lives—together."

"It's best for you and the babe."

"Nay, Benjamin. I shall stay here, near Betsy and Thomas. I'll want Betsy when my travail comes and between your brothers and your father, the chores…."

"You cannot. Thomas is planning to enlist, and Baylis is too—so there will be no able-bodied men about. My father's too feeble to help, and you know everything's just going to get more difficult as your time approaches. Noah is old enough to handle Thomas's chores, but it's too much to expect a twelve-year-old lad to tend to his father's farm and then do for his aunt and grandfather too."

He was only trying to see to my comfort, and I cast about for the right words to express my dismay. "But we've had so little contact with my family since we married. I know I must set aside old disagreements, but to live under their roof is out of the question. I warrant Aunt Jean still does not think us properly wed."

"Your aunt's opinion about the legitimacy of our Baptist practices didn't matter when we married, and it doesn't matter now. Your mother seemed pleased and bade me tell you everyone is looking forward to seeing you and the little ones."

But I sighed at the thought of living with my relatives.

And so, the presence of my extended family diluted my remaining time with Benjamin. We spent our last night together in the large four-poster bed in the chamber I now shared with the children. Though I longed to receive him with an ardor that would bind us to one another even as the miles between us increased, our lovemaking felt furtive and restrained. We were not used to having the children asleep at the foot of the bed and all the rest of the family within earshot.

Long after he fell asleep, sated, I lay watching the flicker of the dying flames on the hearth. Already, I missed him and the liberty I enjoyed as mistress of my own, albeit modest, home.

3

Unexpected Visitor

B aby William's squeal brought me back from my reverie, and I cooed in response as I straightened his smock and picked him up. Benjamin's letters would wait, but my mother would send someone to fetch me unless I returned to the party. Before leaving my chamber, I opened the door a crack and listened to make sure Mollie and Nancy had moved on to a happier song.

On my way downstairs, I noticed Rhoda, my eldest, had also taken leave of the festivities. At the window in the front hall, she blew out one of the bayberry candles standing amid laurel leaves and a scattering of red winterberries on the sill. She inhaled with eyes closed and then touched the smoking wick to the flame of another candle to relight it.

"What are you doing?"

She turned. "Bayberry smells best right after I snuff the flame."

"So it does. Back to the party, love." I put my free arm around her shoulders. In the parlor, Aunt Jean played a sprightly tune on the pianoforte while Mollie and Nancy danced on the polished wood floor.

Rhoda sighed as she watched their skirts swirl. "There's no one to dance with me."

My heart went out to my little girl. She was lonely in this house full of adults with only her brothers, who were too young to be real playmates, for company. No doubt she would have preferred to spend the holiday with her cousin Sadie, Thomas and Betsy's daughter, who was close to her age.

Determined to make the best of things, I stepped around my middle child, two-year-old Elijah, and settled into the wing chair beside my mother's. Uncle William stood near the crackling fire, a cut-glass cup of rum punch in hand, presiding over the celebration in a manner befitting the patriarch of a household full of women, children, and servants.

Rhoda sighed again and leaned on the arm of my chair, chin on her hands. "There's no one to dance with you either, Mother."

Determined to present a cheerful front, I rescued the end of my kerchief from the baby's grasp and stood him up on my lap. "You'd like to dance, wouldn't you, William?" The chubby little boy churned his legs and squealed.

At this, Rhoda frowned. "Elijah and William are too young to care about dancing."

"Come, Rhoda. I'll be your partner!" Seventeen-year-old Nancy saved the day when she danced over to our corner, bowed, and extended her hand. Rhoda's frown turned to giggles. She dropped a curtsey and skipped into the center of the room. Turning the baby so he could watch Rhoda, I bounced him in time to the music and mouthed a thank-you to Nancy. Elijah, who cared naught about dancing, beat one of his blocks on the floor.

A blast of wintry air set the fire flickering as it swept through the parlor. I leaned forward in my chair and saw a dark-haired, broad-shouldered man in the hall shed his cloak and hand it and his cocked hat to the butler. Could it be? A squeak was all I could manage as I rose to my feet.

Aunt Jean heard my soft exclamation and stopped playing. Everyone turned to follow my gaze, and I held my breath until light fell upon the man's face.

"Uncle Thomas!" Rhoda ran to fling her arms around his waist as he came into the parlor.

As my brother-in-law and I locked eyes, I could tell something was very wrong by the way the corners of his mouth turned down. I swallowed hard as I passed the baby to my mother. "We weren't expecting you, Thomas. When did you get home?"

He ignored my questions for the moment. "I thought I saw someone signaling 'one if by land' from the front window as I rode up."

Rhoda giggled. "That was me. I like the smell of the bayberry tapers."

He bent down to her level. "You're shooting up like a weed, Rhoda Stone, and you favor your pretty mother more every time I see you. Before long we'll be beating off your suitors with a stick." He tweaked her nose. "Are you going to introduce me to your little brother?"

Rhoda took his hand and pulled him across the room. "This is our William, Uncle Thomas."

Mother held up the baby with the tight-lipped look of disapproval she wore around my in-laws. Thomas pretended not to notice as he lifted the little boy into his arms.

"Well, hello, young sir! I'd know you anywhere, for you look just like your pa."

The baby regarded him studiously and then broke into a grin, showing his two tiny teeth.

Thomas laughed. "You and your brother will roam the fields and forests with your cousins in a few years, won't you?" He stared at little William for a long moment, as if to commit his face to memory, before handing him back to his grandmother.

My uncle harrumphed and set down his cup. "What are you lads playing at this autumn? Last year, Washington crossed the Delaware to surprise the Hessians at Trenton, but his performance of late has people calling for his replacement. Two defeats in as many months! He should have surrendered after the embarrassment at the battle of Germantown."

When Thomas rose to his full height, he towered over my uncle. It was clear he took offense to the criticism, but he spoke with restraint. "His Excellency seems to have no plans to yield, and we Continentals still have plenty of fight left in us, Mr. Asbury."

"On furlough, are you?"

"Something like that, sir."

"They could have sent your brother home for a spell instead. He enlisted well before you, didn't he?"

Desperate to know why my brother-in-law rode five miles over dark mountain roads to visit, I broke in before my uncle's insults grew worse. "Thomas, would you like a drink to warm you up? Some hot cider or rum punch?"

"Cider would be welcome." When I filled a cup, he took a sip before he addressed the room. "I didn't know I'd be interrupting your celebration. Please, carry on. Anna, may I have a word?"

"Yes, of course." I led him across the hall, hiding the dread clutching my insides.

Aunt Jean and the pianoforte launched into the opening strains of "The First Noel" as Thomas shut the door of my uncle's study behind us. When he knelt to speak to Rhoda, I noticed strands of silver in his dark hair. Now, the harsh shadows cast by the flickering firelight accentuated his hollow cheeks and the worry lines on his forehead, making him look much older than his thirty-five years. "What news? Is it Benjamin? Tell me."

"Ben's alive, last I knew, and should be in winter camp by now."

Limp with relief, I sank into a chair. "Oh! You had me near fainting with fright. I haven't had a letter for over two months, and I want to know what's going on. When the *Virginia Gazette* comes in the post, the news is at least a month old."

"Well, if my brother isn't writing as often as you'd like, it's because we're busy in the army, what with the war on." Thomas delivered what sounded like jest without a smile.

Fear churned in my stomach again. "But how can they spare you? Why are you back in Virginia? And what brings you here tonight? It must be more than to wish us a joyful Twelfth Night."

He rubbed the toe of his boot against the Turkish carpet. "Baylis is dead. I brought his body home."

"Oh no! When was he killed? Thomas, I'm so sorry." The image of Baylis when I first knew him as a lad of nine rose before me. Hard as it was to think of him grown into a young man of twenty, it was harder to know he was cut down in his prime. I couldn't believe I would never hear his infectious laughter again, and he would never find a sweetheart. "Does Benjamin know?"

"They'll get word to him once they settle in camp."

"But what happened?"

"Baylis fell ill with the pox in October. Our unit had to leave him behind with other men who were too sick to march. When we enlisted last spring, Father made me promise to watch out for Baylis, him being the baby and all, but there was nothing I could do for him. Truth is, we lose far more men to smallpox and dysentery than to enemy fire."

I reached out a hand, and he squeezed it, signaling he didn't need to draw strength from me. He'd already reconciled the loss of his brother.

"Early this month, just after he died, we were halted at White Marsh, which was too close to Philadelphia, now that the accursed British occupy the city. They planned to surprise us with a nighttime attack before we headed farther west to winter camp. I heard tell a woman spy—a Quaker, no less—alerted General Washington so we were ready and waiting for them.

"My fellows and I were in the sharp fighting, along with the Maryland lads. Frustrated the Bloody Backs so badly, we did, they took out their wrath on civilians and burned several homes. Once General Howe realized he could neither outflank Washington nor draw him out, he retreated to Philadelphia."

Never one to be still for long, he dropped my hand to pace. "Even in victory, we lost more than a hundred men—twenty-seven were my comrades from Morgan's unit. We were making ready to bury them, along with the ones like Baylis, who died in the hospital. Officers get their bodies shipped back home, you understand, but privates lie in unmarked graves. I decided my brother deserved the same treatment as an officer."

Despite my sadness, my lips curved into a smile. Even Thomas's tragic stories involved some kind of scheme. "But how did you arrange that?"

With a faint shadow of his usual grin, he shrugged and spun out his tale. "There was a considerable disorder as we prepared to move to winter camp. Two skinners were headed to Williamsburg, hauling freight and two officers' bodies sunk in barrels of rum to preserve them. One skinner took ill, so I swapped a week's rum ration for his coat and took his place. Convinced the remaining one to take on an extra barrel and drop me off on the way." He paused, and his pride in his contrivance seemed to fade along with his smile. "At least I made sure Baylis will rest beside Mother in our burying ground."

"But you took such a risk. I read in the last *Gazette* that our officers have orders to shoot deserters!"

He waved a hand to dismiss my concern. "I'm sparing the army the trouble of feeding me all winter. Rations are scarce. When I go back in the spring, hale and well-fed, they'll be glad enough to see me."

"What of the burial? I can help you lay him out if you need me to."

"Snakes, Anna, a body pickled in a cask of rum for a month is no sight for a woman—or anyone. I don't mind saying, one whiff was enough to make me lose my taste for rum altogether. We must wait for a thaw to bury him, but I sent word inviting folks to the funeral in three weeks' time. After that, I plan to spend this winter like a regular farmer, doing repairs at our place and at Father's. Betsy and our young ones are glad to have me home."

"I would be glad to have Benjamin home for good. Visions of the disasters that could befall us keep me up at night. Knowing what happened to Baylis only increases my worry for the rest of you."

He helped me rise. "Ben knows how to take care of himself, and his faith and patriotic fervor will sustain him through the hardships. He and your brothers will watch out for each other." He tilted up my chin, brushing his lips across my cheek. "I'm sure he'd want me to deliver that to you."

Tears stung my eyes again at the thought of a kiss carried across hundreds of miles and I blinked so they wouldn't fall. "Please send my love to Betsy. I miss living next door to you all."

"What? You're not happy to be back in this grand house?" This time a smile accompanied the jest.

He appreciated the humor in my situation more than I ever could. "They're my family, but we don't share the same convictions. It's hardly been a fortnight since we feasted for the day of national thanksgiving decreed by Congress, and my aunt insisted on having another party. It seems disrespectful of our soldiers."

He chuckled. "Come on, Anna. Don't begrudge your aunt a party or two."

"It's not just the parties. I don't want Rhoda to expect slaves to attend to her every need. I want her to believe as we do—it's wrong for one person to own another."

"All right. I admit I'd feel the same if I had to live here and endure your uncle's constant barbs. There's no way I could stay quiet about the immorality of profiting from the forced labor of others. I'm fighting for liberty for all of us, not just those who already had some before the war started."

As he opened the door, I swiped at my cheeks to make sure there was no trace of tears. We were halfway to the entry when King appeared with Thomas's wraps. He thanked the butler, settled his hat on his head and said to me, "Betsy bid me tell you to come visit anytime."

"I will indeed. Good night."

Reluctant to lose his company, I lingered at the window while Manso brought out Thomas's horse. The candles burned low. I whispered a prayer for Baylis's eternal soul, blew them out, and inhaled the bayberry incense, hoping it would sanctify my prayer.

I returned to the party in time to watch Mollie, Nancy, and Rhoda parade figures of the three kings through the house and add them to the tableaux of Aunt Jean's Nativity. Nineteen-year-old Mollie, who found the bean in her cake, was proclaimed Queen. Bless her, when she noticed Rhoda's wistful look, she abdicated and bestowed the gold-paper crown and ribbon-bedecked scepter on her little cousin.

It was after midnight when the family retired, leaving Phillis, Lynn, and King to take down the remaining Yuletide decorations and set the parlor to rights. And so, Twelfth Night ended.

Rhoda refused to surrender the scepter at bedtime until I promised she might retrieve it again first thing in the morning. Little William took his night feeding later than usual and once the children were finally asleep, I had the solitude I craved. With my candle on the escritoire, I unfolded Benjamin's letters that arrived during last year's yuletide season. Smoothing them out with a caress, I prepared to spend a few moments with my love.

November 23, 1776

My dear Wife,

Though I must confess I am still more comfortable with a long rifle than a musket and bayonet, we've spent the last month drilling and training, and I am learning the ways of a regular in the Continental Line. After two weeks of marching to the northeast, we met the main army on retreat from New York.

In the recent fall of Fort Washington and Fort Lee, the British captured over one hundred of our cannon, thousands of muskets, and ammunition. We find we recruits are much-needed replacements for the thousands of casualties suffered in the two defeats.

Though the news sounds bad, do not worry yourself. We are about to go into winter camp, and they will suspend fighting until spring.

Henry's tales of how he tormented you when you were children rival my experiences with Thomas and only increase my admiration for you. Though you have spent much of your life absent from your brothers'

company, they hold you in high regard. I am
honored that they welcome me as family.

Your affectionate husband,

Benjamin

January 1777

My dearest Anna,

Thank you for the gloves. I've worn my
old ones through.

We have returned to winter camp in
Morristown in the state of New Jersey. By
now I assume you've had news of our surprise
attack on the Hessian troops' winter quarters
in Trenton the day after Christmas. You need
have no fear, for your brothers and I are well.
We did most of our fighting from behind the
cover of fences and houses. This feels much
more natural to me than facing our foe on
open ground, lining up, and taking aim at one
another.

During our approach, General Washington crossed the river with Major General Henry Knox's division, while Stephens' Brigade and ours formed the center of the line for the attack.

Many of the men cannot swim, and the sight of the dark water and bobbing ice floes struck more terror in their hearts than the thought of facing the vicious Hessians. Even those of us who can swim did not relish a dip in the cold river. Every man present was soaked and covered in mud before we reached Trenton. We must have been a terrifying sight!

Near the end of the battle, a group of German-speaking Continentals from Pennsylvania called to the Hessians in their language, urging them to lay down their arms. Those in our army who hail from Hesse-Kassel are fighting against their own countrymen, with whom they should have no quarrel.

The battle was soon ended, and decisively so, with thousands of Hessians taken prisoner. We also captured guns, ammunition, and *enough woolen blankets for every man who took part in the battle to have one.*

Write soon, my dearest. I long to hear news of you and the children.

Your Benjamin

His two letters revealed the Continental Army's changing fortunes. Defeats at Fort Washington and Fort Lee meant the loss of men and munitions. Just a month later, the daring attack on Trenton led to an American victory and yielded spoils of guns, ammunition, and blankets.

This year, things looked bleak. As Uncle pointed out, the defeats at Germantown and Brandywine overshadowed the victory at Saratoga. Philadelphia and New York City remained in British hands. Thomas could not downplay the disease, hunger, and want of supplies plaguing the army enough to allay my worries.

There would be a letter from Benjamin soon, I told myself. But what tidings would it bring?

Before drifting off to sleep, I decided not to share Thomas's news about Baylis with my side of the family. I couldn't put the idea in Rhoda's head that men who went to war sometimes did not return.

4

❦

We'll Wish Ourselves Back

A week passed after Thomas's visit and still there was no word from Benjamin or my brothers. Though by day I remained cheerful of face and countenance for the children's sake, I spent the nights in worry and prayer. Sleeping but little, I often tiptoed downstairs before anyone else was stirring to seek a task that would occupy my hands even if it could not lay my anxiety to rest.

Like Benjamin, I believed independence from the Crown would lead to the religious freedom he craved. If I were a man, I would enlist as an army doctor and use my skills to tend the soldiers.

As it was, I had to make my contribution to the war effort from home. Inspired by an article in the last *Virginia Gazette*, I encouraged Mollie and Nancy to join me in canvassing neighbors for donations for the soldiers. We'd spent the past week riding miles over wintry roads. Once the clothing donations came in, we occupied ourselves by sorting and mending the items and knitting mittens and stockings.

Stirring up the coals, I put on a pot of coffee and settled near the hearth with my knitting. The rapid clicking of the needles acted like a tonic on my nerves and another mitten took shape before I heard footsteps in the hall. Uncle came in, as if searching for something lost.

"Where has Phillis gone? I've been ringing that blasted bell for half an hour."

"I haven't seen her this morning, Uncle, but there's coffee ready." I thrust my needles into the ball of yarn and rose to pour him a mug.

I hesitated to ask Uncle for a donation, but it did not look well to collect from our less affluent neighbors without contributing ourselves. Even families with no husbands or sons in the army were generous. When he took a seat at the kitchen worktable, I sliced ham and spread preserves on bread for him. I prepared my appeal while he took a few bites. "Uncle, I fear for the state of the army. Last week Thomas told me there is not enough food and far more men fall to disease than to the enemy's bullets. There must be more ways to help."

The old man sipped his coffee. "War is men's affair. No good comes from telling women the truth about any of it." He gestured toward my knitting. "But since you ask, I must be blunt. Your efforts are for naught. What do you imagine one wagonload of clothes and blankets can do for so many?"

"I refuse to believe that. If everyone gave a few blankets . . ."

"Likely they would never reach the soldiers. Well-meant donations can be stolen and sold on the black market. The longer this revolution drags on, the more likely it is to fail for want of supplies. I only hope it happens sooner rather than later."

"But you cannot wish to remain under Crown rule?"

"We're no better off than we were. The state of Virginia taxes us now, which, if I remember, was considered the basest of insults when done by the Crown."

"But that was different. The King taxed us without proper representation."

"I suppose I can't expect a woman to comprehend the pickle we're in. Congress is paying for the war with a printing press instead of a mint. They pressure merchants and farmers to accept their worthless requisition certificates for food and supplies for the army. Even the vendors with patriotic leanings hesitate to accommodate them. Had the broker for my crops not negotiated better terms for his army contracts, I fear supplying the troops would bankrupt me. This new country is setting itself up to fail before it succeeds."

I folded my arms on my chest, even as I reminded myself raising his ire would not help my cause. "But you must believe in more than money. What about liberty and independence? Two years ago, you fought alongside Benjamin in the Minutemen."

"Yes, because Virginia's economic and cultural prosperity depends on good relations with Great Britain. I fought to return things to the status quo." He harrumphed. "Don't be a goose, Anna. Money is so devalued now that all my wealth wouldn't buy enough food to feed a regiment for a month. Have you considered what will happen if the war comes to this part of Virginia? At the very least, the soldiers on both sides will confiscate our food and supplies instead of paying for them. If it comes to that, I ask you, how will we live? All these twenty years since your father died, it's been my responsibility to protect and sustain both his widow and children and my own family. Mark me—if we win independence, we'll wish ourselves back. Now stop pestering me while I'm trying to eat."

I was not bold enough to point out his shortcomings in his treatment of my family. Protect and sustain? *Indeed.* I fumed in silence as I went upstairs to wake the children. When Father died, Uncle wasted no time putting Joseph and Henry into apprenticeships, which made it impossible for Mother and me to run our farm on our own. He bound me out as a serving maid to one of his business associates when I was but ten years old.

Yet he took Mother and Jeremiah, our youngest brother, into his household with Aunt Jean and the girls, and when it became clear he would have no sons of his own, he named Jeremiah his heir. Jeremiah left to attend William and Mary when he was sixteen, and after he completed his studies, Uncle bought him a clerkship with a lawyer in Williamsburg. The difference in our upbringings and situations left a chasm between Jeremiah and Joseph, Henry, and me.

A hot flush of fighting blood rose within me and I clenched my fists as I stared down at my slumbering brood. Uncle had used my brothers and me as pawns. I vowed to keep the same from happening to my own children, knowing full well if I lost Benjamin and my brothers, I would be powerless to refuse any decision Uncle might make on my children's behalf.

GEORGE ASBURY FARM, STAFFORD COUNTY, VIRGINIA
SEPTEMBER 1758

I was almost ten years old when my father died. Because it was unseasonably warm that autumn, we buried him two weeks before family, friends, and neighbors gathered for the funeral. Everyone brought food and drink, and Aunt Jean and some women from church lent enough dishes to accommodate all the guests. I remember running my finger along the edge of someone's gleaming china platter. I had never seen a gold-rimmed plate before.

With no interest in joining the women clustered around my mother, I crossed the room to listen to a group of men discussing rumors of a peace treaty between the British and the Iroquois and Ohio tribes. The treaty would prohibit white settlement west of the Allegheny Mountains, and I found this news disappointing. My father often spoke of the Ohio country, encouraging the fancy that one day my brothers would venture there. Though I never told him so, I intended to go west one day too.

Uncle William and Uncle James, my father's brothers, conferred away from the other guests, unaware that my oldest brother, Joseph, who stood nearby and out of their sight, was eavesdropping. I tiptoed to join him, and together we strained to hear the murmured conversation.

Uncle William harrumphed. "Every item in George's household, taken and sold, wouldn't come close to satisfying what he owes. If Dunlap calls in the note, it will ruin us all. It'll leave Hannah and the children destitute, and one of us will have to take them in."

"We must encourage Hannah to find another husband," Uncle James replied.

"We can't count on a favorable new match for her and it's bad business to cross Dunlap. Mayhap he would indenture one of the children to pay down the debt."

"You mean work Joseph in the fields with slaves?"

"Nay. Joseph's a steady lad, and George intended to apprentice him to the cabinetmaker in Falmouth."

"But Henry, that young ruffian, is best set on a course that will curb him. He shouldn't spend his youth turned out into the fields, either."

As two women passed nearby, their low conversation and the rustle of their skirts rendered our uncles' conversation indistinct.

Joseph was fourteen, not quite a man but old enough to understand adult conversation. I whispered to him, "Father was in debt?"

His brow furrowed and he held up a hand to quiet me as Uncle William spoke again.

"She's a sharp-witted lass. If Dunlap agrees, that might be the best course of action."

After a pause of introspection, Uncle James replied, "It's a pity there's naught set aside for the boys' educations. Without inheritances, not to mention the matter of a dowry for Anna, you'll scarce find anyone willing to take guardianship of four young ones."

I leaned close to my brother. "What does he mean?"

He kept his voice just above a whisper. "Uncle William explained some of it to me this morning. By law, we're orphans now. The court will appoint a guardian to decide about our futures until we're grown. Likely it will be him."

"But what about Mother?"

"Without a husband, a woman requires the help of a male guardian to make such decisions."

In my anger, I forgot to whisper. "That's nonsense."

"Hush! It may be nonsense, but it's the law."

This new information was more than enough to cause me a sleepless night and my worry increased the following day as we harvested the stunted vegetables from our neglected kitchen garden. While scrabbling through the dirt for carrots and turnips, I wished there was more food left from the funeral.

We were inside for the midday meal when Mr. Mauzy, Mr. Northcutt, and Mr. Goff, who we knew from church, came to the house. They made a list of the dishes and crockery, counted our knives and spoons, and looked through the clothespress and trunk.

Mr. Mauzy dipped his quill into the ink bottle and asked Mother, "Did the slave girl also belong to your husband?"

"No, indeed, sir. She is my brother-in-law's."

Phillis kept her eyes cast down, giving no sign she was listening, but I felt a pang at the thought of her being included on a list of someone's possessions. I regarded her as family.

When the men finished poking around in the house, Joseph walked out to the barn with them. They spent a long time inspecting our stock and looking over the beehives that had been my father's pride. In the end, they made account of everything but the food in the larder. It felt shameful, somehow, to have them scrutinize each item for its value, rather than for its meaning.

Even Henry, usually oblivious to awkward situations, seemed uncomfortable. "Why must they go through our things?"

Mother explained, "It's called an appraisal, ordered by the court. The list of your father's possessions helps the court settle his estate by giving his things away—to pay debts or as gifts."

"What about your things, Mother?" My indignation was still fresh.

Her lower lip trembled before she spoke. "I own nothing, save what I brought to the marriage as my dowry. I'll keep the household items your father said I might have if he predeceased me and my widow's third of what remains."

Henry frowned. "What about us? Will we get to keep our clothes and shoes?"

"Yes, you'll keep your clothes and shoes. But there may be little else after the court settles the estate."

My heart pounded at the thought of saying goodbye to our aging mare out in the barn. "What about Daisy, the cow, and the pigs?"

Mother stood and crumpled her apron in her fists. "No more questions." She hurried from the room, leaving me wondering why it was lawful to take things away from women and children left alone and adrift, with no means of support. And I wonder still.

5

Proud to Wear Homespun

After breakfast Rhoda, my cousins, and I set to work packing the supplies for the soldiers. Mollie tied up a bundle of clothing with twine and frowned at her younger sister. "Nancy, aren't you finished with that pair of stockings yet? Hurry up."

"I'm casting off the last few stitches now."

I parried playfully with a knitting needle. "Yes, hurry up, lass! We give no quarter to shirkers here."

"Aye, aye, General!" Nancy placed the finished stocking on the worktable with a flourish.

"You say 'Yes, Sir' to a general," Rhoda chimed in. "Mother, my stitches on these mittens are crooked. Are they good enough to send?"

"Yes. Look at how your stitches improved with practice. The mittens will still keep a soldier's hands warm."

Satisfied, Rhoda took up her drop spindle. I taught her to hum "Yankee Doodle" as she twisted the wool fibers, for a steady rhythm helps make good yarn. After a turn around the table, she marched away down the hall.

Mollie rolled the stocking up with its mate and some ribbon garters. "How do you stand Benjamin being gone for so long? You never seem to worry."

"That's not true. I worry more than I let on, but I've grown used to his absence. I took it harder when he went to Williamsburg with the Minutemen."

"Father also went with the Minutemen." Mollie said it with pride.

"Yes, he did—and Benjamin told me your father once beat the whole company in a marksmanship contest." It didn't feel right to paint Uncle as less than a hero to his daughters, despite what he'd said to me earlier.

"Tell what it was like to say farewell when the soldiers marched away!" said Nancy. "A good story helps pass the time."

"All right." It was hard not to tread on my cousins' romantic notions about waving one's husband off to battle. "Though I understood how important it was to protect our arsenal in Williamsburg, I dreaded the day Benjamin was to leave. I was nervous about being alone with two little ones, for Rhoda was six, and Elijah but two months old.

"Elijah cried day and night with colic the week before Benjamin left but he fell asleep just before we left home for the parade ground. He was so worn out, poor thing, he didn't stir when Benjamin kissed him goodbye. So many members of Benjamin's congregation gathered around us, shaking his hand and wishing him well, I felt obliged to keep a smile on my face until I thought it would crack from the strain."

"How did you stand it?" Mollie asked. "I would have wept buckets."

I didn't mention that when Benjamin kissed me, I'd leaned in, wanting to feel him close to me as long as possible. I had to turn away when he knelt and embraced Rhoda.

"I thought I'd cried all my tears already, for I cried every time Benjamin was out of the house, and while I was making his uniform. The men chose the slogan 'Liberty or Death,' and I stitched it on the front of his hunting frock. They may have thought it was like a gauntlet thrown down before the British, but I feared it was tempting fate and prayed none of them would have to sacrifice their lives."

Nancy gave an exaggerated shudder. "What if something happened to him?" Did she not know her innocent question weighed on my mind every day?

"I suppose I would have remained at home, hired someone to work Benjamin's half of the orchard on shares, and relied on that and what I earn from tending the sick to get by." I rose to pour myself another cup of coffee. "I declare I was so worried about Benjamin leaving and tired from tending Elijah, it was no wonder I was out of sorts. But had you seen Benjamin run to line up with his fellows, you would have thought he was heading to a picnic, not into battle. The men carried their long rifles and had tomahawks and scalping knives in their belts. They looked savage and dangerous, standing at attention beneath the coiled rattlesnake on their battle flag."

Mollie sighed. "I wish Mother had not insisted we stay home that day. I should have liked to see the militia on parade."

"When Benjamin wrote from the capital, he told me their rough dress and backwoods weapons frightened the fine ladies and gentlemen in Williamsburg."

Both my cousins laughed at that. "Imagine Father mistaken for a backwoodsman!" Nancy said. "He doesn't even ride his own acres anymore."

"Anyway, after the men lined up, a loud crack of gunfire startled me. Elijah woke and spit up on me just as the drummer's cadence signaled for the troops to move out."

"Oh!" Nancy cried. "How mortifying."

"Benjamin recognized Elijah's wail and I could see him watching us from the ranks. His parting view of his family was not the brave, smiling tableaux I meant to give him. Instead, he would remember me with Rhoda clinging to my skirts, Elijah screaming in my arms, and spit-up all over my front."

"Had that happened to me in public I would've died." Mollie mourned for me.

"As soon as the column was out of sight, Rhoda looked up at me with big tears in her eyes and asked, 'Is Father coming home for supper?' That was the final straw. I wailed right along with Elijah."

My cousins looked so downcast that despite my ever-present fears, I laughed at myself to cheer them. "What a ninny I was! Even though I miss Benjamin, I've grown used to him being away. It helps to occupy myself by doing things to aid the soldiers."

Rhoda marched back into the dining room and I turned the conversation to reinforce my message to all present. "Though we do not fight alongside the men, women are vital to the war effort. Instead of guns and bayonets, we're armed with spinning wheels, looms, and knitting needles. What do we say, Rhoda?"

She stopped humming and answered without breaking stride. "A patriot girl is proud to wear homespun!"

Convinced my influence could offset Uncle's attitude about aiding the cause, I folded my arms in satisfaction as I watched Mollie, Nancy, and Rhoda occupied with their tasks. Then King came into the room and interrupted the moment. "Miss Anna, a man to see you. He says he's from your church."

"Thank you, King." When I opened the front door, a man wearing a buckskin hunting frock over a floury apron took off his hat in greeting.

"Brother Kemper, how nice to see a familiar face from home. Won't you come inside?"

"Oh, no, Sister Stone. I must hurry back to the mill. I came about Mary, my brother's wife. She's been feeling poorly, and I wonder, can you please come set with her for a while?"

"Of course. Do you know what ails her?"

"It's the pox. I ain't been in to see her for fear of coming down with it myself. Widow Jenkins has been seeing to her care, but after you tended my little ones when they had the grippe last winter, well, I'd take it kindly if you'd look in on her."

"I'll come right away." If I'd been at home where I belonged instead of here at Uncle's, no one would have summoned the Widow Jenkins to treat my sick friend. "I'll bring Manso to help with the chores. I'm sorry I didn't realize she was ill."

"Yes, ma'am. Thank you, ma'am." He put on his hat as he clomped down the wide porch steps, and I called to King as I shut the door.

"Will you please ask Manso to get ready to accompany me?" As he departed for the stables, I hurried up to my chamber to change into the old quilted stays and petticoat I reserved for work. With my wooden medicine chest under my arm, I gathered apples from the open barrel in the larder and plucked my hooded cloak off its peg on my way out to the stable. Nelly, my pet chestnut mare, greeted me with a whicker, and I scratched under her forelock as Manso led out Charley. Tossing him apples for Charley and himself, I held out another on my palm for Nelly. The mare's lips closed around the fruit, and she crunched as I fetched her tack.

"Miss Anna, I'll saddle her for you."

"It's no trouble. I like to do it myself."

Rhoda joined us, wrapped in a shawl so long it trailed through the hay on the floor. She watched me settle the gleaming saddle on Nelly's back.

"Mother, before you go, may I see Nelly do her trick? Please?"

"We can try, but I've already given her an apple, so she may not be willing." I buckled my medicine chest into the saddlebag, tightened the girth on the saddle, and caught a whiff of apple on the mare's breath as I stood before her. Winking at Rhoda, I dropped a court curtsey. "Your Majesty!"

The mare pawed the ground and knelt.

Left foot in the stirrup, I sang out, "Charmed, I'm sure!" Rhoda clapped her hands as Nelly rose and I swung into the saddle.

"Back to the house or you'll catch a chill. Nancy or Grandmother will hear your lessons and check your copybook if I'm not home by midafternoon. I love you."

"I love you too!"

Nibbling apples, Manso and I headed south on the Winchester Road toward the village of Fauquier Court House, but my thoughts remained with my daughter.

Benjamin and I agreed long ago we would instruct all our children—girls and boys alike—in religious and classical studies and encourage them to undertake any additional subjects that interested them. Though I was likely biased, Rhoda was at least as bright as any child her age. She knew her multiplication table, had a fine hand for needlework, and filled her first copybook with Psalms. She wouldn't have to sneak around and listen at doors to learn about things that interested her, as I did when I was a girl.

Recently, I introduced her to the study of herbs, plants, and the healing arts. In my childhood receipt book, I looked with fond remembrance on the drawings of plants and notes in the handwriting of a different Rhoda, and wished I could tell my mentor all about her little namesake. I meant for my daughter to have the knowledge to follow in my footsteps if she so desired. Communities relied on skilled healers, though my skills did not guarantee me the respect of all.

At Fauquier Court House we took the Rappahannock Road traveling west, and before long we turned in the lane at Kemper's Mill, where the churning water wheel signaled Brother Kemper was back at work within. I dismounted in the side yard and brought my medicine chest into the house.

Steam rose from the kettle hanging in the fireplace as I poured a dipperful of hot water over a mix of yarrow and peppermint in an earthenware mug. While it steeped, I raised the window sash a few inches. The crisp, winter air swirling into the room lifted tendrils of hair from my temples and made the pervasive odors of sweat and body waste more bearable.

Mary Kemper lay weak and listless, the rash and pustules clustered on her face, neck, and arms. I'd seen smallpox many times before, but this time it was my friend who suffered, and would bear the scars.

"Take a sip, Mary. This will ease your fever and make you feel better." With one hand supporting her head, I guided the cup to her lips.

A dribble of tea ran down her chin and she sagged against the pillow, exhausted by the effort. "What of Catherine and the boys—"

Mindful of the blisters, I blotted her forehead with a cloth soaked in goldenseal-infused water. "They are well. Do you trust me to take measures to assure they do not fall ill?"

"Yes, please. I could not bear them to suffer."

I nodded as I smoothed damp strands of hair back from her forehead. "You rest now."

When her eyelids fluttered closed, I took a small blade from my pocket, drew back the sheet, and pushed up her sleeve. The disease's hold on her was weakening. It was the proper time to harvest what I needed.

Heavy footsteps on the stairs spurred me to hurry. What I was about to do was against the law, and woe to me if busybody Widow Jenkins witnessed my actions. Piercing the skin stretched over one of the angry-looking pustules on Mary's arm, I used the edge of the blade to collect the escaping yellowish ooze on a scrap of paper.

"Anna Stone, sakes alive, what do you think you're doing?"

In one motion, I pulled up the sheet and slipped the knife and folded paper into my pocket as I turned from the bed.

The Widow Jenkins clucked with disapproval as she seized control of the sickroom. "I wasn't aware anyone sent for you. You've opened the window. Why is the bed so far from the hearth, and where are my red blankets? Step lively and stir up the fire immediately."

Resolved not to let the old cow bully me into carrying out her treatments, which were mostly rooted in superstition, I stood my ground. "Mary's fair burning up with fever. She should drink my tea and keep a cool cloth on her head." I dipped the cloth back in the gold-enseal water and continued to bathe her arms.

The pitted scars on the widow's disapproving face marked her as a smallpox survivor, and her sharp glance at my smooth cheek insinu-ated that because I'd never contracted the disease myself, I was not knowledgeable. She brushed past me and attacked the smoldering logs with the poker until orange flames burst forth. "We must wrap her in red blankets and move the bed next to the fire until the fever's gone, if we're to rid her of the pox."

Next, she crossed the room and closed the window with a huff. "Dear me, 'twould be better if we had red drapes for the window. She will not recover if you let the fire die and even a child knows fresh air does not belong in a sickroom." Still I refused to move, so she gave the bed a shove toward the fireplace. "My blankets are here, on the floor! She must have kicked them off. Help me swaddle her."

The old woman nudged me aside, panting with the effort as she tucked the blankets around Mary's sweltering body. "Mark me, missus, this treatment kept me from succumbing to the pox forty-five years ago. I'll sit with her now."

My fingers brushed the scrap of paper and the knife in my pocket. I bowed with a deference I didn't feel and gathered up the soiled linens and the chamber pot.

Manso, who often accompanied me on such visits, carried water and built up the fire under a cauldron in the yard so I could I boil the sheets and towels. Once I'd hung them on the line and disposed of the slops, I returned to the sick room for my medicine chest. Widow Jenkins knelt beside Mary's bed, deep in prayer, but it was clear she'd inspected the chest's contents in my absence, for several bottles of tinctures and herbs were out of place. With a sharp glance in her direction, I collected my things and departed.

Downstairs in the keeping room, the rich aroma of stew simmering over the wood fire filled the air. As I joined the Kemper children there, golden-haired Catherine's foot ceased to tap the spinning wheel's treadle, and the bundle of flax fibers in her hand paused on its way to becoming linen thread.

"How is Mother?"

"The worst is past, but you must continue to pray for her recovery." I picked up a skein from the basket near the wheel to admire it. "You have a fine hand, Catherine. I hope my Rhoda will be so skilled when she is your age. The weaver will make you a lovely cloth when you've got enough laid by."

The girl smiled at the praise. "Thank you, missus."

"How do you fare?"

"Well enough. Uncle runs the mill for us and does the chores since Father's been away. My brother helped your slave chop a load of firewood and carry plenty of water so I can do out a wash tomorrow."

"Good. I've boiled the sickroom linens and hung them on the line. You may wash them with the rest of your things." My eyes took in the tidy room. "You manage the household well. Do you attend to your mother at all?"

"Widow Jenkins bade me keep house and keep the boys away from the sickroom." She bit her lip, looking ashamed. "Widow Jenkins says smallpox is a judgment sent down by Providence to humble us and punish us for our sins."

My anger flared as hot as the red wool blankets. How dare that detestable woman put such thoughts in this poor girl's head? I raised my eyebrows and affected a look of surprise. "Really? Then I warrant Widow Jenkins must have sinned mightily when she was your age, for isn't that when she contracted the pox?"

Her eyes widened as she suppressed a giggle.

"The widow's words are stuff and nonsense, Catherine. Smallpox is not a penance for sin and you must pay no heed to such talk. But let me ask you this: when Providence bestows on us the means to protect the ones we love, should we not do so?"

"Yes'm, we should."

"Remember, my husband speaks of this very thing in the pulpit. God gives His children the capacity to gain knowledge and we serve Him well when we use what we know to aid one another." I lowered my voice. "Let me protect you."

Until then, I'd told only Benjamin about the scar on my arm. Untying the cord at my neckline so my shift slipped off my shoulder, I pointed it out. "When I was your age, I served on a large estate in Stafford. One of the other servants knew how to render people immune to the pox. She said I must have the treatment if I wanted to become a healer and made a small cut on my arm. Then she put a smallpox pustule's juice in the wound."

Catherine's eyes grew round. "You didn't get sick?"

"Just a mild fever and rash, and this one scar. Now I can care for those who have the pox without falling ill myself." I brought the folded paper and the lancet from my pocket. "I promised your mother I would inoculate you and your brothers."

She hesitated for a moment, and when she nodded, I cut a bit of the linen thread from a skein and folded it inside the scrap of paper until it was saturated.

Her fingers trembled as she undid the tie on her shift and pulled the ruffled edge aside. With deft movements, I made a nick on her arm and drew the thread across the wound. "You will be a trifle sick, likely for several days. Stay away from others who haven't had the pox until you all feel hearty again. And mark me, don't breathe a word of this treatment to Widow Jenkins, for inoculation is against the law."

"Yes, missus."

Cutting a length of bandage from the roll in my medicine chest, I tied it around her arm. Then I turned my attention to her brother. "Henry, you're next. I have a brother Henry myself. He's off fighting with General Washington."

He scowled as he unbuttoned his shirt. "The war will be over before I get to fight. I could have gone with Father, but Mother said twelve is too young."

"Your mother is right. This earthly life is full of battles and you'll have your share in time. Don't be too eager to seek trouble. Now, let me see your arm."

Peter, the youngest Kemper child, stood clutching a carved wooden horse while he watched the proceedings, and now I knelt down to his level. "Master Peter! Your sister and brother are all done, and you see it didn't hurt a bit. Won't you be a brave soldier like Papa?" I saw repeatedly how a young child who contracted the disease fared far worse than one treated with inoculation.

Catherine took her brother into her lap as I readied my knife. Worried lest he cry out and attract Widow Jenkins' attention, I was quick, and he had no time to whimper. When she turned him loose, the little boy knelt down and galloped his toy horse across the floor.

I wiped my knife on my apron, put it back in my pocket, and handed her a tin from my medicine chest. "If you or the boys feel feverish, brew some of this tea. It will help. Now, if there's nothing else I can do for you, I should start for home."

"We'll be fine. I'll fetch your cloak, missus."

The image of three small headstones that marked the resting places of my siblings in our family's burying ground in Stafford rose before me. Nearly every family knew the pain of watching a child-sized coffin descend into the earth. I had done everything in my power to ensure the health of the Kemper children. I would have to trust the rest to Providence.

6

Clear Course of Action

RAPPAHANNOCK ROAD, FAUQUIER COUNTY, VIRGINIA
JANUARY 14, 1778

The wind whipped my cloak around my ankles as I stepped outside. Manso brought out the horses and I glanced up at the weak winter sun, now halfway down to the horizon. "We must stop at Edwards' and see if the post rider came today." Hoping for a letter from Benjamin, I turned Nelly's head and we set off toward the village.

As soon as we were on the main road, I gave vent to my anger. "How dare she! Manso, I fear next time I see Widow Jenkins I shall lose my temper and speak my mind. I expect her to question everything I do—but now she's put frightening notions in Catherine's head—and ones that malign the poor girl's mother. Why must she cling to misguided superstition instead of embracing treatments that make the patients more comfortable as they heal?"

Manso shook his head. "She's just one of them ladies that don't truckle with nothing she don't already know. She won't have nothing to do with slaves' ways of tending sick folks."

"The woman who trained me in the healing arts was the wisest I ever knew. Her station in life was irrelevant. It's foolish to ignore treatments that work, no matter whence the knowledge came. As foolish, in fact, as believing red blankets and drapes cure smallpox. Do you know what Benjamin would say?"

"I'm sure the reverend's got an opinion. He always do."

I smiled at Manso's accurate assessment of my husband. "He'd say, 'A freethinking citizen is not obliged to agree with anyone simply because the other believes they ought to.' This means I needn't agree with Widow Jenkins. But it also means Widow Jenkins needn't agree with me."

Manso chuckled. "Miss Anna, you never change your opinion for no one. You been like that since you was a little girl."

"Yes, I suppose that's true."

"You and Mr. Henry was always fussing about something when you was children and you wouldn't give in to him nohow. Like to drive Miss Hannah distracted."

The joke was on me, but it felt good to laugh. "That hasn't changed. I can still drive Mother distracted."

As we rode on in silence, my mind drifted to my last childhood squabble with my brother Henry. Though I should have forgotten it long ago, the memory was bound to my father's death—the fatal crack that shattered our family. Suppressing a shudder, I squared my shoulders and vowed that no matter what I had to do, my children's lives would differ from mine.

GEORGE ASBURY FARM, STAFFORD COUNTY, VIRGINIA
SEPTEMBER 1758

Both the doctor and the priest arrived at our house before breakfast. Phillis was then just a girl herself, on loan from Uncle's household to assist us during my father's illness. She read the situation and wasted no time shooing the four of us children out to play on the far side of the hayfield, where the trill of cicadas near the drought-ravaged creek sawed on my nerves like a dull blade on brick.

Henry, who was seven and two years my junior, behaved as though nothing was amiss. He pushed me aside as he ran past, swinging a long stick through the grass like a sickle. "I'm Lieutenant Colonel Washington, attacking Fort Duquesne!" He disappeared into a patch of unmown hay along the path, and though experience taught me to expect an ambush, I still cried out when he jabbed me in the ribs with his stick.

Joseph was used to our squabbling. "Stand and fight like a proper British soldier, Henry. Don't hide in the brush like a savage."

I understand now, that I was not truly angry with Henry. Father's illness was like a great beast lurking in the shadows, ready to strike our family. My brother was an opponent more my size and I took out my frustrations by baiting him. "What if *I* want to be Lieutenant Colonel Washington and lead the attack on the fort?"

Henry parted the grasses and wrinkled his freckled nose. "You can't! You're a girl." He shoved me as he dashed away toward the cover of the trees along the creek bank, leaving me fuming in silence.

Five-year-old Jeremiah clutched handfuls of Joseph's sandy hair as he rode on our brother's broad shoulders. "I wanna be a pirate!"

Joseph set Jeremiah down and the little boy scampered after Henry.

"So are they soldiers or pirates?" Henry tried my patience even on an ordinary day and at the moment my patience was in short measure.

"See here?" Joseph knelt to brush away some fallen leaves and tried to claim my interest by drawing a map in the dirt with a stick. "The pirates—or mayhap the British—will attack from the shoreline." As he stood, he nudged me with his elbow and spoke for my ears only. "It doesn't matter what fancy we spin for the little ones."

He knew too.

As I followed him into the open space above the creek bank, a high-pitched giggle came from the brush. Joseph raised his voice as he made ready with the stick he selected for a sword. "They are fearsome fighters. I have never seen their like in this good colony. Stand ready!"

"Aye, aye, sir!" Even with a sturdy stick in hand and an imminent threat to our coastline before me, I couldn't help glancing back across the fields toward home. I wished I could have stayed there to help. A piping yell signaled our attackers' arrival as Henry and Jeremiah, kerchiefs tied around their heads, charged up the creek bank.

Joseph winked at me. "Methinks it be pirates!"

Little Jeremiah challenged Joseph, who deflected his stick with ease and fought him left-handed. Henry, who was nearly my size, entered combat assuming he'd best me because I was a girl, but I had no intention of letting him. I sidestepped his attack and struck a blow across his rump, sending him sprawling in the dirt and finishing with a verbal jab intended to put him in his place. "Oh, help! Who will save me from such a frightful pirate?"

Jeremiah, outclassed by his sparring partner, giggled as he ran in a circle just out of Joseph's reach. When he dropped his stick, Joseph flipped the little boy over his shoulder and spun around, making him screech with delight. I took my eyes off Henry for a moment, remembering how our father spun Joseph and me that way when we were the little ones.

That lack of attention earned me a blow to the shoulder. Henry had scrambled to his feet, his face bright red. "Come on, then!" He swung at me again, and as we parried, the clack of our sticks grew faster and faster.

Though it was not yet midmorning, the sun blazed as hot as July, scorching through the thin fabric of my gown and linen cap. The cord meant to hold back my hair came undone and tawny strands clung to my sweaty face and neck. I'm sure I made a lovely picture when I stuck out my tongue at my brother. "See Henry dance!"

Angered by my taunts, he lunged in too soon. I accidentally struck him across the face, and he roared as blood spurted from his nose. Lowering my stick, I started to ask if he was all right, but he rushed forward, his stick held out as though he intended to skewer me. I hastened to block his charge and buckled his knee as he passed, so he fell to the ground. Foot on his back, I stood over him, breathing hard.

"Miss Anna!" Phillis emerged from the hayfield and hurried toward us. "You let Mr. Henry up this minute."

Instead I bore down for a moment, pressing him into the dirt before removing my foot. As he got up with a grunt, Joseph and Phillis exchanged a glance.

Phillis was a slave—and no older than Joseph—but she was in charge of us and she knew it. "You all come on now. Playtime's over. Your papa done passed."

We tiptoed into the gray clapboard house, dusty, sweating, and in Henry's case, bloody. Bible in hand, the priest prayed over Father's body in the bedroom. Mother sat stone-faced in the rocker by the window, clutching a lock of his sandy hair.

I knew my life would change once my father was dead. I just didn't know how much.

EDWARDS' ORDINARY, FAUQUIER COURT HOUSE, VIRGINIA
JANUARY 14, 1778

While it did no good to let memories of my father's death plague me so, I could not rid my mind of them any more than I could imagine facing life without Benjamin by my side. Never had he seemed so far away.

Despite my woolen cloak, the damp wind chilled me to the bone before Edwards' Ordinary came into view. When we dismounted in the side yard, I handed Nelly's reins to Manso. "I could do with a bite to eat, and I imagine you could too. Come inside as soon as you have the horses settled."

He nodded as he led Nelly and Charley toward the stable. "I'll be in directly."

"Thank you for the work you did at the Kempers' today. I know it was much appreciated."

"Young Mr. Henry is growing up fast. Knows how to swing an axe. Made the work light."

Unlike most patrons, I entered through the rear door reserved for servants. The Edwards' serving girl was a member of our church. After taking a moment to exchange pleasantries, I handed her some scrip and asked her to prepare a plate for Manso. It was ready when he came in and he took his meal to a stool beside the kitchen hearth, stretching his feet toward the flames. Buttering a slice of bread for myself, I proceeded through the ladies' parlor into the main room, where Mr. Edwards called to me from behind the bar.

"Missus Stone! Post for you arrived a few hours ago."

At last! Scanning the folded letters laid out on one of the scarred wooden tables, my heart leaped when I found the one addressed in Benjamin's hand.

On Publick Service
To Mrs. Benjamin Stone
Carters Run, Virginia

It was nearly an hour's ride home, too long to wait to open the letter. Reading it now would satisfy the hunger inside me food could not. In the ladies' parlor, I cast the scrap of paper and thread I carried away from the Kemper house into the flames and settled into a wing-back chair.

December 26, 1777

My dear Wife,

A week ago, we marched to Valley Forge to take up Winter Quarters and since then have been so occupied with building huts I have not had time to write. Joseph, Henry, Jeremiah, and I share a hut with eight others, and sleep in shifts. We are short of rations, and have been so since our arrival, though the officers say more provisions will arrive soon. I am at present in health, though I lack a warm coat and my shoes are near worn through. I am now a Sergeant. Many of the men resigned when they finished their terms of enlistment, and this made for a great deal of promotion among those of us who remain.

I pray this may find you, the children, and all the family in perfect health. By request of your brothers Henry and Jeremiah, I inform you they have felt unwell these past few days and do not appear to be improving.

There is some stirring of rumors in the camp that Congress is displeased with General Washington's performance at Brandywine and Germantown and instead finds favor with General Horatio Gates. The men of my acquaintance call him Granny Gates for his shillyshallying ways, and they say Gates's victory at Saratoga has puffed up his pride beyond his abilities. Some soldiers fear Congress will try to remove Washington. I am content should they remove almost any general except His Excellency. Congress cannot know of the army's confidence in him, else motions would never be made for Gates to take command.

I should be glad to be favoured with a few lines from you, my Anna. How are the babes? Does Rhoda read the Psalms daily? Is Elijah speaking in full sentences? And does our little stranger, William, still thrive? I dreamed I was holding him and kissing him, and how sweet was his laughter. It filled me with a joy that lasted long after I awoke. I hold you all in my heart and pray for you daily. I will do my duty for my country until I may come home and hold you in my arms.

Until then, I remain,

your Benjamin

A sip of tea eased the constriction in my throat, but it could not calm my pounding heart. Benjamin's letter relieved some of my worries and increased others in equal measure—but it also presented me with a course of action. I must go to him, and right away.

I roused Manso from his stool beside the kitchen hearth and on the ride home urged Nelly onward at a pace that allowed for no conversation. I used the time to gather my thoughts and pray. When I came into the house, the children's voices drifted from the keeping room, but I chose not to join them there and hastened up to my chamber.

Benjamin's moss-green wedding coat, no longer his best, hung in my clothespress. He cut a fine figure in it the day we married. A faint remembrance of his scent lingered in the folds and I held it to my face to breathe him in before I put it on. It was far too large, and the cuffs flapped long and loose beyond my fingertips. His cocked hat, made of good felted wool, sank down over my ears and concealed my linen cap. Tomorrow I'd fetch his extra breeches, leggings, shirts, and his spare pair of shoes from the trunk at our house.

With a wool coverlet spread on the bed, I piled on a change of my underclothes and wrapped them inside. By packing few of my own things, I could bring the warmest clothing for the men and enough food to sustain them. As I headed downstairs with the bundle in my arms, my mind churned out a list of many things to pack. How much could Nelly carry? Everything seemed just as necessary as my medicine chest. Soap, bacon, dried fish, beans, cornmeal, nuts. Maybe some fruit preserves for a treat.

In the larder, my gaze lingered on the salt barrel. The men could not get along without it. Rummaging in the bundle until I found one of my stockings, I opened the barrel and poured in a scoopful. The knit was fine and no salt leaked out so I poured another scoop.

"See here, boy. What are you about?"

At the sound of my mother's tremulous voice, I turned, and Benjamin's hat slid down over my nose. I pushed it back and met her incredulous gaze.

"Saints be, Anna! You startled me. What on earth are you doing?"

"I'm packing. I'm going to Valley Forge."

7

Serve and Protect

M y mother folded her arms on her chest. "Wherever Valley Forge may be, surely you do not intend to go dressed like that?"

"Valley Forge is where the army has made winter camp. It's in Pennsylvania, I believe." Another scoopful of salt slid into the stocking. "And no, of course I don't intend to go dressed like this."

"This war has stayed far from our doorstep, praise God. Why would you court trouble?"

"Benjamin writes that Henry and Jeremiah are ill. I'm going to tend them and bring food and supplies. Where are the clothes Joseph left with us?"

"Worry has made you take leave of your senses, Anna. You cannot possibly travel when little William isn't even off the breast yet."

I tied the stocking closed with a bit of twine. "It is a little early to change his diet to all pap, but I remember Lynn saying her sister's child is but a few months younger than William. I'll send a note asking to hire her away from her situation at the Martins' to stay here and wet nurse him while I'm away. I should be back within a fortnight—three weeks at the latest."

"That long? What about Rhoda and Elijah?"

"I'm not doing this to vex you, Mother. My absence should trouble you not at all. Phillis has helped me care for the little ones since we've lived here and I trust her to take over. Don't you want me to do all I can to help your sons survive the war?"

"Would that I had another son to send. 'Tis no fit adventure for a woman needed at home." My mother wrung her hands, a gesture of helplessness, making me all the more determined to take action.

"I must be the one to go. It's not just for the men—it's for my children. You can't have forgotten when Father died, your wishes regarding us mattered not!"

"Sending you and your brothers from home was harder than losing your father." Tears brimmed in her eyes. "I wish there had been a way to keep us together."

"I regret that too." Did she not realize how easy it would be for our family's history to repeat itself? "You must understand my distress, Mother. Rhoda's past the age of reason. Uncle William didn't shrink from putting me into a situation when I was not much older than she is now. I fear he'll do the same to her if my children and I become his responsibility. Do you think he wants another generation of widows and poor relations under his roof?"

"Who can predict what he will decide? He has not complained about keeping me in his household these many years."

"But it isn't fair to expect him to do much more for us."

"You are rushing into danger without thinking." Her chin trembled. "What if you happen upon ruffians or natives and have no male protection? What if some Hessian soldiers escape the prison camp in Winchester? Everyone knows Hessians violate women and butcher children for sport."

"I'll trust in God to guide me. I warrant I know more of the world than you. I can take care of myself."

She reached for my hand. "A mother expects she may lose sons to war. I've made my peace with their leaving, but I can't lose you too."

Though I would never admit it, her objections pricked a hole in my confidence. Even to my own ears, I sounded less than convincing when I said, "You won't. Good night, Mother."

Phillis put the children to bed while I was in the larder. When I tiptoed in, I reached over the cradle's high wooden sides and touched William's tiny fist to make sure he was warm. Inside the drawn curtains on the big bed, Rhoda and Elijah curled up together like two kittens, Rhoda's well-loved doll, Mariah, between them.

Was I a terrible mother to consider leaving my children? When that worry took hold of my heart, it was hard to remember I must take this risk to give them good, happy futures.

Before I undressed, I scooped coals into the shining copper bed warmer and shoved it under the quilts on my side of the bed. Instead of reading one of Benjamin's letters, I took out a quill and a sheet of writing paper and composed one of my own, short and to the point. I hoped it would never be read.

Benjamin once assured me, because God created me, I could not surprise Him. He knew my nature and what I needed before I asked. Now when I knelt to pray, I did not ask forgiveness for being impatient with the Widow Jenkins. God understood I could not respect someone who put words in His mouth and used Him to frighten people. Instead I asked for a speedy recovery for Mary and that only the mildest cases of the disease would affect her children. For myself, I sought patience and courage to meet whatever challenges lay ahead on the road to Valley Forge and the wisdom to take advantage of any Providence-offered opportunity to control my fate.

Make haste to Valley Forge. The voice nagging me in my dreams echoed in my head when I awoke. Our chamber felt as cold as the frost coating the windowpanes and after stirring up the coals and adding a few sticks, I burrowed back under the covers and let the flames warm the room before rousing the children to help them dress.

I tied the sash at the back of Rhoda's frock coat while Rhoda tied Elijah's and I praised Rhoda's patience, for tying Elijah's sash was as difficult as holding the reins while a frisky pony misbehaved. With William on my hip, we trooped downstairs to the kitchen. *This will be your last breakfast with the children*, a voice inside my head whispered. *Until I return*, I mentally replied.

Rhoda stood at the table, just as my siblings and I did when we were little, but, praise be, my children have never known empty bellies, as Joseph, Henry, Jeremiah, and I did the winter after our father's death. Lynn ladled out porridge while I spread butter and preserves on biscuits and cut Elijah's meat. Because he was not tall enough to peep over the edge of the table, I set his plate and bowl on a chair and tried to keep him from eating his porridge with his fingers while I nursed William.

After wiping the children's sticky hands and faces clean, I handed William to Lynn. "I'll have Manso carry a note to Mrs. Martin asking to hire your sister to wet nurse while I'm away. I hope we'll see her and her baby this afternoon."

"Yes, Miss Anna." Lynn grinned. "I'm looking forward to them staying with us. I thank you for thinking to arrange it."

"Without her, I could not leave. William will thrive in her care and perhaps he won't miss me much, for he is so used to you and Phillis. I must look in on Mrs. Kemper this morning and while I'm out I shall pay a visit to Thomas and Betsy. Is it all right if I leave the children with you now?"

"Yes'm. Miss Rhoda and me got it all in hand."

Rhoda brought her drop spindle from the basket near the spinning wheel in the corner. "I'll spin half a skein while you're gone, Mother."

She smelled like the fruit preserves when I kissed the top of her head. "And I shall see it when I return. Help Lynn with the boys if she needs you."

"Yes, Mother."

Even with my heavy cloak with its quilted lining over woolen petticoats and gown, the wind sliced through my clothing and raised goose bumps on my skin. I shuddered, wondering if I would get used to being out in cold weather on my journey.

KEMPER'S MILL, FAUQUIER COUNTY, VIRGINIA
JANUARY 15, 1778

Delighted to find Mary's brow cooler to my touch, I helped her into a chair and gave her beef broth to sip while I changed the sheets and aired the room. Tears pooled in her eyes as she examined the sores clustered on her arms and the back of her hands. "I know I shall look a fright. I'm not brave enough to ask for a looking glass." She bit her lip. "If my face is anything like my limbs, my husband and children will not know me."

"That's nonsense. Peter and the children will be thankful you've survived. The goldenseal poultices I've been using will help the blisters heal and in time the redness and the scars will fade." I helped her back into bed and laid cloths soaked in the warm herbal brew on her arms, chest, and cheeks. "Mark me, you must pay no heed to Widow Jenkins and her notions. This suffering did not come upon you as punishment for sin. Benjamin would tell you the same if he was here."

"Aye. Thank you. I couldn't account for a sin so great it would take me from my children. I fear this has been a heavy burden on Catherine."

"She is a credit to you. She's managed the house so well while you were ill. You mustn't worry—and you mustn't stir from this bed until the last pustule scabs over. On this the Widow Jenkins and I agree. You could have a relapse and the children need you in good health with their father away. I'm also going away for a spell, but I'll call on you when I return."

"I'll expect you to come by for tea."

"I'll look forward to that."

Before leaving the room, I rinsed my hands and forearms with vinegar and water and whispered the prayer my mentor taught me, asking that God prevent me carrying disease from one patient to another. Downstairs, I looked in on the children, even though it was too soon for them to show symptoms. I hated to think that if any of them grew seriously ill from my ministrations, Widow Jenkins would be summoned to care for them in my absence.

At the Leeds Manor boundary, I turned off the main road to follow the dirt path toward home, and Nelly perked up at the familiar surroundings. She headed toward the log barn, but I halted her in front of the house and looped her reins over the porch railing, disappointed as she that we would not be staying long.

Fallen leaves littered the porch and crunched beneath my feet as I crossed to remove the padlock on the door. Inside, a musty smell met me, and I shivered. With no fire on the hearth, it felt as cold as outside.

We took no furniture or books to Uncle's, only mine and the children's clothing, their few toys, and William's crib. Though I emptied the straw mattresses and packed the linens away in one of the trunks, the rest of our possessions remained in place, a ghostly reminder of what our lives had once been. Originally the tenant house on Benjamin's father's land, it stood empty for several years. Benjamin and

Joseph worked for weeks to make it ready before our wedding and my husband-to-be's desire to please me was clear in every detail.

He whitewashed the ceiling between the heavy beams and scrubbed the fireplace and the floor around the hearth until years' worth of soot stains were removed. My small collection of copper pots and pans gleamed from their hooks on the wall, with a three-legged iron spider and roasting spit ready for use. The trestle board stood in the middle of the room with chairs pulled up on either side.

Joseph sanded and oiled a dish dresser left behind by the house's last tenants until it gleamed like the pewter plates and bowls stacked on the shelves. Our set of six knives and spoons rested in the drawer.

Though it was a modest beginning, I felt rich and content when I surveyed that one room. A grand house did not always make for a happy home.

When Rhoda was a baby, Benjamin and Thomas added two bed-chambers to the structure and sided the house with sawn boards. In the one I shared with Benjamin, I knelt before the trunk and lifted out his folded shirts and breeches. To my disappointment, it was the odor from the cedar-chip sachet, not his scent, lingering in the fibers. But Benjamin's presence was everywhere, like the evidence of the life we built together. To keep my anxiety from consuming me, I thought back to the day he came home from Williamsburg.

STONE ORCHARDS AND FARM, CARTERS RUN, VIRGINIA
FEBRUARY 1776

Benjamin returned unannounced, filthy, and unshaven, but otherwise none the worse for wear. With a cry of joy, Rhoda ran to greet him, but when he knelt and opened his arms to her, she stopped short and wrinkled her nose.

Disappointment flickered over his face and then he laughed. "I suspect I'm a bit overripe." As he rose to his feet, I rushed past Rhoda into his arms, heedless of the grime and the smell. His crushing hug lasted for a long moment and then he laughed again. "You're holding your breath, aren't you?"

"I've been holding my breath since you left." His embrace and whiskery kiss stirred desires I'd kept at bay during our months apart. "But now that you're home, everything's all right." When he released me, I buried my face in my shaking hands for a moment, reminding myself it really was all right.

He set his rifle in the corner, opened his haversack, and brought out a wooden doll dressed in a Turkey-red gown, which he held out to Rhoda. "She came from the capital with me to meet her new mama." His eyes twinkled as he watched her cradle the doll like it was a real infant. "What name do you choose?"

Rhoda studied the painted face. "I shall call her Mariah."

I bent to pick Elijah up off the blanket spread on the floor and held him up for Benjamin's inspection.

"Oh!" The half sigh, half exclamation escaping his lips made me beam with pride.

The baby stuck his fingers in his mouth as he studied his father's face and then reached out to him. It was Benjamin's turn to fight back tears but his smile shone like the sun bursting through a patch of clouds as he took his son into his arms.

"Anna, I knew you would tend to everything while I was gone, but did you have to let him grow so much? He's fair doubled in size."

"I would keep him little, too, but alas, he'll be crawling any day now."

Benjamin bounced Elijah as he walked him around the room, murmuring to him, and my heart swelled as I watched them together. The baby paid rapt attention, as though he understood every word.

When Benjamin made a silly face, Elijah gurgled with laughter and grabbed his father's nose in his tiny fist.

After a time, when Elijah began to yawn, I took him from Benjamin, wrapped him in his blanket, and held out my hand to Rhoda. "Would you like to show Mariah to Aunt Betsy and cousin Sadie? You and your brother may visit there until your father's had time to clean up a little."

I winked at Benjamin over the children's heads as we headed out the door. With Rhoda skipping at my side, we covered the brief distance between our home and Thomas and Betsy's in short order.

At the door, my sister-in-law took Elijah from my arms with a conspiratorial smile. "Tell Ben welcome home from us—and enjoy your reunion. I'll keep the children overnight."

Rhoda had already disappeared into the loft with Sadie and their dolls. I hastened home again, where I found water heating for a bath and Benjamin carrying in the large tub from the barn. While he made trips back and forth to the pump in the yard, I built up the fire and tossed a handful of dried rosemary into the flames. As the pleasant scent filled the room, I hung blankets on the drying line to keep the warmth close around the tub. I then gathered a clean shirt and breeches from the clothespress and placed them on a chair with a towel and the crock of soft soap.

After heating enough water, Benjamin undid the leather cord on the front of his hunting frock and began to peel it off. He'd only been away a few months, but I felt shy in his presence—in part because this darker, more dangerous version of my preacher husband made my pulse quicken. When I left him to undress alone, I heard water pouring out of the kettle into the tub and the thumps as his boots hit the floor.

My heart continued to pound as I took off the kerchief tucked into the neckline of my gown, exposing a little more of my bosom than was considered modest. There was time to primp a little, so I twisted a tendril of hair around my finger and touched drops of rosewater to my wrists and throat. As I straightened the skirts of my plain brown woolen, I wished I'd known he was coming home today so I could have worn a newer gown.

The sounds of his splashing ceased, and he called out. "Could you please add more hot water? There's some left in the kettle."

"Of course." The air was steamy on the side of the blanket near the fire. The tub water, opaque in the dim light, came up above his waist, and my cheeks grew hot as my gaze lingered on his bare chest and shoulders. A blissful expression came over his face as I poured in half of the remaining water. When I turned to go, he caught the hem of my skirt between his fingers.

"Are you away somewhere? Stay and keep a conquering hero company."

"All right. As you like." I couldn't just stand there and stare at him. Pushing my sleeves above my elbows, I knelt behind the tub. "Shall I wash your hair?"

He nodded, and I untied the cord that held his pigtail. He tilted back his head to receive the warm water I poured over the matted, dark strands. I dipped my fingers into the crock of soft soap, massaging his scalp and working the lather through to the ends until he relaxed against my shoulder with a sigh.

"When I dreamed of you and of home, you weren't coddling me as if I was a child."

"But this pleases you?"

"It does."

I giggled and brushed my lips against his wet cheek. "Then whatever other pleasures you've been dreaming of can wait until I wash behind your ears." He grinned and splashed me just a little and I held up my hands in protest. "That's enough of that. I don't want to get wet."

"Let the bugles sound truce, then." He settled back and closed his eyes as I scooped up more water and rinsed out the last of the suds.

The towel was just out of my reach on the chair and before I could turn to get it, he lunged for me. A great wave went over the side, and I squealed as it drenched the front of my gown.

He pulled me close until I was nearly in the tub with him. His lips took mine, and desire rose in me at his taste and the rough prickle of his whiskers against my skin. As the heat from his body blazed through the wet fabric of my gown, more water sloshed out of the tub and soaked my clothes through.

He stood, streaming water, lifted me into his arms, and left a trail of footprints that led to our chamber. He clawed my petticoat up around my waist, and we joined bodies in an urgent coupling that recalled the early days of our marriage, when our appetites for each other were at their peak and we spent the long winter nights exploring the pleasures of the flesh.

After, he helped me unlace. I shivered out of my wet clothes, leaving them on the floor as I burrowed with him under the blankets and counterpane.

"What of the children? When do we need to fetch them home?"

"Betsy said after breakfast."

"Good. Then tonight I shall have you all to myself." He spooned me against his chest and buried his face in the curve of my neck. "After all those mornings rising at someone's command, I warrant I'm not getting out of bed tomorrow until I'm good and ready."

I feigned surprise. "You presume too much, sir. I've had the bed to myself for months, and you've made a right mess of the house since you arrived."

"You'd not share your bed with a brave defender of the colony?"

His lips tickled, and I squirmed away. "Oh, do you know one? Introduce me and then I shall decide."

"You minx!"

We both burst out laughing and I rolled over into his embrace, eager to receive him again. I combed back the lock of hair that was forever falling across his face and, tracing the line of his jaw, brought his lips back to meet mine.

8

I Must Be the One to Go

STONE ORCHARDS AND FARM, CARTERS RUN, VIRGINIA
JANUARY 15, 1778

With the memory of Benjamin's touch as fresh as if I'd just left his arms, I closed the bedchamber door. Though reconciled to the long stretches of separation that stemmed from his fervor for independence, I still ached every day with missing him. Now, hours before my departure, I began to doubt my motives. Yesterday I was certain of this being the best course of action—but was the situation at Valley Forge truly so dire? Did my loved ones' survival depend on me leaving my children and risking my life—or was I about to make an unnecessary, dangerous journey to relieve my loneliness?

Eager to speak to someone who understood what I was about to undertake, I headed across the orchard to Thomas and Betsy's. As I turned Nelly into their fenced barnyard, I imagined the large, oak barrel sitting nearby once held Baylis's remains. The sight of it reinforced my fear that my inaction would lead to more tragedy.

Thomas answered my tap at the door. "Anna! Come in."

"Thank you. I thought I'd take you up on the invitation to visit."

Betsy hurried to embrace me, and we clung together. "My, we miss you and the children. How are they?"

"Everyone is well, but another matter is causing me concern. May I have a word with you both?"

"Of course." Thomas pulled out a chair for me.

Betsy took my cloak. "Sit you down and I'll pour some tea. Can you stay for dinner?"

Luxuriating in the sting as I wrapped my cold hands around the steaming mug, I felt the tension ebb out of my shoulders. In the past ten years, I spent nearly as much time here as in my own home next door. "I'd love to, but I mustn't. There's so much to do. Yesterday I received a letter from Benjamin."

Thomas nodded. "See, what did I tell you? No need to worry."

"I'm not so sure about that. In his other letters, he wrote that he and my brothers were well. I suspect it was not always the whole truth, but he meant to spare me worry. This time, he wrote that Henry and Jeremiah are ill and he lacks warm clothing—so I must assume their situation is desperate. You've said as much yourself, Thomas. I've decided to go to them."

"By yourself?"

When I nodded, Betsy clutched my arm. "No! How can you ever? It's hundreds of miles."

"I can do it." I looked at Thomas for support but he shook his head.

"Traveling those roads is a hardship. You don't want to do this."

"But I must! We've already lost Baylis. I grew up separated from my brothers and now I cannot bear the thought of losing them—or Benjamin. What if he has fallen ill since he posted the letter? How will I live with myself if I don't go?"

The only other time I saw Thomas this serious was when he told me of Baylis's death. He shook his head. "It's an arduous, bone-chilling journey this time of year and I'd advise any man against it."

"I'm not any man."

"Not by a sight, you aren't. If determination alone would get you there, I'd put my money on you. Ben told me once, soon after you married, that telling you 'no' seemed to make no difference at all."

I refrained from mentioning how Benjamin held firm about depositing me and the children at Uncle's against my wishes. "Then you must know your opinion will not sway me, either. Benjamin and I vowed never to stop each other from following our true course." I tried to make light, so they would both stop looking at me as if I'd gone mad. "Don't you think I can read Benjamin by now? Betsy knows—it takes keen observation and a skillful hand to manage men like you and your brother."

Betsy regarded her husband with a hint of a smile. "He's been so glad to be beside his own hearth I've not had a whit of trouble from him for two weeks now. It's like a miracle."

Thomas glanced my way, signaling he noticed how I steered the conversation. "All right, you charmers. There's no need to malign my character. I imagine you'll get naught but grief from your family, Anna, but I see you're bound to go. What can I do to help?"

"I knew I'd find an ally in you." I leaned forward. "Tell me of the roads you traveled and how best to make my way to Valley Forge."

"Mark me, I've not been to Valley Forge, as I left for home before the army made camp. I can get you to Chester County and you can ask your way for the last few miles."

He brought parchment, quill, and ink to the table to sketch a map. "From your uncle's place, take the White Plains Road north to Chinns Crossing, then the Alexandria Road east until it meets the Carolina Road. There's a stretch between Leesburg and the Maryland line that's earned the nickname Rogue's Road, so mind you keep a sharp eye for thieves. If you can, find someone to travel with until after you cross the Potomack. Stay on the Carolina Road through Maryland and into Pennsylvania. Once you reach York, it's another two- or three-day's travel."

"How far in all? A week?"

"It may be closer to a fortnight to reach Valley Forge, depending on the weather and whether Nelly's as willing as you to put the miles behind her. Pray this cold spell lasts. There's naught slows the traveler more than roads mired down in mud."

Betsy frowned. "But a woman can't stay alone in an ordinary. What will you do for lodging?"

"I thought I'd seek churches and inquire after suitable accommodations."

Thomas got up to refill his coffee. "If anything should go amiss, Ben will have my hide for letting you travel alone."

"You're not responsible for me and you've got no right to stop me. I'll be fine."

He retrieved a sealed letter from the mantel. "Father asked me to post this to Mother's Butler cousins in York, to let them know of Baylis's passing. It'll get there just as soon if you deliver it and I know they'll invite you to pass a night with them."

"All right." I took the letter I composed the night before from my pocket and clutched it with both hands. "If something should happen to both Benjamin and me, this expresses my wish that you be our children's guardian. I want you both to be the primary influences in their lives." The thought of Rhoda as a serving girl in a stranger's house, with no one to protect and guide her, made me want to weep. How could I leave without knowing she and the boys would have loving guardians if I did not return?

But Betsy's hand flew to her mouth and I realized I'd asked too much. How could Betsy and Thomas promise to care for three additional children when they could not be certain what fate awaited Thomas when he returned to the army?

Just as I started to put the letter back in my pocket, Thomas reached for it. "On my honor, I'll take responsibility for the children if the need arises."

We made the sober exchange. Neither message contained anything that would prompt a smile.

"Thank you for the map and the advice—and the tea. I mustn't tarry if I'm to get an early start tomorrow." As Betsy and I embraced again, I felt her draw a shuddering breath. I whispered, "Don't cry. I need you to be strong for me."

"Remember when you were a new bride, how you cried worrying over Benjamin getting in a scrap at the courthouse? May I not cry about you doing something ten times as foolish—and ten times as brave?" When at length she released me, her cheeks were wet. "God go with you, Anna. Give Benjamin and your brothers our love and good wishes. We'll see you when you return."

ASBURY MANOR, FAUQUIER COUNTY, VIRGINIA
JANUARY 15, 1778

On the ride back, the late afternoon sun cast long shadows across the frosty hills and fields. When I arrived, windblown, and smelling of winter sweat, I sought nothing more than a seat before the fire. But Uncle called to me as I passed his open study door and beckoned me to come inside. I hesitated before obeying, fearing we were about to revive our earlier disagreement.

He laid two sheets of parchment on his desk blotter as I stood before him. "This morning I heard in town that General Washington has sent a messenger to Governor Henry, informing him of the deplorable conditions at winter camp. He begged the governor's help spurring Congress to give aid without delay. Upon my return from town, your mother spent a quarter of an hour lamenting your intention to travel north alone."

My spine stiffened as I prepared to defend my choice yet again. "I must go. What if the food and medicine I bring are enough to sustain Benjamin and my brothers? Jeremiah is your heir. I'd think at least you'd be worried about losing what you've invested in him."

He raised his gaze to meet mine. "Washington has appealed to the state governors to send as much food and clothing as they can and you think you can save four men with what you can carry on horseback?"

"Yes, I do. I have the skills to help where the need is great. I won't have my children grow up—"

"As poor relations?"

"Without their father." I cringed. Had Mother shared our entire conversation? Bowing my head, I waited for what seemed an eternity until he cleared his throat. "I didn't mean to sound ungrateful. You provide the roof over our heads and the food on the table, but, God willing, that won't be necessary much longer."

He scoffed. "I expected the lads to be home by now. The British capture of Philadelphia should have ended the war. But as long as Washington insists on keeping his army in the field, the soldiers suffer. So do the businessmen."

"I think His Excellency's refusal to surrender shows pluck. They can't give up when they've come this far. I shan't give up either." Should he forbid me to go, I would defy him. Sometimes when in his presence, I had to remind myself I was no longer a helpless child.

He did not speak again until after he dipped his quill into the inkwell on his desk and signed the bottom of a document. "This is a letter of introduction which you may carry with you on your journey." He sprinkled some pounce to dry the ink before he handed it to me, along with a second sheet on which was a list of names and towns. "Present it when you call on any of these associates of mine and they will provide you with lodging as far as Lancaster. And here—you're sure to need more money than you have on hand." He tossed a drawstring pouch of oiled leather on the desk in front of me.

Dumbstruck, I clutched the pages and picked up the money pouch. It was then he held out a third document, folded and sealed with wax.

"In return, you will act as my courier and deliver this to my associate, Andrew Thompson, at his residence in Leesburg. It contains a large bill of exchange. Once he receives the payment, I am sure he will be most hospitable. I expect you to see to the health and welfare of your brother, whom you refer to as my other—investment, when you arrive at the army camp."

It was all so unexpected I didn't know what to say. He gave me a rare smile.

"Do I surprise you? I daresay my brother would have done the same. He would have been proud of your determined nature—that is, until he was charged with reining you in. I take it Nelly is fit and up to the journey?"

"Oh yes. She's a fine horse and I'm fortunate to have her."

"As I surmised when I included her in your dowry."

"Now I must go finish packing."

"Anna?"

"Yes, Uncle?"

"Borrow a riding habit and some decent gowns from your cousins. Determination will take you far, but I won't have you appearing at the homes of my business associates looking like a poor relation—or a plain-wearing Baptist. Do you understand?"

"Yes, Uncle."

"With your husband traipsing around preaching to the country folk instead of studying to become a proper Anglican priest, you'll always be a poor relation, but I suppose you'll have the independence you prize so. Express my regard to Benjamin and your brothers when you see them."

I bowed low. "Thank you."

I opened the drawstring pouch, hands trembling as I pulled out folded notes. He'd given me nearly one hundred Virginia dollars, some tobacco warehouse coupons, and a handful of shillings, more money than I'd ever possessed, and many times what Benjamin earned in a year. As I watched my uncle bend his head over his ledger, I believed I understood who he had become—a man of wealth who relied on bluster to conceal his generous nature.

When I came out of Uncle's study, Nancy laid her embroidery on the settee in the hall and followed me upstairs. "What did Father say?"

"It was a singular conversation." I shoved the money pouch into my pocket. "I feared he'd be vexed but he supports my decision to make the journey. He bade me ask to borrow riding and traveling clothes from you and Mollie."

"At last!" She grabbed my hand, pulling me down the hall to the girl cousins' adjoining bedchambers. "The whole household is talking of nothing else but your journey. You must borrow a ball gown too— just in case."

"Nancy, your generosity is touching, but I'll be tending to your cousins. I warrant there will be no balls or social events."

"It never hurts to be prepared." Her eyes grew wide and she clasped her hands together. "What if you meet General Washington? Or the Marquis de Lafayette?"

"There's no chance of that."

Nancy pouted for a moment and then opened her clothespress. "You must take my indigo woolen. That shade of blue makes your hair look like varnished mahogany. Father brought home the cloth and trimmings before the embargo, so it doesn't count."

"Thank you, but this patriot girl is proud to wear homespun."

"You can afford to say that. You've already got a husband. Will Mollie's brown habit suit you? It's newer than mine and it has such a cunning hat." Nancy hurried into the other chamber and brought back the habit. "She'll never realize you've borrowed it. You need this quilted under-petticoat too. It's the warmest one I have. And I insist you take my good chintz kerchief." The girl's eyes sparkled as though *she* was about to embark on a grand adventure.

"You'd have me take so much finery I won't have room to bring my medicines or clothes and food for the men. Nelly can't carry over two hundred pounds and that must include her tack and me."

"You'll be glad you have a pretty gown when you reunite with Benjamin. Just see if you aren't." She loaded the clothing into my arms and perched the petite peaked cap that went with the riding habit atop my head.

"Thank you, cousin. I appreciate your generosity."

"And don't worry about the children while you're gone. I'll help Phillis and Lynn mind them. Rhoda and I can start her sampler."

Already I felt the ache of missing my little brood.

That evening, I let Rhoda stay up past her bedtime to help pack the supplies. I measured beans, dried fruit, a mixture of walnuts and pecans, dried fish, and cured bacon into separate sacks for her to sew closed.

"I'll tell your father and your uncles how you helped me ready all this good food for them."

"Who feeds the soldiers?"

"The army's quartermaster and commissary department. Sometimes there's not enough nourishing food to feed so many men. We have plenty in our larder and it will cheer them to get good things to eat from home."

She looked thoughtful as she wrapped cubes of pocket soup, made from scraps of dried meat and fat that could be boiled down to make broth. "Mother, will I remember you when you get back?"

Her innocent question wounded me. Did it hurt Benjamin this much when he left? I rolled some clothing into a tight bundle and kept my tone cheerful. "Of course. I'll only be away a short while."

"Not like Father."

"No, not like Father. You remember him, don't you?"

"I remembered him better when I saw Uncle Thomas."

"I did too. Memories fade over time, but something that will never fade is how much your father loves you. You may be sure he thinks of you and prays for you every day, for he tells us so in his letters. When he comes home, you will make new memories with him."

Phillis came to the doorway, bearing a candle, and I nodded in her direction. "You've been a great help, my girl. Now it's off to bed with you. I'll be along soon."

"Will you wake me to say goodbye before you go?"

"Yes." I kissed the tip of her nose. "Good night, sweetheart."

As soon as she was out of my sight, a wave of loneliness washed over me. Aside from the times I stayed away overnight tending to someone's illness or assisting at a birth, I'd never left my children for more than a few hours.

The food parcels and clothing bundles went into larger sacks treated with linseed oil to repel moisture. A small piece of oilcloth would protect the letters I carried on behalf of Thomas and Uncle William.

Bending over the pot of melted rosin and lard simmering on the crane over the fire, I dipped a rag into the slimy mixture to waterproof my boots. When I spied my mother hovering in the doorway, I girded myself for yet another battle.

"Anna, I implore you. Stay home. Don't endanger yourself."

"I appreciate your concern, but I've made my plans. I have Uncle's blessing."

She pressed her lips together until they nearly disappeared, an expression of displeasure bound up in my earliest memories. Then she left without another word.

What right did she have to judge my decisions without expecting I would also hold her to account? She was unable to stop Uncle from removing us from her care, one by one. Before I left to begin my indenture, she seemed to worry more about how I would comport myself, and whether I would be a credit to Uncle, than any mistreatment I might suffer at the hands of my employers. From the age of ten to seventeen, she could neither influence nor help me.

Why then, when I returned to Uncle's house as a young woman, was she astounded at my independent streak and my unwillingness to accept her authority? While I was away, my experiences opened my eyes, and I learned women who found ways around the strictures of society could protect one another and do more than just survive.

DUNLAP PLANTATION, STAFFORD COUNTY, VIRGINIA
MAY 1759

In the months after my father's death, I saw my uncle grieve. I saw him scheme. I watched him take responsibility for supporting two families. But I never saw him nervous until the day he delivered me to the Dunlaps. I didn't understand the circumstances leading to my indenture, but now I knew my father's last three tobacco crops had been poor, and Mr. Dunlap, his broker, paid the rent on our farm and loaned my father money on which to live. Someone had to repay that debt, and it fell to me. I would serve in the Dunlap household for seven years. If I did not satisfy, the debt would come due at my dismissal.

When we arrived at the estate, we halted in the circular drive and I slid out of the saddle. The house seemed impossibly large. What if I got lost inside it? Fear took hold of me and I had to choke back a sob when a slave came for the horses and led away Daisy, my last link to home. Once she was off to the barn, I had no choice but to follow Uncle to the door where a butler wearing a braid-trimmed coat answered his knock.

The foyer alone was larger than our whole house, and I forgot to feel frightened as my eyes darted about, taking in flocked wallpaper, walnut wainscoting, and what appeared to be a machine-made table and bench. I was so busy trying to see everything I bumped into Uncle as we followed the butler into the parlor.

There, I found riches beyond my imagining—oil portraits, silver candlesticks, a bright, patterned Turkish carpet, and shelves full of leather- and cloth-bound books. A woman about my mother's age, dressed in a silk gown the color of evergreen boughs, set down her embroidery and folded her hands in her lap as we drew near.

My uncle bowed. "Good day, Lady Dunlap. May I present my niece, Anna?"

The woman looked at me but addressed my uncle. "How old is she?"

Eager to please the lady who lived in this beautiful house, I dropped a quick curtsey. "I'm almost ten and a half, ma'am."

Her pursed lips showed she was not pleased but my attention strayed yet again when a gentleman wearing a powdered wig joined us and my uncle bowed lower than the first time. "Mr. Dunlap, sir!"

Though I turned and curtsied, my new master never even looked at me. "Asbury. I have some business to discuss with you." When he led the way out, I followed, unwilling to lose sight of my uncle so soon.

Lady Dunlap rang a little bell, which brought the butler back in time to intercept me. She spoke to him as though I was too stupid to understand her. "Take her to the kitchen."

I broke into a trot trying to keep up as he strode down the hall past a room that looked as though the family used it only for eating, left the house by the rear door, and crossed the yard.

In the brick summer kitchen, the air was redolent with savory aromas that set my stomach rumbling. A woman servant stirred something simmering in a pot hanging over the fire. Another was slicing a ham, and a third was pulling loaves of light bread out of the bake oven on a wooden peel. Bowls and platters crowded the worktable in the center of the room—as much food as was at Father's funeral.

"Here's the new girl." The butler departed.

The woman by the fire turned toward me. When I bobbed yet another curtsey, she looked amused. "Put on your apron, child."

In my bundle I found the apron, made of a piece of homespun from Mother's scrap bag, and tied the twine around my waist. When I presented myself again, they were all piling serving bowls and platters on trays. The first woman, who seemed to be in charge of the kitchen, handed me a bowl of yams and shooed me. "Go on now—take this to the dining room."

Trotting after the other women, I carried one dish at a time. When we brought in the last, the family and Uncle William had assembled to eat. I hesitated, not sure where to sit and the daughter, who was about my age, smirked and whispered something to one of her brothers.

Uncle gave me an encouraging nod but then looked away. It was a moment before I realized I was not welcome at their table. My eyes filled with tears of embarrassment and I hurried from the room. I knew no servants, black or white, other than Phillis and Manso. As I crossed the yard, I realized they never ate at the table with my family, and I assumed they hadn't with Uncle William's either. I never thought about why. Perhaps it was not only about skin color, for it seemed I was not good enough to dine with the Dunlaps. Yet I had not changed since yesterday.

As I entered the summer kitchen, there were two plates on the cleared worktable, filled with generous portions of the same food we just served the Dunlaps and Uncle William. My mouth watered until I had to swallow. Surely everyone in this household, whether master or servant, was a stranger to hunger and want. The woman motioned me toward the bench pulled up to the table.

"Sit, girl, so I can bless the food."

Thankful, I scooted onto the bench and we bowed our heads. After my whispered "amen," I picked up my spoon. "I'm Anna. Anna Asbury."

Her large, dark eyes met mine. "I'm Rhoda."

My mother named her first son Joseph, after her father, and her first daughter Anne, after her mother, our Hardwick grandparents. My older sister Anne died before her first birthday and Mother modified the name for me when I arrived. I sometimes wondered what they would have called me had Anne lived.

When my daughter was born, I named her in honor of my surrogate mother, the strongest woman I have ever known.

9

Well Begun Is Half Done

The night before my departure I lay awake listening to all the little sounds the children made—the sighs, the scuffling as they searched for a warmer or cooler spot, the open-mouthed breathing of deep sleep. We were settled here. They would be fine during my short absence.

Before dawn, I lifted baby William out of his cradle. It was earlier than his usual waking time. He yawned, looking up at me with eyes half closed as we settled into the chair near the hearth. I untied the drawstring on my shift and though still drowsy, he latched on. I crooned to him as he nursed, wishing I could capture this moment to share with Benjamin.

When he was full and dozing again, I laid him back in his cradle and dressed by the light of the glowing coals in the fireplace.

The more clothes I wore, the fewer things I had to pack, so I drew on two pairs of wool stockings, tying the ribbon garters just below my knees. Over my shift went my quilted stays, which I preferred for riding. I couldn't endure whalebone poking me for two hundred miles. I doubled up on wool under-petticoats, too, and tied on my pocket, which had the drawstring bag of money and my sheathed knife inside.

Though Uncle had every right to expect his courier to reflect well on him, I always believed traveling clothes should be one's oldest, most comfortable, and in the winter, the warmest. Now I felt obliged to wear only my cousins' clothing. Uncle's barb about my being plain-wearing stung a little. Though Baptists favored simple dress, I told myself my gowns were not as severe as those worn by Quakers.

I had nothing against pretty clothes. Had I not married in a fashionably trimmed gown striped in yellow and red? Now, as a matron, my gowns were serviceable gray, brown, and blue, with little adornment. No matter how my clothing changed, I still held to my vow to care for Benjamin for better or worse. I wondered, when I made the final tally of my life's adventures, into which column this one would fall.

Mollie's elegant riding habit, cut in military style, had black velvet panels on the front with a row of brass buttons down each side. The cream-colored chemisette's frilled jabot spilled out of the jacket's upstanding collar. In the looking glass, a fine lady stared back at me with huge gray eyes as I pinned on the black hat trimmed with two pheasant feathers and a ribbon cockade.

When I parted the curtains around the bed to gaze down at Rhoda and Elijah, I nearly changed my mind about leaving. Rhoda stirred and opened her eyes when I brushed a wisp of hair off her forehead. "Must you go now, Mother?"

"Yes. Be good and help care for your brothers. I shall return as soon as I can."

She wrapped her arms around my neck and held me so I could barely turn my head to kiss her cheek. Even then she did not let go and a sob escaped her lips when I pried her arms off my neck. With trembling lip, she turned over and snuggled closer to her brother. As I let the curtain fall, I heard her take a shuddering breath. The sound broke my heart.

Boots in hand, I fought back my own tears as I tiptoed from the room and downstairs. Phillis had breakfast waiting, but the porridge, ham, and bread and butter threatened to stick in my throat. I washed it all down in a hurry with two cups of Hyperion tea, a common substitute for the Chinese teas I and other patriot women proudly refused. I did not let on, but I feared I'd never learn to prefer the taste.

"God watch over you, Miss Anna." Phillis handed me a canvas haversack. "I packed enough food for a few days, if you're sparing."

"Thank you, Phillis." It felt natural to embrace her. "Thank you for breakfast and for seeing me off." I slung the haversack's long strap across my body and fastened my cloak.

Manso was waiting for me by the back door and I held a lantern to light our way as he carried my bundles. It was wetter and not as cold as the day before, but Nelly reacted to the damp, chilly air swirling into the barn with flared nostrils and a toss of her head. She balked when Manso led her out of her stall and stamped her foot as he loaded the heavy bundles. Disdaining to make things easier, she refused to bow even when I coaxed her with an apple, so I led her to the mounting block, feeling heavy and awkward in all the extra layers as I settled in the saddle.

She reared when I touched her flank with my heel, so I reined her down and counted to ten to give her time to reconcile herself. After that, it took just one tap of the crop and we departed under clouds portending a day of soggy travel. I put her into her rack gait, which was slower than a canter but so smooth I would not need to post, as with a trot. I could not push our pace while the roads were slick.

Without doubt, Nelly was the smartest horse I ever owned. Maybe I spoiled her from time to time, but I knew well the difference between serving a heartless taskmistress and one who rewarded efforts with genuine affection and thanks.

A cold drizzle struck my face as I left my uncle's land and headed past the Leeds Parish glebe lands, farmed by citizens for the benefit of the parish priest. Benjamin believed, should the United States win its independence, compulsory support of the Anglican Church would become a thing of the past. Under the current system, priests lived well on tithes and the profit from the glebe lands' harvest yield.

This was not true for Benjamin and his fellow Baptist ministers. His income from serving several churches in the rural areas of Fauquier and Culpeper counties, where a better-than-average annual tithe was twenty-five cents, was negligible. That never mattered to him, for we did not require an income from his preaching. We had several acres each in wheat and corn, a kitchen garden, and some stock. The yield from our apple and peach orchards bought the necessaries we could not raise or grow.

Some women knew little of their husband's finances, but Benjamin and I always went over accounts together. Even though his income was modest, I didn't allow myself to think overmuch about our long-term financial situation until Uncle put that bag of money in my hand. Despite my occasional disagreements with my relations, we were fortunate to be living where the children and I wanted for nothing. Still, I did not ask for extras and never expected Uncle to provide more than a place to live while Benjamin was away.

I had an income, of sorts, from tending the sick. When my patients paid in produce, chickens, or small game, I turned the food over for the benefit of Uncle's household. Coins and scrip I hoarded, but my nest egg would not go far if our other sources of income dried up.

Every man in my family, save Uncle, abandoned his business interests to go off to war, and now his words rang in my ears. How would we fare if the war came to Virginia and left our homes ravaged, our wealth destroyed, and our men dead on the field?

ASBURY MANOR, FAUQUIER COUNTY, VIRGINIA
OCTOBER 1776

Once Benjamin made up his mind to deposit the children and me at Uncle's, neither my reasoned arguments nor my cajoling could sway him. As I would not resort to tears to get what I desired, I packed with a heavy heart.

When we departed our home after breakfast the next morning, I rode Nelly apace with Benjamin and the children in the wagon. Nelly misbehaved, even though it was slow going, and I blamed my unhappiness and impatience for her skittishness. Alone, she and I could cover the five miles to Uncle's in less than an hour. Most of the roads winding through the foothills of the Blue Ridge Mountains in this part of northern Virginia were little more than dirt paths dotted with stumps and boulders, so it was faster and easier to travel on horseback, or even on foot, than by wagon.

With the loaded wagon, our trip took nearly three hours. When we arrived, I was glad to climb out of the saddle. Manso took Nelly's reins, and Jacob, one of Uncle's other slaves, untied our two milch cows from the back of the wagon and drove them to pasture. Benjamin handed Elijah to me, climbed down, and let Rhoda jump from the wagon into his arms. As we walked toward the house, the last of my good humor fizzled. Uncle's raised voice reached my ears even before King opened the front door. The butler looked flustered as he took Benjamin's hat.

"Reverend Benjamin, Miss Anna, we'll serve dinner as soon as I can announce it to the master." He inclined his head toward the study.

Benjamin nodded. "Perhaps it will help if we announce ourselves first."

Inside, we found my uncle, his face purple with rage, bellowing as he waved a sheet of parchment under the nose of a red-haired young man. Joseph stood by, looking reluctant to intervene. The young man, I realized with a start, was our brother, Jeremiah. I hadn't laid eyes on him in six years, since he departed for his studies at William and

Mary. A reedy youth then, he had grown up, and gave all appearances of prosperity in a well-tailored coat and knee breeches, silk stockings, and shoes with shiny silver buckles. I would not have recognized him had I passed him on the street.

He cut across William's diatribe. "Uncle, I'll not sign."

My family and I looked on, as yet unnoticed, as Joseph put his hand on our brother's arm. Jeremiah pulled away. "I'm twenty-four, Joseph! I'm old enough to know my own mind, and still he treats me like a child." William brandished the paper at him again and when Jeremiah spied us in the doorway, he brushed Uncle's hand away and pleaded for Benjamin's support. "See? Didn't I tell you yesterday how obstinate he's being? He won't give up on the idea of engaging a substitute for me, but I'm going with you."

William let out another roar, and I cried out, "Jeremiah, please— you'll drive him to apoplexy!"

Elijah began to wail, and Rhoda, unused to heated words, ducked behind my skirts. Benjamin took Elijah and settled him in his own arms, shushing him as he stepped into the group of men and addressed his youngest brother-in-law. "But we discussed the other side of this as well, did we not? William is expecting you to take over some of his business holdings now that you've finished your studies and your clerkship. He's long been grooming you for this, Jeremiah." He paused. "Your uncle has shouldered the load and supported two families for most of your life. Should you not honor your obligation to him for all he has done for you?"

Jeremiah looked shamefaced as he addressed our uncle. "Of course, I appreciate everything you've done for me. But to hire me a substitute? It's like you think I can't look out for myself."

Benjamin had, without effort, positioned himself between the two men. So calming was his presence that the tension began to ebb away and even Elijah quieted when he spoke again. "Jeremiah, you know William considers you his son. He raised you in his house, which you'll inherit someday. It's a grand legacy but I warrant his primary worry is losing you to circumstances beyond your control. I don't have such a patrimony for Elijah, but I know it would tear my heart out to send him to war."

Uncle's harrumph signaled his tacit agreement and for a moment it looked as though Benjamin had diffused the situation.

Then Jeremiah delivered the final blow. "I cannot enter that contract, Uncle. It's too late. I've already signed my enlistment papers."

William ripped the substitute contract in two and threw the pieces at Jeremiah's feet. "Out! The lot of you!"

We all fled into the foyer like naughty children. I glanced back into the study, watching as my uncle sank into his chair and put his head in his hands.

As I closed the door behind me, a hearty laugh rang out, and I turned to find a sandy-haired, freckled man at the entry, two large canvas sacks slung over his shoulders. He dropped the sacks and hurried to clasp Joseph's hand.

"Joseph! It looks like Uncle's come up in the world since I last saw him. I didn't expect a hero's welcome, but when I heard all the hollering, I thought it prudent to wait to announce my presence." His face lit up when his gaze fell on me. "Anna? Saints be!"

"Henry?" I rushed into my brother's arms and he swung me around with ease. "It's been nigh eighteen years! What brings you here at last?"

"Joseph wrote that he was going with the Third. The recruiters over in Stafford are after us night and day to enlist, but I figured I'd rather go with this lot, so I sold my interest in the shop." He gestured at Benjamin. "Are you going to introduce us?"

Joseph clapped Benjamin on the shoulder. "Meet the man who won our sister's heart. Ben's fearless in battle . . ."

"As he must be!" Henry flashed the same mischievous grin that annoyed me so much when we quarreled as children. Not angry at all, I played along, putting my hands on my hips, but stopped short of sticking out my tongue at him.

". . . Plus, he'll pray for your soul." Joseph finished. "He's the best of the best. It's bully to have you with us again, Brother."

Now that the shouting seemed to be over, Rhoda's curiosity emboldened her to speak. "What's in the bags?"

"Shoes and boots." Henry smiled at her as he stooped to untie one. "Who might you be?"

"Rhoda, sir." She bobbed a quick curtsey.

"Well, Miss Rhoda, I believe you may call me Uncle Henry." He brought out a pair of shoes. "These are first quality—not like what they issue to the army. I should know, as I made them myself."

Joseph inspected them. "But won't you regret selling your interest in the business?"

Henry tossed me a pair of ladies' riding boots. "Here. See if these will suit you." To Joseph, he said, "The cost of raw materials keeps going up. I couldn't take an army contract at the price they offered and still deliver a product that would last more than a few months, so I thought I'd try my hand at soldiering."

Uncle took dinner alone in his study, but for the rest of the household, it was a jolly meal, with all of my brothers together around the table for the first time in our adult lives. Henry's personality had not changed since I last knew him, but now I found his sense of humor akin to Thomas's, and much to my liking. His disposition rounded out Joseph's steady, good nature and Jeremiah's youthful rebelliousness. I could not recall my mother ever looking so happy as she sat between Joseph and Henry.

At the end of the meal, Phillis brought out a frosted cake, made as a surprise for my twenty-eighth birthday, and I insisted it also serve as a going-away treat for Benjamin and my brothers. I hadn't expected to see all four of them off to the army at the same time and found my feelings quite in sympathy with Uncle's. Had Jeremiah given in to Uncle's wishes, I'd have one less brother at war to worry about now.

10

Waterlogged

Dawn did little more than turn the eastern horizon above Fish-back Ridge a paler shade of gray. Had not a gust of wind blown my hood back as Nelly and I topped a rise, I might have missed the flicker of movement on the road behind me. It was too dark to recognize the rider, and with Thomas's warning about rogues at the forefront of my mind, I nudged the mare's ribs, though I could not urge her to go much faster without the risk of breaking her leg. The rider behind me slapped his horse's rump and as he drew nearer, his shout carried on the wind. "Miss Anna!"

I turned in the saddle and slowed Nelly to a walk. "Manso? Whatever are you doing?"

He reined in Charley as he came up beside me. "Miss Hannah sent me to watch over you. She said likely you give up and come home before dinner."

"Oh, did she? Well, I daresay I'll be in Leesburg by this evening. You shan't follow me all the way to Pennsylvania."

His voice was pleading. "Miss Anna, you can't travel by yourself. It ain't safe and it ain't proper." One knotty, veined hand clutched the reins as he put on his tattered hat.

"You shouldn't be out in this weather without warm gloves."

"Never mind that. I'm used to it. What if there be soldiers about?"

"I might ask you the same thing. Soldiers from either side are likely to take you into the army. Did Uncle give you a travel pass?"

"No'm. Miss Hannah sent me."

"Then you must go home! You'll be in terrible trouble if you're caught out here alone without a pass."

"I'm supposed to be with you, Miss Anna."

"The longer we linger arguing, the longer it will take me to reach shelter this evening."

"Miss Hannah gonna scold me." His unhappy expression revealed his torment, caught between my mother's orders, his worry for my safety, and the dangers he faced.

After a bit more back and forth, Manso, grumbling, consented to turn back. I believed it was because I asked, rather than ordered, him to obey. Sheltered beneath an ancient fir tree, I watched until he was out of sight and dallied several minutes longer to make sure he did not double back to continue following me.

As Nelly and I emerged, a splash wet my cheek, followed by another. I brushed the raindrops away and squinted at the steel-gray sky. The scattering of drops was a last-minute warning before it began to rain in earnest. I urged her back off the road and closer to the bank of the Little River, where the tree branches arching above us were thick enough to protect us from the downpour.

All too soon, the road crossed the river and forced us back into the open, where the wind whipped my cloak and the cold rain numbed my cheeks. Nelly splashed through the shallow ford and picked her way through the churned-up mud at the water's edge. Her hooves made sucking sounds as she pulled them out of the ooze. Unable to find secure footing on the icy bank, she whinnied as we slid backward toward the water's edge.

I dismounted, feet squelching through the muck as I led her up the hill and over to a grassy area where I found a flat stone and a stick to scrape out of the concave bottom of her hooves. When I finished, I surveyed my smudged petticoat, cloak, and gloves in dismay. "I suppose it'll be easier to brush off once it's dry, won't it?" She snuffled against me as I patted her flank. "I think we shall both walk for a while."

I lived in Stafford County until I was seventeen. In that time I made but two notable journeys. One, when I was ten, to begin my indenture, and the other when my time in service ended in 1766 and I removed to Uncle's grand new estate in Fauquier, the next county to the west. His fortunes increased tenfold in my years away. No longer a servant, but neither the young lady of the house, I was not sure how to behave. Jeremiah and my cousins did not remember me and they were too young to have a circle of friends into which I could enter.

The adults trotted me out to church and social events, determined to find me a match from among the young men of the county's planter class. But I distrusted young gentlemen, for I saw how my master and his elder son preyed on the help to satisfy their carnal urges. In my limited experience, wealthy men were naught but brutes in well-tailored clothes. As the law would allow any future husband of mine to do whatever he wanted to my property, our children, or me without my consent, I reckoned I was better off without a husband.

When my young cousins fell ill with scarlet fever, I tended them, and word of my skill as a healer spread among the neighbors. Before long, someone came knocking at Uncle William's door nearly every week to ask for my help. In this, I found purpose and a sense of accomplishment. The remedies I copied into my receipt book under Rhoda's tutelage eased the sufferings of my neighbors. Poring over my pages of notes with new enthusiasm, I gathered herbs to steep in brandy for tinctures, and blended others into medicinal teas.

At first, my mother and Aunt Jean protested against my riding out alone to tend the sick but as time passed, they refrained from mentioning it. Potential suitors ceased to appear at Uncle's dining table. Content, I thought myself as free as I could be.

That was before I met a man who offered me more freedom within the bonds of matrimony than I could have hoped to gain on my own. Until I met Benjamin Stone, I knew no one who embraced the idea that liberty was for everyone.

CARTERS RUN BAPTIST CHURCH, FAUQUIER COUNTY, VIRGINIA
SEPTEMBER 1766

Joseph, my thoughtful big brother, noticed my reserve around Uncle's acquaintances and invited me to accompany him to services one Sunday so I might meet some of his friends.

At Carters Run Baptist Church, the little crowd in the clearing buzzed with lively conversation, punctuated by an occasional burst of laughter. This came as a surprise, for at other churches I attended, people dressed in their best and signaled their piety by their sober silences and frowns. I arrived in my new striped yellow polonaise to find all the women and girls wearing simple homespun. Several of them cast curious glances my way and I wished Joseph had known to mention I would blend in better in an everyday gown.

Most of the men also wore rough clothes. One, dark-haired and suntanned with a tomahawk stuck in his belt, seemed so rugged he would be at home among the native tribes. I shrank back a little as he drew near. He stood in stark contrast to my sandy-haired brother, whose knee breeches and linen shirt marked him as a tradesman.

To my surprise, Joseph greeted the swarthy young man with a smile and a handshake. "Thomas, good Sabbath. This is my sister, Anna. Anna, this is my friend Thomas Stone."

He swept off his hat in a courtly gesture completely at odds with his appearance. "Miss Asbury, how nice to make your acquaintance." A blonde young woman smiled in welcome as she joined us and he put his arm around her. "This is my wife, Betsy."

"Good Sabbath." Feeling silly for misjudging him, I dropped a hasty curtsey. As I rose, I locked eyes with the young man who stood just behind Thomas and Betsy. He, too, was dark haired, lanky, and tanned, but was dressed in a linen coat and breeches. The breeze ruffled a loose lock of hair that fell across his forehead and his dark eyes sparkled at me when he smiled. I nodded to acknowledge him but kept my face sober, as was proper for the Sabbath.

Joseph offered me his arm as everyone filed inside. "That's Thomas's brother, Benjamin," he murmured.

My eyes darted around the unadorned meetinghouse. Rows of backless benches filled the space on either side of a narrow center aisle and a simple table stood on a raised platform at the front of the room. It was nothing like the ornately carved interior of Aquia Church in Stafford, the site of my christening, and the décor was not the only difference. Here, men and women sat together, instead of on opposite sides of the room, and there were black faces among the white.

As Thomas and Betsy filed in behind Joseph and me, I glanced sideways to see if Benjamin followed. Instead, he made his way to the front of the room and laid his Bible on the wooden table. An older man joined him to deliver the opening prayer and lead the hymn, and then placed a hand on Benjamin's shoulder. "Brother Stone has asked to lead the meeting today."

As Benjamin began to speak, his gaze fell upon me. Transfixed by his earnest and confiding manner, it seemed he directed his discourse as though he and I were the only ones present.

"When I was nine years old, thoughts of death, of judgment, and of future punishment began to oppress my mind. I resolved to live free of sin and to work until I received pardon for whatever childish transgressions I committed. I sought to be an exemplary Christian, but somehow, vowing to avoid sin did not hold for long."

Thomas spoke up in a solemn voice. "I warrant I may have had something to do with that."

Several men in the congregation snickered.

Had I not been watching Benjamin so closely I might have missed the wounded look that crossed his face before he recovered. "You did indeed have a hand in my frequent need to repent, Brother."

This time I joined in as everyone in the congregation laughed at Thomas's expense.

Benjamin continued with growing confidence. "My resolve to live a model life fell short. I am not a child anymore and I understand that full redemption comes to those who believe in the Son. We need not be perfect to receive His grace. We must only believe.

"But we still have obligations. I say to you, we must not avoid risk out of fear. We must use our intellect and our gifts to see to the earthly—and the spiritual—comfort and well-being of our brothers and sisters."

People around me nodded, and so did I, wondering if Joseph told his friends I was a healer.

Benjamin spread his arms for emphasis as he went on. "Some may call this sin, to dare to act so our own will, rather than His, be done. But our Creator, the One who first loved us, knows our hearts and minds. He smiles when His children help and serve one another, because in this way, we also serve Him."

A latecomer opened the door at the back of the meetinghouse and Benjamin paused in his discourse. "Good Sabbath. All are welcome." Then the light faded from his eyes, and he set his stance as though preparing to ward off a physical blow.

I looked over my shoulder at a young man who stood in the doorway, wearing a linen coat with embroidery on the hem and cuffs and two rows of brass buttons down the front. He stepped into the room and sneered as he glanced around.

"I came to watch you all go into your frenzies."

Before Benjamin could respond, Thomas spoke up. "We completed the frenzies part of the service about ten minutes ago. Another time, friend."

"Nay. I hear tell Baptists preach blasphemy and tell their converts they may indulge in any abomination without fear of punishment for their sins." At least a dozen young men, all wearing clothes marking them as the sons of planters, came down the aisle and grouped around him. In the simple, country church, they looked foppish and out of place. The first one's eyes roved the young women in the congregation and lingered on Betsy and me. "Makes us wonder what goes on during your meetings."

Benjamin cleared his throat. "You are misinformed."

"You're not even a proper priest," the young man shot back. "Your false doctrine unleashes moral depravity on the pious people of Virginia."

Thomas's laugh sounded more like a warning. "Says one who spends more time in his cups than at worship. I know you, Adam Whitaker. You'd not recognize a pious man if you tripped over him on your way out of a tavern."

"Are you calling him the sinner then?" Another of the intruders pushed his way to the front of the group of men as he challenged Thomas. He gave the congregation a disdainful look. "I see you even allow pagan slaves at your prayer meetings."

Benjamin's chest rose and fell as his anger swelled, but he kept his voice under control. "We welcome all who desire instruction in the ways of our faith." He addressed the congregation. "Brothers and Sisters, fear not when men criticize us, for spiritual dissent is the first step toward religious freedom."

"Offensive noise." Whitaker scoffed as he continued up the aisle toward the front of the room. "We came to root out the rabble."

I clutched Joseph's arm, my gaze darting between Whitaker and Benjamin, but again Thomas spoke, rising to his feet to reclaim Whitaker's attention. "The only offensive noise is coming from you, you puffed-up—"

One of them passed wind. As the others guffawed, Thomas retorted, "Oh, that was the most intelligent thing I've heard from you lot since you arrived."

The men who filled the aisle spread out to hold the congregation back as Whitaker approached the platform. "We're going to take your boy preacher out for a dunking. Stay back unless you want a martyr to your so-called faith." He made a grab for Benjamin's arm, but Benjamin wrenched it free. Another rushed forward and took a swing at Benjamin, who deflected the blow and landed one on the man's jaw, sending him reeling back. Two more advanced and together the four overpowered Benjamin. I stifled a cry as Whitaker punched him in the stomach. As they wrestled him off the platform, the men of the congregation attacked the interlopers.

Betsy pulled me out of the way. The bench in front of us tipped over with a crash as Thomas and Joseph disappeared into the fray. Rather than quail at the sight of thirty men and boys all brawling at once, my mind flew to tally the inevitable black eyes, scratches, and bruises. How long it might have gone on I cannot say, but when someone tossed a hornet's nest into the center of the room, the brittle paper shell burst as soon as it hit the floor. A swarm of angry insects poured forth, and more benches tipped over as congregation and interlopers alike fled the building.

Outside, I waved away hornets and scanned the crowd until I spied Thomas and Joseph helping Benjamin up the steep creek bank. Downstream, Whitaker, who also had a dunking, hurried after his retreating fellows.

I ran to Joseph's side, Betsy at my heels. "Is he all right?" Benjamin was soaked to the skin and a watery rivulet of blood ran from his nose. Keen to examine him for injuries, I reached out, but when Thomas and Joseph let him go, he fell to his hands and knees at my feet.

Thomas snorted. "He's fine. That Whitaker's all mouth and no trousers."

Benjamin's shoulders trembled as though he was crying. Then he sat back on his heels, pushed his wet hair out of his face, and scowled at his brother. "You should have let me handle it. You riled them up with your insults."

Thomas looked surprised, but still he reached out to clasp Benjamin's hand and pull him to his feet. "I couldn't leave off. They were a proper bunch of pompous windbags."

Betsy glanced from brother to brother and took her husband's arm. "Come. 'Twas not the first time they've disturbed worship and it won't be the last."

Though Thomas looked cowed at first, he did not let his wife lead him away without adding, "Ever thus, eh, little brother? I suppose I shall always fight your battles for you."

"Nay." Benjamin rose to his full height and looked his brother in the eyes. "Mark me, you only make things worse, Thomas. Part of my role as preacher is dealing with opposition. I must do it my own way, without your interference." He stalked away into the trees, leaving me wishing I had the right to take his arm and offer comfort.

11

Cider

Though I knew most of the roads in Fauquier, neighboring Loudoun County was unfamiliar territory. Relying on Thomas's rough map, I passed a blacksmith, a dry goods store, and a sawmill before stopping to water Nelly in front of Chinn's Ordinary, a three-story fieldstone tavern at a crossroads.

Even with no sun to gauge the hour, it had to be past time for the midday meal. I knew I should push on and eat the food Phillis packed for me, but my legs and back ached from being in the saddle, and I was so cold I couldn't get the thought of hot food out of my mind. When the stable boy came out to take Nelly's reins, I read the bill of fare written on a slate board propped beside the door.

The cost of food for man and horse—one shilling three pence—was enough to give me pause. Heavens! That amounted to a day's wages for a farmhand. As I hesitated, two men left the tavern. My stomach rumbled at the aromas of cooking drifting out in their wake and decided the question.

Inside, nearly a score of men occupied a long dining table in the center of the room. No families were about, and no women save one harried-looking serving girl. My sodden cloak scattered droplets of water as I shook it out and hung it on a peg near the door. I trailed after the serving girl as she carried pitchers of drink to the main table. "Is there a ladies' parlor?"

"No, missus." She did not break stride as she tilted her head toward a corner of the room. "You can take the small table, yon, and fill your plate from what's set out over here."

"Thank you." Peeling off my gloves, I washed at a bowl set near the door. As I crossed the room to my table, I watched a man grope the serving girl through her skirts as she refilled his mug. My sympathy went out to her. Had I no home to return to after my indenture, I might have shared her lot in life. What a pity she must endure such rough treatment. I felt glad and guilty in equal measure for my social standing.

As I watched the men bolt their meals, belch, and pile more food on their plates, I despaired of getting anything to eat. Mother never would have allowed us to behave that way and I doubted my ability to match their rudeness. But if one must push and shove to get food at this place, so be it. I took up my plate and approached the main table.

Reaching past their shoulders, I speared a slice of a meat pie with my knife and dipped up a ladleful of the stew. As my fingers closed around a golden square of cornbread to dip into the broth, someone else's fingers sought my rump through my layers of clothes. I flinched, slopping stew over the side of my plate and into another man's lap.

"I beg your pardon!" My words were meant to upbraid one and apologize to the other. The rumble of laughter following me to my seat across the room made my face grow hot and I kept my eyes on my food as I ate.

Though I did not frequent ordinaries at home, I sometimes stopped in to collect post or warm up after a long ride. The owners and most of the regular patrons at Edwards' in Fauquier Court House were members of Benjamin's congregation or my patients. While there, I could hold my head up and fear no untoward comments or advances.

Not so here, where I was unknown and traveling without escort. I regretted sending Manso home. I also regretted paying so much for this unpleasant meal. When some of the men left their places at the table, I rose to fill my plate again.

One of them cast a glance my way and wavered on his feet as he drained his mug. "I didn't realize I'd stopped in at Eve's Custom House, you, lads?" He inclined his head toward me, which led to guffaws from some of the other men.

Another called out in protest. "Here, shut your gob and be on your way. She can hear you."

The first man wavered. "What if she does? That's as fine a doxy as I've seen in these parts. A little long in the tooth, maybe, but a sight better than the usual fare."

Clammy sweat started under my armpits as several of the men stared at me. I felt like a rabbit caught in a trap. The kitchen maid seemed to have vanished. Would shouting for help summon the proprietor of the establishment?

"Here, love—how much for a quick tumble? I got some clink." The drunken man brought out his money pouch and shook it.

My anger flared. "Sir, take leave at once or I'll have my husband shoot you for the blackguard you are."

"She's wearing a ring, lads. I bet she'll show me how she earned it." He took a step closer, making lewd movements to suggest the skills I must have used to snare a husband while some of the other men jeered.

I reached behind me for something with which to defend myself. My hand closed around my mug, and I flung the contents in his face. The other men hooted as I left him wiping cider out of his eyes and hurried to the door, snatching my cloak off its peg as I went. Their laughter rang behind me as I picked up my skirts and ran for the stables.

Though I arrived gasping, the boy who brought Nelly out and tightened the girth on her saddle seemed to notice nothing amiss. As he gave me a hand to step up, I wondered if he could feel me trembling. "How far to Leesburg?"

"Near eighteen miles, missus."

My heart sank. I'd traveled just under twelve and most of that along familiar roads. Rain was still falling and the gray clouds hanging low in the sky made it nearly as dim as twilight. "Do you know the time?"

"Happen it's about a quarter past two. Most of the regulars who board here have long gone back to their labors and there's naught left but the drunks and layabouts."

I'd noticed as much. "Thank you. Please give this to your master." I paid him in scrip, turned Nelly's head, and departed in a rush. Once we were back out on the churned-up, muddy road, the dainty mare faltered and dropped to a walk.

Even after I was well away, my shame and anger flamed hot. Our society offered few opportunities for women to advance their education and support themselves. Men like those might assume women served but one purpose, but was not my intellect and my potential equal—nay, superior—to theirs? It was infuriating to consider how they must treat their wives, if indeed they found anyone who would consent to marry them.

Head bent against the wind, I guided Nelly into the rows of an apple orchard, where she found better traction in the short grass. I meant to find a chamber in which to express milk while I was at the tavern. Now I dismounted and stood in the shelter of the trees, shivering as I unfastened the riding habit's jacket beneath my cloak. The gnarled trees were bare, the falls long carried off by woods creatures, but Nelly was no stranger to orchards. Her velvety lips searched the ground for stray bites of fruit as I expelled the milk that should have fed little William this day.

The lingering scent of rotting fruit brought me back to the time when I found what I most desired in an orchard. I blessed my brother Joseph's intervention, for without his help, I might not have married the man who was right for me.

STONE ORCHARDS AND FARM, CARTERS RUN, VIRGINIA NOVEMBER 1766

"Anna! Come have a turn."

I couldn't believe my luck as I joined my friends at the Stones' kitchen worktable. Thomas and Benjamin's sister, Elizabeth, a coltish thirteen-year-old, greeted me with an enthusiastic embrace and Betsy patted the seat beside her. Mary Kemper and her little daughter Catherine were among other women and girls I knew from church.

I'd been attending services with Joseph for about a month when word of the trouble at Carters Run Baptist reached Uncle and he forbade me to spend any more Sundays there. Dispossessed of contact with Joseph's friends, I fretted. I had just turned eighteen and I'd enjoyed my first taste of a social life. The people I met there—especially the Stones—were much more to my liking than the ones in my uncle's circle of acquaintances.

My exile ended when Joseph sent Uncle a note begging to spare me for a few days, saying someone paid him for a carpentry job in apples. He needed me to see to the drying and preserving. When Uncle gave his consent, I hid my smile, wishing I could leave right away.

My mount was ready to go but I was the one chafing at the bit when Joseph arrived the next day. As soon as we were away, he grinned at me. "All work and no play makes Jack a dull boy. We must go claim the apples at the Stones' first. They're having a cidering party today."

When we arrived, he helped me down from the saddle. "Why don't you go inside and say hello? You have an admirer who's been fair bursting, waiting to see you." He wandered over to hail Thomas and a group of men throwing hatchets at a target, leaving me wondering which of the Stones might be anticipating my arrival. Benjamin was nowhere in sight among the men, but I dismissed the notion it could be he when I found the kitchen filled with women and girls. Obviously, it was his sister who was excited to see me.

I sat and took up an apple and a knife. "What must I do?"

Elizabeth leaned her elbows on the table, resting her chin on her hands. "Peel your apple in one long piece, then close your eyes and throw the peel over your shoulder. It will land in the shape of your true love's initial."

I shook my head. "Let Betsy or Mary go first then."

Betsy laughed. "It's a game for unmarried girls."

"Why?"

"It wouldn't do at all for my peel to form the shape of a letter other than T, now, would it?"

One of the other young women raised an eyebrow. "Might take Thomas down a peg, though."

This brought giggles from everyone at the table and I joined in at the thought. Elizabeth hovered nearby, watching me work. When I shut my eyes and threw the peel over my shoulder, everyone craned their necks to see.

Betsy winked. "Sure and it's in the shape of a B."

I studied the squiggle of peel on the floor. "I think not."

"Oh, there's no doubt. B it is."

They waited to hear what I'd say—Benjamin was the only eligible bachelor I knew whose name began with a B. I must carry the jest further or be the brunt of it. "I'm sorry, Betsy, what I feel for you is naught but friendship. I could never come between you and Thomas."

Over the burst of shocked laughter, Elizabeth cried out, "No! The B stands for Benj—" She clapped her hand over her mouth, which brought even more hilarity.

What was so funny about the thought of Benjamin? Surely he did not favor me. We barely spoke during the few times we met at the social hours before and after services.

Betsy nudged me with her elbow. "Anyone with eyes can see it."

Elizabeth beamed at Betsy. "The only good thing about having brothers is when they marry, I get sisters-in-law! Now come, Anna. I'll show you the cider mill."

She grabbed my hand and pulled me outdoors, leading the way to the mill built into a hillside. Baskets of falls stood inside the upper story. "The wagons and carts stop here, on the upland path, to unload. We pour the apples through that opening in the floor into the masher."

Bees buzzed about and the sweet scent of crushed fruit wafted up from below as Elizabeth leaned over the short wall and pointed below. "The workings of the mill—the important part—is there."

Just then Benjamin came into sight, walking beside a black horse yoked to a wooden lever, and Elizabeth's freckled face lit up with a mischievous smile. "Come on!" As she hurried to lead the way, she skidded on the steep path and landed on her bottom nearly under the horse's nose.

The horse gave a frightened whinny. Nine-year-old Baylis, who was also within, laughed at his sister, but Benjamin stopped the horse and helped her to her feet.

"Elizabeth? What are you about?"

She dusted herself off, as unapologetic as a kitten who has just shredded the drapes. "Anna wanted to see how the cider mill works."

Benjamin blushed when he saw me and rolled down his sleeves. Seeing him flustered signaled Elizabeth's instincts were correct.

Dropping my gaze, I stroked the black horse's muzzle. "Yes, please, if it's not too much trouble." The fruity smell hung even heavier inside the shed's lower level.

He cleared his throat. "No trouble at all. Dobbin here, supplies the power that runs the gears. The wooden cylinders turn toward each other to draw the apples down from the hopper and crush them. When, like now, the mashed apple clogs the holes in the cylinders, we clean it out." He took up a long wooden pole, cleared the upper workings, and stirred the mass of crushed fruit in the wide barrel below the mill. "There's enough ready for the press, so if you'd like, I can show you how the process works through to the end." When I nodded, he put the pole aside. "I helped Father build this mill when I was Baylis's age."

Enchanted by Benjamin's enthusiasm and his knowledge, I watched him work with his brother to put down a layer of clean straw in a barrel with holes bored near the bottom. They set it over a trough and used wooden shovels to spread a thick layer of the pomace over the straw, repeating the process until the barrel was nearly full. Then Benjamin put on the lid. He stepped back as Baylis, full of boyish enthusiasm, seized a long hand-lever and ran with it in a circle, causing a large, wooden screw to descend into position over the barrel top.

"Now Baylis presses the lid down until the juice runs out below." We joined Elizabeth behind a short wall, out of the way.

Baylis kicked up his feet and rode the momentum of the lever as it made another revolution. "This is easy work!"

"I used to love that part too." Benjamin grinned as he watched his brother.

Baylis was halfway around again when the screw reached the barrel top, and the lever jerked to a halt. Bravado gone, he found he had to pull hard. Though only a trickle of cider ran into the trough, his face grew red with effort.

Benjamin teased, "What ails you, Baylis? Pull!" The boy strained at the lever and when he could go no further, Benjamin vaulted the wall with ease and headed for the press. Instead of taking hold of the lever to help, he retrieved a tin cup hung on a peg, held it in the dwindling stream of juice, and carried it back to me. "Guests get the first sip." Our eyes met over the rim of the cup. His crinkled in the corners when he smiled.

"Ben, I give. 'Tis too much for one man." Baylis slumped over the hand-lever to prove his point.

Benjamin turned his attention back to Baylis. "Then make room. Two will get the job done." He took hold of the end of the lever and Baylis took the middle. The boy's feet scrambled in the straw, but Benjamin braced his legs, muscles straining, and did the bulk of the work as they brought the hand-lever another full revolution around the press. The screw drove the cover down, and apple juice coursed into the pan. I smothered a smile. He was showing off for my benefit.

Elizabeth, who missed none of the nuance in Benjamin's display, spoke up. "Baylis, go add more apples to the hopper. I'll take a turn minding Dobbin. Thomas said I could this year." She gave her younger brother a little shove and he ran up the hill.

Benjamin seemed ready to shoo her away, too, like he would an insect buzzing around the vat. "Why take on more work? Doesn't Mother have plenty for you to do in the house?"

"I just thought"—she gave me a sly look— "Anna might like you to walk her back to her brother."

My face flamed as I clutched the tin cup.

"Oh." Her words gave him the desired nudge. "Anna, I'd be failing in my duties if I didn't make you feel welcome. May I escort you?"

Hanging the cup back on the peg, I gave the horse's nose a final pat. "Yes, of course." He led the way out of the shed and when I glanced back at Elizabeth, the girl's grin nearly split her face.

Benjamin's arm brushed against mine twice as we made our way up the steep hill. His touch sent a pleasant shiver down my spine but I felt too shy to start a conversation. It was a relief when he broke the silence.

"I've been reading the published journal of Major George Washington, regarding his exploits in the late war."

Was he attempting to woo me with such a strange overture? Whether or not, I gasped with delight at the mention of the familiar topic, and my words spilled out with no effort at all. "At the Forks of the Ohio! It sounds like such a savage place, does it not? Still, my father dreamed of seeing the land on the other side of the mountains. He spoke of it during the early days of the war, certain once the British reclaimed the land beyond the Blue Ridge, his children's future would lie to the west, in the Ohio country."

Benjamin seemed pleased by my response. "I don't know any other girls who are interested in the lands to the west."

"According to the tutor where I used to live, history, geography, and political theory were not suitable subjects for girls."

"A pity. I should encourage you to learn about anything you choose."

"Would that you had been the tutor. As it was, I had to take matters into my own hands."

"How?"

"I borrowed books without permission and read them at night. Sometimes I listened at doors." His surprised expression made me giggle. "The tutor's voice carried. I suspect he didn't realize I could dust or sew or spin in the next room and listen to a lecture at the same time."

"Joseph told us you are a healer. Did you also learn that by listening at doors?" He was smiling, jesting with me, and just like that, we warmed to each other.

"No. The tutor knew Latin and Greek, but he was useless on the topics of healing and herbal remedies. One of the other servants taught me."

He paused beside the split-rail fence bordering the orchard and picked an apple off a tree, studying it as he spoke. "My parents never learned to read or write but our pastor recognized my interest in books, and Father hired him to instruct us children. Thomas did not enjoy our studies the way I did and I think it bothered him that his younger brother excelled at something when he did not. Of my siblings, it was only I who wished to attend university."

"And did you?"

"No. I've worked on our farm all my life. Last year, when I turned twenty-one, Father gave me the eighty acres adjoining Thomas's land, and we tend our orchards together." He spoke with such sincerity I realized he was taking me into his confidence. "'Tis a fine start. But I want more than farming and plan to continue my scholarly pursuits. My future lies in the church, to help others recognize their worth in the eyes of the Lord. Some of my mentors say fits of anguish beset them as they contemplated their call but I feel no doubt at all about what I must do."

"How long must you study to become ordained?"

"The Baptist Church is less formal than the Anglican Church and does not require ordination. I'm studying theology with the preacher Elijah Craig." I must have looked blank, for he laughed. "Have you not heard of him?"

"No. What's humorous about him?"

"Some say Brother Craig will only teach me to end up in trouble. Earlier this year, he was jailed after he led the Baptists in a revolt against paying taxes to support the Anglican Church. He's been arrested half a dozen times more for preaching without a license."

"And you intend to follow in his footsteps?"

"I have no wish to spend time in jail. If I do not let my enthusiasm lead me into unwarranted conflict, I daresay I will do as much to advance our faith as the fieriest outlaw preacher."

"I would say 'tis admirable to serve others."

"You do, as a healer."

"As you say."

He polished the apple on his shirt and when he offered it to me, it was my turn to laugh. "Aren't you sending Joseph and me home with bushels I must stew and dry? I don't need even one more apple."

"You can never have too many apples, Anna—and we grow the best in the county. Try it."

"You eat them uncooked?"

"Of course. We always have a ready supply. They're delicious this way."

"We eat them stewed or baked in pies. My mistress preferred a tansey."

"I favor pie and tansey. But try this one just as it is."

It was perfect. Unblemished. When I bit through the red skin into the crisp flesh, a dribble of juice ran down my chin. He wiped it away with his thumb and I trembled at his gentleness and familiarity. Gazing up into his twinkling brown eyes, I decided I might consider taking a husband who supported education for women—and had hard muscles and a soft touch, like this young preacher.

12

Tories, Soldiers, and Spies

A t the edge of the windblown orchard, I climbed the rail fence and got back into the saddle. Nelly and I struck out across a desolate tobacco field where the rain pattered on the soft, rotting stalks. Tobacco, my uncle's crop, was treated like cash in Virginia but I preferred apples.

By late afternoon my cloak was heavy with rain, and even after the clouds rolled away, moisture seeped through and penetrated every layer of my clothing. When there was but an hour of daylight left, the clear sky brought with it a temperature drop, leaving me chilled to the bone. I had to find shelter for the night.

Tendrils of fog crept up from the sodden ground as the sun sank below the horizon. The mist gathered until it was thick as combed wool and I could see only a few yards in front of me. Nelly and I might be the last beings alive on Earth. Could even God find me in this mist? Surely this day's travel was the worst I would face.

As Nelly plodded along, I thought I heard voices, though I could not tell from where they originated. Worried I might pass potential lodgings without realizing, I took heart when the hulking shape of a building materialized a short distance away. The burble of a stream and the shadowy forms of two men rolling barrels off a loading dock onto a wagon all signaled a flour mill.

One man laughed. "And then my brother David says in his letter, says he, 'damned if the Bloody Backs didn't come in, bold as you please, and—'"

Whatever he would say next was lost to me. I heard only the click as someone nearby cocked a pistol.

"Who goes there?" demanded a man's disembodied voice.

I halted Nelly, afraid to speak.

A second voice sounded as if it came from farther away. "You, on the horse. Come forward and show yourself."

Were these men the unsavory types Thomas warned me about? I couldn't risk them taking a shot and wounding Nelly or me. "I prefer to keep my distance, thank you." I tried to decide whether, and where, to flee.

"A woman." Indistinct mutters followed, filtered through the fog.

One man in the wagon called, "You must have a great need of flour to be about in this weather, missus. Show yourself."

"Nay. I dare not when there's a pistol pointed in my direction."

"You wouldn't be a decoy for those brigands, now, would you?"

"No." Before I thought the better, I blurted, "And I'm no doxy, either. I'm a patriot."

An explosion of laughter seemed to come from every direction.

The man on the wagon spoke again. "I've known patriotic doxies, but just as you say, madam. Now give us your name since you won't show us your face."

"I am Mrs. Benjamin Stone, of Carters Run." As another murmur rippled through the mist, I could sense them closing in on me.

A voice came from my right. "Stone, you say. Would your husband be Thomas's brother?"

"Yes, he is."

"Well, then you're among friends, missus. We all know Thomas well. I'm kin to the Jackmans, his wife's people. He makes a fine hard cider, Thomas does. But what brings you so far from home? You must look sharp, for it's not safe abroad here at night. We're picketed to guard this shipment of flour."

Four men moved closer until they were just visible through the waning day's darkening mist. Could I trust these as-yet faceless strangers? Nelly sidestepped and I tightened my hold on the reins.

"I'm on my way north to tend sick relations and I need shelter for the night. Are there Redcoats about?"

The shadowy man in front of me answered, "We've seen none but I heard they steal from honest folk to feed their troops without offering to pay a shilling."

Another chimed in, "Though to be fair, the Continentals can offer little more."

Yet another voice came from behind me. "It's not the armies that plague us. At least, not yet. Of late, brigands came to town brandishing clubs, thinking to get their hands on our supplies. Last time, when they found they couldn't get the salt they wanted, they thrashed some of the shopkeepers and terrorized the lot of us before hieing off to the east."

I twisted in the saddle. "Should I fear their return?"

"Can't say for sure but folks are mindful and guarding their property. You'd best get indoors, missus, so no one mistakes you for one of their band."

"Yes, I must. Is there a parsonage nearby?"

The man on the wagon said, "No parsonage but you could inquire at the Widow Champe's place. She and her daughter take in the occasional boarder."

Another cautioned, "She may be skittish of strangers, though."

There it was. If I'd made the eighteen miles to Leesburg, I'd have a safe place to stay at the home of Uncle's business associate

Mr. Thompson. How could I have fallen so far short on this day's travel? "Where will I find Mrs. Champe?"

The man on the wagon pointed. "This road runs alongside the creek. Her place is the brick house just past the ford. Tell her the Mercer brothers sent you."

"Thank you very much." Shivering as the heat of my bravado burned away, I pulled my hood closer.

As Nelly splashed through the shallow ford, candlelight shone through the mist like a beacon. Moments later I slid off Nelly's back for what I hoped was the last time that day and knocked at a two-story brick house. A woman about my mother's age opened the door a few inches, holding a candle aloft.

"Mrs. Champe?"

"Yes. Who wants to know?" Her voice betrayed fear.

"The Mercer brothers at the mill said I might secure lodgings here tonight for my horse and myself. I am Mrs. Benjamin Stone from Carters Run."

"And where's your husband, missus?" She craned her neck as if she expected to spy him lurking in the shadows.

"He's in Pennsylvania with the Third Virginia, ma'am."

"My son Johnny joined up with Lee's Legion back in seventy-six." Mrs. Champe peered into the darkness and the fog beyond me for a moment longer before she nodded. "Patriots are welcome here. Costs two shillings for you and your horse."

"Oh, thank you, ma'am."

"Go around to the barn and I'll send my Polly out to you."

Nelly's head drooped with fatigue as I led her toward the log barn. A girl about Nancy's age came out of the house with a lantern, led the way inside the barn, and hung the light on a peg driven into one of the hand-hewn posts. "What's your horse's name?"

"Nelly." I stroked the mare's muzzle before tying her to the post and removing the saddlebags and the bundles.

"Poor tired girl. She's so pretty. We'll have her settled before Mother gets supper on."

The barn's other occupants—a black horse and a spotted cow—kept it cozy with their body heat. Nelly would pass a comfortable night here. My fingers tingled as I unbuckled her girth strap and hung her saddle and soaked blanket over the short board wall of the empty stall.

Polly pitched fresh hay into the stall and manger box. "I'll draw a pail of water and fetch some oats. The brushes and combs are on the shelf yonder."

I found a hoof pick among the brushes, which did a much better job of cleaning out the mud than the rock and stick I used earlier. After attended to Nelly's hooves, I brushed the sweaty marks off her back and flanks and worked my way down her legs to remove the caked-on mud. As Nelly snorted and nickered, I answered her as though I understood her meaning, because I always believed I did. "You're welcome. How I wish I had someone to take charge of my toilette. I'm as muddy as you."

Polly returned with two wooden pails, set the one half-full of water within Nelly's reach, and poured oats into the manger from the other. Then she attacked the mud caked on Nelly's fetlocks and when we finished, the mare's coat gleamed in the lantern light. Before we departed, I scattered a bit of salt from the supply in my stocking for her. "Rest well, sweet girl. I hope we'll have better traveling weather tomorrow."

"You can leave anything you like in the barn overnight. We always lock it."

"Good. The saddlebag is all I need."

As soon as we entered the house, the full impact of my fatigue left me lightheaded. I sat the saddlebag at the foot of the stairs. It was all I could do to wash my face and hands before I staggered to one of the straight-backed chairs at the table.

Mrs. Champe set down a bowl of stewed vegetables and took her seat. As soon as she finished the blessing, the old woman all but shook a finger under my nose. "If I were your mother, I'd have insisted you stay at home, missus. Even though the war hasn't come back to Virginia since our men drove Governor Dunmore out, it's dangerous on the roads. Have you heard they're sending prisoners of war farther south instead of keeping them in Pennsylvania and Maryland?"

"Yes, ma'am, I heard they were sending Hessian prisoners to Winchester."

The old lady harrumphed just as vehemently as Uncle William, and I stifled a giggle at the similarity. "We'll soon be overrun with British prisoners too. Washington insists our troops treat them well, to prove we're not savages. Still, the British believe your husband and brothers—and my Johnny—are naught but traitors. They subject their prisoners to the worst abuses."

She went on without giving me time to respond. "You'd better watch yourself as you travel, missus, and keep your thoughts to yourself. It's not easy to tell the patriots from the traitors and scoundrels. Some folks are so riled up that if you take issue with any opinion or insult, they'll call you a Tory to justify violence against you."

"You think other patriots pose a threat?" I thought of my experience in the tavern.

"Look sharp and trust no one." She glanced at her daughter. Polly's face reddened. "I ran off one of her suitors last year when I learned he was a Loyalist. Loyalists are bad enough, but woe to you if you meet enemy soldiers. Tories, soldiers, and spies are everywhere."

"I thought it was only the British who would destroy patriots' homes and property."

"Mark me, invading armies never destroy what they expect to keep and enjoy. That goes for homes, chattel, and the women of their enemies. Although," her eyes lit up with mirth, "did you hear how the other Mercer boy, David, outsmarted one of the British officers?"

"No, ma'am. What happened?"

126

"David's a miller too—in Pennsylvania. We heard the tale last time we went to buy meal. The officer came in with a foraging detail, bold as you please, and stole six barrels to feed his troops without offering to pay a shilling."

"How awful! What did the miller do?"

"As they tell it, there was naught poor David could do but let them take the barrels—but as they were full of the lime he'd planned to use to whitewash the inside of the building, the bread the British baked must have given them quite a surprise." The old woman took a sip of coffee. "Serves them right for stealing from good, honest folk. I hope they all broke a tooth."

Too weary to linger over coffee, I thanked Mrs. Champe for the meal and rose to retire. Polly showed me to my chamber, where she built up the fire and left water for washing. As soon as I was alone, I sank down on the bed, head in my hands. All my worries and doubts rushed at me like an incoming tidal wave.

My mission, noble and selfless yesterday, now seemed impetuous and full of folly. Why did I not harken to those who tried to caution me? Why did I not believe I would face threats to my safety at every turn?

On the whole, Mrs. Champe was no different from my own mother—full of worry and admonition. When my children were grown would they think me a silly old woman? I hoped they would seek my wise counsel.

Though it seemed I did everything wrong today, it was not too late to begin again tomorrow.

If my mother was here, she would insist I return home, but then, she rarely gave me credit for having sense God gave a goose. When I was younger, I was foolish enough to let her influence me toward what could have been the biggest mistake of my life. Had she been a more reliable counselor, I never would have decided to break off my engagement to Benjamin.

ASBURY MANOR, FAUQUIER COUNTY, VIRGINIA
SEPTEMBER 1767

A few days after the cidering party, I returned to Uncle's. It wasn't long before a note arrived from Joseph, asking where I left his paring knife and to please reply at my earliest convenience. I remembered leaving the knife in the drawer where I found it, but before I could puzzle over this odd request, I realized there was a second, sealed note within. It bore my name in an unfamiliar hand. When I opened it and saw the signature, my heart leaped.

> Dear Miss Asbury,
>
> Please forgive my boldness. I asked your brother to send his note so I might enclose mine.
>
> Your absence is felt at meeting. Elizabeth, in particular, speaks of you often.
>
> Joseph told me that your uncle has forbidden you to attend our services, but I hope you will make up your own mind about whether you would like us to forge a friendship.
>
> I enjoyed discussing the Writings of the Journal of Major George Washington with you. How inspiring that a man so youthful could

make such a contribution to his country. If you care to correspond, we can discuss other topics that fall within our mutual interests.

I hope this finds you in good circumstances and that your duties with regard to tending the sick are not too arduous.

Your humble servant,

Benjamin Stone

I hastened to my chamber for quill and ink and giggled with pleasure as I penned my response.

Dear Mr. Stone,

Your lines I received with gladness, for I found our conversation at your family's cidering party most agreeable. I should be pleased to correspond. Have you read the works of the Scots philosopher, Adam Smith? I learned of his theory of the invisible hand while listening to a lecture last year and would be pleased to discuss it with you in future letters.

An article in one of my Uncle's old issues of the Gazette stated that since the Stamp

Act was repealed last year, the citizens of
Boston need no longer take to the streets
burning stamp distributors in effigy and
destroying property. Yet the Townshend Acts—
particularly the tax on tea—do nothing to
put down years of people's frustrations and
resentment. I fear the situation will grow
worse before it improves.

I ate my fill of apple slices while preparing
Joseph's supply for drying and find that I
have come to prefer them uncooked.

Please pass my greetings along to your
family, especially to dear Elizabeth.

Your friend,

Anna Asbury

All that winter and the following spring our correspondence
passed by messenger two and sometimes three times a month and
ruined me for any other suitor. Benjamin's letters were full of interest-
ing news, funny stories about people I knew, and a hint of flirtatious-
ness that challenged me to come up with suitable replies. In return,
I told him about my patients and it pleased me when he asked after
them and congratulated me on my successes. Through our letters we
learned each other's minds and temperaments. Despite his obvious
interest in my friendship, he made no lover-like overtures, and never
expressed a desire to ask for my hand.

Though by summer I was certain I would wed no one but him, I still wasn't sure I wanted to marry at all. My life was full and satisfying just as it was.

During one of the hottest July days in memory, I rode circuit through Fauquier tending patients. The blacksmith's wife suffered from typhoid and little Catherine Kemper was recovering slowly from a bout with the measles.

At McFeely's smithy, the ashes in the forge were cold. Odd for a weekday, I thought as I turned my mount into the fenced-in stable yard and paused at the pump to bathe my perspiring face. As I started up the steps, the Widow Jenkins came out on the porch, took me by the arm, and propelled me away from the house.

"You must not enter."

"Why ever not? I was here yesterday and promised to return. Has Laura grown worse?"

"She is no better, and now Mr. McFeely is ill. It's not appropriate for an unmarried woman to tend him." She looked me up and down before adding, "Unless it won't bother you to see sights unfit for virgin eyes."

I pulled my arm from her grasp. "I will not let you decide who gets my help."

"You must, for propriety's sake. Now be off, Miss, or I'll speak to your mother and aunt about you. I declare you'll never catch a husband if you continue to traipse all over the county without escort. I'll see to the care of the McFeelys from now on."

There was nothing to do but retreat. I could not risk my family forbidding me to continue in my vocation, but I fumed as I headed back to the stable and swung into the saddle. My horse's ears went back as I dug my heels into his ribs.

When I arrived at the Kempers', I spied Mary's husband, Peter, up to his waist in the millpond, mucking out below the waterwheel. As he hailed me, Benjamin emerged from the other side of the wheel.

He sloshed toward the bank as I dismounted and shaded his eyes with his hand as he peered up at me. "Your face is so red you look as though you might have the measles yourself. Are you quite well?"

I blotted my perspiring forehead. "I'm fine, though I warrant you've found the coolest job to be had this day. How is your family?"

"Everyone is well. It's very nice to see you."

Glad my face was already flushed, I smiled. "And you as well. I must go look in on Catherine."

"When you're finished, may I escort you to your next appointment? Peter and I are all but finished here."

"Yes, that would be lovely."

When I emerged from the house, he was ready and waiting, his clothes nearly dry. "Where are you heading next?"

I put my medicine chest in my saddlebag. "I'm done for the day and can go home."

"Very well."

Peter brought our horses from the stable and Benjamin gave me a hand up before swinging into his saddle.

As we passed through the village a few men called greetings and raised their hats to us. I liked the feeling of being seen in Benjamin's company. The ride was pleasant enough, though Benjamin spoke little. When we neared the turnoff to Uncle's, he halted beside a stream. "There's a spring here that stays cold year-round. Would you care for a drink?"

I fetched a tin cup from my saddlebag and followed him into the shady glade, where the water was as refreshing as he said. As we lingered, neither in any hurry to leave each other's company, I realized he'd been saving his words until the moment was right. He took the cup from my hands, set it aside, and stood before me with his heart plain on his face.

"The months since we met have been the happiest of my life. I hold you in the highest regard and admire your strength, your kindness, your determination, your intelligence, and your beauty. I'd like it very much if coming home meant coming home to you, Anna." Tears brimmed in his eyes as he knelt in a gesture of respect and surrender. "Will you join your life with mine and be my wife? I could be in no better hands."

He surely planned his proposal with the same care he applied to the remarks he delivered from the pulpit—but it was for my ears alone.

"Yes. I'd be honored to be your wife." He seemed so sure about wanting me and though I took no time to consider my choice, I required one assurance. "Benjamin, after we marry, may I continue to tend the sick?"

"Of course. We'll make a good team. Someone knowledgeable must tend to the physical health of a community, just as a pastor nurtures his flock's spiritual health."

It meant the world that he agreed without hesitation, and before he could get to his feet, I threw my arms around his neck. Our lips met, and I felt a hundredfold the same tingle of excitement I had when he'd wiped the apple juice off my chin.

He seemed quite as surprised by my impulsive gesture as I was. "Shall I see you the rest of the way home?"

"No. The drive is just up there. I can manage."

"Shall I speak to your uncle?"

I kissed him once more. "Let me speak to him first."

Though I had accepted Benjamin's proposal without their counsel or consent, I expected Mother and my aunt and uncle to be pleased, if only because marrying would get me out from under Uncle's roof. At first they seemed so, but when I mentioned my plan to keep on with tending the sick after the wedding, my mother's skeptical response sowed seeds of doubt.

"It doesn't matter who you marry, whether it be the son of one of your uncle's friends or this backwoodsman who has caught your fancy. Once wed, you must do your husband's bidding and bend to his will. This young man may encourage your whims while you are courting, but he only does it to win you. What kind of man would permit his wife to go out among the sick to tend them? He will expect you to stay at home and see to your own family."

"How can you say that when you've never met him?"

"Consider the married women you know, Anna. Which of them can do as she pleases? Any husband will be the same."

Her mournful tone vexed me, but should she not know the truth about marriage better than I? The words festered like a sore in my soul until I convinced myself it was better to stick to my original plan not to marry. The note I sent to Benjamin expressed only my change of heart without giving a reason.

Once the messenger was on his way, I shed tears of regret. Benjamin was never anything but kind to me. I didn't want to hurt him. Would he accept my refusal without comment? At most I thought he might send back an angry note of his own. I did not expect him to come galloping up the drive to Uncle's the very next day.

Though I quailed at the thought of facing him, I came downstairs when I heard him ask King to summon me. As I descended the stairs, knees quaking, he raked back the hair that had come loose from its queue and held out his hand. His voice was gentle. "May we please speak in private?"

Up close, his appearance signaled his inner turmoil. His stock was askew and a day's growth of stubble darkened his jaw. The sadness and hurt in his red-rimmed eyes put me in mind of a dog kicked by a beloved master. Blinking back tears, I nodded.

Outside, we walked far enough from the house we could speak without being overheard. Over his shoulder, I glimpsed Mother and Aunt Jean watching us from the parlor window.

"You first." His voice was hoarse.

I couldn't look him in the eyes. None of my own words could explain why I hurt him, and my mother's rose to my lips. "I shall have to give up everything to be with you."

His shoulders sagged. "As soon as I saw your uncle's house, I realized that was the reason you changed your mind. I didn't know he was such a wealthy man. Joseph is of humble circumstances, so I thought what I can offer you would be enough. I could never provide the kind of home you deserve." He flushed and stared at the ground. "Forgive me, Anna. I believed we would suit one another but now I see I did not consider all the facets of the situation."

His despondence broke my heart. "Houses and possessions matter not! Do you not know me better than that? I don't belong here at my uncle's. I want to devote myself to my vocation but as an unmarried woman, I face limitations. Married, I could tend anyone without fear of stigma—except if we marry, I must give up my life to assume a place in yours." My tears spilled over. "I don't know what to do. I fear I like you far too much."

Looking both distressed and confused, he brought out his handkerchief and dabbed at my cheeks. "How can you like me too much?"

"After I finished my indenture, I had but little time to enjoy my liberty. It ended the moment I expressed tender feelings for you. Now you and my uncle will shut me out of your negotiations and strike a bargain for me as if I were a horse or a cow—or a slave. And I shall go from one household to another as I am bid."

He stared at me. "Has our courtship not been one of tenderness? Do you not know I love you, Anna? If you care for me, let's figure out how to meet halfway."

"I love you, too, but there is no halfway. I'm the one who must give up everything."

"Who says this?"

"You will. Won't you? From what I've seen of marriage—even among couples who care for one another—it's not unlike slavery. The wife belongs to her husband and she must work to eat."

He no longer looked like a kicked dog, and I shrank from the anger in his voice. "Mark me—for I will not explain this again. My grandfather's mother died in childbirth and he loved the nanny who raised him, for she was all the mother he ever knew. When he grew old enough to understand what it meant for her to be enslaved, he vowed never to own another person. My father does not own slaves. Nor will I. Why would I subjugate you, the woman I revere above all others? If you think I don't care for you a thousand times more than I could care for a horse or a cow, you have me entirely wrong. I warrant you know nothing of me."

"Well!" My blood coursed hot as I defended myself. "Do you think I would insist you pursue another line of work so I could live in a monstrosity like my uncle's house? I'd happily live in the tenant place near your orchard, if we were both able to carry on our work."

His chest heaved as his hands closed around my shoulders and he pulled me close. The crush of his lips on mine communicated both his passion for me and for the work we would do together. Then he held me at arm's length and fixed his gaze on mine. That kiss was a pact, sealed for all eternity by what he said next.

"Anna, I would never seek to own you, only to love you. I want you to be my foremost partner, in every sense of the word."

"I want that too."

"Have we reached an accord, then?"

"Yes. I believe we have."

"And you wish to proceed?"

"I do."

A smile spread across his face as he squared his shoulders. "Very well. Shall I speak to your uncle now?"

"Please."

"Does December suit for the wedding?"

Could he sense the desire burning in my chest as I gazed up at him? "That's too far off. Can't we have the banns read in time to wed in November?"

His smile grew wider. "November it is."

13

Secrets, Lies, and Treachery

I may not have wanted Benjamin to become a soldier, but I wanted him to be my husband. Kneeling beside my bed in Mrs. Champe's house, I prayed God would sustain him and my brothers and grant me the wisdom to avoid trouble on the road. Then I crawled under the covers, fell into an exhausted sleep, and woke at first light feeling stiff and sore. When I hobbled downstairs for breakfast, I moved like one of my hostess's rheumatic contemporaries. Even lifting my spoon required effort.

My cloak, brushed to remove the worst of the mud, toasted before the fire. After I ate and prepared to take leave, I enveloped myself in the warm folds with a sigh, knowing it would be hours before I would feel so comfortable again.

When I stepped outside, a blast of cold air shriveled the insides of my nostrils and took my breath away. Thomas said to hope for clear, cold weather, and by those standards it was a fine day for travel. In the barn, Polly helped me saddle Nelly and secure my bundles.

"How far is it to the Carolina Road?"

"Naught but a mile to the next crossroads."

Stifling a groan, I hauled myself into the saddle and Nelly's breath blew out in white puffs as she trotted past the house and onto the road.

Polly joined Mrs. Champe and waved goodbye from the front porch. The old lady called, "Be wary of strangers!"

"Yes, ma'am, I will."

"And don't forget, missus—keep your politics to yourself!"

Once on the Carolina Road, I was truly on my way. I would follow this course all the way to Pennsylvania.

Though I couldn't help but give everyone I met a suspicious glance, I was glad there were plenty of travelers about. The road wound through shaded stretches Thomas claimed earned it the nickname Rogue's Road, but it was unlikely highwaymen would bother me while I was in the company of post riders, peddlers with carts, and drovers with herds of sheep. A closed carriage drawn by a matched team passed me going south and I turned to stare after it. No one in Fauquier had so fine a rig. I hadn't seen one like it since I left service at the Dunlap home.

Midmorning, I halted Nelly at an ordinary, winced as I dismounted, and led her to the water trough. While she drank, I stretched my legs and wandered over to read the broadsides pasted on the front of the log structure. One announced Congress's call for a day of national fasting to beg forgiveness for the many sins prevailing among all ranks.

Indeed. Little time had passed since Congress set aside the eighteenth of December as a day of thanksgiving to celebrate the victory at Saratoga. Perhaps Congress should concern itself more with feeding the troops than telling civilians how we should eat and pray. Only fools would attempt to direct the activities of every citizen in the country.

Certainly, no woman who managed a household with children would believe it could be done.

I had never been on my own and responsible for only my mount and myself. A man could be alone and independent his whole life if he chose. This solitude would be my pleasure—or my travail—for only a few weeks.

Just as I had not considered how differently men could conduct their business and themselves, I wondered if men understood the role their wives and mothers assumed in the structure of society. Benjamin and I depended on one another but he would never need me the way our children did. As their mother, I was their protector since before I knew them.

Stone Orchards and Farm, Carters Run, Virginia
November 1768

Stumbling out of the house, I clutched my shawl around my shoulders and made it halfway to the privy before I stopped to vomit into the dry grasses beside the path. After two months of morning sickness, often lasting all day, I despaired I'd ever be able to keep down a meal. I pressed my forehead against the bark of a young tree and willed my stomach to quiet. For once, I was too warm nearly all the time, and I welcomed the chill morning air curling in under my shawl.

"Anna? You're unwell again." Benjamin, clutching his napkin, came up beside me.

My stomach heaved, but there was little left to come up.

"You don't have to come outside in the cold to spare me. I share the blame for your condition, do I not?" He handed me his napkin to blot my perspiring forehead and wipe my mouth.

As we walked back to the house, he put his arm around my shoulders and even that simple gesture sparked a surge of desire—blunted though it was by my queasy stomach. Betsy teased me on my wedding day, saying Benjamin and I would have a merry time getting to know each other as husband and wife. I blushed, even while hoping she was right—and she was. We kept so much intimate company in the first weeks of our marriage I was disappointed when my monthly arrived. When my courses continued on schedule through the spring and summer, I tried not to envy Thomas and Betsy their two children.

Listless and unwell in late September, I thought I had contracted a mild case of the grippe, but when my nausea hadn't abated by my twentieth birthday in October, I realized at last, I was with child. Now, when I could feel the soft swelling of the life growing within me, my nausea was still just as likely to interrupt my dinner as my breakfast. Inside, I rinsed my mouth and spit into the slop jar before coming back to my half-eaten meal.

Benjamin took his place across from me and gave me a wary look. "Are you going to do it again?"

"It's not a regular sickness." I took a bite, and then another.

Now it was he who looked as if he might be ill. "I warrant I shall never get used to you running away from the table to void your stomach and coming right back to finish your food."

Suddenly ravenous, I continued to eat. "Once I void, I feel fine, though I'm ready for this sickness to end. Betsy said hers was over before she began to show. Both times."

"Are you well enough for me to leave you? Thomas and I planned to do repairs on the cider mill today?"

"Yes. No need to coddle me."

He rose and put his fringed buckskin frock on over his shirt. When he pressed a kiss on my forehead, his hand slid over my belly, and he bent to speak to my midsection. "Take pity on your ma, little one."

After he was gone, I sighed as I poured myself a mug of mint tea. Already I felt sapped of strength, and the day had just begun. Though I wanted more than anything to build a family with Benjamin, it came at the price of fatigue and discomfort.

Rhoda was worth every bit of that discomfort—as were my sons when they arrived. After bearing three children, I was used to my body undergoing the changes that came with pregnancy. The uncertainty and worry during the birthing were something no woman could ever cast off.

Perhaps the closest thing men could experience was the uncertainty and worry of trying to create a new nation—and I could not help them until I reached Pennsylvania. I made such a poor start yesterday. Now Uncle's errand would slow me again. I resolved to deliver the letter to Mr. Thompson and continue my journey in haste. There could be no more delays.

LEESBURG, LOUDOUN COUNTY, VIRGINIA
JANUARY 17, 1778

The sun was nearly overhead when I reached Leesburg, half a day behind schedule. I called to a woman who was picking her way down the icy street with a market basket on her arm. "Good day, missus! Could you direct me to the Thompson residence, please?"

"North of town, about a mile," said the woman, her eyes taking in my mud-spattered ensemble. "You can't fail to see the sign."

I nodded my thanks and clucked to Nelly. At least it was on the north side of town. With any luck, I could make the crossing into Maryland and find lodgings before dark.

As the woman predicted, the large sign announcing the Thompson estate was impossible to miss. As I guided Nelly toward a grand, brick house set well back from the road, I counted eight windows across each of two stories, not including the transom and sidelights around the front door.

A liveried groom met me in the circular drive and took Nelly's reins. I thanked him and rummaged in the saddlebag for the packet of letters before he led her off to the stables. Alone on the drive, I straightened my skirts and brushed at the new mud spatters on my cloak before climbing the porch steps. The butler opened the door the moment I knocked.

"Good day. Could you please present this letter of introduction to Mr. Thompson on my behalf? I am here to deliver correspondence to him from my uncle."

The butler gave me a quick once-over and left to seek his master without a word or a smile. While waiting in the foyer, an uncomfortable thought plagued me. The butler and the sullen groom disparaged me.

Their uniforms cost a great deal more than the clothing I borrowed from my cousins, which was, in turn, far nicer than my own. But that was a poor excuse for failing to smile or acknowledge my thanks. I squared my shoulders, eager to satisfy my obligation to Uncle and leave this dour place.

The butler returned with a man whose lined face and thinning gray hair suggested he was in his fifties, but there was no stoop to his shoulders, nor paunch around his middle. His presence was like a physical blow, and nearly took my breath away. He put me in mind of my former master, whose commanding air bound his subordinates to accept his orders—and his cruelty—without question.

Under his gaze, my hand flew unbidden to my hair, though there was little I could do to improve my windblown state. I tried not to let my gaze flicker toward my mud-spattered clothes and reminded myself that mud or no, I was my uncle's emissary. I bowed. "Good day, Mr. Thompson. My travels brought me through Leesburg, and my uncle, William Asbury, bade me deliver this to you."

He accepted the letter. "Will you stay and take refreshment?" His tone suggested the invitation was perfunctory and he did not wish to entertain me. The butler's mouth pursed, signaling his disapproval.

"No thank you, sir. I must be on my way." While bowing to take my leave, a woman's voice called my name and I straightened in surprise. On the second-floor landing overlooking the foyer, my eyes beheld my former master's daughter.

14

Where Loyalties Lie

"Isabel Dunlap?" Though I had not seen her in a dozen years, I would have recognized her anywhere. When she was little, she was wont to do things like dribble honey on the floor, knowing I would be the one to clean up the mess. For a moment I wondered if recalling memories of my youth conjured her here.

She hurried to descend the stairs and took my hands. "How good it is to see you!"

"I thought you were in Stafford." As I tried not to recoil, I puzzled over why she would be glad to see me.

"Oh, yes. I came to Leesburg when I married." She turned to Mr. Thompson. "Anna and I knew each other when we were girls."

The connection seemed to raise me a notch on his scale but not enough for him to welcome me. He addressed Isabel. "See that you're ready in plenty of time this evening. I don't want to be late."

She inclined her head. "Yes, of course."

He bowed to me and took his departure.

As soon as the door closed behind him, she leaned close to whisper, "He need not know you were once our serving-maid. How long can you visit?"

Still disbelieving she could be interested in my company, I stammered before I answered. "I only stopped by on an errand. I intended to reach Maryland today and I don't imagine the ferry across the Potomack runs after dark."

Her eyes widened. "But where will you pass the night? There are no suitable inns near the Potomack crossing. I'll have your trunk brought in. Did your husband accompany you?"

"No, I'm traveling alone, and in haste. On horseback."

"But you have another gown with you, I hope?" She continued without waiting for an answer. "Never mind. You shall borrow one of mine." She tilted her head as she regarded me. "On horseback, you say. In winter? But how far are you going?"

Mrs. Champe's admonition echoed in my head, and I heeded it. "A day's ride north or so. I'm needed to tend a sick relation."

"Well, at the very least, you must eat before you continue on your journey." She tucked my hand into the crook of her elbow as she led me toward the staircase. "I'll have the maid bring a meal up to my chamber."

I opened my mouth but she would hear no protest as she prattled on. "To see you floods my mind with memories. Do you remember when the tutor found that copy of *Pamela* and lectured Mother about keeping a closer eye on me because reading novels incited lust in young ladies?" She giggled. "Mother never admitted the novel was hers and not mine. Honestly, when did I ever choose to read?"

My feet followed, though I had no wish to visit with this woman, who I remembered as a vapid, spoiled girl. Perhaps another topic would distract her. "Shall I meet your husband?"

Her smile took on a fragile quality. "Oh, but you have. Andrew is my husband." I nodded without comment. Isabel, who should have had her pick of eligible suitors, ended up with a man twice her age. We continued up the stairs and into a bedchamber as big as the main room in my house, a maid following at our heels. Upon Isabel's murmured instructions, the maid fetched a towel and spread it over one chair set near a tea table.

Isabel said to me, "Now take off your cloak and let me look at you."

Even as I obeyed, I chided myself for following her orders. I was mistress of my own home now. Nearly a dozen years had passed since I left service in her father's house. As soon as I removed my cloak, the maid took it and departed, holding the muddy garment at arm's length.

"I warrant you haven't aged a day since I last saw you." Her voice sounded sad.

"Oh, but you flatter me, for after three children I assure you the yellow gown no longer fits. I wore it for my wedding, though."

"Did you? Yes, I suppose cotton would be suitable for a country wedding. Was there ever such a tantrum over a gown? I thought Mama would skin me alive for making a fuss. 'The pleats are crooked! I'll not be seen in such a rag!'" She affected the petulant tone I remembered well.

"I reset the pleats. It is still a beautiful gown."

"Please, sit." Gesturing toward the chair covered with the towel, she sat opposite as she continued her reverie. "I recollect that was the spring my brother Theo went riding alone and his horse threw him. He broke two ribs. Such a stir in the household!" She reached out to squeeze my hand. "No one but me ever noticed how you spied on us and our tutor. Do you find, as I do, you remember best that which you learned by listening at doors?"

Just then the maid returned bearing a tray and Isabel burst into giggles. The maid gave her mistress a wary glance as she set the tray on a table and scurried out.

My hostess's last remarks pricked my already fragile dignity. What could she mean by mentioning things from the distant past? I drew myself up. "There is no longer any need to hide my desire to learn. My husband and I often engage in intellectual discourse. I read anything I choose and will encourage my children to pursue studies that interest them."

She nodded, not really listening, as she poured two cups of tea. "I couldn't bear to part with the last of my Chinese blend, so I saved it for serving company."

Telling myself I would have refused it under other circumstances, I sipped the fragrant tea and ate the cold meat and cakes she served me. How strange to be disparaged by the servants and fawned over by their mistress. The only explanation I could fathom was Isabel was unendurably lonely. A short visit would not hurt my timetable and I suspected, contrary to her warning, there were suitable accommodations near the Maryland border, provided I was not as picky as my hostess. "Tell me about your family."

She shook her head, setting her earbobs dancing. "It's not a happy tale. My brother Richard died of the influenza while he was in his second year at William and Mary. Father died the following year and Theo abandoned his studies to take over the businesses, not that he ever cared about his education.

"To everyone's surprise, he managed things well enough. It was his Loyalist leanings that proved to be his undoing. The rebels confiscated everything after they drove the governor out. Theo left Virginia for England. The shame of it all nearly killed Mother."

Though I did not mention my husband was one of the rebels who drove her brother away, I felt a great deal of satisfaction in knowing.

Isabel continued, "My husband is from Norfolk. Though he is no Loyalist, the rebels destroyed his home and business when they fired the town. He rescued Mother and me from financial ruin when he purchased some of our former business interests."

She lowered her voice, even though there was no one else to hear. "It took Andrew's good reputation to rescue ours. I cannot credit what my brother was thinking. Admitting one's Loyalist leanings might be acceptable in New York, but in Virginia it was social suicide. After Andrew and I married, Mother came with us to Leesburg, but she was never the same. She passed about a year ago."

I thought of the thick stack of scrip Uncle gave me to sustain me on the trip. I had spent but little. My heart swelled as a plan took form. "What about Rhoda? Is she still part of your family? I'd love to see her if it's not too much trouble."

Isabel looked puzzled. "Who do you mean?"

"Your family's cook, Rhoda." I could feel my breath coming faster. If Isabel and I could agree on a price, I could make arrangements to send Rhoda back to Uncle's with a note, explaining how I came to purchase a slave. "She was the one who taught me—"

"Oh, her. I couldn't say what became of her, though I believe Mother sold her after Father died. Mother never liked her."

"I see." Pressing my lips together to fight back tears, I prayed Rhoda found herself in better circumstances and changed the subject. "When did you marry?"

"It's been almost two years. Andrew was a widower." She glanced down at her cup. "I have stepchildren older than me."

With a notion to cheer her and make it easier to excuse myself, I looked around the room. "I see no evidence of any downturn in your fortunes. My recollection of your father's house is it was grand but not so well-appointed as this."

"It is better than Father's, isn't it? I daresay we're among the wealthiest in town." The mention of her circumstances restored Isabel's good humor. Before I could rise, she poured more tea. "I ordered only a light meal because our hosts will provide more food and libations than their guests can possibly eat this evening."

With a sigh, I realized I'd have to rely on the tact I developed as a minister's wife to make my escape. "I've enjoyed our visit, but I'm already behind schedule. I'd feel awkward going to a party without being invited."

"Nonsense! The bride's father owns half the businesses in town. He is hosting their second-day party at his tavern. I warrant no one will notice one extra guest." She got up, opened the armoire, and brought out a coffee-colored silk à l'anglaise, embroidered with creamy vines and leaves. "You must wear this tonight."

"I must be on my—"

"I'm not used to taking no for an answer, Anna." She laid the gown across the counterpane. "No one, not even my husband, will recognize this as mine. I have more gowns than I can wear."

With the air of someone who has prevailed in battle, she rang for the maid. "You should rest so you'll be fresh for this evening. Your things have been brought up to your room. I'll send a maid to you later, when it's time to dress."

Alone in my room, instead of resting, my emotions ran from anger to reproof. Why did I agree to play the fine lady and accompany Isabel to a social event where I knew no one and which interested me not at all? Was it the desire to prove I could stand on equal footing with her, even though she and everyone else in her household judged me as too lowborn to be worthy of their association?

Unused to the defiant pride rising in my breast, my need to prove I could navigate in Isabel's waters extended my delay. Though I believed I put unpleasant memories of the Dunlaps behind me, this renewed acquaintance with Isabel reduced me to a state of insecurity.

But for Uncle, I never would have stopped at this place. More unpleasant memories rose to my thoughts. I nearly forgot I was married in a gown that should never have been mine at all.

DUNLAP PLANTATION, STAFFORD COUNTY, VIRGINIA
JUNE 1761

In the weeks before I went into service in the Dunlap household, my mother kept up a steady stream of advice and admonitions meant to curb my natural impulses, like "Remember child, when you serve, you must not speak until spoken to," and "After a time, this new place will feel like your home, but you must always remember you are not their equal."

Her litany of warnings included a cryptic one I was too young, at ten, to understand: "Give no inlet to familiar conversation and pray that you may avoid the temptations that befall a young woman without a mother's watchful eye to check her."

While I served the Dunlaps, I had no temptation other than my forbidden thirst for knowledge. Oh, how I envied the children their lessons. On days when I dusted, scrubbed floors, or cleaned the ashes out of the upstairs fireplaces, I planned my tasks so I would be close enough to listen near the schoolroom door. I daresay I had no trouble keeping up. When I heard one child make an incorrect answer, I longed to call out the right response and earn the tutor's praise.

In the afternoons, Theo, Isabel, and Richard went riding while their teacher retired to his room and took his ease. It was then I would bring my dust cloth into the empty schoolroom to attend to the rungs of the chairs, the windowsills, and the mantel. The faster I finished, the longer I could look at the books. There was nothing to read in the kitchen and I dared not touch any of the leather-bound volumes on the parlor shelves.

One fateful day I lingered, so engrossed in a Latin grammar text I forgot my chores as I turned the pages of engravings of the Roman emperors. No one in my family knew a second language, though my father picked up a few phrases that helped him communicate with the friendly natives in our area. But Latin, so said the book's introduction, was the foundation for other languages—Spanish, French, Italian. I drew in an excited breath at the discovery.

"Is it knowledge you seek, girl?"

The tutor's voice startled me and I dropped the book. Hoping he would recognize my inquisitive mind, I stooped to pick it up and opened it to the page I'd been reading. "If you please, sir . . ."

He strode across the room and reclaimed the text as though my touch would sully the pages. "You should select something more suitable." He opened a glass-front cabinet and handed me a small wooden frame with printed parchment secured beneath a transparent sheet of horn. "Best to begin at the beginning."

He thought me ignorant. Had he never noticed me lingering outside the schoolroom door? "Oh, but I know my letters ably, sir. Even my youngest brother no longer uses a hornbook. At home, I would read from the Bible and my father's volume of Shakespeare."

He raised his eyebrows at my eagerness, and I forgot my mother's counsel that I should refrain from speaking out of turn. "My uncle said I was to learn many things during my indenture."

He scoffed. "I am sure your uncle meant many things suited to your station in life. You already know how to read the Bible. I assume you can do sums?"

"Yes, sir."

"That is more than enough. A girl has no need for classical studies." He took the hornbook back and put it and the Latin grammar in the cabinet. "It seems to me the most valuable lesson you could learn, miss, is your proper place—and that place is not in this schoolroom."

Tears of humiliation welled in my eyes. I forgot to curtsey. I barely kept my dignity as I fled down the stairs and out the back door. When I burst into the summer kitchen, sobbing under my breath, Rhoda looked up, startled. "What's the matter?"

Anger and embarrassment threatened to choke me and I had to calm myself before I spoke. "The tutor caught me looking at a schoolbook. He thought I couldn't even read! He said the best thing I could learn is my place." I slumped on the bench and leaned my elbows on the worktable.

Rhoda's face softened, even as her words stung. "It's best to keep what you know to yourself. He's afraid you gonna make him look bad—like he ain't working hard enough to teach the master's children." She sat on the opposite bench. "You can read. Can you write too?"

"Yes, of course."

"I can't. The master I had when I was young taught me to read a little, but I wasn't allowed to write. You're better off than me—and a lot of folks. You can always keep learning."

"But how, when the schoolmaster won't let me read anything more difficult than a hornbook?"

"I ain't got books here, but I can teach you about herbs and medicines for healing. Midwifery, too, when you're older. My first master was a physician who bought my mama specially because she knew about herbs and healing. He was always reading and liked to make his own remedies. I tended his medicinal garden and learned from both of them."

Interest piqued, I sat up straighter. "I'd like that. When my father died last year, I never knew what ailed him. If you teach me about healing, in return, I'll teach you to write." Before she could answer, I hurried up the ladder to the loft where I slept and brought back my box of personal things. At the worktable, I took off the lid, brought out my receipt book, and handed it to her. "Mother said I must write everything I learn about running a household in here."

Rhoda ran her fingers over the thick cardboard cover before she opened it and stared at the writing on the page. "That's an L. Lem-on. Lemon—what does this say?"

"It says 'Use lemon thyme for indigestion and asthma.'"

She pointed to a blank spot on the page and handed me the book. "Write down 'Use marigold heads for cuts and sprains.'"

I brought out my quill and the precious bottle of ink my mother gave me and complied. Once the ink dried, I turned to a fresh page farther along in the book. "Now, let's practice the ABC."

Everyone knew there were laws in the Bible governing the practice of slavery. I did not understand why that lot fell to certain people and not others—or why women of any race or color could not make life choices for themselves. It seemed to me Rhoda was the smartest, most competent person at the Dunlap estate. The more I learned, the more I found to question.

In the months following, Rhoda's handwriting mingled with mine on the pages as we filled a section in the receipt book with descriptions and drawings of different herbs, flowers, and plants. She improved her reading and learned to write so rapidly I wondered why her first master, who taught her many things, did not teach her to write.

When our lessons progressed from plants to actually tending the sick, my quill scratched on the page while she gave instruction.

"The typhoid can fool you. It has so many symptoms, it's hard to diagnose. But the way to know for sure is the person's sweat smells like baking bread. And the typhoid, it can catch you, too, if you ain't careful. When you're attending to the sick, it's important to be clean. Every time you leave the sickroom, you rinse your hands and arms with vinegar and water and say a prayer to chase the sickness away."

"How does vinegar do that?"

"I don't know for certain, but wounds heal better when they're treated with vinegar, and food preserved in vinegar brine doesn't spoil. With God's help, it all works together somehow."

One afternoon when I was twelve, Rhoda interrupted my labors over a sketch of a goldenseal plant, corked my inkbottle, shut the book, and shoved everything out of sight behind the cornmeal sack.

"Go on now and get more purple coneflower." She pushed a basket into my hands and shooed me out the door. Confused, I set out to do what she asked, knowing few remained where we collected them just the day before. When I returned, the kitchen was empty, so I started back outside, intending to seek Rhoda in the garden but when my ears pricked up at an unfamiliar sound, I tiptoed to investigate.

Expecting to find one of the other servants stealing food, I looked into the larder. Instead, I saw the master holding Rhoda against the wall. Her skirts were up around her waist and he was thrusting himself against her. I had never seen a man take a woman before and did not understand what was happening. When realization dawned, my hand flew to my mouth, and that small movement drew Rhoda's attention. As her eyes met mine over his shoulder, a fearful expression spread over her face. Mr. Dunlap rutted against her, grunting. She gave a slight shake of her head and her mouth formed the word "go." I turned and fled.

I stayed away until I saw the master head back to the big house and when I returned to the kitchen, Rhoda and I did not speak of what happened. Though I didn't realize it until much later, as I grew into a young woman, she directed my tasks so I would have minimal contact with the master and his sons. Rhoda did everything she could to protect me from them, though she was unable to defend herself.

Isabel and I grew up in the same household, but I assumed she was an innocent, sheltered from the things I saw. She mentioned her brother Theo's riding accident. Was she trying to elicit a reaction from me—or did Rhoda conceal our secret so well Isabel never learned the truth of what transpired just before I left my position?

DUNLAP PLANTATION, STAFFORD COUNTY, VIRGINIA
JUNE 1766

When I was seventeen, the temptations my mother warned me about were as far from my mind as when I was a child. Thanks to Rhoda,

I had not attracted any male attention and my only thought was to be free of my servitude. With a week before I was to leave, I grew careless—guilty only of lingering in a doorway to watch Isabel and her brothers practicing with a dancing master to prepare for an upcoming ball.

Isabel excelled at dancing. She and her younger brother, Richard, were well matched and looked lovely doing the minuet. Theo struggled with the patterns of the quadrille and behaved in a fractious manner to mask his embarrassment. As I stifled a giggle, the diminutive dancing master mopped his brow with his handkerchief, called for a short recess, and hurried from the room. I turned my attention back to Isabel and Richard, moving my feet to mimic their steps.

"You'd be comely in a proper gown." Theo spoke, so close to my ear I jumped. He spotted me in the hall and left the parlor through the dining room, so he could come upon me unseen. At first, I entertained the possibility he was inviting me to join as their fourth to better balance the couples but before I could gather my wits, he seized me by the shoulders and pushed me into a curtained alcove.

Theo stirred nothing in me but revulsion. My status in the household was no higher than Rhoda's and I knew he did not expect me to refuse him. My thoughts ran ahead of what was happening as I sought a way to escape. Though he was at least a head taller than me, Theo was naught but an overgrown lad, and none too bright if I was to believe the kitchen gossip. I raised my chin and pretended I was not frightened. "You'd better go back to the parlor. From what I could see, you need all the dancing practice you can get." I pushed his hands away and shouldered past him, back into the light. "You could use some lessons in manners too."

Taking to my heels out the back door, I ran at top speed, but as I rounded the side of the house he caught up and pushed me against the rough bricks. Hidden from view, he placed his hands against the wall on either side of me.

"I'll take some lessons from you. I bet you know lots of tricks." He moved closer until his whole body blocked my flight. As his face filled my vision, one hand cupped my breast, squeezing to the point of pain. I twisted in his grasp, fighting to break free, and my knee caught him in the groin. When I realized how much it hurt him, I kneed him again, leaving him doubled over as I ran for the kitchen. But Rhoda, my protector, was nowhere in sight.

There wasn't time to climb the ladder to the loft. I was only halfway up before he was upon me, grabbing me around the waist and flinging me facedown on the worktable in the same motion. I heard fabric rip as he pulled up my skirt and my hand closed around the handle of an iron trivet near my head. Aiming over my shoulder, I struck, just grazing the side of his head. Before I could swing again, I felt the shock of a blow to his body and heard the crunch of breaking bone. Theo lost his grip on me, groaning as he fell to his knees. I turned in time to watch Rhoda swing an iron frying pan and render him unconscious with a clout to the head.

Frozen with shock, I panted, still gripping the trivet, as Rhoda sprang into action.

15

Intrigue

Deep in the grip of that memory, my heart nearly beat out of my chest when someone rapped at my door.

"Just a moment, if you please." Once composed, I admitted the maid in charge of my toilette. She stood over me while I took a sponge bath, loathe for her mistress's gown to touch my body while any trace of mud remained. Then she dressed my hair and after a few adjustments with a needle and thread, Isabel's coffee-colored silk fit as though made for me.

Delivered to my hostess, I stood self-consciously while she clapped her hands in delight. She beckoned me to join her before a long pier glass, which faithfully reflected her shining, golden curls and her rose damask polonaise. The dignified looking stranger beside her had a neckline that exposed daring décolletage, an elaborate coiffure, and a hint of rouge on her cheeks and lips. I could not decide if I looked like a high-priced doxy or a woman who would command a gentleman's respect. Would Benjamin think me attractive this way? Would he even recognize me?

We rode to town in a closed carriage much like the one that attracted my attention earlier. Tension tightened around my head like a vise at Isabel's unceasing prattle until it was all I could do to smile as she squeezed my arm and declared to Mr. Thompson, "I shall introduce Anna to all my friends and make her feel most welcome."

He only nodded. As he escorted us inside the handsome fieldstone tavern, Isabel pulled away from his touch. He, equally uninterested in remaining at his wife's side, excused himself and disappeared into the crowd. The moment he was out of sight, she transformed from an unhappy wife into a carefree coquette.

"There are the bride and groom." She pointed with her fan.

I was glad to see the glow of love on their faces, for it reminded me of how I felt the day I married Benjamin. Poor Isabel. It was clear she had no affection for her husband.

She plucked at my sleeve. "Come. I'll introduce you." But instead of conducting me to the happy couple, we joined a group of matrons to whom she presented me as a girlhood friend from Stafford. With nothing much to contribute to their conversation, I found myself at the edge of the circle, listening while the other women commented— not always kindly—about the gowns and the hairstyles of the women present. I soon had my fill of their gossip and stifled a yawn before Isabel finished whatever she was saying and dragged me away to the buffet table. It was, as she predicted, laden with food.

It was pleasant to sip rum punch and nibble at the good things to eat but before long I grew restless. Out the window, the setting sun reminded me I had traveled only a few miles in my long journey that day. It would take more than a fortnight to reach Valley Forge if I kept to this pace. Annoyed at myself, I barely heard Isabel's murmured commentary about the women in her circle of friends—their domestic arrangements, their scandals, and many other things that interested me not at all. Then a male voice broke through my thoughts.

"My dear Mistress Thompson, has your husband left you unattended again this evening?" A man in a powdered wig and mustard-colored brocade coat bowed over Isabel's hand.

Isabel giggled like a schoolgirl. "Why, Mr. Emory, you know Mr. Thompson never misses an opportunity to conduct business at social events." She inclined her head in my direction. "May I present my friend, Anna? We knew each other as girls. In Stafford."

"Charmed, Anna from Stafford." He bent over my hand as well, though he immediately turned his attention back to Isabel. "If I was fortunate enough to possess your husband's army contracts, I should also be occupied night and day. But I am not and I fear he'll not be back to claim you for hours. May I have this dance?"

"Yes, of course." As she stood, Mr. Emory took the punch cup from her hand and placed his lips where hers had touched the rim, draining the last of the drink before escorting her to the center of the room.

Smothering a smile, I watched him lead Isabel away. How Thomas would relish making fun of the man's satin dancing pumps and clocked stockings! My mirth vanished when I noticed the matrons in Isabel's circle of friends begin to whisper behind their fans. They stared at Mr. Emory's hand, which lingered on Isabel's lower back in a manner suggesting intimacy rather than solicitousness.

This was intrigue worthy of the French court, not the likes of Leesburg, Virginia. Isabel and Mr. Emory did not return after one song but stayed out in the center of the dancing crowd, leaving me alone for what seemed an age. Why did she insist I attend this party, only to desert me? With a jolt, I realized she had not introduced me properly because she never asked my husband's name.

Isabel's friends turned their glances my way and rather than remain where I would be the subject of their whispered comments,

I made my way through the crowd to the far side of the room and took my time refilling my punch. There was no one I cared to converse with, so I found an inconspicuous spot near a group of younger women. Watching the ones who held their babies made me long for my own children. How could I have gone hours without even thinking of them? As soon as I pictured little William, my breasts, overfull and pushed high by my borrowed stays, throbbed in response.

I should have heeded my body's first warning. A moment later one infant began to cry, and I felt the tingle as my milk let down. Horrified, I watched dark spots form on the silk as I leaked through the front of the gown. Fleeing past the catty bunch of matrons and into the kitchen, grabbed the first towel I saw and stuffed it in my bodice while I unfastened the stomacher partway. Then I expressed into the towel until the pressure eased.

Even after my efforts to tidy my gown, the damp spots were conspicuous. Remaining out of sight until they dried was my only option. Then I would find Isabel and prevail upon her to leave at once.

Heavy footsteps crossed the kitchen and paused outside the larder. As I shrank back into the darkness, I overheard a hushed conversation between two men.

"It's true he's always put a healthy markup on the prices and delivered a mere three-quarters of what they purchased. The commissary agent gets his share to keep his mouth shut and reconcile the books."

"But he's not selling this shipment?"

"He's selling what's above—but what's below must go inside the prison walls unseen."

When the men's footsteps faded, I crept out of the larder to the window. Under the full moon's illumination, I watched two men load long, wooden crates into a freight wagon and then fit planks over the crates to conceal them. I'd seen boxes that size and shape before, at the parade ground—full of rifles. Were these men smuggling guns into a prison?

Moonlight shone on the silver hair of the man who joined them. When he turned, I recognized the hawk-like visage of Andrew Thompson.

Mind whirling, I tried to puzzle out what I saw and heard as I hastened back to the party. I forced myself to nod and smile as I threaded my way toward a refreshment table. While pouring a glass of punch, I realized with dismay that the damp spots on the silk were still visible. Perhaps no one would notice. I folded one arm across my front, nails digging into my other arm as I tried to take a casual sip.

"There you are!"

I jumped and slopped punch on the gown.

"My dear, are you ill? You're white as a sheet." Isabel hovered at my elbow, the very picture of a concerned friend.

There was no need to fib. "I feel faint."

She handed me a handkerchief to blot the punch. "Then we must summon the carriage and take you home right away."

"I'm sorry to make you miss the rest of the party."

"It's all right. There's another tomorrow evening and all next week. Come along." She took my arm.

"Should we summon Mr. Thompson?"

"I usually leave before he does and send the carriage back. He won't find it unusual."

With one servant off to call the carriage and another to fetch our cloaks, we waited by the door. I scanned the crowd for Mr. Emory. He was speaking to a group of men and though he glanced our way, he did not come to bid Isabel goodbye. On the ride home, I felt quite ready to rid myself of her company. "Thank you for taking me to the party. I'm sure I'll sleep well tonight after all the excitement and my travels."

She looked surprised. "I hoped you'd want to stay up and gossip. We barely had time together at the party."

Fatigue and irritation got the better of me. "We would've had plenty of time if you hadn't disappeared with Mr. Emory. There was talk about the two of you."

Her face colored. "I'm sure I don't know what you mean."

"Has no one mentioned your behavior to your husband?"

"When I looked for you, my friend said you disappeared for a time this evening." Isabel folded her arms on her chest. "Were you spying on me? Or perhaps you dallied with someone, knowing your husband was unlikely to find out?"

How dare she accuse me of her own crime? "I beg your pardon. I am a woman of honor. Anyone with eyes can see Mr. Emory acts like a suitor and you invited his attentions. Surely Mr. Thompson would call him out if someone made him aware."

She scoffed. "No one will tell Andrew. Why may I not take pleasure where I find it? Doesn't your husband ignore you too?"

"No, he does not."

"Yet I would say he does, for you're here by yourself and you won't say why."

Her assumption that Benjamin was no better husband than hers filled me with anger. I burst out, "Benjamin is a soldier serving in the Third Virginia." Immediately I regretted it.

Isabel regarded me with suspicion. "The Continentals?"

"Yes, the Continentals. Your husband's reputation rescued you from the taint of your brother's Loyalist leanings. He's an avowed patriot who does business with the Continental Army, isn't that right?"

The carriage halted in the front drive and she pressed her lips together as if to indicate we should not speak in front of the butler. Inside, she followed me up to my chamber and shut the door.

"I know nothing of my husband's business."

"That's hard to believe." Dropping my voice to a whisper, I sought to confirm my suspicions. "Does my uncle know Mr. Thompson is a

Loyalist—and that he's misappropriating goods and funds intended for the army?"

"Ask me no more, Anna!" This time Isabel's distress was real. "I knew nothing about Andrew's business when we married. I must stand by him, or it will ruin all. You'd do the same."

"Benjamin would do nothing so dishonorable, nor would he expect me to act simple and ignore what's going on right under my nose. Where are the guns bound for?"

"I do not know. You must say nothing. If Andrew finds out, he will have you silenced. You don't know how powerful he is."

"If you and Mr. Emory don't shrink from cuckolding such a powerful man, I see no reason to worry for my own safety." My hand shook as I opened my chamber door. "I believe I've had enough gossip for one night. Don't trouble yourself to see me off in the morning."

Locking the door behind her, I wedged a chair under the doorknob and undressed without summoning the maid. Free of rouge, my hair long and loose, I surveyed myself in the looking glass in my room. This time, I recognized myself.

It's not just servants and slaves whose circumstances force them into subservience. Even someone born to privilege, like Isabel, could be brought low. She might believe she exchanged poverty and shame for financial security and a wardrobe of expensive silk gowns, but I saw only a woman who sold herself into a loveless marriage. She was complicit in the schemes of her husband who was defrauding the army and causing the soldiers to suffer.

What a fool I was to have thought Isabel an innocent. I pulled the bed curtains closed and burrowed beneath the covers, but more long-buried memories rose to torment me and sleep would not come.

Dunlap Plantation, Stafford County, Virginia
June 1766

As I stared down at Theo's motionless form, I dropped the trivet on the worktable and hugged myself to quell my shaking. Rhoda knelt to run her hands over the back of his head and feel for the pulse in his neck. Then she fetched the bottle of opium tincture from the larder, poured some into Theo's mouth, and let his head fall back to the floor.

"He's gonna live. I didn't hurt him that bad. After I'm gone you lock the door. Start supper like nothing's wrong. Don't you stir from this kitchen and don't let anyone else in until I get back, you hear?" When I nodded, she left, and I watched her pick up her skirts and run in the direction of the stables. Then I locked the door behind her and leaned against it for a long moment, resisting the growing urge to kick Theo while he could not defend himself.

Then I, too, went into action. From the cold cellar, I brought up eggs and butter. As I cored apples and sliced them into rings, the familiar task comforted me, and my hands ceased to shake. I whisked the eggs with nutmeg, lemon juice, and rosewater, and poured it all over the apples in the cast-iron skillet, Rhoda's weapon of choice. Apple tansey was Mrs. Dunlap's favorite side dish.

While the tansey baked, I sliced bread, fixed platters of cold meat and cheeses, and dished up several kinds of fruit preserves. We had cakes left over from one of Mrs. Dunlap's card parties and when everything was assembled, I felt no one could criticize the meal. I arranged lemon slices like flower petals on the finished tansy and was dusting it with a sprinkle of white sugar when someone pounded on the door. Stepping around Theo, I hurried to press my ear against it. "Who's there?"

Rhoda answered. "Let us in."

I threw the bolt and Rhoda entered with the stableman and another man I didn't know, who bore two long, stout poles and a horse blanket. Both regarded Theo with fear in their eyes.

"Don't worry. I promise he won't remember nothing." Rhoda cut strips of canvas for them to lash the poles together and commanded, "Tell it back to me again."

The stableman replied, "Master Theo's horse come back without him this afternoon. I went looking and found him layin' in the pasture, down by the creek."

"That's right. And that's all you say, cause that's all you know."

The other man frowned down at Rhoda. "You're crazy."

"Hush. I know what I'm doing."

"But do you know what will happen if they find out we're lying?"

She glanced at me before answering. "Yes. I know." She took his face tenderly in her hands and kissed him on the lips. "Thank you." Then she put her hands on her hips. "Now get."

"Yes'm." The men laid the blanket across the makeshift litter and rolled Theo onto it. He groaned but did not wake.

Rhoda called over her shoulder as she followed the men out. "Serve the supper—though likely they ain't gonna eat it because they'll be fussing around the sickroom. I'll send for you later."

I nodded. Rhoda was so in control of the situation I would not have dared to disobey.

From that evening on, Rhoda scarce let me out of her sight and no one objected when she claimed she needed my help to care for Theo. With the two of us in full-time attendance and administering regular doses of opium, he slumbered on and on, with only brief, incoherent spells of waking. Rhoda made no mention of the opium's role in Theo's treatment and bound his cracked ribs and applied poultices to the lump on the back of his head.

Mrs. Dunlap, moved to hysterics at the sight of her injured son, alternated between hovering in the sickroom and prostrating herself in her chamber, and required nearly as much tending to as the patient.

Two days after Theo's injury, while on my way to the sickroom bearing a covered tray for Rhoda, I heard Isabel shouting and crying in her chamber. I set the tray on a side table in the hall and when I tapped on her door, it swung open. Isabel, her face tear-stained, threw a striped yellow gown to the floor and kicked at it. "The pleats are crooked! I'll not be seen in such a rag!" Her mother, who sat weeping in a chair, looked more lost and defeated than I could have imagined possible for a woman in her position. They had not noticed me. *Spoiled girl*, I thought as I eased the door closed. Isabel couldn't stand anyone else commanding the center of attention—for any reason.

The days and nights spent in the sickroom blurred together until one morning the butler came for me. "A man's here to fetch you home."

I hadn't even thought to count the days and suddenly I was free. I wanted to shout for joy and dance out the door. Instead, I nodded. "Thank you. Please tell him I'll gather my things and be down directly." I locked eyes with Rhoda and she gave a single nod. She protected me to the last. I would take leave with no hint of scandal with the master's son and emerge with the terms of my seven-year contract fulfilled, beholden to no one.

Just then Mrs. Dunlap, who had been dozing in a chair beside Theo's bed, spoke. "Wait. Anna, you cannot go."

Blinking, I stammered, "But, ma'am, I...."

"Nay. You cannot." She burst into tears. "I never sent to the haberdasher for your clothing."

According to my indenture contract, I was owed freedom dues. The Dunlaps were to provide me with a new gown, two sets of underthings, and a new pair of shoes upon leaving. I was also entitled to a set of copper pans and a small cash payment meant as a start to my dowry—so I might begin again in servitude as someone's wife.

The copper pans were already in my possession, and the plain, gray linen uniform I had on was enough to get me home. "Oh, Mrs. Dunlap, under the circumstances . . ."

"I will honor our terms. Wait here." She got up, wiped at her tears, and returned with Isabel's discarded yellow gown and some Virginia dollars. "Take these. I will have the rest of your clothing sent to your uncle's home."

I shoved the money in my pocket and ran my fingers over the crisp, bright-colored gown. It came as an unexpected boon, for it was more fashionable and costly than anything I could have expected Mrs. Dunlap to order for the likes of me. "Yes, ma'am. Thank you."

Rhoda followed me back to the kitchen and waited at the work-table while I folded the gown and tied it and my few possessions into a bundle and retrieved the box where I kept my receipt book, quill, and ink. When I climbed down the ladder from the loft for the last time, I caught her wiping away tears.

In my eagerness to be gone, I hadn't realized how hard it would be to leave her, and my eyes welled. "I wish I could write to you."

"Ain't no way you can do that."

"But I must do something for you after all you've done for me." I drew in a breath. "I know! I'll buy you. That's what I'll do."

"You can't do that, either."

"Why not?" I dug out the folded bills. "This is a start. It might take a while to save the rest, but I'll figure out a way."

"The master will never sell me. Besides, even if he did, you'd be taking me away from my husband."

"That man who came back to the kitchen with you? I never knew you were married. Why didn't you say something?"

"It's a secret. We done jumped over the broom—but the master, he wouldn't let us live together, even if he knew."

"Does your husband know your other secret?" We never spoke of what I saw the master doing to her.

She looked away for a moment. "He knows."

"I can't just leave you. I must do something." Tears escaped my eyelids.

She gripped my shoulders so hard it hurt. "Promise me you won't come back here trying to help when you'd just be making things worse."

"You deserve so much better. You've been a mother to me." A sob escaped my lips. "You taught me and you saved me. God bless you and deliver you."

She enfolded me in her arms, the first and last time we embraced. "Godspeed you, Anna. Now go live your life. I'll live mine."

I wiped away my tears as I crossed the yard. I didn't recognize the figure sitting on the lumber wagon's high seat, nor did I care. Until he hailed me.

"You look just like Mother."

Then I stared in amazement. "Joseph? You're a grown man!"

"So I am, little sister and you're nearly grown yourself." He jumped down and pulled me into a hug. "It's so good to see you. Let's go home."

For seven years, Rhoda taught, nurtured, and defended me with a zeal that served as the model for how I mothered my own children. Her determination to protect me from Theo's assault meant I could give myself to Benjamin on our wedding night without reservation and take pleasure in our physical relationship. I wished I could have told her I wore the yellow gown for my wedding. She would have understood, better than anyone, it was a symbol of my uncompromised virtue.

16

Potomack Peril

The creak of wagon wheels and the jingle of chain and harness startled me from my reverie, and I pushed aside the bed curtains. The moon had set and from my window I spied men bearing torches. They met two arriving freight wagons and lit the way around to the rear of the house. Enveloping myself in the dark folds of my cloak, I hastened to my chamber door, removed the chair, and turned the key in the lock. Below, I heard another door open and close. Determined to know more about this shipment of weapons, I melted into the shadows as I crept down to the dining-room window, where I concealed myself in the heavy portieres to watch the scene in the yard.

The men loaded more long, flat boxes into the second wagon and lay another false bottom to conceal them. They passed a bottle as they loaded crates and barrels above the hidden compartments.

"Thompson, you've recouped the losses you suffered in Norfolk ten times over, have you not?" I was positive it was the man I overheard in the tavern's kitchen.

Another man laughed. "If the war drags on for five or six more years, he'll be able to buy half the state."

The first man added, "It does little good for our officers to break the jail unless they can dress as civilians and arm themselves against the rebels. I appreciate our host's generosity."

Thompson added, "The funds from our venerable friend in Fauquier arrived this very day to promote our venture."

One man, whose twang suggested he was a backwoodsman, lifted an oak cask into the back of a wagon. "And ours. Don't think you can kimbaw me in the name of your cause. I'd be obliged if you could sweeten the deal a little—for I'm not getting my usual fee."

Another in the party laughed. "I'm working up a powerful hunger, too, if you get my meaning."

Thompson supervised as the men tied off the last of the load. "You may all avail yourselves of whatever will slake your appetites before you go. Outside of the main house, of course." He gestured toward the slave cabins in the distance.

One man rubbed his hands together in anticipation. "Yes, and if you please her, mayhap she'll cook you breakfast besides."

The others laughed, and Thompson said, "I think you'll find any of my wenches amenable. With any luck, you'll end up increasing my holdings." The men hooted as they headed off toward the row of slave cabins.

A hot flush of disgust and rage swept over me. The men in the yard were cheering about the prospect of forcing themselves on defenseless women, while I stood by, powerless to do anything to stop it. All the times I deferred to William's decisions or tolerated his bad humor, I should have spit on him instead. He played me for a fool and involved me in a scheme to outfit British prisoners with guns and supplies that should have been going to our own soldiers.

How I wished I could rip up the bill of exchange I'd delivered on his behalf. For one wild moment I thought to dash the tainted scrip he'd given me into the nearest fireplace, but I thought the better of it. Instead, I would spend it for the benefit of my family, and if perchance

I could undo his treachery, so much the better. A plan formed in my head: I would figure out where those wagons were headed and alert the authorities in time to prevent them from reaching their destination.

Before I could return to my chamber, I heard two, maybe three sets of footsteps in the hall. A nearby door opened and closed. A moment later I heard Thompson say, "These bear the official seal that will get you through the checkpoints. Make haste on your journey."

The footsteps continued to the back door and my panic surged. The wagons would be out of sight before I could dress and go in pursuit. Soon flickering candlelight passed the dining-room door and a single person mounted the stairs. I waited until I heard a door close upstairs before I left my hiding place within the portieres.

Thompson left the key to his study in the lock and the soft click as I turned it sounded as loud as if I'd dropped an entire ring of keys into a brass bowl. My knees trembled as I stepped into the room. The coals on the hearth gave off just enough light to avoid tripping over the furniture. I lit a taper and held it over the papers on the desk, searching for the letter from my uncle. When I found it, I scanned it, and then took a fresh sheet of writing paper and a quill and copied it. I would see justice done.

The wagons moved out as I tiptoed upstairs to my chamber and dressed with all haste. Surely Providence delayed me here so I might witness this wrongdoing. I might not defeat the whole British army, but I vowed those guns would not reach their destination. Shoving the copy of William's letter into my pocket, I gathered my bundles and clung to the shadows as I headed for the stables in case any of the men were still about.

As much as I wanted to be off at a gallop, I forced myself to walk Nelly past the house. On the main road, I turned south, toward Leesburg. If the wagons were headed for the prison camp at Winchester, I would soon overtake them. The sun was just coming up as I arrived at the tavern where we attended the party. Some guests, still dressed in their finery, straggled out as I hesitated but there were no freight wagons in sight. Perhaps they went north. If so, I could use the letter I copied to prevail upon a magistrate to have the wagons stopped and searched. I wheeled Nelly around and retraced our route.

Bells rang in the steeple of Goose Creek Anglican Church as we raced past.

I reached the southern shore of the Potomack River so quickly I would've had no problem making the crossing yesterday. Again, my anger flared at Isabel's lies.

Pale tendrils of fog rose from the water as Nelly made her way down the muddy path to the water's edge. The ferryman, just returned from a trip across, poled his flatboat to bump against the narrow ramp extending onto the bank where it bobbed in the waves washing toward the shore.

I called to him. "Did two freight wagons just cross here?"

"Yes, missus. Busy morning, for the Sabbath. Most Sunday crossings are churchgoing folk."

"I must cross right away, if you please."

He clomped down the ramp, which rocked under his weight, and leaned against the gate at its foot. "That'll be sixpence."

I paid with scrip. The ferryman pocketed the note and swung open the gate, but Nelly balked as I tried to urge her up the ramp. I pulled the reins to the left, circled, and tried again. This time she reared, nearly unseating me.

The ferryman made a grab for the bridle and missed. "How now, missus! Get that beast under control."

I reined Nelly down, but she would not be still. "Come on, girl. I know you're frightened, but we must hurry."

I dug one heel into her ribs, and she jumped forward, as if to spend as little time on the unsteady ramp as possible. The raft rocked and she reared again, going up, until I lost my balance and fell backward into the river. I cried out at the initial shock and as I sank, the paralyzing cold held me in its grip.

I bounced off the sandy riverbed and though I churned the water with my arms and legs, I rose slowly and had to gasp for air the moment my face broke the surface. The weight of my wet hair dragged my head below again. The river was not deep, but my waterlogged clothing was so heavy I couldn't right myself. Terror-stricken, I thrashed harder as water flooded my mouth and nose. I might as well have been under glass. My shoulder slammed against a submerged boulder as the current swept me downriver.

When my head surfaced again, I took a breath and screamed for help. Though only a few moments had passed, my numb arms and legs were useless. A splash of water covered my face. When I went under again, black clouded the edges of my vision and my lungs felt like they would burst. Then I jerked to a halt. Something had hold of me.

I felt a mighty heave and staggered up, gasping and coughing up water, my hair a curtain over my face.

"Up you get, missus!" The ferryman had plunged hip deep into the frigid water and chased me downriver until he could seize hold of my arm. Now as he supported me around my middle, we both shook so I feared we would fall back in. He panted as he sloshed through the water with me in tow. "Hurry along now. January's no time for a swim. We must get you across without delay so my wife can tend to you."

My skirts hung heavy around my legs and I stumbled over every rock and branch beneath the water's surface as he dragged me toward the shallows and half-carried me up the ramp and onto the raft.

His fingers shook as he unclasped my cloak and let it fall to the deck with a thud. As I pushed wet strands of hair out of my eyes, I saw Mollie's plumed cap bobbing in the shallows. Then it swirled away on the current.

"Quick, now, take off the jacket too."

My own fingers all but useless, I peeled off in my sodden gloves and fumbled with the brass buttons. He had to help me take the jacket off and the wind cut through my remaining layers, setting my teeth chattering as though I had the ague. He wrapped me in a heavy blanket and seized his pole, pushing us away from the ramp as I collapsed on a crate. Nelly nudged my wet face with her muzzle.

I mumbled through my numb lips. "It's all right. I'm not angry. I know the ramp frightened you."

In this dangerous and undignified manner, I left Virginia for the first time in my life. As soon as we arrived at the Maryland shore, the ferryman tied up the raft and rang a bell mounted at the dock. The ferryman's wife bustled out to meet us and together they supported me inside, where I stood quaking like a leaf in high winds, dripping water all over the floor.

The ferryman's wife asked, "Do you have more clothes with you?"

I could barely form the words needed to reply. "Y-yes. The bundle behind my saddle."

The ferryman returned with the bundle and my wet cloak, dropping both on the floor beside me. "I put your beast in the barn, missus."

As he went upstairs to change, his wife poured a mug of tea and shoved it into my trembling hands. Then she bustled about, setting a chair before the fireplace and hanging a curtain of blankets on the drying line strung across the room so I could undress in private. After placing a stack of towels and more blankets on the chair, she left. "I'll be back, missus, as soon as I make sure my husband's all right."

"Thank you." I dreaded taking off the heavy blanket I wore across the river, for it seemed to be the only thing holding in my body's heat. I told myself I would warm for a moment and undress as soon as the ferryman's wife returned. Soon I heard her footsteps, and I rose and let the blanket fall at my feet.

She spoke from beyond the curtain as I started on the chemisette's buttons. "Sure, and you're not the first to go overboard, but it's such a cold morning. 'Twould have been better if you'd fallen in on this side of the river."

I was far too miserable to appreciate the joke, but she went on without pausing. "Ladies rarely cross alone. Where is your husband?"

"He is a clergyman."

"A clergyman husband who gives you leave to travel on the Sabbath?" Disbelief was clear in her voice.

I managed to speak without my teeth chattering. "The matter is urgent and could not wait until he could accompany me." It was never my nature to be wary of kind, motherly women, but could I trust anyone?

"Well, you've met my Arthur. I'm Dorcas Nelson." She did not pause long enough for me to respond. "Where did you say you were going?"

"To care for a sick relation."

"But what town?"

I recalled one place on Uncle William's list. "Ceresville."

"They got no one who can tend the sick in Ceresville?"

I didn't answer but focused my efforts on removing my boots. I dumped the water out and stripped off the haversack and the rest of the riding habit. I untied Nancy's quilted petticoat and felt my spine lengthen as its sodden weight left me and it fell to the floor. Tossing my pocket on top of the heap, I gasped as I remembered what it contained, and hastened to draw out the folded parchment. The water ruined my copy of Uncle's correspondence to Thompson. In frustration, I threw the paper into the flames, where it hissed and turned to ash.

Without that evidence, how would I stop the smugglers? Now I would have to find a magistrate, relay what I could recall of the letter, and swear out a warrant on them for thievery and conspiracy. But first I must find the wagon. There was no time to waste.

17

Hunter and Prey

I let the heat from the fire warm me on all sides as I toweled myself dry. Wrapped in a blanket, I dug through the bundles for my other set of clothes and toasted my spare shift before the fire, downing the rest of the tea before I put it on. Then I realized I had but one dry stocking. The other was full of salt. My toes looked as white and bloodless as if I was Lot's wife, made of the same stuff. I waved my quilted stays close to the flames as I wiggled my toes. The stays were not as wet as my outer clothing. Perhaps they'd soon be wearable.

As soon as I could feel my feet, I rolled on the damp stockings, but my toes turned to ice again in my wet boots. The moisture that lingered in my stays seeped through my shift when I pulled the laces tight.

Nancy's indigo woolen, cut fashionably low over the bosom, was not appropriate for riding but it would have to do. I tucked the chintz kerchief into the neckline and buttoned Benjamin's wedding coat over it all, leaving my hair long and loose. Hairpins straggled in my tangled curls but I couldn't take time to search and pick them out.

I rolled up my wet things in my cloak and stuffed everything into the sack that had held my change of clothing. Perhaps I could dry them once I stopped for the night.

When I emerged from behind the curtain, Mrs. Nelson raised an eyebrow at my new traveling costume. "No need to hurry off, missus. Stay until you're proper warm or you'll catch your death."

"It's not my death I'm worried about."

She shook her head. "Just as you say, then. Be careful out on the roads."

My boots squelched as I crossed the room, reinforcing Mrs. Nelson's objections.

In the barn, Nelly knelt on command in what I imagined was an act of contrition, and we were soon underway. With barely a mile behind us my stomach growled, reminding me I'd eaten no breakfast—and the river ruined the rations in my haversack. Though I shuddered at the thought of another meal like the one I endured at Chinns Crossing, I could go hungry until I reached an ordinary. The provisions for the men were undamaged but none of it was ready to eat. Even the nuts would have to be shelled.

As Nelly and I followed the fresh wagon tracks from the ferry crossing, the foothills of the Blue Ridge Mountains gave way to wider vistas but still yielded no sight of the wagons. My frustration grew when I met no travelers who might give me news. I should have overtaken the smugglers by now. The road passed through rolling stubble fields and into a pine forest where the thick branches cast everything into shadow. I was so busy planning what I would do when at last I overtook the wagon I failed to notice an approaching rider until he emerged from the woods and came up on my right side.

"Whither away, mum?" The man's stench was more pervasive than the smell of the horses and I tried not to wrinkle my nose. His clothes were filthy and torn and he showed rotted teeth as he leered at me.

Determined not to show my fright, I tucked my riding crop under my arm and fished a coin from my pocket. "I have little, sir, but I can offer you alms."

A second rider, just as odorous, came abreast of me on the left, crowding his horse close. He made a grab for Nelly's bridle, and she whinnied as he pulled at her head.

The first man scoffed at the offer of a coin. "What you got in those bundles? We ain't et for a few days."

The man who held Nelly's head leaned closer. "Ain't had no gentle company neither."

"Nor will you!" Fear and revulsion drove me as I grasped the riding crop's handle, drew it from beneath my arm like a dagger from its sheath, and brought it down across his wrist with all my might. He howled in pain. As his grip on the bridle slackened, I swung my arm back to apply the crop to Nelly's neck, and my elbow caught the other man square in the face.

He roared and Nelly bolted into the clear with no encouragement. I kept my eyes forward as the thunder of hoofbeats came up behind us. The road, sheltered from the elements, was dry, but it twisted this way and that through the trees, concealing what lay ahead. I lay flat on Nelly's outstretched neck and prayed God would lead me toward anyone who could come to my aid.

Gaining ground on an uphill slope, I topped the rise and spied a third rider trotting toward us. Unlike my pursuers, he wore a clean, wool coat and gleaming boots, his hair powdered and curled under his hat. As I drew near, he pointed a pistol at the advancing riders. I reined Nelly to the side to get out of the line of fire. The other two halted a short distance away.

"See here—what are you about?" He fixed a stern gaze on the men. "Haven't I told you what would happen if I caught you molesting travelers on this road again?"

The one I struck with the crop mumbled, "Yes, sir."

He kept the pistol trained on them as he turned to me. "Did they hurt you, madam?"

I took a deep breath, trying to slow my galloping heart. "No, sir. But I thank Providence you were riding this road."

"Do you live nearby?"

"I'm a stranger here. I'm traveling to meet relatives."

He nodded in greeting. "Magistrate Alexander Smith, of Frederick, at your service."

A magistrate! Relieved, I smiled in return.

He motioned to the two men with his pistol. "I will conduct this lady into town and this time I'll be drawing up charges against you both." They hung their heads as they guided their mounts around me.

I nudged Nelly forward and stole another glance at the magistrate as we rode. Nearly as old as Uncle William, Magistrate Smith carried himself with authority and his presence cowed the other men. After a few minutes, my heart slowed to a normal pace, and I decided to tell him about the smugglers as soon as the two highwaymen were in custody. "How much farther to Frederick Town?"

"Just a few miles."

As we splashed across a shallow creek, the magistrate pointed off to the east. "That's the Monocacy River, through those trees. Do you see it?"

I looked in that direction and a second later I heard the click of the pistol's hammer next to my head. In shock, I turned toward the sound, and my blood turned as icy as the Potomack. The magistrate had his pistol leveled at me. As the other men turned their mounts to hem me in, panic closed my throat and I panted in little gasps, like an animal caught in a trap. They no longer looked meek.

Smith's polite tone did not change. "Now, missus, hand over the riding crop."

The man I elbowed in the face held out his hand and when I surrendered the crop, he raised it as if to strike me and even the score. I held my arm in front of my face to ward off the blow but Smith shook his head.

"There's no need for violence." He holstered his pistol, took the reins from me, and led Nelly as he turned downhill on a narrow path shrouded in evergreen boughs. Smith's accomplices moved in behind me, single file, and when I glanced back, I could no longer see the road.

My gaze darted about as I searched for some avenue of escape. If I leapt to the ground and tried to run, the wooded terrain would make for slow going. Could I outrun them? If I did, where would I go? My chin trembled at the thought of leaving Nelly behind if I fled. Knowing I couldn't abandon her, I took stock of my assets.

The contents of my medicine chest were unlikely to interest them. Uncle's money was in my pocket along with my knife. The knife was a weak weapon against three men, but it was better than nothing. I drew Benjamin's coat closer around me so I could reach into my pocket unseen and move the blade to my waistband. Then I spoke. "You may have my money." I was glad my voice did not shake.

The man I hit with the riding crop chuckled. "No question about that, mum."

"My supplies are but a small amount of food and clothing bound for some soldiers and not worth your interest."

Smith, who rode so close to me his knee brushed against mine, smirked. "Only the best for our barefoot heroes."

At his mocking tone, my fear gave way to anger. I pictured Benjamin and Joseph, living in a drafty hut without warm clothes or proper food, and Henry and Jeremiah lying ill in some camp hospital. These blackguards would take everything—unless I could offer them something better. I vowed to do whatever it took to survive, whether it meant escape or submission.

I pretended I was bargaining with a clerk at the general store, not with three highwaymen for my life, and began by asking more than I expected to gain. "The money is to ransom myself."

Smith was my best hope for mercy. His two henchmen were only feral, snarling animals, and his leadership was all that stopped them from taking what they wanted right here on this deserted path.

But hope faded when Smith reached over and pinched my cheek between gloved fingers, forcing me to look at him for a long moment. "You're not leaving until we've partaken of everything we want."

My insides quailed and I squeezed my eyes shut as I continued to bargain. "'Tis true, I have more to offer you, sir." I must convince him to go after the more lucrative prize. "Two freight wagons traveling ahead of us on the main road are full of supplies stolen from the army and a hidden cache of rifles besides. Surely that would be more profitable for you than the pittance I carry."

Smith halted and I noted the gleam of interest in his eyes. "I saw two wagons pass. But how do you know they carry such cargo?"

"I observed them loading it last night in Leesburg."

"Oh, so there's a spy amongst us honest rogues? If so, you're no better than we. You're worse."

Ignoring the barb, I kept my tone businesslike. "I will lead you to them—in exchange for my liberty."

The men behind me laughed again. One said, "Sure we'll be taking the liberties rather than giving 'em."

"I'll be giving her a taste of my sugar stick," said the other.

"Here—I'm first this time!"

Smith fixed them with another hard look. "Silence, you jackals. Madam, I applaud your courage, but we do not bargain with women— or spies." He motioned with a tilt of his head. "If you'd be so kind as to dismount."

I closed my fingers around the handle of my knife and vowed I would not sully the memories of Benjamin or my children by thinking of them while I was at the mercy of Smith and his men. Instead, I would fight, and curse my uncle's name for involving me in his treachery.

Before I could move, something whistled past my ear and landed with a sickening, sticking sound. Smith, the hilt of a knife protruding from his chest, toppled backward out of his saddle.

A heartbeat later, a stone struck the man closest to me on the head, knocking him senseless, and he, too, fell to the ground. The rogue at the rear turned his horse and retreated up the narrow path. Two giant, bearded men in green uniforms emerged from the forest. One of them spoke in a harsh, unfamiliar tongue and pointed up the road.

"Fange den anderen."

The other caught hold of one horse's mane, swung into the saddle, and headed after the retreating highwayman. The first man advanced toward me. *"Lass mich Sie helfen."*

Hessians. All the warnings I heard rang like bells in my head. I could barely breathe, let alone think what to do. Had I escaped the highwaymen only to fall prey to the soldiers with the most brutal reputation of all?

Nelly sidestepped and bumped against Smith's horse, causing it to snort and buck. I wrapped one arm around Nelly's neck, desperate to keep my seat and seize the dangling reins.

As the soldier drew near, he motioned that I should come to him. I sat up and drew my knife. "Stay back."

His chuckle told me I posed no threat. Seizing my wrist with a practiced twist, he flipped the blade from my hand. In the same motion, he pulled me from the saddle so my back was against his chest, one arm around my waist and the other across my throat.

Locked in the grip of the hulking man who held me as easily as my daughter held her doll, I gasped for breath and kicked, feet dangling inches above the ground, as a third man emerged, panting, from the trees. He was a good deal older and shorter than the others and dressed in civilian clothes.

"Are you all right, madam?" He spoke English with an accent suggesting he hailed from the same place as these soldiers. "Do not fear. No harm will come to you now." He spoke to the soldier and motioned with his hand. *"Du kannst Sie jetzt hinlegen."*

The soldier released me with surprising gentleness, but I wobbled as my feet touched down. The soldier put a hand under my elbow and asked, *"Gehen Sie gut?"*

Gut? Good? Almost certain he asked if I was all right, I nodded.

The tall soldier pushed past the horses to where Smith lay on his back and pulled the knife from the dead man's chest with a grunt. He stepped over Smith to the other man, who was stirring, and plunged the knife into his neck.

In my time I'd seen people die of illness and watched animals butchered but I'd never witnessed murder. At the spurt of blood, the world tilted, and my empty stomach heaved. I fell to my knees, vomiting bile into the underbrush, horrified that I was glad both men were dead. When at last I wiped my mouth, the older man helped me to my feet and escorted me out of view of the corpses.

I felt my knees give way again and I drew a sobbing breath as he helped me sit with my back against a tree. Blackness clouded the edges of my vision and I leaned forward with my head between my knees. After a few moments, I stopped feeling as though I would faint.

He patted me on my back as he spoke, as though comforting a child. "Madam, I am Christopher Ludwick, of Philadelphia. My commander in chief is General George Washington. Corporal Wertenberger, whom you have met, and Private Brumbaugh, of the Hesse-Kassel Jäger Korps, are prisoners of war under my charge. You may count on our protection. Do you understand?"

I nodded. "Yes."

As I sat up, he reached into his haversack, produced a cloth-wrapped loaf of bread, and handed it to me. "Here. Eat this."

I broke off a bit. It tasted good and as I ate, I felt my strength return. I was just finishing when Private Brumbaugh came into view, riding one horse and leading another.

Ludwick called out to him, *"Ist er tot?"*

"Ja. Er ist tot." When he dismounted, the corporal motioned to him and together they dragged the two bodies into the underbrush.

My companion spoke in a soothing tone. "You need not fear the other highwayman. He is also dead. May we see you somewhere, madam?"

"Oh, no!" With a jolt, I remembered what I'd been doing before my encounter with Smith and his men. "You cannot help. I'll never find them now." I was one heartbeat away from a breakdown.

"Whom do you seek?"

I sobbed out my answer. "The smugglers."

"I heard you mention supplies stolen from the army while we were tracking you, but I thought you were spinning out a tale. What smugglers? Where are they bound?"

"I don't know. I was following the wagons—"

"Following? By yourself? *Mein Gott!* Have you taken leave of your senses?"

I managed a shaky laugh. "I was so incensed, I didn't think."

"Then let me assist you. We shall alert the proper authorities in Frederick." He stood and extended his hand to help me to my feet.

Despite all the excitement, Nelly had not strayed. Perhaps she wasn't willing to desert me, either. I located my riding crop a few feet from where she stood and Corporal Wertenberger returned my knife before giving me a hand up into the saddle. The soldiers and Ludwick took the other three mounts, and we were soon headed north on the Carolina Road. Private Brumbaugh pointed at Nelly and said, *"Das ist ein shönes Pferd."*

"Shoones fair?" I repeated what I heard, and the men laughed.

Ludwick explained, "He said you have a fine horse. *'Ein schönes Pferd.'*"

"Tell him thank you very much. Nelly has been my pet for years."

"You can tell him yourself. Say *'Vielen Dank.'*"

My tongue stumbled over the unfamiliar words and I laughed along with the men.

Corporal Wertenberger addressed me. *"Wo kommen Sie hier?"*

I shot a questioning look at Ludwick.

"He asks where you are from."

"Northern Virginia."

At that, Private Brumbaugh spoke while Ludwick translated. "He says that he has seen the men of Virginia. They are tall, well-formed, and have very good teeth."

It was true of the men in my family. "Please tell them their accuracy at throwing matches that of my husband and his brothers, who often throw hatchets and stones at targets for sport."

Ludwick passed along my words, listened to Private Brumbaugh's response, and nodded. "Many of the soldiers in their units were woodsmen before they joined the army."

"I've never seen a British soldier. How do the men of Virginia compare?"

Ludwick relayed my question and this time he translated for Corporal Wertenberger. "He says he can tell you about the British, for he has fought beside them for nearly a year. British soldiers can march for days on end and when they go against an enemy, they do not worry about their lives. Their only vices are swearing, drinking, whoring, and stealing, and these they do more so than the Jägers."

The men laughed and I joined in, though it wasn't a joke. The ragtag Continentals were challenging hardened, professional British soldiers and Hessian warriors.

"I cannot thank you all enough for coming to my aid. We always heard that Jägers—"

"Are inhuman, bloodthirsty savages? Monsters who burn homes, violate women, and kill children?"

I glanced at Corporal Wertenberger before nodding.

"They've heard the same about Americans." He smiled. "Based on what happened to you today, which would you say is closer to the truth?"

Outside Frederick, we passed a half-finished limestone structure and there I got my first sight of red uniforms and British soldiers. Ludwick nodded toward the complex. "They were building those barracks for the Maryland militia, but since our victory at Saratoga last fall, it has housed captured Conventioneers—British officers. They keep the Hessians in a prison closer to the center of town."

I stared at the barrier and the guards around the perimeter as we passed, wondering how easy it would be to smuggle rifles inside to the prisoners.

When we reached town, there were no soldiers picketed around the large storehouse that served as the Hessian prison. Instead, two young boys with rifles, not even in uniform, stood guard.

We bade farewell to Brumbaugh and Wertenberger, who dismounted and walked inside without being hailed or searched, as though they were walking into the village tavern.

"Are they all bound by honor to remain here? It looks as though the inmates could overpower the guards with ease."

"Where would they go? The prison paroles them to work and attend religious services, even to forage and fish to supplement their rations."

"But aren't the townspeople afraid with the enemy at liberty?"

Ludwick shook his head. "They treat them like kinsmen, mostly. The whole town of Frederick speaks German and many of the residents here hail from Hesse-Kassel."

Herr Ludwick spoke the truth. As I looked around, I saw other men in green uniforms on the streets, coming and going as they pleased. He called to the young guards and issued instructions in German. One boy hurried inside the building and the other led the highwaymen's horses away.

When the camp commandant came out and conducted us to his office, I relayed what I saw and heard in Leesburg and turned over the list of names Uncle provided.

Ludwick added, "Just last month British prisoners started a fire in the barracks at Lancaster in an attempt to escape. Now the Loyalists could be planning to arm them."

The commandant nodded. "I will alert the commandant who oversees the British prisoners here in Frederick and send dispatches to other prison camps in the area. Do you have any additional information?"

I neglected to mention Uncle's part in the conspiracy, and now, when I had the opportunity, I found all I could do was shake my head. If the authorities apprehended Thompson's smuggling ring, Uncle would cease to profit from their activities. I told myself the blow to his finances was enough. For now.

18

Respite

As we left the barracks, Herr Ludwick asked, "Where will you pass the night? May I escort you somewhere?"

"I don't know." I explained how I learned of the conspiracy, making a leap of faith by revealing Uncle's part in it, and finished with, "I planned to seek lodgings at his associates' homes, but now I fear calling on any of them is out of the question."

He nodded. "I agree you should have no more to do with your uncle's business. This evening I am staying with friends who have a large farmhouse. Please come with me. They are most hospitable. I daresay you will have a chamber to yourself."

"That's very kind of you. Are you sure they won't object?"

"Not at all. Now, we have at least another hour's ride ahead of us before we arrive, and I find your situation most curious. I know how you discovered the smugglers, but would you tell me why you are traveling alone?"

"All right, if you like. I'm sure it will pass the time."

"And I never caught your name."

I hesitated for just a moment before I replied. "Mrs. Benjamin Stone. Anna."

"*Schön, Sie kennen zu lernen,* Anna. It is a pleasure to know you."

"And you, sir. My story is this: I received a most distressing letter last week from my husband at Valley Forge. Since the commissary cannot procure enough to feed and outfit the troops, I am bringing all the food and warm clothes I can carry. Two of my brothers there are ill and I plan to tend them when I arrive."

"You have medical skill?"

"I learned when I was a girl."

Ludwick nodded. "I share your concerns about feeding the troops. Last year, I volunteered my services to the Continental Army as Baker General, but they soon sent me on a different mission. I infiltrated the prison camp at Staten Island in New York and spoke with Hessian soldiers. When I described the affluence and independence enjoyed by their former countrymen in German-speaking communities in Pennsylvania, hundreds deserted."

"Goodness!"

"I also hope this will help ease the army's food shortages. Fewer prisoners to feed, *ja?*"

Surprised by what he said, I tried to be fair-minded. Brumbaugh and Wertenberger had not hesitated to come to my aid. They treated me with respect and were eager to be friendly. But I could envision my mother, aunt, and uncle's consternation at the very thought of Hessian soldiers turned loose to live among us.

"You hail from Virginia. Very good soil for tobacco." Ludwick drew a paper tobacco packet from his pocket and handed it to me. "See the label?"

"I can't read your language."

"It says the United States government will give fifty acres and the promise of religious tolerance to any Hessian soldier or prisoner who lays down his arms."

This was a matter on which I did not have to consider my position. I gave a hot retort. "Religious tolerance for our enemies? But how can that be? In Virginia, my husband and his fellow Baptist clergymen are tormented, abused, and jailed for professing their faith and for nurturing it in others. Why are men who fight against our country given more religious freedom than we whose families have lived here a hundred years and more?"

"I may not give you an answer that will satisfy you. But I would say Hessian soldiers sent to fight in a war that means nothing to them have more sympathy for slaves than for people who are free. Though they fight for the British Crown, the British soldiers have abused the Hessians until they believe themselves inferior. This is not much different from how one treats slaves, *ja*? Better to invite them to join us."

I thought about Benjamin and his family's objections to slavery and gave a reluctant nod. "We would prefer to see slavery abolished everywhere."

Ludwick nodded. "The Hessian soldiers have found life without a monarchy to their liking. They think we Americans are quite the anarchists."

I felt my fury ebb away. If we gained independence from the Crown, liberty would belong to people of any nationality who wanted to build up America. Wouldn't it? "I suppose someone must always be the first to blaze a trail. Do you remember two Septembers ago, the Continental Congress passed a resolution declaring the thirteen American colonies the thirteen United States?"

"Yes, of course."

"Not long after, the Virginia State Assembly called upon Benjamin and his fellow preachers to help inspire the men in their congregations to enlist and fight the British, even though the state's persecution of Baptists and other dissenters had not abated. Why, I ask you, should my husband help raise troops to support Virginia while Virginia authorities continued to harass him?"

"That does not seem fair."

"It took a petition placed before the state's General Assembly, demanding toleration and an end to the harassment aimed at dissenters, to put things right. Benjamin and his brother were among the Baptists from Fauquier County who signed the petition. Over ten thousand signatures from Baptists and their supporters came from all corners of the state. If Virginia wanted an army, the Baptist clergy would help raise it—in exchange for religious liberty."

"Ah, then we are in the same boat, as they say. Is your husband as enthusiastic a soldier as you?"

"Yes. I suppose he is more so."

When we arrived at the home of Herr Ludwick's friends, a tall, broad-shouldered young man came out to greet us, and they embraced. Ludwick spoke in rapid German, gesturing toward me, and the other man nodded at once. He took both horses' reins and motioned we should go inside, where an elderly woman, several adults, and children whom I assumed were all of one family hailed Ludwick as one of their own. Again, after a brief word, the adults smiled and made gestures of welcome to me. A blonde young woman gestured that I should sit close to the fire and warm myself. Though the house was indeed spacious, I assumed Ludwick was mistaken about me having the luxury of a chamber to myself. Still, I was so glad to be someplace where I felt safe, I would be content to sleep on the floor before the fire.

As Ludwick continued to speak to the adults, they all turned to look at me in astonishment. One woman gasped, while others made indignant noises, and I realized he was retelling the events of the afternoon.

Herr Ludwick's friend who saw to the horses came in carrying my bundle and saddlebags and I hoped I remembered how to say it. "*Vielen Dank.*"

He smiled and nodded in return. At the oldest woman's direction, he took my bundles upstairs. One of the other women shooed the men across the big room and while meal preparations continued, the one who first interacted with me came and sat, pointing to herself. "Klara. Klara Hartmann."

"Anna Stone."

"Anna, *Sie sind mutig*—brave."

"*Danke*, Klara, but it was Herr Ludwick who is *mutig*. I should have been more careful." I mimed looking around.

Klara pointed at Benjamin's coat. "*Haben Sie einen Ehemann?*" She gestured at herself, pointed at the ring on her finger, and then at the young man who greeted us when we arrived. "*Der is mein Jacob.*"

"A husband?" The words sounded similar in both our languages.

"Yes. Benjamin. He is a soldier." Again, I mimed. "I go to him."

"*Und Kinder?*" She pointed at one of the children and back to me.

I held up three fingers.

Klara held up one finger and patted her belly. "*Amerikanisches Kind.*"

"That's wonderful!"

"We are all *Amerikanische, ja?*"

Before I could agree, the oldest of the women called, "*Kommen Sie!*"

After a good meal of sausage, potatoes, and a briny, cooked cabbage I never tasted before, Klara motioned for me to sit while the women and girls cleared the table. When the family gathered in the parlor for evening prayers, I bowed my head and found the rise and fall of the unfamiliar words comforting as I thought back on the events of the day.

Though I failed yet again to make a full day's travel, I was lucky to be alive. I found relief and comfort in Herr Ludwick's care and in this family's welcome. They spoke a different language, but they thought of themselves just as American as my family and me.

After prayers, most of them put on wraps and departed, leaving just the old woman, Klara, and Jacob.

Ludwick explained, "In the old country, land was not so readily available. All the family would have lived together in a home smaller than this. But here, even though their lands conjoin, and they spend the day together on the Sabbath, every man has a house for his family. Is very good, right?"

Klara took a candle and beckoned for me to follow her upstairs, where she led me into a cozy room already warmed by a fire on the hearth. She lit more candles as I undid the bundle of wet clothing. When I hung the cloak and riding habit on pegs set in the wall, Klara held her nose and began to giggle. Everything reeked of river water. I picked up a stocking and wrung it out over the slop jar in the corner and we both burst out laughing. I opened the bundle that hadn't fallen in the river and took out a pair of Benjamin's breeches, holding them up to my front. "Should I wear these?"

"Klara, Anna, *was geht hier vor?*" Ludwick stood in the open doorway with his own candle, smiling at our mirth without understanding the joke. "What goes on here?"

Still giggling, Klara hugged me and kissed me on both cheeks. "*Gute Nacht, Mutiger.*" She took her candle and departed.

"Her Jacob was a Hessian prisoner, you know."

"He was?"

"Yes. He and Klara met at church while he was furloughed from the prison."

"It's like a happy ending in a fairy story. Herr Ludwick, thank you for bringing me here. This was such a pleasant evening."

"Your day began as a tragedy and ended well."

"Except I fear my riding clothes won't be dry by tomorrow morning."

He pointed at the breeches in my hand. "But you have clothes for a man. Tomorrow it is no problem. You dress as a man, *ja?* We shall travel together and I will see you to Hanover."

I had not considered dressing to conceal my sex but his plan made perfect sense. "Yes, thank you. I would appreciate the escort, and your good company."

"You are most welcome. *Gute Nacht.*" He closed the door behind him.

The indigo gown was the only clean, feminine garment I had left. It was better to dress in Benjamin's clothes and save the gown to wear the day I would arrive at Benjamin's aunt and uncle's house in York.

I poured out water from the kettle on the hearth to wash and express the diminished supply of milk my body produced. With the bed warmer toasting the sheets, I blew out all but the bedside candle and sighed as I got under the covers. The wavering light from the fireplace cast huge shadows into the corners of the room and as I waited for sleep to come, I pondered the many ways we develop loyalties and create the lasting bonds of family.

Klara and Jacob grew up worlds apart yet, because Jacob was taken prisoner during the war, they found each other and fell in love.

Isabel's union with Mr. Thompson was also brought on by the war. Surrounded by wealth, she was lonely and miserable.

As for Benjamin and me, we would never have met had Uncle's business with Mr. Dunlap not taken him west from Stafford to Fauquier. And but for my delivering Uncle's letter to Mr. Thompson, I would not be here this night, under the protection of one of General Washington's spies, and welcomed by these kind strangers.

Nothing was happening the way I expected.

Joining my life with Benjamin's has not altered who I am. From the moment we wed, he was at once my anchor and the one who made the liberty I craved possible. He vowed he would come back to me and I'd had no hesitation about going to him. But I never thought I'd be swept up in such intrigue on the way. I was glad to have the treacherous part of the journey behind me.

I much preferred to recall the harmless intrigue prefacing my wedding day.

STONE ORCHARDS AND FARM, CARTERS RUN, VIRGINIA
OCTOBER 1767

Once again, Joseph acted to bring Benjamin and me together, but I am sure Thomas would, if asked, claim credit for all that transpired that day. Joseph arrived at Uncle's unexpectedly on a golden autumn morning and hailed me from the kitchen doorway. "Can you take time away from your tasks? We've all but completed the repairs on your house and I'm here to escort you over to inspect my craftsmanship."

"Yes, I certainly can. It's to be my home in two weeks and I've barely set foot inside it." I pushed the cast iron hook holding the kettle away from the flames so my blackberry preserves could simmer unattended.

He sniffed the air as he crossed the room. "Go put on a clean kerchief. I'll keep an eye on the preserves." At the hearth, he crowded me out of the way as he reached for the spoon. Forgetting a young lady of nineteen and soon to marry should act her age, I put my hands on my hips and stuck out my tongue at him. We both burst out laughing and I hurried to my chamber, heart singing at the prospect of an afternoon in Benjamin's company.

Rather than just put on a fresh kerchief, I changed into the yellow gown, reasoning that Benjamin would see me in work clothes often enough once we married. My fingers flew as I fastened the bodice and adjusted the cords to drape the overskirt in puffs above the petticoat's ruffle. In the looking glass, my face was clean and my auburn curls subdued inside my cap.

Out in the barn I saddled a three-year-old chestnut mare called Nelly, a recent addition to Uncle's stables. The roads were dry, so Joseph and I rode the five miles in short order, and as we drew near the tenant house by the orchard, I saw Benjamin up on the ladder leaning against the gable end, working bareheaded and coatless with his sleeves rolled up to the elbows. The mud-and-straw daubing he used to fill the gaps between the logs and make the house weather tight smudged him from head to toe.

Turning at the sound of our approach, his smile lit up his tanned face when he saw me. He jumped off the ladder and wiped his hands on a rag before helping me down. His hand lingered at my waist for longer than was proper and I let him steal a kiss as soon as Joseph wasn't looking. We had spent so little time alone during our courtship. Soon I would have him all to myself.

Joseph was busy giving the gable end of the house a critical inspection. "Did you get more mud on yourself or the walls?"

"Ah, you malign me when you neglect to tell Anna I've been wearing these same work clothes for a week." Benjamin, grinning, released me and threw the rag at Joseph.

Joseph caught it and bowed, flourishing the grubby thing as if it were a lace handkerchief. "My apologies. You're the neatest dauber I've ever seen. Ever."

"Thank you, friend. It's a title to which I aspire." Benjamin laughed as he took my arm. "I don't mind doing the lowly tasks and leaving the fine work to your brother. I want our home to please you and Joseph's master trained him well. I know it's not as grand as you're used to, but in a year or two we'll be able to side it and paint it, like Thomas and Betsy's house."

"A grand house doesn't guarantee a pleasant home."

"True, and ours will be very pleasant."

As I stepped over the threshold, sunlight streamed into the room and I inhaled the tangy scent of the fresh lumber used to repair the roof. On the trestle board, a pitcher of late-blooming daisies, goldenrod, and bittersweet berries made a cheerful splash of orange and yellow in the room. My eyes lingered on the bedstead on the far side of the fireplace, already made up with the linens from my trousseau. "It's just enough, isn't it? The flowers brighten the room."

"Betsy sent them over with Thomas earlier."

"Her baby is due any day now, isn't it?"

"Thomas said she has a few weeks yet." He moistened his lips and gazed down at me with undisguised longing. "You know, you brighten this place more than any blossom ever could."

"Thank you, kind sir. I look forward to becoming mistress of this fine establishment in two weeks."

He took a step to close the distance between us and laid a gentle hand on my cheek. "Why wait when we can marry today?"

The energy communicated in his touch sent a thrill through me and my skin grew hot. "But how? Everything's arranged. The priest has only announced the banns in church once. We have two more weeks to wait."

"Not if Brother Craig marries us in the Baptist faith. We can go to him now, in secret. It will make being married even sweeter, knowing we've not had to compromise our convictions to see it done."

"Tell me true. Is this act of nuptial defiance your idea or your brother's?"

"Indeed, 'twas Thomas who forged the plan." He ran his hands down my arms and they came to rest at my waist as he whispered close to my ear. "But now that you're here, I find I scarce can wait another day or even another hour, to make you my wife."

I watched his chest rise and fall and dropped my gaze again. I didn't want to wait any longer, either. My heart was pounding so that, with any small encouragement, our wedding and bedding could end up occurring in the wrong order.

He went on. "Thomas would have done the same if he'd thought of it. Brother Craig's tobacco barn will serve as the chapel, if you agree. Will you?"

Rather than admit I'd already warmed to the idea, I tilted my head as though still considering. "So, Mister Stone, let me understand. You would marry me to make a political statement? Am I but a pawn?"

"My dear Miss Asbury," he pretended affront. "You are no pawn but a queen, for you make me want to take risks. For you, I would defy the Crown, the priest, and your family—not necessarily in that order—to marry you and begin our lives together as we choose. Now, what say you? Will you be Missus Stone before day's end?"

His lips touched mine, gently at first, then with a growing urgency that left me breathless. When his hands slid up from my waist, I pulled away, holding a finger to his lips to check him as one more objection arose in my mind. "Mother won't be able to hold her head up if the clerk refuses to record our union in the courthouse register—and they will refuse if we're married by someone other than the parish priest."

"What does that matter as long as we know God smiles on us?" He caught hold of my fluttering hands. "The government should have no role in marriage. As long as the King is head of the Anglican Church, every dissenter who wishes to wed in Virginia is under the government's boot heel.

"Be my partner in this fight, Anna. Together we'll strike a blow for liberty, so someday our children may think, speak, and worship as they please under the law's protection."

I looked down at the sun-browned hands clasping mine and nodded. "Yes."

We were a team, in our hearts, even before we stood before the preacher. I considered our elopement rebellious. I wonder what that girl would think of the woman I've become.

19

In Disguise

I watched Benjamin dress thousands of times. On him, breeches and shirts and waistcoats with a dozen buttons down the front seemed natural and right. Contriving to make his clothing both fit and disguise my frame was more difficult than I expected.

My shift bunched up in the crotch of the breeches, so I shed it and tied Nancy's chintz kerchief around my torso before putting on my stays. Benjamin's shirt was large enough to hide my curves in its linen folds, and when I buttoned the waistcoat over it all, my body looked like a boy's.

His shirt fell almost to my knees and I wrapped the tails around me before I stepped into the breeches. Even with the front flap buttoned and the back lacing tied as tight as it would go, the breeches rode low on my hips. Unaccustomed to wearing anything but petticoats and stockings below my waist, I disliked the way the shirttail and the rough, woolen breeches felt against my legs. No wonder men and women walked differently. I buckled the woolen leggings over my stockings and riding boots and put on Benjamin's coat, which still smelled of my dip in the river. With my hair pulled back in a long tail, I placed Benjamin's cocked hat atop my head.

Ludwick was sipping coffee at the table when I came into the kitchen. Klara applauded, and the old woman nodded her approval. I started to curtsey but then checked myself. As I bowed, the hat slid down over my nose, which set them laughing.

My traveling companion took the hat and rolled up a newspaper, wedging it inside the brim so it would fit better, and produced a linen queue bag to complete my ensemble.

"Oh, thank you. My hair is so long, even pulled back, that I feared it would give away my disguise." Klara helped me coil the length of my hair down inside the bag and tied it to the leather lacing that secured the tail at the nape of my neck.

After breakfast, I embraced Klara, wishing our acquaintance had not been so brief. "*Vielen Dank.* I appreciate your family's hospitality."

"*Auf Wiedersehen,* Anna. Safe journey."

A few inches of snow fell overnight, and residual flurries dusted our hats and shoulders as Ludwick and I crossed the yard to join Jacob and our horses. Nelly cocked her head and I laughed. "Yes, Nelly. It's me."

The mare nickered in response. At the mounting block, I found it easier to get settled in the saddle, though my legs quickly grew cold without my usual layers of petticoats.

We passed other riders and pedestrians on the road and no one mistook me for a doxy. No one gave me a second glance. At worst, I would be thought a runaway boy in ill-fitting clothes. It came as a jolt that in my disguise, I had both anonymity and independence. I could do almost anything I pleased while dressed this way. That is, except stay in a tavern where I might have to share a bed with strangers in a common sleeping room.

"Herr Ludwick, yesterday you asked how I came to be on the road. Today, I wish to know how you found me in the forest?"

He laughed. "That was easy. Anyone could have tracked you, for you took no pains to conceal yourself."

"But with this load of provisions, how I could be anything but conspicuous?"

"There are still ways to protect yourself. For one, stay alert and do not move so quickly that you fail to notice trouble. Keep your head up while you ride and look three or four rods ahead. Did you realize you passed us before the first of those blackguards came upon you?"

"I did?" That was disconcerting news.

He chuckled. "You see my point? Traveling by yourself is dangerous. As a woman, you cannot expect to overpower an attacker."

I thought of the ease with which Corporal Wertenberger relieved me of my knife. "As I determined."

"So you must use stealth and trickery to avoid trouble. You are fair-skinned, so in the dark, cover your face. If you think you are spotted, freeze, for the eye detects movement. If a threat is close by, breathe through your mouth."

"But how did you and the others get close without Smith and his men noticing?"

"First off, we knew to be silent. You and those men were making such a stir we could have walked up and joined your party with none of you the wiser. You must expect trouble, *ja*? If you sense danger, let your fear guide you. Do not ignore it."

What other tricks did I have at my disposal? My healing knowledge was useless in a confrontation. It was a shame none of the medicines I carried would ward off an attacker.

The temperature rose above freezing and the snow melted to slush by the time we stopped for the noon meal at a public house in a Quaker settlement. Here, in contrast to the ordinary I visited my first day on the road, the clientele was sober and respectful of the serving maids. The women's plain dress differed little from what I usually wore at home, so Uncle was right about that, I supposed. I wondered what he would think of my attire if he could see me now.

I was curious to ask questions of the Quaker women but did not feel comfortable speaking to them while in my disguise. Back on the road with Ludwick, I could not be silent. "Before I met my husband, I knew only the Anglican Church. The Baptist doctrine's liberty of conscience appealed to me. In Maryland the Catholics and the Lutherans do not attack one another. And here, in Pennsylvania, you say you have toleration?"

"Yes, that is correct."

"If there cannot be one Christian denomination on which we all agree, why do we not simply leave everyone to choose, rather than persecute? The Quakers seem content to stand apart."

"And are you acquainted with any Friends?"

"I am not but I have read some scholarly works published by Quaker women."

"Toleration does not eliminate discord. Though the Friends extend more opportunities to women, there is much about them you would not like, Anna."

"I think a person's actions matter more than their professed doctrine. Though women are the guardians of religious life in the home, religion—and wars—are the dominion of men. The Quakers are pacifists. No woman wants to send a husband, brothers, or sons to war."

"*Ja*, but are you familiar with Thomas Paine's *Epistle to the Quakers*?"

"Of course. Benjamin brought home a copy of *Common Sense* the summer before last, and I read it all—including that essay in the appendix. I said no woman wants war. I didn't say we should never resort to it. And I am wife to a soldier."

"In Philadelphia, I have many acquaintances who are Friends. As you and your husband consider yourself patriots, do you not find the Quakers' refusal to aid the Continental Army a threat to the

Revolutionary cause? Quakers send none of their men off to fight, yet they pay substitutes—and they sell goods to whichever army can best pay for them. In this way they are complicit, for their actions prolong the war. Is that fair to your husband, who has volunteered to fight?"

I sighed. "I don't know. It is difficult to hold religious convictions that differ from the majority. Yet Benjamin has always said religion should not drive a wedge between us and others. He hopes once we achieve independence, we shall also have freedom to worship as we please—in all the states."

"My friend General Washington believes the nation that proselytizes least governs best. Perhaps we shall soon find out if that is true."

I could not see how our nation could exist without embracing the faiths of all who called the United States home. I thought of our sweet little sons and wondered if soldiering lay in their futures. Hard as it was to let Benjamin go, I knew that should I have to watch Elijah and William march away someday it would rend my heart in two.

Yet I would be proud if my sons grew into men like their father, willing to put themselves in harm's way to advance the cause of liberty.

STONE ORCHARDS AND FARM, CARTERS RUN, VIRGINIA
AUGUST 1776

A few weeks after Benjamin returned home from his service in the Minutemen, Washington's troops drove the British out of Boston. At this news, I hoped the conflict was drawing to a close and our lives could return to normal, but things were soon to escalate again, and a radical new idea took hold.

One spring evening Benjamin, brimming with excitement, brought home Mr. Paine's pamphlet, *Common Sense*, which he read aloud to me by candlelight. "'How came the King by a power which the people are afraid to trust and always obliged to check? Such a power could not be the gift of a wise people, neither can any power, which needs checking, be from God.'" His dark eyes shone with excitement. "Mr. Paine put into words what I have thought for some time. It is a matter of common sense."

I finished drying the last dish and sat at the table with him as he continued.

"The Anglican Church obeys the King of England. If we follow our consciences, we must seek independence from the Crown. And here it says, 'America would have flourished as much, and much more, had no European power taken any notice of her.'"

It felt like treason, to suggest America would thrive without Crown rule. For the first time, I wondered, *Should Americans want independence?*

"I thought it would be enough to restore the way things were before the late war, but with more religious liberty. Now, I don't believe we should stop there. It's our Christian duty to oppose tyrants." He stood and placed the pamphlet between two of his books on the mantel.

Just weeks after Elijah's first birthday at the end of July, the Continental Congress sent copies of a new declaration to all congregations in the colonies.

Benjamin received the document midweek and, treating it with the same reverence he would have afforded a rare religious text, he set about studying it before writing his sermon. When he stood before the congregation that Sunday, he led the service with more than his usual enthusiasm.

"It is written, in Paul's first letter to the Corinthians, 'For as the body is one, and hath many members, and all the members of that one body, being many, are one body: so also is Christ.'

"This is also true of our nation, for surely there is more that binds us as Americans than drives us apart. I ask you, what would you be willing to sacrifice to secure a future free from Crown rule for your-selves and your children?

"In Thomas Paine's *Epistle to the Quakers*, he asserts that all men dislike violence and want peace, but there comes a time when vio-lence is inevitable. Mr. Paine writes that total separation from England solves the problems we face."

He unrolled the parchment. "This is a copy of our Continental Congress's Declaration of Independence. The original is on its way to England and King George. I am privileged to be the one to share this message with you.

"'In Congress, July 4, 1776. The unanimous Declaration of the thirteen United States of America: When in the Course of human events, it becomes necessary for one people to dissolve the politi-cal bonds which have connected them with another, and to assume among the power of the earth, the separate and equal station to which the Laws of Nature and of Nature's God entitle them, a decent respect to the opinions of mankind require that they should declare the causes which impel them to the separation. We hold these truths to be self-evident, that all men are created equal, that they are endowed by their Creator with certain unalienable Rights, that among these are Life, Liberty, and the Pursuit of Happiness.'"

As he read, I scanned the faces of the people in the congregation and saw the dawning excitement I experienced a few months before. But now, fear overshadowed my excitement. What would indepen-dence from England and Crown rule mean? What would it cost to gain it? Benjamin read the crimes of the King. When he came to, "'He has plundered our Seas, ravaged our Coasts, burnt our Towns, and destroyed the lives of our People,'" his voice shook for a moment, and he cleared his throat. I saw the tears in his eyes, and a combination of pride, patriotism, and fear caused the tears pooling in my own.

My pride swelled at Benjamin's commitment to change and for what our nation accomplished outside the grasping hand of the King.

I saw enough of what Crown rule did to us to want independence too. But I feared war would force families like ours into long separations. If we lost, what would happen to the men who rebelled?

As I watched my husband stand before his congregation, I could almost see the fresh flames burst forth from the smoldering coals of his ideals.

That night, when the children were asleep and the windows thrown open to the night sounds of frogs and katydids, Benjamin spread the Declaration out on the trestle board and weighed down the corners of the parchment with candlesticks. He traced his fingers over the words. "Many great statesmen hail from Virginia—among them Thomas Jefferson, the author of this declaration. I marvel that King George will see the signature of my cousin, Thomas Stone of Maryland."

I leaned against him. "Do you wish you had pursued the law and become a statesman?"

"Nay. I understand my role in what is to come. Just imagine what possibilities may be open to us if this challenge to the Crown leads to our independence. We're living in wondrous, dangerous times." He ran a hand through his hair. "I warrant I shall not sleep tonight. I'm that excited."

His elation put me in mind of the day we married and just like then, I was there to fan the sparks of his passion. I brought his callused palm to rest against my cheek. "Then neither of us shall sleep."

He needed no more encouragement. He cradled my face in his hands and his kiss ignited a blaze deep within me. The flames spread until I felt nothing but the desire to draw him in and receive his unrelenting energy.

20

Reinker's Tavern

Ludwick and I rode in silence for some time and I cast a sidelong
glance at my companion, my face still flushed at the memory of
that summer night in Benjamin's arms the Lord used to give us baby
William. I cleared my throat. "I warrant this part of Pennsylvania looks
like a different country. It's hard to believe we are still in the United
States." The houses in Hanover charmed me and I turned in the saddle
trying to see them from every angle as we rode down the high street.

Ludwick explained, "Half-timber houses were practical in areas
with limited access to stone. They are very popular in Hesse-Kassel.
A masonry ground floor, half-timbered above, was the best use of
the available building materials. Those who came here from Europe
brought the style with them."

"Benjamin's father built ours of dressed logs, and a few years ago
we sided it with clapboard. If I had known about this style of house-
building, I might have suggested my husband and my brother try to
fashion ours more in this way."

Late that afternoon we turned into the stable yard at the Sign of
the Horse Inn. Ludwick jumped down from the saddle and embraced

a strapping teenaged stable boy and then sent him on the run toward the kitchen door.

I shook my head in disbelief as I dismounted. "Do you know someone in every town?"

He laughed. "As a solitary traveler, I like to make friends whenever I can—especially ones who may help me in my mission for His Excellency."

"How does the stable boy help your mission for General Washington?"

"It is not he, but his grandfather, who is—ahh, and there he is! Herr Reinker is the owner of this establishment."

The stable boy returned with a man about Ludwick's age. He smiled through the pipe clamped between his teeth and welcomed Ludwick with a hearty embrace. My question went unanswered.

My companion gestured toward me and spoke in rapid German. When the inn's proprietor looked me up and down and nodded, Ludwick turned to me. "You shall have a private sleeping chamber this night. Your secret identity is safe."

I paid eleven shillings six pence for the private room and clean sheets and thirty pence more for hay and pasturage for Nelly, remembering I paid Mrs. Champe only two shillings for overnight lodgings just days before. But no matter. I would be safe—and anonymous—on my last night in Ludwick's company.

Though the men would have carried my bundles upstairs without my assistance, I insisted on carrying my saddlebag. Herr Reinker stoked the fire before placing the key in my hand and leaving me to freshen up. With water on to warm, I got my cloak out of the bundle containing my wet things, hung it on a peg set in the wall, and dabbed it with lavender oil. It would not be clean, but with any luck it would smell better and be dry enough to wear the next day.

Wearing Benjamin's clothes served to make the day's travel easier. I did not expect them to also bring me closer to him in spirit but I could almost imagine him here with me. I rubbed a smudge of dirt off one of the brass buttons on his coat, with a fond remembrance of the first time I saw him wearing it. He emerged from our house, washed and changed and ready to escort me to the preacher. This shade of green, deliberately chosen, signaled a celebration, and I was glad I wore my yellow gown.

CRAIG FARM, CULPEPER COUNTY, VIRGINIA
OCTOBER 1767

The rest of our wedding party gathered in Elijah Craig's tobacco barn. As Benjamin, Joseph, and I rode up, we found Thomas and the preacher lounged in the doorway, passing a bottle of whiskey between them.

Betsy, heavy with child, pushed herself up from the bench under the barn's awning to embrace me as I drew near. "Don't worry. They're not drunk. I wouldn't let them do anything to ruin your day."

"I'm glad you're here to stand up with me. You look well."

She smoothed her shawl over her swollen belly. "Thomas is hoping for a brother for our Noah, but I wager it's a girl this time. Everything is ready for my lying-in, so today I baked a cake and picked more than enough wildflowers for the bridal bouquet. May I make a wreath for your hair with the extras?"

"Yes, please." I unpinned my cap and as Betsy wove the flowers through my curls, I wished I had a wedding favor for her. A pair of gloves, perhaps. I promised myself to present her with such a gift at the next opportunity.

She took a step back to admire the effect. "Perfect! I'm so glad we're going to be sisters."

"As am I."

The men's conversation rose to my ears as Thomas threw an arm around Benjamin's shoulders and pushed the bottle into his hand. "So, a pretty girl catches a young man's eye and he asks her, 'Which way to your bedchamber, miss?' And she replies, 'Through the church, sir!' Today, brother dear, your fine filly of a bride will lead you to hers through the barn!"

He affected two voices—one high, one low—as he told the story and the other men laughed as Benjamin nearly choked on his mouthful of whiskey.

"Thomas!" Betsy admonished and then said to me by way of apology, "He's after remembering all the bawdy jokes he ever knew."

Thomas grinned at his wife, claimed the bottle, and took another drink.

I winked at Betsy and addressed my future brother-in-law with my sweetest smile. "I'm so pleased to be recognized as a thoroughbred, even if it is by the barnyard swine."

The laughter rose again, this time at Thomas's expense. He took off his hat with a flourish as he bowed to me and I returned his courtesy.

Brother Craig took the bottle. "I believe Thomas has had enough fortification." He offered it again to Benjamin, who shook his head. "Very well then. Shall we begin?"

Inside, Brother Craig set down the bottle and picked up his worn Bible. The curing tobacco hanging from the rafters framed Benjamin and me in a golden-brown bower as we stood before him. It was just as Benjamin desired—a simple, personal service conducted by a man who knew him well, rather than a half-hearted recitation of liturgy done by a priest of my uncle's choosing.

"As we gather to celebrate the wedding of Benjamin and Anna, we may view the formation of their new family as a little society, in which each member has a role to fulfill. I charge you, Benjamin, to be a strong, wise, and affectionate husband. Anna, as the partner of his life, you must strive to cultivate the charms of modesty and kindness that encourage Benjamin's love and affection. It is not the joining of hands, but of hearts, which constitutes marriage in the sight of God. That alone sanctifies and perfects this most solemn and sacred connection.

"Be loving toward one another. Have no separate secrets, but instead open out your whole hearts to one another. As you begin your life together, we pray your children will inherit the virtues embodied in both of you and live up to your good example. Anna, wilt thou have this man . . ."

I clutched the bouquet, glad to have something to keep my hands still. As I made the responses, my voice sounded far away. Benjamin's gaze never left my face and I watched his lips move when it was his turn to repeat after Brother Craig. It was almost over when I began to comprehend what we just promised. We might be happy all our days or desperately sad. Whatever our lot, we would face it together. Tears filmed my eyes as I wished our time together would never end.

Benjamin's heart was plain on his face as he repeated after the preacher. "With this ring I thee wed, with my body I thee worship," — he reached into his waistcoat pocket and brought out a gold band — "and with all my worldly goods I thee endow."

A single tear spilled down my cheek as he slid the ring onto my fourth finger. When Brother Craig pronounced us joined for life in the sight of God, Benjamin rubbed his thumb across the gleaming gold band and kissed me on the lips. Then he grinned, all nervousness gone, and shook the preacher's hand. "Thank you, Brother Craig. This means a great deal to us. When I'm appointed, I'll do the same for others of our faith."

I added, "Yes, thank you. We're most grateful."

"It was an honor, Sister Stone." He kissed me on the forehead.

"Oh, are we all kissing the bride, then?" Thomas seemed eager to resume the frivolity but I saw a worried look cross Betsy's face.

Joseph spoke up before I had time to ponder my new sister-in-law's reaction. "If we are, I'm to be next." He followed the preacher's example and kissed me on the forehead.

Thomas gave me a cheeky grin as he leaned in for his turn, but his kiss was as proper and respectful as the others.

Out in the afternoon sunshine, Betsy took my hand. "I can help you put your house in order before we have dinner." She lowered her voice. "Has your mother spoken to you about what to expect?"

"So far, her only advice has been, 'Modesty must be preserved, even at the moment appointed for its loss.'"

"Well, as you can see, I'm fair fixed to answer questions—better so than your ma, for I have recent experience."

At that, I giggled. My new sister-in-law and I were the same age, but Betsy was indeed the more experienced. She often said things in a way that made me blush. "I'm not worried about tonight—but what about after? Benjamin is the first man I've known who regards me as his equal. Will that change after I submit to him?"

It was Betsy's turn to giggle. "Ben? Nay! He'll not lose interest in your mind once you're in his bed—and don't mistake his gentle ways for lack of an appetite. You two will have a merry time of it, you'll see."

REINKER'S TAVERN, HANOVER, PENNSYLVANIA
JANUARY 19, 1778

Footsteps in the hall outside my door brought me back from my reverie. The water in the basin had grown cold while I sat holding Benjamin's coat in my arms and I poured the tepid liquid back into the kettle to heat again. Once washed, I adjusted my costume and descended for dinner. Ludwick was already in the public room in the company of our host and I joined them at a small table near the kitchen door. I wore the hat downstairs but as none of the other men kept theirs on indoors, I hung it on a peg on the wall. Even with my face exposed, I felt comfortable and inconspicuous in the dim, quiet corner.

The kitchen maid brought us mugs of ale and plates of sausage, potatoes, rye bread, and the briny cabbage dish Ludwick called sauerkraut. I wrinkled my nose at the plate before me but dug in with enthusiasm. "It tastes better than it smells."

Ludwick laughed. "I quite enjoy the smell. It reminds me of home."

After dinner and a second mug of ale, I was content to sit by as Ludwick and Reinker chatted. One hour passed and then two, and the candle on our table burned low. The rise and fall of their words and the hum of the other patrons' conversation lulled me into a stupor.

I came fully awake when Ludwick nudged me with his elbow. "Will you enjoy a pipe with us?"

I stifled a yawn. "No thank you. I'm afraid I'm not that much of a man yet."

Ludwick made a comment to Reinker and they both chuckled. Every seat in the place was taken, with many more men standing nearly elbow to elbow. It was a good time to make my exit.

"Shall I see you to your room?" Ludwick rose from his seat.

"Yes, please. I feel uncommon tired. I warrant I shall have no trouble sleeping tonight."

As I pushed back my chair, a shout on the opposite side of the room drew my attention, and Ludwick's head snapped in the same direction. A tall, broad-shouldered man rose from his chair, tipping it over, and swept the dishes and mugs off the table in front of him.

As I watched, I wondered if this man was like the brigands in Aldie, come to rob the tavern. Because I could not understand what was being said, I could only guess what sparked his aggression.

A look passed between Ludwick and Herr Reinker and the tavern keeper shoved his way through the crowd toward the disturbance. The brute who started the trouble seized another man by the lapels and dragged him across the tabletop. Then he shook the man until his teeth were surely rattling in his head and struck him a clout that sent him reeling backward. When the hapless man fell to the floor, I cried out and started toward him to render aid, but Herr Ludwick took me by the arm and hustled me ahead of him into the kitchen.

A moment later, the tavern keeper's wife and the kitchen maid hurried in after us. Frau Reinker took a cloth-wrapped bundle from her apron and worked it deep into the flour barrel, while the kitchen maid collected the knives, rolled them in a towel, and hid them away.

From the doorway, I watched the large man take a long draught of ale, cast the mug aside, and waver on his feet. Perhaps he was so far gone with drink he was on the verge of losing his senses. I hoped he could be brought to a settlement without more violence, but as Herr Reinker approached with his hands open, showing he held no weapon, the big man picked up a chair and smashed it across the table, brandishing one of the splintered legs.

At this, about half of the tavern's patrons rushed out the front door, slipping on the spilled food and drink in their haste.

When he brought the chair leg down on the table again, Herr Reinker took another step toward him, attempting to pacify him. The drunken man swung the chair leg and grazed the tavern keeper's head. Old Herr Reinker reeled back, blood coursing from the gash as he fell against one of the tables.

It might have gone far worse for him had the husky young stable boy not rushed in and flung his arms around the brute's waist, the way I saw men at home wrestle—catch as catch can. The force of the boy's attack spun them around in the space between the tables. The chair leg clattered to the floor and the drunken man threw flailing punches against the boy's sides. When they fell against one of the tables, they went head over heels onto the floor, landing near the kitchen door.

As they staggered up, the madman struck the stable boy a stunning blow and then reached for his club. He stepped over the helpless stable boy toward the old tavern keeper, who backed away.

Herr Ludwick grabbed one of the serving trays, dashed from the doorway and came upon the drunken man from behind. With a slicing motion, he used the tray to buckle the man's legs. As he fell, his chin struck a table's edge, and he collapsed, insensible.

21

The Healer

My eyes swept the room, taking in the four injured men. I dashed upstairs, fetched my medicine chest, and when I returned, I cast off my coat and rolled up my sleeves as I knelt beside the stable boy. I called to Ludwick, who clutched the tray as he stood like David over fallen Goliath. "I need hot water and clean cloths."

He relayed my instructions, and the weeping kitchen maid scurried to obey. She was back in an instant with a pile of towels and a basin and joined me at his side. It was obvious she and the young man were sweethearts. I let her help while I cleaned his cuts and made compresses sprinkled with tincture of myrrh for his bruised ribs and the swelling around his eye.

What was the purpose of the fight? I wondered as I made a poultice of yarrow powder and pressed it to the gash on Herr Reinker's head to stanch the bleeding. I knew nothing of the conflict that sparked the brawl—and my trip thus far taught me to take no one at face value.

Frau Reinker watched my every move and my treatment seemed to meet with her approval. I gave her a reassuring smile. "He's going to be all right, though I expect he'll have a powerful headache for a day or so."

Herr Ludwick translated for me, and with tear-shimmering eyes, she nodded and patted my shoulder.

The brute's first victim was not hurt as badly as the others, likely because he elected to stay where he fell and not draw any more of the drunken man's ire. I cleaned a cut on his lip and when I found no other wounds, let him leave in the company of some comrades.

With the drama at a close, Herr Ludwick brought me a mug of ale. "I could recommend you for a position as a surgeon's assistant. You kept a cool head."

"I've cleaned up after a brawl or two." I took a gulp and clenched my trembling fist around the mug's handle.

Some of the men who fled the fight filtered back into the tavern, along with the magistrate of the town. At his orders, a few of the patrons trussed up the drunken man and hauled him out to the jail. As they were leaving, a boy of about twelve shoved his way past them, looking confused at the disorder. When he spotted Frau Reinker, he tugged on her sleeve to get her attention, and what he said upset her all over again.

I asked Ludwick, who was looking on, "What's the matter?"

"That's the tailor's apprentice. His mistress is in labor and she asks for Frau Reinker to attend her."

I stood. "I am a midwife. I'll go if Frau Reinker prefers to stay with her husband."

Ludwick translated and once the matter was settled, spoke to me. "I shall accompany you and the boy, to translate."

"Does Herr Reinker need you here?"

The tavern keeper spoke up and Ludwick nodded. "They will suspend business for the night and bar the door once we go."

I picked up Benjamin's coat and took his hat off the peg. "Then let's away."

The boy led us down the dark, narrow streets, while Ludwick held the lantern.

My curiosity consumed me. "What was the fight about?"

"Naught but a dispute between tradesmen. Happily, it had nothing to do with me or my dealings with our host."

He unlocked a door and we followed him into a storefront. A woman's moan cut through the silence. The boy's eyes widened and he gestured for us to hurry. In a keeping room at the rear of the store, two children sat huddled in a blanket on a wooden settle near the fire.

I looked around. "Where is the woman?"

The boy pointed at a narrow staircase, nearly hidden in the shadows. Together, we climbed the stairs by lantern light. In the candlelit bedchamber, we found a woman kneeling on the bed, clinging to the wooden footboard. The evidence of her preparations lay nearby—plenty of towels, scissors, a ball of twine. Water simmered in a cast iron pot hung over the flames on the hearth. She looked up as we entered but before I could introduce myself, she sobbed out something. I looked to Ludwick.

He murmured, "She asks why the boy has brought men when she needs a woman. She thinks we are the undertakers."

I hoped the few words I knew in German would comfort her. "*Mutig. Mutiger Frau.*" I called her brave, as Klara called me.

The timbre of my voice revealed what my shadowy form had not and the woman relaxed before my eyes.

Ludwick spoke to her in a soothing voice, then said to me, "I told her you will bring the child. I am only here to translate until you know her situation and then I shall take leave. What do you need to ask her?"

"First I must know her name."

He relayed my question, and the woman gasped out, "Margaretta."

"*Sehr gut*, Margaretta." I pointed to myself. "*Ich* . . . Anna."

In the ensuing back-and-forth conversation, Herr Ludwick apologized for the delay and explained Frau Reinker's husband was ill and so I, a guest at the tavern, was here in her stead.

I said, "Fear not—I have helped deliver many a babe in the past ten years. Indeed, my first was on the night I became a bride."

The woman gave Ludwick an incredulous look and when she asked her question, he turned to me. "I fear I have mistranslated—she asks if you were delivered of your own child on your wedding night?"

I laughed. "No, it was my sister-in-law's child. Her travail started after she stood up with me at my wedding. My special day ceased to be about me once my niece, Sadie, decided to make her entrance into the world."

He hastened to relay what I said and Margaretta's laugh turned into a gasp as the next contraction came on. As she began to pant, Ludwick looked discomfited. We were definitely in my territory now. I patted his shoulder. "You've helped a great deal. Now leave us so I may attend to Margaretta."

He nodded, only too glad to be dismissed. "I'll be downstairs if you need me."

Once he was gone, I approached the bed. "Now, Margaretta, let us see how soon we'll be welcoming your little stranger."

STONE ORCHARDS AND FARM, CARTERS RUN, VIRGINIA
OCTOBER 1767

On the way home from our wedding, as was the custom, Thomas spared no jokes at Benjamin's and my expense. "Tonight, we'll make Ben ride a fence rail up and down the orchard rows before we serenade the happy couple at the shivaree!" He launched into the opening lines of a bawdy song.

Benjamin raised a hand to stop him. "Brother, truly—we've had enough excitement for one day."

"You haven't even made it to the marriage bed yet!" Thomas howled with laughter.

I felt my face grow hot. Joseph and Betsy joined in Thomas's laughter but Betsy's mirth ended in a gasp.

Instantly Thomas sobered. "What's the matter? Are you all right?"

She nodded. "I felt a pain after the ceremony and another just now. It's likely nothing."

But her contractions continued and when we reached their house, Thomas helped her from the saddle and put a protective arm around her.

She sighed as she paused to massage her lower back. "With Noah my travail took almost a day but I think the pains are coming faster this time." Before he could reply, she cried out and doubled over, wrapping her other arm around her belly. He lifted her into his arms in a flurry of skirts, her shawl trailing behind them as he carried her up the porch steps. Over his shoulder, he called to Benjamin, "Fetch Mother."

Benjamin turned his horse's head, clapped his heels against its sides, and was off like a shot.

Joseph asked, "Want me to go for Betsy's ma?"

"Yes," Thomas called, kicking the door shut behind them as Joseph rode off to do his bidding.

Nelly sidestepped nervously in the wake of the rapid departures. I reined her down and patted her neck. "Easy, sweet girl. I guess it's just you and me."

Thomas hurried back out on the porch. "Anna? Come in—Betsy wants you. I'll stable your horse."

I slid out of the saddle and hurried past him on trembling legs. Inside, I found Betsy in the bedchamber, slowly undressing. "What can I do?"

"Help me take the counterpane off the bed, spread the oilcloth pad on the mattress, and unlace me. I must put on an old shift instead of my good one." Betsy untied the waist tapes on her petticoats and let them fall to the floor and I picked them up to fold them. She gasped again and a splash wet the floor between her feet. "This baby is surely coming today."

Before the tasks were complete, Benjamin's mother came bustling in and appraised Betsy with an experienced eye. "Let's walk you about for a bit before we settle you into bed." Mary Stone turned her beaming smile on me. "Anna, my dear girl!" She gave me a quick hug and kissed me on both cheeks. "Benjamin told me you'd just come from the preacher and I couldn't be happier. What an exciting day! Now, why don't you go start some water to boil and brew some raspberry leaf tea?"

"Yes, Mother Stone." Just like that, I was part of the family.

I was pouring steaming water through the strainer into an earthenware mug when Betsy gave a sharp cry of pain and I jumped, knocking it over. Chiding myself for being a ninny, I grabbed a towel to soak up the spill. Though I tended people with all manner of illnesses, midwifery was work for matrons, so I was never before summoned to a baby's arrival. The sounds emanating from the next room were terrifying and they were a part of married life that, until now, was shrouded in mystery somewhere in the distant future. My hand shook a little as I carried the mug into the bedroom, where our mother-in-law was helping Betsy settle back against the pillows.

"See what you have to look forward to?" Betsy tried to joke as she suppressed another groan.

Mary Stone chuckled. "Hush, Betsy. Poor Anna's eyes are as big as saucers already. No need to try to frighten her." She turned to me. "Don't worry, child. It's the most natural thing in the world."

REINKER'S TAVERN, HANOVER, PENNSYLVANIA
JANUARY 20, 1778

Ludwick returned before dawn with Frau Reinker, and she relieved me of my duties a few hours after Margaretta's daughter made her entrance into the world. Eyes gritty with exhaustion, I plodded back to the tavern, bid Herr Ludwick good night, removed my jacket, breeches, and boots, and crawled into bed. Once I was under the covers, my body relaxed, but sleep would not come.

There was much to celebrate in life and much to fear. Of all the things, good and bad, leading me to this point, I could cling to loyalty and family above all others.

I smiled as I turned over and plumped my pillow. Though my wedding day wasn't anything like my vision of it, I say with certainty we could not have made a better start, and were, as Betsy would say, fair fixed to weather everything to come.

STONE ORCHARDS AND FARM, CARTERS RUN, VIRGINIA
OCTOBER 1767

Had Betsy wanted, I would have stayed at her side until she delivered. When her contraction eased, I asked, "If you have a girl, what will you call her?"

"Sadie. We'll call her Sadie."

"That's a lovely name." As I helped her take a sip of the raspberry leaf tea, the door opened and her mother came in, removing her wraps. While the two grandmothers stood off to the side in hushed conversation, Betsy looked up at me.

"Go home. Take the cake with you. I'm sorry I ruined your wedding supper."

"You didn't ruin anything. I'll stay if you need me."

"No. Ben's waiting for you. You mustn't stay here with me on your wedding night."

I kissed her perspiring forehead. "God keep you. Next time we see each other, you can introduce me to your new babe." In the kitchen, I cut the cake in half and wrapped one section to carry home in a borrowed basket. Outside, I found Benjamin sitting with Thomas on the porch.

Benjamin jumped to his feet like he'd been scalded. "Is everything all right?"

"Yes." I glanced over at Thomas, who, though he stayed seated, also hung on my words. "The pains are getting harder, but Mother Stone and Mrs. Jackman have everything in hand."

Thomas chuckled. "We can postpone the shivaree, unless you want me to—"

"No, really. Stay here." Benjamin pulled him to his feet and the brothers embraced. "My wife and I will see you tomorrow."

The sun was soon to disappear behind the ridge and our long shadows moved ahead of us and we headed past the apple orchard. When the log house came into view, I stopped for a moment to admire the golden glow that shone from the windows. It looked like a cozy home and I realized with a jolt it was. It was Benjamin's. And mine.

He looked at it too. "I'd just returned from kindling the fire. I hope it's had time to warm the room." He took my arm again. "Why, you're shaking."

"I'm a little chilled." This day—and the wedding—happened so fast. Had they missed me at Uncle's and wondered where I went? Had my blackberry preserves turned out all right? Even though I believed I was ready to be Benjamin's bride, I could not deny the connection between what I was about to do with Benjamin and what I saw of Betsy's travail. Nor could I shut my mother's grim predictions for my future happiness and the memory of Theo Dunlap's attempt to force himself on me from my thoughts.

"Let's get you inside." Benjamin could not know of my inner turmoil as he picked up the pace and all too soon the house stood before us. "This wasn't the wedding day you expected but we can keep to some traditions. Shall I carry you over the threshold?"

When I nodded, he swept me into his arms with ease and shouldered open the door. Besides building up the fire now snapping on the hearth, he'd laid the table with the pewter plates. When he set me down in the center of the room, it was as though he placed the final piece in a puzzle.

He closed the shutters and pulled in the latchstring while I fumbled with the clasp on my cloak.

I felt poised on a precipice, knowing in a moment I must gather the courage to jump, and sought delay. "Are you hungry? We didn't eat."

He shook his head. "I only hunger for you."

Our second kiss as a married couple was as gentle as the one he gave me before the preacher. The moment had come to give myself to this man, and the dark longing in his eyes made my pulse flutter with nervous anticipation. Benjamin was gentle. I trusted he would never hurt me. It would do him—and me—a disservice not to cast away the worrisome thoughts.

When I put my arms around his neck, his mouth opened against mine and his embrace tightened. The buttons of his jacket pressed against my bodice and I could feel his readiness through the layers of my skirts.

He drew back and smiled down at me, his voice heavy with emotion. "If you knew how many nights I have fallen asleep with you on my heart."

"How many?"

He bent to kiss the curve of my neck. "All of them. Since the day we met. You should wear flowers in your hair more often."

I removed hairpins, spilling the waves down my back.

He tossed aside his best coat without a care where it fell and I could see him tremble as I untied the knot in his stock. His nervousness emboldened me as I unwound the length of silk and his collar fell open. Tracing my fingers down to undo the buttons on his shirt and waistcoat, I pressed my palm into the dark, curling hair over his heart. "You must help me learn how to please you."

His chest rose and fell under my hand. "And I shall be your most willing pupil." His hands ran over my bodice until I thought I would melt under his touch. Then he laughed. "For my first lesson, show me how to get you out of this."

"We have much to learn, do we not?" Any tension that would have held me back was gone and only the excitement of discovery remained. I unhooked the top closure on the front of the gown and then he moved my hands away, his fingers growing more confident as they traveled toward my waist. He pushed the gown off my shoulders, and my breath strained against the whalebone stays as I fumbled for the waist tapes on my petticoats. They joined the gown in a pool around my feet while he gathered my hair aside to unlace the stays. He did not loosen them, as I would have, but pulled out the cords until they came completely away, leaving me in just my shift. The barrier between us was gone.

Submitting to him turned out to be the easiest thing in the world.

The next morning, a persistent knocking pulled me from sleep. I opened one eye and in the faint light filtering into the shuttered room, I saw a few scattered flower petals on the pillow. For a moment, I forgot where I was.

Beside me, Benjamin stirred and rolled over to wrap himself around me. "Maybe whoever it is will go away if we ignore them."

His day's growth of whiskers tickled the side of my neck, making me squirm with pleasure. He pulled the neckline of my shift off my shoulder, running his fingers over my skin. "How did you get this little scar on your arm?"

Before I could answer, Thomas's voice came from outside. "Wake up!"

I stifled a giggle as I turned to face Benjamin and he held a finger to my lips to shush me. Our legs entwined under the covers.

The knocking continued. "By all the saints, Ben! I know you're in there."

He raised himself on one elbow and shouted back, "We said no shivaree, remember? Come back later. Tomorrow." He touched my cheek and spoke only for my ears. "Or never." He claimed my lips again and at the tantalizing press of his body against mine, I wished we could deny the existence of the world outside our door.

But when the kiss ended, I whispered, "He must bring news about Betsy and the baby."

Benjamin called out, "We'll be over later to see the baby." He grinned conspiratorially, resuming the kisses and pulling the hem of my shift a little higher up my thigh. It was almost too daring to carry on so with Thomas just on the other side of the door but I didn't want Benjamin to stop. I moved against him in a subtle signal of assent and he rolled on top of me.

Thomas's voice grew louder. "That's not why I'm here—though mother and daughter are both doing well, thank you very much for asking." There was a pause. "Are you going to make me keep shouting through the door?"

"Why not? You're doing a masterful job of it so far."

"Fine. The sheriff came with a posse to arrest Brother Craig after we left yesterday. They dragged him from his field, took him before the magistrate, and had him thrown in jail for preaching schismatic doctrines and disturbing the peace." He snorted. "Of all the ridiculous . . . Anyway, I heard about it in town this morning when I saw Betsy's mother home."

That news ruined the moment and Benjamin's shoulders sagged. He muttered, "I thought the parish's thugs only did the Lord's work on Sundays. They usually arrest dissenting preachers in their pulpits, not in their fields." He raised his voice. "All right. I'll be over soon and we'll see about his bail."

Thomas retreated off the porch and Benjamin flopped onto his pillow.

I pushed back my tangled hair as I sat up. "Did they arrest Brother Craig because he performed our wedding?"

"I don't think so. They arrest dissenters without cause all the time. As Brother Craig says, 'The followers of the Lamb are esteemed ever thus.'"

"If you and Thomas protest, they could arrest you too."

He was silent for a moment. "So be it. I'll follow the path of Brother Craig and the other dissenters to prison if need be. I'll always fight for liberty, for without equality, liberty is our best hope for the future."

"I daresay we shall never forget our wedding day."

He pulled me close again. "Help me remember, Wife—once more before I go."

Of course, Benjamin had to go. From the first day of our married life, I understood he would always answer the call of liberty. When he and Thomas returned that afternoon, Benjamin dismounted slowly. I flew down the porch steps to meet him and he flinched when I threw my arms around him. Judging from the state of his wedding clothes, he'd been brawling in the dirt. A shiny purple bruise ringed one eye above a gash on his cheek. He didn't react when I felt around his eye socket but when I reached inside his coat and pressed on his side he pulled away, insisting, "It's nothing."

"What happened?"

Thomas touched his fingers to a cut on his lip, checking for fresh bleeding. "They roughed him up a bit but he's seen worse."

"Indeed, I think I've seen worse from you, Brother."

Thomas nodded as he flexed his right hand. "But we gave as good as we got."

Benjamin explained, "The magistrate called the sheriff and had us removed from the courthouse. Some of the deputies set upon us after."

"What of Brother Craig?" I looked down and realized I was clutching a handful of Benjamin's coat.

"We went to the jail and spoke to him through the bars on the window. We told him we'd post bail but as the court has refused to call the case to the bench, he languishes."

"Can they do that?"

"They've warned him before not to preach without permission so they say he must wait until there's room on the docket to hear his case." Benjamin glanced at his brother. "That was when the trouble started."

Thomas shrugged. "I merely pointed out to the magistrate that refusing to call the case violated common law and the writ of *habeas corpus.*"

"Yes, but the magistrate didn't appreciate you standing up while court was in session to tell him so."

"He did appear somewhat vexed." Thomas turned to me. "Your husband was brilliant. He should study law. He told the magistrate the church should fear us dissenters."

Benjamin shook his head. "I've chosen to study God's law, Brother—and you have it backward. I told the magistrate that if the Anglicans' beliefs and practices were truly superior, its followers should have no need to persecute those who disagree—and no man has the right to force another to join a church. Not the Anglicans, nor we."

I looked from one to the other. "You're both lucky you didn't end up in the cell with Brother Craig for insulting the magistrate."

Thomas laughed. "Luckier than you know. Last night the jailer crowded the cell with drunkards who were expelled from the ordinary and encouraged them to beat up Craig. They did and when they had him down, they pissed on him too. They've all been before the bench, paid their fines, and departed, yet Craig's the one who remains in that stinking place for disturbing the peace."

"Is there no way to get him released?"

Benjamin shrugged. "He could sign a bond saying he won't preach for a year but Brother Craig prefers jail to denying his faith. Besides, it's a promise he's sure to break. He'll preach through the bars on the window until they decide to let him out. Since we couldn't post his bail, we passed him some scrip to help pay for his food and bedding."

"There's naught more we can do for him today." Thomas clucked to his horse and headed across the orchards toward home.

Benjamin put an arm around my shoulders and kissed my forehead. "Such a worried expression you wear. It's going to be all right. We dissenters are like chamomile—the more we are trodden, the more we spread."

22

Conflict in Congress

Wooly-headed from lack of sleep, I woke to the sounds and smells of breakfast preparations and could not remember where I was. Benjamin's coat and breeches were draped over a chair and I sat up to look for him before I remembered. Then my thoughts ran to the events of the previous night and to Margaretta and her child. The little girl was healthy and vigorous and as I held her, I realized how faint my memories of holding William and nursing him had become. Now, when I could express only a small amount of milk, I felt a lump form in my throat. Had concealing my sex caused the last of my milk to dry up? I pushed the thought away. I sounded like Widow Jenkins, grasping at superstition rather than logic and reason.

Did my children miss me—or was I now absent from their thoughts? How soon before we would be reunited?

First things first. At the end of today's travel, I hoped to arrive in York, just twenty miles away. Dressed in the blue gown with my hair pinned up, I gave my familiar reflection an approving look before I joined Ludwick for breakfast in the tavern's dining room. It was so late only a few patrons remained.

He looked surprised at my attire. "Did you not enjoy traveling in disguise? Our business takes us in different directions today, so you must continue alone."

"I enjoyed the liberty, but I should not be in disguise when I meet my husband's relatives for the first time. It's but a short day's ride to York and the weather is fair, so plenty of people will be on the road." I caught sight of the stable boy, who was sporting a spectacular black eye, as he left the kitchen and headed outside. "I trust Herr Reinker is also recovering from his injuries?"

"Yes, I had breakfast with him earlier. Aside from a headache, he is well."

After the meal, we walked to the stable together. "You're never going to tell me about your alliance with Herr Reinker, are you?"

He laughed. "I'm afraid you'll just have to wonder. It has been a pleasure traveling with you, Anna."

I held out my hand. "I'll miss your company as well. Thank you for everything you've done for me. I wish there was some way I could repay you."

Instead of bending over my hand, Ludwick clasped it as if I was a man. "Heed my advice and be observant as you travel. Listen to your instincts, for instinct is reason traveling at a gallop. Be cautious in all things. And Godspeed." He gave me a hand up and then clambered into his saddle, turned the horse's head, and headed off to the north. I guided Nelly onto an eastward course on the Monocacy Road.

The previous day's snow melted, making a slushy, muddy mess of the road. I took pains to keep my cloak close around me, fearing I would be spattered from head to toe before I arrived at Benjamin's aunt and uncle's home. When I stopped at an ordinary for dinner, I paid the stable boy a shilling for Nelly's fodder, and sixpence to reset one shoe and scrape her hooves clean while I ate.

Inside, I held my head high and acted as though I had every right to eat in the tavern. To avoid trouble, I requested the serving girl bring a filled plate to me, so I need not go among the rougher sorts to take food from the communal dishes. Self-respect and confidence, I realized, would not lead me awry in my dealings with others. Nor would kindness. I gave the girl an extra coin for her trouble.

Late that afternoon, I buried my nose in my crooked elbow as I crossed a stone bridge spanning a slow-moving creek. Breathing through the fabric of my cloak, which smelled of river water and lavender, was not entirely pleasant but it filtered out the odors from York's tanneries, distilleries, and other manufacturing interests. As I walked Nelly eastward on the muddy high street, I heard a group of women speaking German outside a shop. When I caught familiar words here and there, I thought I might stop and try to engage them in a brief conversation. Before I could make an overture, I heard applause and cheering nearby. Curious, I urged Nelly on until we came upon a large crowd gathered in front of an ordinary.

This public house was constructed in the half-timbered style I admired in Hanover, except the first story was of dressed logs instead of stone. I wondered if I could draw the complicated pattern of brickwork between the dark beams on the upper story well enough for Joseph and Benjamin to replicate it. Perhaps they, too, saw buildings like this while on the march with the army.

A thickset officer on a white horse sat above the crowd. His jowls swelled over the collar of his immaculate blue coat, which had a buff collar and cuffs. Even to someone with my limited knowledge of military insignia, his gold epaulets and rows of brass buttons signified his importance. His entourage numbered at least a dozen soldiers, all dressed nearly as splendidly as he, and a half-dozen servants.

He raised a hand to the crowd, begging their silence. I nudged Nelly forward to be sure and hear what he had to say, in case he had news of the situation at Valley Forge. When the clamor subsided, he spoke. "The Continental Army in the northern theater has, of late, surrounded General Burgoyne on all sides and destroyed half of Britain's forces in America. This gross reduction of His Majesty's troops is the completest victory of the war."

Swept up in the crowd's excitement, I cheered along with them. Again, the officer waited for the din to subside.

"The northern army has humbled the pride of the haughtiest nation in the world! If we have not, by this lesson, taught Old England humility, then she is an obstinate slut and bent upon her own ruin."

This time I remained silent as the crowd roared its delight. I didn't care for the man's tone or how he waved and smiled, basking in the adulation for what had to be a minute and more. When he dismounted, the crowd parted for him as he strode toward a closed coach on the street. A footman opened the door for a haughty-looking woman in a fur-edged cape and the officer escorted her inside the ordinary.

I nudged Nelly's flank and guided her into the thinning crowd, hoping to ask directions to the Butler residence. One gentleman heading inside the ordinary said to anyone who would listen, "There's the true antidote to what ails the army!"

One of the other men agreed. "He would procure all the necessities for the troops—and do it without Washington's whining and complaining!"

Once I heard what they were saying I hesitated, not sure I wanted to speak to either of them. The pageantry and excited adulation I just witnessed put me in mind of people's behavior in the presence of royalty. Was it not wrong for Americans to regard one individual as ordained by God to be better than another? Benjamin was risking his life to fight for the end of those beliefs. I decided I did not care for that officer, whoever he was.

The gentlemen went into the ordinary, while the women in attendance headed up the road to the market square. As the soldiers and servants began sorting out the luggage tied to the roof of the coach, I wondered if any of them knew the town of York well enough to give directions.

"Excuse me, madam. Do you require assistance?"

I jumped, startled out of my thoughts by a tall, portly man who hailed me from the opposite boardwalk. Though drawn to the cadence and flat vowels of the man's speech, I was glad we were not alone as he started across the muddy street. The memory of my encounter with the highwayman posing as a magistrate was still fresh.

"I'm looking for my aunt and uncle's residence. If I may say, you sound like—home, sir."

The man smiled as he drew near. "I'm a native of Virginia."

"As am I."

He took off his cocked hat and bowed. "Benjamin Harrison. Your servant, madam."

"The Congressional delegate?"

"The same." He seemed surprised I knew who he was.

"It's an honor to meet you, sir. I am Mrs. Benjamin Stone, from Fauquier County. Can you direct me to the Samuel Butler home? I was told it is near Christ Church."

"I can. I also live near Christ Church, and the Butlers are my close neighbors. Will you permit me to escort you?"

"Yes, thank you, sir. I appreciate your kindness." I touched Nelly's flank again and kept pace with him as he walked beside me on the boardwalk. When I returned home, I would be sure to mention this encounter to Nancy, though I suspected she would not consider this gentleman exciting. Meeting a young and dashing officer, like the Marquis de Lafayette, would impress her more.

"Have you come from Fauquier in this weather to visit the Butlers?"

"No, sir, I'm bringing supplies to my husband and brothers at Valley Forge." One of Nelly's front hooves landed in a puddle, and muddy water splashed Harrison's cloak. "Oh dear. I'm sorry."

"You cannot help the weather or the state of the roads."

"Sir, if I may ask, who was that officer who spoke in front of the ordinary? The one applauded by the people."

"You mean General Gates?"

"*That* was Granny Gates?" I gasped and covered my mouth, horrified that I spoke the general's unflattering nickname, but Harrison laughed.

"I see someone you know holds an opinion on Gates."

"The opinion is mine, sir, though I didn't mean to be disrespectful. Both my husband and my uncle have mentioned him, and I've read about him in the newspaper. My husband wrote me that some would prefer to see Washington replaced with Gates." When I saw the appraising look on Mr. Harrison's face, I feared I gave offense and tried to explain. "My husband holds General Washington in the highest regard. He wrote in his most recent letter that appointing Gates as commander in chief would be a mistake. We often discussed politics at home and since he has been away in the army, we have continued our discourse in our correspondence."

He nodded. "Stone. Are you related to my fellow delegate, Mr. Thomas Stone of Maryland?"

"He is my husband's second cousin. I must tell you, sir, it was a grand day when my husband read the Declaration aloud to his congregation." I looked about as we approached the square filled with market stalls. "And this is the largest town I've ever seen."

"Is it, though?"

"I lived in Stafford when I was a child and for a time near Falmouth, though I never visited the city. Our family owns apple and peach orchards a few miles southwest of Fauquier Court House."

"I shall soon return to Berkeley, my family's plantation near Richmond."

"How nice. I suppose you must miss home."

"Those of us called into the service of our country must endure temporary exile from those places and people most dear to us."

"And hardship. When my husband wrote of the shortages faced by the army, I canvassed my community for donations, but I feared what we collected might not arrive soon enough if shipped by wagon—indeed if it arrived at all. I came with what I could carry, hoping to sustain him and my brothers until more provisions arrived."

He was staring at me again. This time I was sure I insulted him and I dropped my eyes and adopted the tone of deference Benjamin hated. "I do believe that Congress and the commissary are doing their best to feed the troops, sir. But I have seen firsthand that men can be scoundrels and take advantage of others' generous natures."

He snorted. "Congress itself has a fair number of scoundrels. I have been a delegate since the beginning, when our purpose was to debate, share ideas, and come to the conclusions that would best serve the needs of all the people. Now, Congress also attends to the business of the war. But the new delegates—and some old as well—do not understand they are elected to serve the people. Or else they have found it convenient to forget."

At the square, we turned south on George Street. He stopped across from the stone church, and gestured toward a narrow, two-story brick house with black shutters.

"This is the Butler home."

"Thank you so much for seeing me here."

"It was my pleasure, madam. Will you be continuing on your journey soon?"

"Oh, yes, first thing tomorrow." I slid out of the saddle and looped Nelly's reins over the hitching post at the edge of the walk.

"If you will permit me, I shall wait while you make sure they are within."

"Yes, thank you." I rapped with the brass knocker. The woman who answered looked so much like Benjamin's mother I caught my breath before I spoke. "Mrs. Butler? I am Mrs. Benjamin Stone of Fauquier County. My brother-in-law Thomas bade me stop on my way to Valley Forge . . ."

The old woman's cheeks rose like plump apples as she smiled. "Anna? Come in, child. What a lovely surprise! I can scarce believe you're here." She folded me into her arms as though she'd known me all her life and spoke past my shoulder. "And greetings to you, Mr. Harrison. Will you take tea with us this evening?"

"Indeed, Miss Lydia, I would find that most agreeable. I must stop at home first and shall return if that suits you."

She nodded and he tipped his hat to us and continued down the boardwalk.

Mrs. Butler ushered me inside and called to an old gentleman seated before the fire. "Samuel, come meet Benjamin's Anna!"

Tall and spare, gray-haired Samuel Butler rose to his feet and clasped my hand. "Did you come all the way from Virginia, lass?"

"I did, sir. I've been traveling for close to a week."

"Samuel, could you please see to Anna's horse?" After he shrugged into his overcoat and went out to the street, she shut the door behind me and took my cloak. "Let me look at you, dear. Cousin Mary and I were as close as sisters when we were young. Samuel and I moved north all of twenty years ago, when Baylis was just a babe, but I knew the rest of her brood well when they were young ones. Come have a seat by the fire."

She gestured toward a chair and when I sat, she took the chair Samuel vacated. "Elizabeth wrote to us about your marriage. She said her mother was overjoyed, and you were the perfect wife for her quiet boy. Elizabeth described you and your darling babe so well in her letters I feel as though I already know you. I suppose your little one is growing up fast. Is she as pretty as you?"

I had not realized Benjamin's aunt regarded me as an intimate acquaintance. "Dear me, Mrs. Butler, I'm not ready for Rhoda to grow up yet. She's but eight years old. And don't all mothers think their children are beautiful? Benjamin and I also have two sons, Elijah and William."

"You must call us Aunt Lydia and Uncle Samuel, dear. Have you traveled far today? Of course, you have. Sit and rest while I get tea ready." She hung the teakettle on a hook over the flames and kept up a steady stream of talk as she bustled back and forth from the kitchen to the parlor. "I want to hear everything about the family. How is old Thomas faring? Of course, you'll pass the night here with us before you continue on your journey."

My smile faded as I took Thomas's letter from my pocket. "I bring sad tidings about Baylis. He succumbed to the pox last month in Pennsylvania."

Tears shimmered in the old woman's eyes as she accepted the letter and laid it on the mantel. "I'll have Samuel read it to me later when I can grieve in private. For now, I would prefer to enjoy your visit, my dear."

When Uncle Samuel ambled back in from the stable with my things, he left the bundles and saddlebags near the stairs and stood before the hearth warming his hands. Aunt Lydia headed for the kitchen. "Now I shall lay out our tea, though Mr. Harrison is running late."

While she was in the rear of the house, an insistent knock sounded at the front door. Uncle Samuel did not alter his unhurried pace on his way to the entry and when he opened the door, Benjamin Harrison barreled over the threshold without being invited in.

"Samuel, please forgive my rudeness, but there is a matter I must discuss with Mrs. Stone without delay. May I speak to her privately?"

The old man shut the door. "If it's all right with her."

Curious, I rose and met him in the hall. After Uncle Samuel returned to the hearth, Harrison drew me into the shadow of the staircase and held out a sealed letter, speaking just above a whisper. "There is a conspiracy afoot against the commander in chief that threatens the outcome of the war."

I caught my breath. "Are the troops at Valley Forge in danger?"

"Mark me, this scheme threatens everyone who is part of the revolution. My message must reach Washington as soon as possible—and with the utmost secrecy. You say you are leaving first thing tomorrow. Will you see it into his hands?"

"Directly to General Washington?" As William's courier, I had unwittingly furthered his and Thompson's treachery against the cause. Now I could absolve myself. I stood a little taller as Harrison went on.

"By morning, there will be men about with orders to stop and search every courier, so I can't send it by one of my regular men. It's likely no one will suspect a woman is carrying anything of import."

Dread clutched at my insides. "How far to Valley Forge?"

"About eighty miles. I cannot guarantee your safety."

Thomas estimated it was two days' ride from York to Valley Forge, but eighty miles was two days of hard riding. My heart plummeted. When I first set out, I found traveling fewer than twenty grueling, and I never managed more than thirty in a day. I could not count on favorable weather or dry roads.

His eyes searched my face. "Will you assist me?"

I took the letter, turning it over in my hands. "Yes, sir, of course I will, but what does the message—"

"It is better if you do not know the letter's contents, in case you are stopped. I must not tarry. Please give my excuses to Lydia and Samuel and say nothing to them of this errand."

I nodded.

"I will send out a decoy courier just before dawn. You should depart thereafter and proceed through town as though you are continuing on your journey. Do you understand?"

"Yes. You have my word. I will see the message into General Washington's hands."

"Thank you, madam. You are doing a great service to your country. Now I must bid you good night."

He left as abruptly as he arrived and as I shut the door, my quickened pulse thudded in my ears. What a singular request! I peeped through the curtains at the window beside the door and watched Harrison bow to a group of men coming from the high street. They stopped to speak but after a moment, the men all brushed by him and left him standing alone on the walk. Now alert for any signs of intrigue, I wondered if they were among the conspirators.

There was a plot against General Washington. Whatever could it be? Mr. Harrison made it plain the letter's contents were none of my business, but I had never known a temptation that burned as hot as this. No one—save I—would be the wiser if I read the message. I slid my thumb under the wax but could not bring myself to break the seal.

Even the highwaymen outside Frederick viewed spies with contempt. Was I such a rogue I would violate the congressman's trust? No. I was merely a courier. I put the letter in my pocket and returned to the parlor.

"Is everything all right, dear?" Aunt Lydia patted the seat beside her. "Why did Mr. Harrison hurry away?"

"He apologized for not being able to stay. Some urgent business arose."

"A pity. But what was his business with you?"

They both looked at me curiously. Clearly, I must give some explanation. "Well, when he escorted me here this afternoon, I mentioned my brother, Jeremiah, recently finished his clerkship in Williamsburg. Mr. Harrison was acquainted with the solicitor, and—" I faltered, not used to spinning out falsehoods at a moment's notice, "—he asked me to pass along greetings on his behalf when I see my brother at Valley Forge." I gave them a weak smile and as Aunt Lydia filled my teacup, I doubted they found my explanation plausible. What if I had to lie convincingly to discharge my errand for Mr. Harrison? Did I have the makings of a spy?

23

What Could Go Wrong?

CAROLINA ROAD, YORK COUNTY, PENNSYLVANIA
JANUARY 21, 1778

I spent the night tossing and turning, tormented by my fear of being discovered, my desire to read the letter's contents, and the worry I might fall into a deep sleep and get a late start. For the next two days, every minute counted. Just before dawn I dressed in the blue gown again, for now I must present myself as a woman so I might pass unmolested by the conspirators' agents who were told to search couriers. Shivering from both cold and nervousness, I left the house, prepared to carry the weight of this additional responsibility for the final third of my trip.

As I led Nelly out of the stable, someone's shout fractured the pre-dawn silence. A man on horseback left Mr. Harrison's house at a gallop and headed toward the high street. I swung into the saddle, more than willing to let the decoy courier draw attention. Passing the church and approaching the square at a walk, I saw the other rider's horse rear, whinnying in fright as two mounted Continental soldiers and a civilian on a gray horse surrounded them.

The soldiers dragged the courier out of the saddle, dumped the contents of his haversack on the ground, and held a lantern up as they pawed through the pile. I pulled my hood closer around my face and passed by without altering Nelly's pace, as would anyone who did not want to get involved, but out of the corner of my eye I saw the man on the gray horse watching me. If he turned out my saddlebags, he would find no letter, for I had concealed Mr. Harrison's note in my stays.

Somewhere beyond the houses and outbuildings, a rooster crowed. I started, and when Nelly reacted to the change in my grip on the reins, I put her into her rack gait and did not look back.

A few moments later, pounding hooves galloped up behind me but the soldiers and the man on the gray continued past, overtaking another rider and treating him in the same rough manner. Again, I averted my gaze and kept moving, praying Mr. Harrison's assurance that no one would suspect a woman courier was correct. York was about a mile behind me when the sunrise turned the eastern horizon orange. The road was in good enough condition to put Nelly into a canter.

Within the hour I came upon a small market town where vendors busied themselves setting out their wares. Wagons, drovers with herds of goats and sheep, and people on foot clogged the street. I slowed Nelly before we reached the crowd and a moment later, the man on the gray stallion galloped up beside me and blocked my way.

"You know the Butlers?"

My heart pounded, but my tone was as haughty as Aunt Jean's. "That is no business of yours. Let me pass."

"Don't lie to me. You are a Virginia relative of theirs. Harrison says there has been a mistake. He wants his letter back." He made a grab for Nelly's bridle, but I pulled the reins and turned her head, so he grasped empty air.

"I know not what you mean—and I didn't lie." I regarded him through narrowed eyes, and he looked surprised, as though he expected it would be easy to frighten me.

We stared each other down. As he shifted in the saddle, his broad shoulders strained the seams of his dark coat. His unshaven jaw and oft-broken nose accentuated the malevolent look on his face as he extended his hand. "Give it to me."

This was no time to stand my ground. It was time to run. I applied the crop and Nelly leapt forward, dodging the gray and skimming over the ground like a bird about to take to the skies. When I dared to glance back, I saw him following, but at a distance. He knew my destination. Doubtless there would be many places to overtake me on the road. I must keep my wits about me and best him one situation at a time.

Plunging into the market crowd, Nelly scattered a herd of sheep. They milled about, bleating, and blocked the road behind us. Another look back revealed my pursuer edging his way between the sheep and a man pulling a two-wheeled cart. I sawed at the bit and Nelly turned, plunging into a narrow alley between two buildings. We flew past outbuildings and stables, forded a shallow creek, and circled behind a massive stone mill. Concealed in a clump of trees beside the mill race, I surveyed my surroundings. The ribbon of road wound through open fields to the east as far as I could see. I would be visible and vulnerable once I left this hiding place.

From my vantage point I had a clear view of a blacksmith, a stationery, and an ordinary at the eastern edge of the main street. When the gray galloped into view, I remembered Ludwick's advice, and remained motionless as I watched the man rein his horse down and scan the landscape in every direction. Though he looked directly at my hiding spot, he did not see me. I smiled with satisfaction as he dashed his hat against his leg and turned back to the ordinary. Dismounting, he looped the horse's reins around the hitching post, flung open the door, and went inside.

Herr Ludwick was right and I blessed him for his instruction, for I would need to resort to all manners of trickery to protect myself.

I spied a man driving a wagon and two women on horseback who would soon pass me on their way out of the village. I unclasped my cloak and turned its blue plaid lining to the outside. Pulling the hood close around my face, I started Nelly at an unhurried pace, following the wagon track that led from the mill back onto the main road. There I fell in with the other travelers and tried to stay close enough that I looked as though we were all one party.

I kept with them until they turned off at a crossroads a few miles out of town. By then the terrain turned to rolling, wooded hills, which better concealed me. I rode hard for an hour and more, never daring to hope my pursuer would give up the chase. Nelly slowed as the road rose steeply before us. We crested the hill and I groaned aloud when I beheld the vista before me.

Another river ferry.

Two flatboats tied to a short dock bobbed in the shallows. Floating ice chunks stretched to the horizon. Even from my position on high ground, I couldn't see the opposite shore.

On the slope leading down to the river's edge, skinners had camped overnight and now many of them were cooking over small fires. I turned Nelly toward the ramp and she threaded her way through dozens of freight wagons and carts, riders, and people on foot. When I spied several soldiers in Continental uniforms waiting near the wooden gate, I considered asking for their help, but Mr. Harrison hinted the conspiracy came from inside Congress. My pursuer was in the company of soldiers when I first saw him, so anyone could be part of the plot.

I halted Nelly behind someone's canvas tent and scanned the crowd for the man on the grey horse, but there was no sign of him. When two ferrymen in heavy coats and boots clomped up the ramp, the crowd swarmed toward the riverbank, and I breathed a sigh of relief as I urged Nelly into the throng.

"See here, missus! You can't go to the head of the line! Where's your number?"

I turned, startled. "What?"

A skinner regarded me with disdain as he pointed at the number 27 scrawled on his wagon with chalk. "You get your number from the ferryman. We got here early yesterday." He slapped the reins on his team's back and urged them forward to block me from getting ahead of him.

The crowd was too large to count. "How many can cross at once?"

The skinner on the next wagon over, marked with the number 28, said in a twangy voice, "No more'n two wagons on each ferry plus a horse and rider or two. You'll be here all day and likely tomorrow, too, missus."

That man's voice sounded familiar. I wondered where I saw him on the road earlier. "Is there another crossing nearby?"

"Sure." He pointed with his whip to the north. "There's Vinegar Ferry and Anderson's." His whip swept to the south. "Or McCall's. You could cross at any of them."

"Are the crowds the same at all the ferries?"

The man on wagon twenty-seven spoke up. "Expect so, but I've no wish to find out. The ice has made the crossing treacherous and yesterday they took no one across."

I bit my lip but stood my ground. One of the ferrymen unlocked the gate, and the group of soldiers crowded to the fore, filling the first boat.

I could see no other women on horseback in the crowd. I was too conspicuous, even after turning my cloak. My heart froze when I spotted the man on the gray horse high on the hill, scanning the far side of the crowd, and as his gaze turned my way I knew the moment he recognized me. Without hesitation, he reined his horse to the right, forcing his way through a crowd of people on foot. I kicked Nelly's flank with one heel and urged her closer to the water's edge.

People, animals, and wagons moved in a crush toward the remaining boat, slowing the gray's progress. A horse and rider followed two men on foot up the ramp. As Nelly wormed her way toward the front of the line, I kept the man on the gray in view.

The skinner on wagon 28 yelled at me again. "Oi! We're next. I'll not be kimbawed by a woman. You need to take a number!"

Realization flooded my mind like someone doused me with icy river water. That man—with his strange expression, spoken in the backwoods twang—was one of the smugglers! The impassible river detained the pair overnight. It was not too late to keep the cache of rifles from its destination.

As my thoughts tumbled over each other, my pursuer closed in to intercept me. A man on foot shouted in protest as the gray horse knocked him off balance and my pursuer snarled a reply. Several people turned toward the angry voices.

Seizing the moment, I struck Nelly with my crop. The mare leapt forward, dodged the wagons at the head of the queue, and clattered up the ramp past the startled ferryman. I reined her down hard before her hooves touched the boat, and she skidded to a stop in the center, nearly sitting on her haunches. The horse already aboard reared in fright and one of the foot passengers climbed up on the railing to avoid being trampled. As the ferry rocked, ice chunks bobbed all around us and waves splashed against the muddy riverbank. Ripples extended toward the distant opposite shore.

A roar of protest arose from the crowd. One of the smugglers threw a half-eaten apple at me in frustration while the other stood up, gesturing with his whip. The ferryman, bracing the rocking boat with his long pole, shouted, "See here! What kind of trick is that? You must get back off. All these people have been waiting...."

I reached into my pocket, thankful I had hard money to offer, and my fingers closed around the coins Uncle gave me. The ferryman stomped over and seized Nelly's bridle. When I leaned down to speak to him, the tremor in my voice was genuine. "Please. A man has chased me all the way from York this morning, and I fear for my safety. I must cross now. See him, there, on the gray?"

The ferryman looked over his shoulder. "He your husband or something?"

My pursuer's face darkened with anger when he realized I was talking about him and I gave him a defiant look in response.

"Perish the thought. My husband is a clergyman serving in the Third Virginia. I am on my way to him at Valley Forge. I've never seen that rogue before today. Please, help me put some distance between us." I handed the ferryman enough coins to pay for several trips and then added another.

He scratched the back of his neck while he considered, then nodded and pocketed the money. "That one comes across often, and I've thought he was up to no good."

I sighed with relief and dismounted. "Thank you. God bless you."

He motioned to the smugglers. "Come aboard, and I'll hear no more of your bellyaching. This lady has urgent business. She's paid your fares for your trouble."

I must share the ride with the smugglers! My heart pounded out of my chest as the wagons rumbled aboard, but I took a calming breath. There was no chance they could know I was at the Thompson residence that night. Perhaps I could learn something of their destination by eavesdropping. I stood as close as I dared.

As the ferryman shoved off from the dock, the boat rocked again, but less violently. Nelly stamped her hoof and I stood at her head, keeping tight hold of her bridle. This fearsome river looked deep and I had no wish to find out how cold it was.

The boat's prow nudged the shining ice in front of us, separating it to expose dark, jagged ribbons of water beneath. Ice chunks of all sizes slid over one another, bumping and tilting as we passed. Behind us, the water's surface rolled in our wake. Ahead, the opposite shore was only an uneven, gray line in the distance.

I asked the ferryman, "How wide is this river?"

"The Susquehanna? Near a mile across."

I nodded, wishing I hadn't asked. The crossing took almost an hour, during which time the smugglers made no mention of anything hinting at where they were headed. By the time the ferry docked on the opposite side, I desired nothing more than to lead Nelly down the ramp and onto solid ground. The crowd waiting to cross to the western shore was just as large as the one we'd left behind. I found a mounting block and swung into the saddle.

Well away from the riverbank, with the skinners' wagons out of sight behind us, I began to giggle. "We did it, Nelly! We got away." My excitement turned to uncontrollable laughter and then, unbidden, the tears came.

Nelly shook her head, jingling her harness, and I wiped my face with my sleeve. "You're right. I'm being a ninny and after we bested him too. I promise I shall weep no more. That awful man may know where we're going but we have a head start. We'll have the protection of Benjamin and the rest of the Continental Army before he can catch us."

Benjamin. Even though it was comforting to think of him, he could not shield me from whatever dangers still lay between us. Determined to waylay the smugglers and outwit my pursuer on my own, I squared my shoulders and urged Nelly onward as fast as I dared.

24

A Trick or Two

At a military checkpoint on the western edge of Lancaster, I waited in line, my anxiety increasing with each passing minute. How long before the smugglers would arrive and join the queue? I shrank from accusing them face-to-face. And what of my pursuer? He could be nearing the Susquehanna's eastern shore at this very moment.

When it was my turn to be questioned, the soldier there gave me an appraising glance. "Madam, I must inspect your belongings and papers."

"Papers?"

"Yes, missus. All identity papers and bona fides."

He was certainly not getting a look at the letter concealed in my stays. "Search if you must. I am on no official business for the army. I go to tend a sick relative." I lowered my voice. "But I must speak to whoever is in charge here and inform him of something I witnessed on the road."

He motioned me out of the line and off to the side. While a second soldier went through my saddlebags, I told the first one all I knew of the smugglers, emphasizing that he could identify them by the chalk numbers on their wagons. Then I waited while together they examined the contents of my medicine chest and flipped through the pages of my receipt book. When they insisted on searching in the pockets of the clothing in my bundles and opening the food sacks, I felt I could not refuse, and hoped they would search the smugglers' wagons with as much zeal for the task.

It was much later than I expected when at last they allowed me to tie up the open sacks, repack, and continue through the checkpoint.

On the eastern edge of Lancaster, I left Nelly at a livery to rest a spell and paid a shilling for feed. Across the street at a stationery, I purchased a bottle of ink and a quill. I brought my purchases, the letter from Harrison, and my receipt book into a tavern where I was the sole occupant of the ladies' parlor. Ordering a meal and a pot of tea, I brought a candle close and laid Harrison's sealed letter on the table before me.

Yesterday I felt my desire to read the letter might drive me mad. Now I had a good reason to give in to my temptation, even though it meant breaching Mr. Harrison's trust.

I could not risk losing the message entirely. My pursuer stood a good chance of stealing it before I reached Valley Forge. Barring that, some officer at another checkpoint might confiscate it and think me a spy for the enemy. I must, I reasoned, make a copy and conceal it well. Without a pang of conscience, I heated my knife over the flame and pried off the wax seal, unfolded the sheets of parchment and smoothed them flat. Quick as snuffing out a candle, my excitement turned to disappointment. The message was naught but a jumble of letters and numbers.

Still, it must mean something to Mr. Harrison and General Washington. I copied the message, one half at a time, onto two separate pages in my receipt book. I labeled the new entries *Tinctures to Treat Rheumatism* and *Lye Soap,* and then refolded the packet, using the heated knife to melt the seal and re-affix it.

Hoping I'd done enough to safeguard the message, I tucked the original into my stays.

Nelly, refreshed from her rest, splashed across a shallow ford of the Conestoga River near a crossroads village called Zooks Corner. The sun was low in the sky as we left the Carolina Road and turned onto the northern fork of the Kings Highway. As I rode, I wondered what my pursuer would say to the soldiers when he reached the checkpoint. How would he state his business? Would he inquire whether the soldiers saw me? They would likely remember me, a woman traveling alone. I must change my appearance as soon as I could find a place to stay.

In Earl Town, the narrow main road followed a ridgeline and had several sharp bends in it that made me think of a nursery rhyme I sometimes recited for the children.

There was a crooked man, and he walked a crooked mile. He found a crooked sixpence upon a crooked stile. He bought a crooked cat, which caught a crooked mouse, and they all lived together in a little crooked house.

When I halted Nelly in the side yard at the Sign of the Blue Ball Tavern, I was annoyed to find no lanterns lit and no stable boy about. There was barely enough fading daylight filtering into the stable to see. I must be quick about attending to Nelly's needs. I led the mare inside and unsaddled her, rubbed her down, and turned her into an empty stall where I brought in a water bucket, pitched some hay into the manger, and added a scoopful of oats.

Settling myself for the night required my disguise. I carried the clothing bundle into an empty stall at the rear of the stable. In the darkness, I pulled on a pair of breeches under my gown and then stripped it off along with my petticoats, shivering as I buttoned Benjamin's waistcoat and put his coat and leggings over it all. My middle was lumpy where my shift bunched up, but perhaps no one would notice. I slapped the hat on my head and stuffed my other garments into the bundle, planning to leave it and my saddlebags in the stable until I secured a place to sleep.

Senses dulled by fatigue, I failed to survey my surroundings as I plodded out of the stable. I hadn't gone but a few steps when a newly arrived rider dismounted, jumping to the ground in front of me. I started, and when he tossed me the horse's reins, I caught them automatically.

"Rub him down well, lad."

The familiar voice made my hair stand on end with horror. It was my pursuer who stood mere inches away. Could he hear my heart as it thudded against the letter concealed in my bosom? I broke out in a cold sweat as I nodded, not daring to look up or speak.

Noticing nothing amiss, he strode away into the tavern, but my legs trembled as I led the gray inside the stable. Out of sight, I leaned against a rough stall door, my breath coming in gasps as I fought to bring my panic under control.

Though he did not recognize me in the dark, he might, even in my disguise, if he spotted me inside the tavern. My fear gave way to anger. I arrived first, but he, not I, would spend the evening eating and drinking beside a blazing fire. Must I huddle in the dark stable, fearing to go inside? Should I risk going in search of another place to stay?

The gray horse bumped his nose against my shoulder and brought me back from my thoughts. I could not let the horse languish, even if his master was my enemy. I unsaddled him and slipped off his bridle, dropping the tack on the ground outside the stall. As I filled his manger and moved in a water bucket, a plan formed in my mind. Tasks completed, I headed for the rear of the tavern where I tapped on the door. A kitchen maid about my mother's age answered.

"Pardon me, missus."

She gave me but a glance. "What is it, lad?"

"I seek a meal and a place to sleep, but—"

When she gave me a second look, her eyebrows shot up in surprise. "You're no boy, are you—lass?"

I lowered my voice. "No." I produced a coin. "I can pay for the meal and lodging, but I cannot go among the men."

"Running away, are you?"

Everyone assumed the same. Now I hung my head and shrugged, hoping to garner sympathy. She tutted and motioned me into the kitchen. "You can eat in here and bed down in the larder tonight. It's warm in there, and I'll make sure the master doesn't spot you." She ladled stew into a wooden trencher and put a few squares of cornbread on the edge. "Sit you down here." She pointed to a low stool in a corner.

When I sat, the worktable hid me from view of the public room. I held the trencher on my knees, and after I spooned up the stew, I mopped the last of the gravy with the cornbread. At the doorway, I made certain my pursuer was in the public room, then dashed to the stables and brought in my bundles, which seemed to reinforce the kitchen maid's theory I'd run away with what I could carry.

"Stow those in here." She pointed toward the open larder door as she headed into the dining room with a laden tray.

When she returned, I pointed out my pursuer. "See that man? I'd like to buy him a bottle of wine, without him knowing it came from me. Can you see to it?"

She fetched a bottle from the bar and left it on the table. "I'll bring it out after I serve this platter." As soon as I was alone, I uncorked it and hurried to my medicine chest for my bottle of opium tincture. I poured in half the contents. When she returned a few moments later, she put it on her tray with a clean glass and gave me a shrewd glance.

"You ain't running away from your husband."

"What makes you say that?"

"I seen a fair few who did, and you ain't like them. You ain't beat up or nothing. And I never seen a wayward wife buy her man a bottle of wine." Her eyes narrowed. "You act more like a spy."

Though it was not the first time I heard the accusation, this time words failed me.

She continued to prod. "You out giving aid to them soldiers?"

"Are there soldiers about?"

"Aye. The Lobster Backs. We see far too many of 'em in these parts, but you can't always tell them for what they are. They break prison in twos and threes and change garb so a body can't tell whether they're friend or foe. They pass this way, going to New York or Jersey. I warrant they don't go direct to Philadelphia now that our gents are at Valley Forge."

"If I was a spy, I would only give aid to our Continental soldiers, of that you may be sure."

"A wise general would use women as spies." The woman enjoyed sharing her opinion. "Menfolk think we're fit for nothing more than minding children and cooking vittles, but we're a sight smarter than they know."

"With that, missus, I would agree."

When she left with the tray, I dared not watch lest he look around for the sender. Alone in the kitchen, the minutes ticked by and I wrung my hands as I waited for her return. When at length she came back with a tray of dirty dishes, she chuckled. "See your gent out in the keeping room already slumped over the trestle, snoring fit to wake the dead. He must've had his fill of ale before he started on the wine. Full as a goat, he is! Looks as if you're safe for the night, missus."

I nodded, thinking it couldn't happen to a more deserving fellow.

In the larder, I opened one bundle and folded a blanket into a mattress under the table. As I huddled in my cloak behind a barricade of baskets of potatoes and onions, my prayer was simple: *just get me there.*

Again, I slept but little, alert to any sound. Up long before the kitchen maid stirred, I stuffed fruit, bread, and cheese into my haversack so I would not have to stop to eat on the road and left a coin on the worktable.

The moon was set and the faint glow of starlight on the paddock was not enough to light my way. Not willing to risk stumbling over some unseen obstacle in the dark, I lit a taper in the coals, placed it in a lantern, and, with the nippers and hammer I brought with me in hand, I let myself out the back door.

In the stable, Nelly whickered in greeting from her stall, and once I lit a second lantern, I led her out, saddled her, and reached into my haversack for an apple. The gray stallion looked on jealously as Nelly took the treat and I climbed up on the wooden partition between the stalls and held another out to him on my open palm. The horse's lips closed around it and he crunched as I spoke to him in a crooning voice. "I don't blame you for yesterday's troubles, my handsome boy, but now I must slow you and your master down."

Manso had taught me to care for Nelly's hooves and though I could not size and set shoes like a blacksmith, I knew how to remove them. I stepped around a steaming pile of manure as I cross-tied the gray inside the narrow stall. He thrust his nose into the manger box and rooted around as I picked up one of his front feet and, holding it between my knees, used the nippers to loosen both ends of the curved iron shoe. A smart tap from the hammer to bring the shoe back against the hoof exposed the ends of the nails, and I pulled them out one by one, congratulating myself for doing as good a job as Manso would.

"See here boy—what are you about?"

My head snapped up before I remembered to take pains to conceal my face. The first fingers of daylight cast my pursuer into silhouette as he wavered on his feet in the barn doorway.

In a panic, I wrenched the shoe free and flung it behind me into the hay beneath the manger. As he approached, his bleary-eyed expression sharpened to one of recognition.

"You! Where did you come from?" He slapped Nelly on her rump and she clattered out of the barn, snorting at the rough treatment. "Give me that letter."

Size matters not when you find the weak spot. Ludwick's words echoed in my head. I released the gray's foot and took a step back, putting more of the horse between us, though it hemmed me in at the back of the stall.

He leered as he came a step closer. "Don't make me drag you out and search you for it."

Ducking around the ropes holding the stallion fast, I whispered, "I'm sorry." Then I jabbed the final nail I took from his shoe into the tender spot beneath his elbow. He tossed his head and bucked, kicking both back feet into the aisle. As I climbed into the manger and swung one leg over the partition separating the stalls, the man's oath rose above the horse's whinny and I saw him arc through the air and land with a thud, sprawled on the barn floor. I dropped the nippers and hammer into the empty stall and scrambled over.

As the gray stallion snorted and slammed against the sides of his stall, I gathered my tools and dashed past my pursuer, who lay bleeding from a gash on his forehead and wheezing as his chest spasmed.

Outside, I looked around wildly, relieved to see Nelly had not ventured out of the tavern's side yard. She shied away from me as I drew near. "Come on, girl. We must go." My pulse pounded in my ears but I forced myself to act as though we had all the time in the world. I stretched out a hand for her reins and she sidestepped, bumping against the water trough. "One more day. We can do it." She bobbed her head and I patted her nose. "That's right. Here we go." Reins firmly in hand, I began to coax her toward the mounting block at the gate.

Blood streaming down his face and murderous rage in his eyes, my pursuer launched himself through the barn door and staggered across the yard toward us. There was no time to think. Using the edge of the water trough for leverage, I stepped up, pushed off, and leapt into the saddle. Stirrups swinging, I gripped with my knees, applied the crop, and we hurtled past his outstretched hand.

VALLEY FORGE

25

Journey's End

A s I recognize my pursuer outside the White Horse tavern, I pull at the reins. Nelly wheels around and we plunge back into the darkness. Too little moonlight filters through the trees to see, but Nelly seems to know where she's going, so I lean into her neck and hang on.

This time there is no doubt he's behind me. He swears, and shouts, "Stop! Enough of this foolishness! We'll both break our necks in the dark."

But I cannot stop. I will not stop. Up ahead the trees thin and I catch my breath. There's a flicker of light in the distance and I rise in the saddle to look. It's a small fire. I must be close now, so close. I hear my pursuer urging his horse on and I do the same. He, too, knows there is little time left to catch me before I reach the army's camp. Now, how to find the soldiers?

As if in answer to my thoughts, someone at the side of the road shouts, "Halt!" as he springs out of the underbrush.

Nelly rears and I scream as I try to keep my seat. Within seconds, I am surrounded. One of the men grabs for Nelly's bridle and hisses, "Shh!"

"Who goes there?" demands the voice of the one who first commanded me to halt.

My fear, so familiar now, does not leave me cowed. Instead it drives me to answer boldly. "Who are you? Have I reached the Continentals' camp?"

The man standing beside my stirrup sneers. "That's not how it works, my dear. The men with the rifles ask the questions."

We'll see about that. I wish I could kick him in the ribs for scaring the life out of me. "Rifles? Are you lads some of Morgan's Sharpshooters?"

The tallest of the men steps closer and stands at Nelly's head. As he peers at me in the darkness, seeming to take my measure, I refuse to improve my disheveled appearance. When he speaks, I realize he's young—perhaps just seventeen or eighteen.

"Madam, I think the sergeant was clear. You're coming through our picket line at night. Before you get any answers from us, you must satisfy our curiosity. Who are you? What business have you here?" He is direct without being menacing. Though I think he's too young to be in charge, he's the one I speak to.

"My name is Anna Stone. I must see General Washington right away."

At that, the men laugh, and the tall, young soldier shakes his head. "Is that all? You just want to speak to the commander in chief? Well, that's a relief. I thought you might have some outlandish request."

Thank goodness I'm used to Thomas and his cheek. "I've been riding hard—pursued all the way from York. It's critical I speak to the general without delay."

"How do we know you're telling the truth? You could be a spy."

I sigh. How many times has someone accused me of spying since I left home? It's been at least once a day, by my count. This time I suppose it's true, but I'm trying to help the very men who detain me. "If you're in the Sharpshooters, perhaps you know my brothers-in-law.

One died of the pox last month, and the other brought his body home at Christmastide."

The tall soldier pats Nelly's muzzle. "What are their names?"

"Thomas and Baylis Stone."

The soldiers mutter words I can't make out.

"What else do you need to know before you'll let me pass? My husband and brothers are here, in the Third Virginia. Summon one of them and they can vouch for me."

From the darkness, a horse's whinny carries on the wind, and I twist in the saddle and peer into the darkness behind me before pointing. "There! That's the man who's been following me!"

The tall soldier issues orders to the men. "You four—go persuade our other guest to join us. Mo, you remain here with me and see to Mrs. Stone's safety."

As the others disappear into the shadows, the tall soldier and the one called Mo stare past me into the darkness, rifles raised. The tall soldier says more to himself than to me, "We'll see what this is all about."

I know he wonders if I'm a diversion so others may breach the lines, and I remember how the men back in Aldie feared an attack by the brigands. Shivering in the chill wind, I jump when the pop of a pistol breaks the stillness and turn in time to see the flashes as two rifles fire in return. Galloping hoofbeats fade into the distance.

When the other soldiers come back, one shrugs. "Whoever he was, he didn't care to take advantage of our hospitality."

Nelly snorts, her frozen breath shining in the moonlight. The tall soldier continues to stare into the darkness behind me until I grow too impatient to be deferential. "Do you still not believe me?"

He gives me another appraising look. "What's so important that you must see the general?"

"At York, Mr. Harrison instructed me to discuss the matter with none other than the general himself, soldier!"

"That's Lieutenant to you, woman," barks another.

I've had enough talk, and leap at the bait. "After what I've endured to bring this message, I will not stand for your sharp tongue, sir! I'm no soldier you can order about. Now let me pass." I saw at Nelly's mouth with the bit.

"That's enough!" the tall soldier shouts and I have a flash of Joseph stepping in to break up a childish squabble between Henry and me. "Mo and I will take the lady to headquarters. When I pass the guard-house, I'll send some lads up here to reinforce you. It's a strange night. You may need help."

"'Tis strange indeed." It was the soldier who was short with me. "'The time is out of joint. O cursed sprite, that ever I was born to set it right!'"

I can't resist being pert. "Surely a man who can quote Shakespeare has some gentlemanly qualities. You should let them show more often."

This draws chortles from the other soldiers.

"That's not the first time someone's made that observation," he concedes.

The tall lieutenant adds, "You really must see him perform *Henry the Fifth* while wearing nothing but war paint and a breechcloth."

"I'm afraid I must decline your kind offer." The things young men would say!

As the soldier who first admonished me to be quiet leads Nelly into the darkness, I hear him speak to the lieutenant for the first time.

"How you gonna explain this?" The mellow tone of his voice reminds me of Manso and for the first time, I am close enough to my goal to imagine returning home. Once I thought only to complete my mission of mercy and return to my family, but I shall never again be the woman I was. On this journey, I inhabited the world of men—and with success, I might add. Will I be disappointed to return to my old roles of wife, mother, and healer, now that I am also an adventurer?

The lieutenant breaks into my thoughts when he answers, "I have no idea. I'm hoping my personal history with him will help."

I take heart. Perhaps I will see the commander in chief without delay. "You know General Washington?"

"Yes. He and my father fought together against the French and Indians."

Softly I say, "At the Forks of the Ohio."

As we continue down the path, a solitary figure approaches and tips his hat. "Good evening."

At the sound of his voice, Nelly whinnies and tears free from the soldier's grasp. I can only hang on as the mare lunges toward the man, nearly knocking him to the ground.

"What in blazes?" he cries.

Though I've never heard him use that oath, I know his voice. "Benjamin!" In a flash, I'm out of the saddle and leaping into his arms.

"Anna?" He staggers on impact but keeps his feet as I kiss him full on the lips. I don't care that the other soldiers are watching. All my hardships cease to matter. Nelly prances around us and nudges us with her nose.

"Easy, Nelly!" Benjamin shoves her muzzle aside and speaks as though he's just awakened from a dream. "Can it be you?" He touches my face, reassuring himself I'm real. "What in the world are you doing here? Where are the children?"

"They're at Uncle's. What of Henry and Jeremiah?"

"Both still in the hospital, but they are expected to recover."

"Oh, thank goodness. I feared I wouldn't get here in time and we would lose them. Your letter came right after Thomas brought Baylis's body home. I have medicine and food, and warm clothes for you."

He pulls me back into his embrace and I sigh against his chest. "I'm so sorry about Baylis."

He is silent for a long moment. "War means sacrifice. I shall miss him all my days on Earth, but I take comfort in knowing nothing disturbs the peace his soul now enjoys."

"Thomas feels the same. When he came to Uncle's on Twelfth Night, I could tell the loss devastated him." Drawing back, I look him in the eyes. "I also have a message from a congressman in York I must see delivered to General Washington."

"What?" Befuddled, he shakes his head. "For Washington? But why? How did you—"

"I've been riding hard, for the message is urgent. These men were on the picket line and they're taking me to the general's headquarters now. I'll tell you everything later, I promise."

The tall soldier speaks up. "Lieutenant Hawke and Private Jones, Morgan's Rifle Corps."

Benjamin keeps one arm around me as he reaches out to shake the lieutenant's hand. "Sergeant Stone, Third Virginia. Thank you for escorting my wife."

He turns to me as he continues to take stock of my situation. "But wait. Were you without escort on your journey? How did you find your way here?" He holds me at arms' length. "Are those my clothes?"

Now that I am in his presence, all the problems plaguing me on the trip matter not, and I laugh at the astonishment on his face. "I'm fine. Tired and dirty, but fine."

"You're a sight. I'm surprised you found a warm reception at the picket line."

I cast a glance at Lieutenant Hawke, and he chuckles. "Your wife is persuasive, and her story is just crazy enough to be true. May I suggest we press on to headquarters?"

Elated to be this close to my husband and also to delivering the letter, I clutch Benjamin's arm, wanting to tell him everything at once. I begin with what's happened in the last few hours. "Then I saw lights in the distance and I could hear someone speaking German as I rode up. I said, '*Was geht hier vor?*' because I learned a little from the Hessians and the family I stayed with in Frederick Town, and it seems everyone in York speaks German too. The grandson spoke English and said they were taking out the bodies of some soldiers who died of a fever. I feared I was too late, but none of the poor boys in the field hospital was Henry or Jeremiah."

Outside the two-story stone house serving as Washington's headquarters, Lieutenant Hawke speaks to the guards while I turn my back and fish Mr. Harrison's letter out of my stays. Hawke beckons us into the entry, where he whispers something to the sentry, who nods and goes into a room off the narrow hallway.

I remove my hat because the men have all done so and feel my skin flush as my body adjusts to being inside and out of the bitter weather. When the door to Washington's office opens, Benjamin and Lieutenant Hawke salute. My body snaps to attention too. Is this the end of my mission?

26

The Message for Washington

"At ease." A young, red-haired officer turns his gaze on me where I stand between Benjamin and Lieutenant Hawke. Again, I resist the urge to smooth my hair and try to look more presentable.

"You are the wife of Sergeant Benjamin Stone of the Third Virginia Regiment?"

"Yes, sir."

He glances at Benjamin, who nods.

"How did you come to be here?"

"On horseback, from home, to bring food, medicine, and clothes to my husband and brothers. While I was in York, two days gone, Congressman Benjamin Harrison gave me a message and bade me deliver it in haste to His Excellency. I wish to present it to him now."

He folds his arms on his chest as he gazes down at me. "You've come here unannounced and claim you have a message for the commander in chief. Tell me, why should I believe you and grant you an audience with the general?"

I see I must prove myself again and I feel my face grow hot as my anger flares. Benjamin starts to speak on my behalf but I place a hand on his arm to check him as I address the officer.

"I may ask you, sir, why I must answer the same questions over and over. Mr. Harrison bid me deliver his message to General Washington—and no other. I do not know who you are but I should trust you because you wear a uniform?"

The officer opens his mouth to retort, but I cut him off.

"The message is genuine, sent—and carried here—in good faith. Why would I do anything treacherous that would endanger my loved ones? I vow I shall burn the dispatch if I cannot fulfill my promise to Mr. Harrison and any consequences will lie with His Excellency's gatekeeper, not with me." I raise my chin. "Do you not think the commander in chief should read and evaluate the message for himself?"

He stares at me for a long moment before he retreats to the office. As soon as the door shuts behind him, Benjamin runs a hand over his face and stifles a laugh. "You don't know who that is, do you?"

"No. How could I?"

"Lieutenant Colonel Alexander Hamilton keeps close counsel with His Excellency and it actually *is* up to him whether you gain admittance."

I exhale slowly. "Oh. I suppose I could make apology."

Then the door opens and Hamilton gestures us inside the paneled office where General George Washington rises from his chair to greet us.

Despite my frustration, awe sweeps over me as I stand in the general's presence and tears flood my eyes as I bow. "Your Excellency."

"Sergeant and Mrs. Stone." He inclines his head and fixes his gaze on me. "I understand you have brought me a message from York?"

"Yes, Your Excellency. From Mr. Benjamin Harrison." My hand shakes a little as I hold it out. He lays the letter on his desk.

"Thank you, madam. You came to us from Virginia, I believe?"

"Yes, sir. Fauquier County."

"I know that area very well. You must have been traveling for days. Can you stay long enough to spend the Sabbath as our guest?"

Why doesn't he read the message? My heart sinks, but I try to answer without letting my disappointment show. "Yes, thank you."

"Very good. A detail leaving Monday can escort you back to Virginia."

"That's very kind, but unnecessary. I know the way home."

"I insist. No doubt Sergeant Stone will be happy to accompany you as part of that detail. We will, however, need him back."

I shall have more than a week with Benjamin at my side. A smile spreads over my lips. "Thank you, Your Excellency."

"Upon its return, the detail will escort my wife here. Though she is more comfortable at home at Mount Vernon, she insists on arriving in time to celebrate my birthday next month."

Inspiration strikes as I see a way to further signify my good intentions. "I did not realize your birthday was approaching. Will you excuse me for just one moment?" I hurry past the sentry at the door, Benjamin at my heels, and find what I'm looking for in the bottom of my saddlebag. Inside, I present my bulging stocking to the commander in chief of the Continental Army.

"Please accept an early gift. It's salt."

Washington bows, acting as though receiving a woman's stocking full of salt is not at all unusual. "I thank you for such a valuable gift. I will share it to benefit as many soldiers as possible. You reinforce my belief that the women of Virginia are the cleverest and most resourceful to be found. Now, may I do anything to see to your comfort?"

"I wish to visit my brothers and reassure myself they are recovering from their illness." I drop my gaze, but can't help asking, "Also—may I know the contents of the letter?"

He avoids my request but I suspect he's trying not to laugh. "I see Lieutenant Hawke was not exaggerating. Had they detained you at the picket line much longer, I am sure his men would have been taking orders from you, and I believe Lieutenant Colonel Hamilton would concur."

"I cannot attest to that, sir. Fear and worry may have driven me to assert myself in a manner that could be described as commanding." I nibble my lip as I glanced at Benjamin, who is trying to maintain his composure. Then he makes bold to speak.

"Your Excellency, my wife is being too modest. She is accustomed to asserting herself, and I am accustomed to having a strong partner by my side. I had not realized how much I missed her until I laid eyes on her."

"You seem to have made a wise choice of partner, Sergeant." As Washington bows to me once again, he smiles. "I hope you have a comfortable stay."

I cling to Benjamin's arm as we walk past the parade ground to the enlisted men's quarters. He holds Nelly's reins in his free hand, though it isn't necessary. The mare follows us like a dog as we pass row upon row of the roughest-built huts I've ever seen. When we're nearly back to the picket line, a man in a grimy, torn jacket hails us from an open doorway. I do not recognize Joseph, whose face is half-hidden behind long whiskers, until he speaks.

"We heard someone chased a woman into camp. Why am I not surprised to learn it was you?" As he comes near, I see he has wrapped rags around his patched shoes and up his calves to serve as leggings. He looks me up and down and shakes his head. "You look worse than we do."

I let go of Benjamin's arm and hug my brother. "You don't recognize Benjamin's coat and breeches? He wrote to me and said Henry and Jeremiah weren't well. I feared it was smallpox."

Benjamin shrugs. "I didn't want to worry you, as I believed there was nothing you could do. I should know by now nothing deters you." He puts his arm around me and kisses my forehead. His smile communicates far more about what he is thinking than does the chaste touch of his lips.

The sidelong glance I give him in return says I can't wait to be alone with him, either. But first things first. "How are Henry and Jeremiah?"

"Come see for yourself." We three fall into step as we cross the camp and Joseph takes over the conversation. "The boys caught the pox while we were waiting for the governor's permission to inoculate Virginia troops. Every time we get new recruits, we get outbreaks."

Benjamin gives me a reassuring squeeze. "But don't worry—now that our physicians have permission to inoculate, most of the new recruits are well enough to fight by the time they receive supplies and weapons."

When we reach a log structure more than twice the size of the enlisted men's huts, Benjamin fetches the medicine chest from Nelly's saddlebag without being asked. Joseph takes hold of her bridle. "It won't do to let her stand out in the cold while you visit the boys. I'll unload your bundles and then take her to the livery and see her settled."

Mindful of all we've accomplished together, I press my forehead against hers for a moment. "Don't let the army commandeer her. Promise?"

"I'll make sure they know she's just visiting." He leads Nelly away and I follow Benjamin as he ducks through the low doorway and heads toward two cots in a corner near the fireplace. Relief sweeps over me at the sight of my brothers and I bend over Jeremiah first. The pustules crowd close on his face and neck and under my hand, his skin is burning hot. Henry appears to be resting easily and feels only a little warm.

A red-haired young woman comes to us from the other side of the room and I ask, "Have you been seeing to my brothers' care?"

"Yes, missus."

"I'll want some hot water to make tea for them. How long since the pustules started to scab?"

"Almost a week for Henry. His case was among the milder I've seen this winter but as you can tell, Jeremiah's is serious. Henry was feeling poorly when they arrived in winter camp. Jeremiah was here a week before he began to show symptoms. His rash developed just after the new year."

She leads the way to the hearth where a copper teakettle steams beside a few flatirons and fills two mugs. I add my herbal mixture and while it steeps, we carry the mugs back to my brothers.

"Do you sweat the patients to treat the pox?" I hope whoever trained this girl did not use the Widow Jenkins' methods.

"No missus. My father is one of the army surgeons. We found cooling feverish patients helps more than sweating them, so we use snow and cold compresses to keep their fevers down. There's a chill in here, no matter what we do. I understand you rode all the way from Virginia?"

I stand tall inside Benjamin's jacket. "I came over two hundred miles."

"Well done!" The girl's eyes light up as though she would not shrink from such an adventure. "I'm Ruth Hawke, from Massachusetts. I've traveled with the army for two years, but never such a distance in so short a time. My husband, Gideon—Lieutenant Hawke—stopped by and told me the story. He said you were riding a blue streak!"

I laugh. "It's easy to do when someone's chasing you. My mare, Nelly, and I find ferry crossings much more difficult. Mrs. Hawke, this is my other brother, Joseph, and my husband, Benjamin."

"Please, you must all call me Ruth." She turns to Benjamin. "Gideon knew two Stone brothers in Morgan's unit."

"Thomas and Baylis are my brothers. Baylis died of the pox last month before we made winter camp. He was just a few years older than you."

Ruth nods. "I'm sorry for your loss."

I squeeze Benjamin's hand and address Ruth. "I'm sure you see so much death. The number of ill and injured men . . ."

"More than I have time to count." Ruth looks around the crowded hospital and her gaze comes to rest on us. "You're a devoted sister and wife. Will you be staying until your brothers are well?"

"Devoted? Stubborn and bossy, more like." A raspy voice comes from behind us.

Ruth turns and puts her hands on her hips but she smiles as she retorts, "Well, soldier, it seems you're feeling better. You haven't displayed ginger like that since you arrived to occupy that cot."

I'm so relieved to find Henry on the mend I can't remember why I ever found his teasing annoying and he seems just as glad to see me. I help him sit and hand him the mug. Jeremiah cannot raise himself, so Ruth puts a hand under his head and holds the mug to his lips. Both my brothers are too thin, like all the men in the room. My practiced eye tells me Henry will chafe at his inactivity long before the last of his rash clears and they allow him back to his duties.

"I shall stay with them tonight." I look around the crowded room. "Ruth, you have more than enough to occupy you. I hope Jeremiah will improve and set my mind at ease before I leave with the general's detail on Monday."

Ruth casts a knowing glance at Benjamin. "That's not much time to spend with your loved ones."

I sit beside Jeremiah and cool his skin with a wet cloth as I murmur to him. "Uncle expects you home at the end of the war. I came all this way to care for you. You must not disappoint us. Do you understand me?"

He gives me a weak smile, but he does not realize the full weight of my words. Jeremiah must return home to take over Uncle's interests, as planned. When he does, I will tell him all I observed and make certain he severs our family's business dealings with Thompson and his cronies.

After he is asleep, I shift my chair to give two stretcher-bearers room to edge past with a body.

Ruth murmurs, "Be sure to save his blankets. Leave them to be boiled so we may use them again." One of them nods, and when they are gone, she comes to sit beside me. "I feared we would never get the pox under control in camp, but thankfully now we have permission to inoculate the new recruits. Smallpox inoculation is legal in Massachusetts, and both Gideon and I received the treatment as children. It's tragic that many of the men arrived here and fell ill, when it could have been prevented."

I nod in sympathy. "Even though it's illegal in Virginia, I inoculate whenever I have the opportunity. I was also inoculated when I was young and it has been a blessing to be able to tend the sick without falling ill myself."

"My shift is over soon. The attendants will keep watch over your brothers through the night. You've had a long journey and you shouldn't exhaust yourself."

"I know, but I'm so lately arrived I can scarce think of leaving them yet." I produce a tin from my medicine chest. "Here's more of the tea I use for fever."

She thanks me as she places it into her apron pocket and pauses before she speaks again. "Gideon has been my sweetheart for a long time, but we were married just a few months ago. Every minute we have together is precious, for a soldier's wife never knows what the next day will bring. You should spend as much time with your husband as you can. Would you like to clean up first at my quarters?"

She's right. Washington has Harrison's message. My brothers are resting. It's high time I spent some time alone with Benjamin. To Ruth, I reply, "Yes. I'd like that very much."

27

Camp Wife

Ruth and Gideon share quarters with two other officers. Their hut's single room is smaller than my chamber at Uncle's, with a blanket hung across the middle to give the newlywed couple a bit of privacy. When I survey the state of my soiled clothes, I'm mortified. Everything is grimy and smells of sweat, horse, and river water.

Ruth takes it all as a matter of course. "I'll have someone wash them for you in the morning. Everything should be dry in time for your trip home." She wraps up the dirty clothes and grabs a bucket in her free hand. "The men are on watch until midnight. I'll fetch water so you can bathe and lend you some of my things to wear while you're here."

I want to hug her for her kindness but decide it's better to wait until after I've washed.

When I emerge, scrubbed pink and glowing from the heat of the fire, my bathwater is the color of wet ashes. The feel of the fresh linen shift Ruth leaves toasting near the hearth is a luxury I took for granted until two weeks ago and I am sure I could want nothing more than the simple, russet-colored woolen she lends me to wear. As I dry my hair,

281

the glints of firelight in the dark strands match the gown. I finish putting on the clean stockings—heavens, clean stockings—and my boots just as Ruth returns. I emerge from behind the curtain with a flourish, like an actor stepping on stage.

"That color becomes you!"

"I imagine it also looks lovely on you."

Her pale skin flushes. "Sergeant Stone is waiting for you outside. Here, you may take this shawl. Your hair is still damp. Do you have a cap?"

My insides flutter as I settle the shawl on my shoulders. "My cap is not fit to wear without a good scrubbing but I'm used to being outdoors and will be fine for such a short walk. Benjamin will keep me warm." I embrace her with as much affection as I would Betsy. "Thank you for everything you've done for me and for my brothers, Ruth."

The fluttery feeling grows more intense as Benjamin leads me across camp to his quarters. Is it the fact I'm wearing a young wife's fresh clothing that makes me feel like a bride? Every soldier we pass glances at me as if he can read my thoughts. If tonight proves to be anything like the last time Benjamin and I reunited, I'll not be able to thumb through the memories later without someone recognizing wanton pleasure in the smile on my lips.

Benjamin pushes open the rough door of his hut. As I step inside, the flutter in my stomach plummets and my smile dies. Joseph and the two other soldiers who huddle around the fire fill the space in the tiny, smoky hut.

Though I nod to each soldier as Benjamin makes introductions, I forget their names as soon as I hear them—and then I remember why I have come.

"You all must be hungry. I've brought food from home."

Their faces light up. In a flash, I'm untying the sacks of nuts and dried fruit and cutting strips of bacon to lay in the spider that stands over the flames.

It's a poor meal compared to what I would serve at home. I lack the time to boil beans or soak the dried fish until it's ready to fry. While the men eat every morsel I set before them, I unpack the other bundles and give Benjamin and Joseph the clothes and blankets I've brought.

All the men linger around the fire. Benjamin seems reluctant to ask them to give us some privacy but I'm not about to renew relations with my husband with strangers—or my brother—in the room.

When I glance at Joseph in dismay, he rises to put more wood on the flames and then nudges the man nearest him. "I hear there's a card game down the way again tonight. You fellows fancy a wager? I have some rum left from my rations."

The other two shrug and get to their feet, and Joseph, without appearing to, shepherds them toward the door.

As he passes, he murmurs, "The general has forbidden us to wager our rations, but I'll risk it just this once. It's not every day my little sister comes visiting and needs time alone with her husband." He ducks under the doorway and then turns back to Benjamin, his thin face lighting up in a mischievous grin. "You want me to stand sentry?"

"No." Benjamin shuts the door in his face.

The moment we're alone, Benjamin reaches for me, and the flame of desire sweeps through me anew. His hands burrow into my curls, drawing the strands between his fingers as his lips take mine. He cradles my head with one hand and his other arm presses me against him until I feel his heartbeat as though it is my own. He whispers, "If you knew how often I dream of rolling with you in our featherbed at home."

"How often?"

"You never leave my thoughts." His kisses trail down my throat to the scooped neckline of my gown. My sigh is pure bliss as I rise on tiptoe, arching my back as I melt into him. How I've missed his voice and his caress. His hands move down my back, seeking my curves through the folds of the petticoat.

I let my hands wander over his body as my own thoughts flit to our featherbed at home. As I consider what making love will be like on one of the rough, narrow bunks set into the log walls, I imagine getting splinters in places I'd rather not. "Which of these do you occupy?" I point at one bottom bunk, which is only about a foot and a half below the one above it. "Please tell me it's not that one. How does a man fit in there?"

He laughs. "We built these huts in haste, you know. The width of the logs varies, and we set the bunks where we could. Believe it or not, I've seen others with worse miscalculations. That bunk feels too much like a coffin and I warrant no one sleeps there if he can help it, but we're all lean enough we don't need leverage to extract ourselves in time for roll call."

He sweeps me off my feet and cradles me against his chest as easily as he did on our wedding night. "How do you feel about heights, then? I'll toss you up and we'll be like two spoons in the top drawer."

Is he jesting? I bite my lip as I consider his plan and he bursts out laughing again. "If you could see the look on your face." He sets me down and drags a threadbare blanket and a thin straw mattress off the top bunk. "I'm sorry there's no luxury to offer you, but you arrived unannounced. Honestly, it's not that bad."

"Liar. It is that bad. You've just grown used to it, though I favor the dirt floor above my other options." I add the wool coverlet from home and Ruth's shawl to our bedding.

"Soldiers are used to sleeping on the ground. What more could I desire now that you're here to share my new blanket?"

When he draws me down beside him before the fire, there is no tenderness in our embrace, nor any pretense at seduction, only our raw hunger for one another. It doesn't matter the straw mattress does nothing to cushion the hard-packed floor beneath us. I care not that the side of me nearest the hearth is too hot, the other too cold. As his hands move over my flesh, I know how well fed I must feel to him, just as he, who has always been hard muscle and sinew, now seems far too thin to me.

This connection is what I've longed for. After a year and a half apart, my body remembers the rhythms and the tune as though we played it together only yesterday. As my passion peaks with his, I wonder if we will make another child tonight.

After, I waste no time covering myself and gathering the blankets and shawl around us. A few minutes ago, I didn't notice—but the hut is drafty.

As we lie face to face, he runs his hand up my leg under my shift. I drape that leg over his hip to pull him a little closer. How I've missed his familiar touch! He often enjoys talking after making love and now I bask in the familiarity and hang on his every word.

He traces the outline of my lips. "You are a singularly beautiful woman. I consider myself the luckiest of men you consented to wed me. But of all the memories of you I carry in my mind, I vow I shall treasure most of all the sight of you arriving in camp, disheveled, spattered with mud, and dressed as a boy."

I laugh, embarrassed. "I was not beautiful then."

"On the contrary. You were beautiful in the way of a wild creature. Now that the initial shock of your arrival has passed, I find I am not at all surprised you made the journey." He presses his lips to mine. "Is there is anything you cannot do?"

"I couldn't bring your new son to meet you."

"But I shall see him when I escort you home."

"Oh, Benjamin, he's so much like you. Sometimes I wonder if we shouldn't have named him for you, or George, after my father, rather than for Uncle. I hope the name does not sour his disposition."

"You and your uncle haven't been getting on well, then?"

"No, and once I return, I'm moving back to our house. I'll manage fine until you return, and mark me, I'll hear no objections."

His jesting tone turns to one of concern. "But surely it's not that bad. What's happened?"

I feel a flash of annoyance but then I remember he doesn't know—and I don't have to keep Uncle's treachery a secret. I can open my heart to him and tell him anything. By the time I reach the part where Ludwick and the Hessians rescue me from the highwaymen, I'm sobbing in his arms, and his hold on me has turned hard as iron.

"I thank Providence for sending you deliverance on the road and I promise you, Anna, I will see you and the children settled back in our home before I return to camp. Can you forgive me? I passed over your objections before, believing I knew what was best for you."

"Of course. If I hadn't embarked on this journey, I would have been in no danger—and things may have gone much worse for you. Can you forgive me?"

"Always." He wipes away the last of my tears. "Now, tell me all about Rhoda and Elijah."

My smile is watery, but genuine. "They've grown so, you'll not recognize them. I used acorns and pebbles to teach Rhoda to multiply and divide last summer and now she can't get enough of arithmetic. She has a fine hand with both needle and spindle and treats her brothers with kindness. Well, nearly all the time. I began teaching her of herbs and plants, and she shows great promise. But she misses you and is lonely for playmates her age. She asked if she would forget me before I returned. You must make time to reconnect with her during your visit home."

"And what about Elijah?"

"Elijah is nothing like the other two. He has an adventuresome spirit and runs, rather than walks, everywhere. I take more pains to keep him out of trouble than I ever had to with Rhoda and he gets into all kinds of mischief in Uncle's big house. Before Twelfth Night, Phillis went into the parlor to prepare for the party and found Elijah-sized footprints in the dust on the mantel."

"The little scamp." He laughs, more pleased by our son's fearless-ness than I.

"We could not credit how he climbed up there or how he walked across without falling, but I thank the Lord he was not hurt."

"Elijah sounds as if he takes after Thomas."

"Or Henry—or both! I fear he'll lead us on a merry chase before he's grown. Who can say what his future will hold?' I roll onto my back. "Or any of our futures. I hope General Washington has read the letter from Mr. Harrison. I wish I could have made sense of it."

He raises his head to stare at me. "Did you dare look at it? What did it say?"

I shrug. "It was nonsense. I copied it into my receipt book, because I feared someone would intercept or damage the original. The book is in the saddlebag."

He rolls over, grasps the saddlebag's strap, and pulls it toward us so I can retrieve the book and his brow furrows as we turn between the two pages containing the message. "It must be a cipher—a code. I suppose there's no way to know if His Excellency will accept the origi-nal, with you as an unknown courier. A spy can do much good for the cause and much harm to the enemy."

"I didn't go unnoticed for long, believe me. I still can't believe I got the message here at all." I tear out the pages. "I've no need of it now. Washington will choose either to read it or discard it and that will be that." I lean across Benjamin to hold them over the flames, and when they catch, we watch the fire consume the writing until there is noth-ing left.

"When I think of how many times you put yourself at risk, I'm flooded with concern over things I didn't know I needed to worry about."

I pull the blankets higher and snuggle close. "The rest of the story of my journey is an epic tale—and it will keep. I promise I'll entertain you with it on the way back to Virginia."

28

The Board of War's Visit

CONTINENTAL ARMY CAMP, VALLEY FORGE, PENNSYLVANIA
JANUARY 23, 1778

The bugler who blows reveille could be standing right outside our hut—the loud, unexpected notes penetrating the darkness set my heart racing. My eyes fly open, and I sit bolt upright as Benjamin stirs beside me. Though I lie back down, it takes me a few minutes to relax. The pile of glowing coals in the fireplace gives off the only light. "What time is it?"

He spoons me against his chest. "Time to wake up."

As he holds me, the camp comes to life outside the hut's walls. Somewhere, not far off, I hear retching. Closer, someone makes water on the ground.

Benjamin ignores all of it and covers my face with kisses before he leaves the warmth of our shared blanket. "You need not report for roll call, but I must. His Excellency and Major General von Steuben want to make sure we look sharp. We expect a delegation from the Board of War today or tomorrow." He stirs up the coals and puts a few sticks on the fire before he dresses. "Oh, and our bunkmates who were on picket duty last night will be home soon."

"Do you have time for breakfast?"

"We rarely eat before roll call."

I reach for the strap of my haversack. "Wait. Take this."

His lean face takes on the look of a hungry wolf at the sight of the cheese and bread I offer. He tears off a great mouthful of the bread with his teeth as he shrugs into his tattered jacket and picks up his musket on the way out the door.

I must dress before the other men arrive, though I would rise regardless, for there is nothing appealing about lying abed on the dirt floor. It takes me little time to put on Ruth's russet woolen, my stockings and shoes, and wrap myself in the shawl which is still warm from our bodies. His old blanket is sorely in need of laundering, but it looks as though a good scrubbing will reduce it to rags. I wrinkle my nose as I hang both it and the blanket from home over the side of a bunk to air.

Using a handful of kindling, I sweep the old straw, litter, and dried leaves the men have tracked inside onto a piece of bark, and the bits send up sparks as I dump them into the fireplace. Crumbled mint leaves sprinkled in the corners will discourage mice and I toss a handful of dried lavender into the flames to freshen the air.

When the other men troop in, I make a hasty introduction, offer them some of the bread and cheese, and then leave the hut. The wind whips my hair around my face as I watch the ranks assemble on the parade ground. Redoubts surround the flat field spreading out before me in a depression in the earth.

In daylight, the camp is both a sorry and a glorious sight. Most of the men wear mismatched, torn, and inadequate clothing. But I see something remarkable. I see an army of volunteers and I swell with pride at all the husbands, fathers, sons, and brothers who are taking a stand for freedom.

Around the perimeter of the parade ground, I note some half-built huts, tents, and lean-to shelters among the completed cabins. In the darkness the night before, I did not realize the structure in which I'd slept was good accommodations.

From the top of the rise I spy another group of cabins and tents set farther away. There, women wrapped in shawls stir the contents of kettles hung over campfires while poorly clothed children dart in and out of sight among their meager lodgings. How hard life must be for women who, with children in tow, follow their men to war.

The encampment is many times larger than York, and given what I know of the privations here, I expected to find a prevailing attitude of despair. But Valley Forge hums with activity and industriousness.

What will become of its inhabitants if the officers do not heed the message I delivered? Benjamin said the men revere Washington. Would his removal lead to mutiny—and if that happened, which side would Benjamin choose? If the British catch wind of such a thing, they could attack while the Continental forces are in disarray.

I give myself a little shake. It will not do to fret about the worst that could happen. I must be like the soldiers, trust the commander, and do what I can do to further the cause.

When Benjamin, Joseph, and their bunkmates return, I am frying more of the bacon. A simmering pot of beans will be ready for supper.

Joseph sniffs the air as he ducks through the doorway. "So this is what a woman's touch does for these huts? Anna, you may stay as long as you like."

One man whose name I can't remember grins at me. "I'm glad you're here, ma'am. I can't take one more meal of soup with burned leaves and dirt in it."

Joseph pretends to look affronted, but he cannot keep a straight face. "I'll thank you not to criticize my cooking."

At that, everyone laughs as they crowd around the hearth and mix their daily ration of flour with water to make what they call fire cakes. While the cakes bake on the stones, I bring out a crock of preserves. The men spread a thick layer over the flat, tasteless bread, and the rapture on their faces as they eat the simple fare rewards me for my trouble.

Benjamin wipes the last crumbs from his lips and licks his fingers, his gesture showing these men have learned to waste no sustenance. "Be sure to remind the fellows on watch the commanding officers expect us to have our cartridge boxes filled at inspection."

Joseph asks, "Do they think we'll need to fight while we're in winter camp?"

"I think they're just teaching us to prepare, like proper soldiers."

But I wonder if Harrison's letter warned Washington to prepare for trouble.

After the meal, the other men leave for picket or fatigue duties. Benjamin escorts me to the hospital, where today it is his duty, as a chaplain, to visit and offer comfort.

Outside, the path to the hospital smells worse than a privy, as men relieve themselves wherever they please. I hold the end of the shawl to my nose as we pass the carcass of a dead horse. "It's a pity that they left that poor beast too long for its hide to be of use."

Again, Benjamin takes the filth, death, and decay around him as a matter of course. "At roll call this morning, they formed details to see to the removal of dead animals. I'm sure it's hard to understand, since you've just arrived, but it takes time for men to adjust to army life. The new recruits sometimes balk when they must take their turns at fatigue duties, like digging latrines and keeping the camp clean."

"Do they also dislike using the latrines once they are dug?"

He laughs. "If they do, I think it's because they're unused to obeying orders. I've spoken to many frontiersmen from Virginia who went to war assuming their individual liberties would remain unchecked, for they knew nothing else. You know how it is at home. Discipline falls like a heavy yoke on these young fellows' shoulders and sometimes they rebel in small ways, but their commitment to the fight is true. It's hard to be patient in winter camp when we're all bored, hungry, and in need of warm clothing and supplies."

The sound of construction comes from all directions. "You're going to preach on a Friday—so do the men work on the Sabbath?" It was not a criticism, for I broke the Sabbath myself when circumstances warranted.

"Yes. At first it bothered me, but now I'm used to it. The other chaplains and I agreed to hold services whenever it was most convenient, rather than on a specific day of the week. I warrant we share the word of God more often this way, anyhow."

"Sabbath or no, the work cannot cease!" I'm horrified at the thought of anything prolonging the sufferings of these soldiers. "I'm sure God understands, even if the situation here is beyond human comprehension. Why are some men still in unfinished quarters?"

"There weren't enough tools to go around and some are just getting their turn with borrowed hatchets and augers. Ours was one of the first finished. We who share it are all old men compared to most of the others, and decent shelter was more important to us than time spent in leisure. We also had Joseph to superintendent the job and he kept us hustling." He chuckles. "He even had the good grace to say my daubing skills have improved since last we worked together."

I cannot make light of their situation. "How can Congress expect you to carry on like this? How will you live through the winter, let alone fight, without adequate food, clothing, and shelter?"

"Anna, the news is not all grim. Just this day, they relieved soldiers who are tailors by trade of their other duties, so they may repair and sew uniforms from recently procured cloth." He puts his arm around me. "A soldier's life is one of privation."

"This is not privation. This is an outrage. When I was in York, I saw the luxury in which General Gates travels and heard how Congress complains about princely accommodations compared to what you must endure. Congressman Harrison told me of the delegates' reluctance to allow more funds for the army. The only explanation for their cruelty is they do not comprehend the reality of your situation here."

"That will change once the members of the Board of War review the camp. Then they can address the problems."

"But what if they remain coldhearted?" I look up at his profile, so familiar and dear to me, and wish I could do more to help him. "There aren't even enough blankets."

"It would be easier to shield you from the reality if you could not see it for yourself."

"Uncle said the same before I left."

"And in this he is right. None of us want to worry our families. Men from the Virginia regiments who elect to leave once their enlistments expire must surrender their blankets before they're mustered out. They leave them behind for those who remain."

"But it will take at least two weeks to travel on foot back to Virginia. The temperatures have been tolerable during the day, but it's below freezing at night. How will they get along without blankets?"

"They will have to find shelter, just as you did on your journey here."

When he pauses, I look up at him, letting him see the tears in my eyes. "Will you be giving up your blanket?"

"Nay. I can't give up my blanket, for I can't give up the fight yet. After the smallpox outbreak at the end of the year, desertions have been high. The men fear the pox more than they fear the British, and many panicked and fled. I fear some were already ill and carried the disease away with them."

"But, Benjamin, can't you . . ."

"How can I ask others to stay and not be willing to remain myself?" His convictions have not changed since he first took up arms against the British.

When we arrive at the regiment hospital, I am cheered to see Henry sitting up, taking some broth. One of the doctor's assistants helps Jeremiah, spooning his portion into his mouth. I walk with Benjamin as he stops at every cot, speaking to those who are well enough to converse, praying over those whose circumstances are grave. When he moves to the center of the room, I sit on the chair between my brothers' cots and take their hands in mine. How I've missed listening to my husband offer words of comfort.

"My brothers and sisters, you have been called on to make great personal sacrifices and endure extraordinary privation to see our dream of an independent new nation become a reality. May we find comfort in the text of Psalm ninety-one, 'Thou shalt not be afraid for the terror by night, nor for the arrow that flieth by day; nor the pestilence that walketh in darkness; nor the destruction that wasteth at noonday. A thousand shall fall at your side, ten thousand at thy right hand; but it shall not come nigh thee, because thou hast made the Lord thy refuge.'

"If to love God and man were engraved on every human heart, we would not willfully violate God's commands. The want of this love causes the greater part of the moral evils in this world and it is ignorance that fosters those evils. I believe wherever the Gospel goes, the law goes with it."

He bows his head and I close my eyes and let his voice wash over me as he prays. "Heavenly Father, we ask that You grant every man and woman who supports the efforts of the Continental Army strength and wisdom to serve You without stumbling or stain. Keep them and their families safe and sound during these days of separation. Lay your healing touch upon the wounded and the afflicted and protect our soldiers in the battles yet to come, that they might return to their homes to serve You in peace and quietness. Through Jesus Christ our Lord. Amen."

When I open my eyes, a young soldier advances down the aisle toward me.

"Missus Stone?"

"Yes."

"You're wanted at headquarters, ma'am."

Benjamin and I follow the messenger out of the hospital and down the path to headquarters, where Lieutenant Colonel Hamilton is waiting. He bows to me in greeting, bolstering my hopes. "Good afternoon, sir. Am I to see His Excellency again?"

"No, madam, it was I who summoned you. The general is preparing for other visitors, and he is reticent with all but his intimate acquaintances."

"Oh. I see."

"Please do not interpret that as a lack of esteem. I can always tell if someone who is not close to him is lying. When they say, 'Washington told me—' I can be sure it is not true." His expression softens as he continues. "I understood your disappointment last night when the general didn't seem interested in the dispatch. You risked your life to bring it to him and I cannot blame you for wanting satisfaction for your trouble. I can tell you this: General Washington has read your message. It pertains to the actions of certain men in positions of power, both in Congress and in the army. Their treachery will be brought to a halt before it raises the concerns of the French."

It was as Harrison said. The way Benjamin tightens his arm around me signals he is hanging on Hamilton's words too.

"For I daresay, we must let nothing impede the finalization of an alliance with France. The scoundrel who followed you was in the employ of the general's enemies in Congress. He eluded Lieutenant Hawke's men, but he will have to return to York and report that he failed in his task."

Pride swells inside my chest and I make a low bow to atone for my sharp words the day before. "It was an honor to help, sir."

"My dear madam, the commander in chief owes you his thanks, to which I humbly add mine." He bows once more before he escorts us to the door.

On our way up the path, Benjamin asks, "Are you sorry we burned that copy of the message?"

"Yes. I suppose it would have made quite a keepsake from my journey."

We step aside to allow soldiers escorting five men on horseback to pass and then linger to watch Washington and Hamilton emerge from headquarters to greet them. Another officer, a slight man with a weak chin, hurries over as the men dismount. Benjamin takes my hand as if to carry on, but I resist, wanting very much to hear what they say. "That's the Board of War's delegation, isn't it?"

"It appears so."

"I don't see Gates. I wonder why he's not here?"

Benjamin shakes his head. "I cannot say. That man"—he indicates the weak-chinned officer— "is probably wondering the same thing. He is General Conway, the recently appointed Inspector General of the Board of War and a close ally of Gates. He and Washington, it's said, do not get on well."

They are out of earshot but now that I know what I am watching, my amusement grows as Conway maneuvers, trying to be the first to greet the members of the committee. One delegate, a heavyset, well-dressed young man, holds what must be a scented handkerchief to his nose, though the stench of the camp is much better here than near the enlisted men's huts. Another man, standing at the back of the group, looks about to weep.

I sniff. "Conway tries too hard. It must bother him that he's naught but a Bantam rooster next to His Excellency's great height. I warrant he cannot compete with Washington's natural air of command, either. But did you notice? It is Lieutenant Colonel Hamilton who does most of the talking."

Benjamin chuckles as he plucks at my shawl. "Come along. We shouldn't stand here gawping."

"Why? Are you afraid they'll think I'm a spy?"

Though we laugh, I'm fair consumed by my curiosity. Are the men in the delegation players in the conspiracy? I want to know more.

When we return to the hut, my clean laundry has been delivered. After an evening meal of hearty bean soup with chunks of bacon in the broth, the men in Benjamin's hut thank me and take their leave. Joseph, last to depart, winks on his way out.

Just as before, Benjamin wraps his arms around me the moment the door closes. "One tumble did not slake my thirst for you." His kisses send a delicious thrill up my spine. He murmurs against my hair, "I vow from the moment I left this morning I've been counting the minutes until we could be alone again. Lieutenant Hawke is lucky to have his wife with him in camp."

"That may be, but it torments her to know every time he's in battle. I think I prefer to hear about your exploits when they're well in the past."

"I could say the same about yours. But I assume you wouldn't like to stay and assist the doctors in camp?"

"If I had no children at home, I might. I admit it's not as bad here as I expected." To temper my admission, I toss my head, playing the coquette. "Though I fear I may have given in to you too easily last night, sir."

"Did I forget my manners?" He traces a line down into my décolletage with his index finger and unties the lacing on the front of my borrowed gown.

"A forgivable offense, considering our long separation."

"You must re-civilize me."

"I will—just not right away." I take hold of the frayed lapels of his coat and pull his mouth down to mine.

Monday morning, I rise at reveille to wash and dress in the clean riding habit. Dawn breaks over the redoubts as Joseph, Benjamin, and I make our way to the hospital so I can bid goodbye to Henry and Jeremiah.

Joseph stays with us as we report to the detail's assembly place at the western edge of camp. On the way, we pass the parade ground where the visiting Board of War delegation huddles, shivering in their heavy coats as they watch the poorly clothed soldiers drill under von Steuben's direction.

The men of the Virginia regiments whose terms have expired stand in line before the paymaster's tent. When each squad of twenty men departs, they leave their blankets in an ever-growing pile on the ground. We follow them toward the picket line where I arrived in such haste just a few days before.

I pull Joseph aside and hand him a thick stack of scrip—most of what remains of Uncle's gift to me. "I hope this will help sustain you through the rest of the winter. Take care of yourself and the boys."

"I will. You have done much to sustain us already. Give our greetings to the folks at home." He kisses me goodbye.

A soldier holds Nelly's bridle and when she sees me, the mare bobs her head and paws the ground. I pat her muzzle but do not give her the command to kneel. Instead, I let Benjamin give me a hand up into the saddle and sit ramrod straight as he swings onto his mount. Joseph salutes, and Benjamin returns it.

My soldier husband reaches out to squeeze my hand. "It's been a while since I've traveled any other way than on foot. I warrant I must get used to being in the saddle." His smile warms me like the summer sun. "Let's go home to see the children."

29

Harrison's Gambit

Two days into our journey, as Benjamin and I stroll up the high street toward The Plough, I hear someone call my name. Congressman Harrison waves as he hastens across the churned-up street, dodging a wagon and a pair of men on horseback. Too excited to bother with the steppingstones, he joins us on the boardwalk, his shoes, stockings, and cloak spattered with mud.

"Missus Stone! What a delight to see you again." Beaming, he clasps both my hands in his and brings them to his lips.

I bow. "Thank you, sir."

"Did you hear I am to join your traveling party tomorrow?"

"Yes. We will be glad of your company. May I present my husband, Benjamin?"

Harrison extends his hand. "Sergeant Stone, your servant, sir. If I may say, your wife is a singularly brave woman."

But Benjamin refuses to shake. Instead, his chin juts out as he puts a possessive arm around my waist. "I well know my wife's determination and grit. But how dare you take advantage of her and put her in harm's way, sir?"

Harrison's good cheer fades and I speak up on his behalf. "Mr. Harrison did not send me on the errand to endanger me. I was proud to help."

"He could've gotten you killed."

"Oh, come now, Benjamin. All's well that ends well. The important thing is Washington received the letter." I shrug at Harrison. "The journey was more harrowing than I expected."

Before Benjamin can reply, the congressman gestures toward the tavern. "I must hear all about your journey. Will you join me as my guests for supper? I imagine you might like to know more details of the situation necessitating you taking such a risk." He lowers his voice. "Let me assure you, men in and out of Congress were maneuvering against Washington in favor of the hero of the Battle of Saratoga."

At that, Benjamin's eyes light up. He will not refuse the opportunity to learn more. He is as curious as I—and wild horses could not drag me away from this meal.

Harrison opens the door and gestures us inside the tavern where we gather around a table near the fire. Harrison signals to one of the serving maids and she brings a carafe of Madeira. He pours three glasses for a toast.

"To the cause of liberty and those who risk their lives and fortunes to further it and in particular to Missus Stone, for her bravery and resourcefulness." Both men raise their glasses to me.

Harrison shifts his considerable bulk in his chair. "Now, if you please—tell me what transpired on your journey."

I tell the story, though Benjamin raises an eyebrow at me when I gloss over some of the worst moments. Then I ask, "How did they know I was the courier? Their man was following me within an hour of my departure."

He admits, "Some of the conspirators saw me leave the Butlers' the night before. They must have been watching Samuel and Lydia's house the next morning."

Benjamin looks peeved again. "So you endangered my elderly aunt and uncle too?"

"Not at all, sir. Let me explain how we came to this critical juncture. I'm sure you understand the members of Congress hail from all parts of the United States—and they do not share one voice. Far from it. Their opinions vary as does the flora of the fields." While Harrison is speaking, the serving maid bustles past our table but he fails to catch her attention.

"My congressional term ended in December and I should have been on my way back to Virginia before the New Year. But I could not go. When I served as chairman of the Board of War in 1775, I promised to support Washington, my friend and fellow Virginian, in his role as commander in chief and keep him and the Continental Army in the best circumstances. But just two years hence, the Board of War has become a vehicle for criticizing, rather than aiding, him." He leaned forward. "Three men who would see the commander removed and replaced with another now control the Board of War."

"General Gates." Benjamin's face was grim.

"Yes. Another, General Conway, is a gossip who stirs up trouble, but it is General Mifflin who is the master of this conspiracy. That blackguard abandoned his responsibilities as quartermaster and left the army's supply chain in a state of complete disarray. Yet because he and his friends sit on the Board of War, he bears no repercussions for his negligence. I suspect his failings as quartermaster were not because of honest mistakes but because he appropriated supplies meant for the army and sold them on the black market. It is he who is to blame for much of the army's discomfort this winter, sir."

"But how could anyone do such a thing?" I keep my voice low, but I want to scream in frustration. Will the vile natures of men never cease to surprise me?

By Harrison's expression, he agrees with me. "Replacing Washington was part of the plan to mask corruption in the army's departments.

But that was not the only faction interested in seeing a different general as commander in chief."

The tavern maid pauses at our table long enough to set down bread and cheese. "Begging your pardon for the delay, sir. The cook is out of sorts. General Gates ordered a feast put out for his guest of honor with no notice to speak of, and we're all a-scramble. May I bring you more wine while you wait for your meal?"

"Thank you. This and another bottle will sustain us until you are able."

I get her attention and lean in, eyes wide and open to gossip.

"Who is the general's guest of honor?"

"Why, it's the Marquis de Lafayette, missus. He's every bit as handsome as the rumors would have it and so elegant with his French manners." She drops a hasty curtsey and rushes back to the kitchen. The men commence eating, but I only desire more of the story. "Who else, sir? Who else is conspiring against the commander?"

Harrison swallows a mouthful and takes another sip of wine before he continues. "Well, now that the British commander Howe is at the center of the social scene in Philadelphia, he has excited the Quaker businessmen and merchants by proposing a way to resume transatlantic commerce. They, eager to refill their empty coffers, pressure their delegates in Congress to appoint a new commander in chief who will bring the war to a speedy end. They clamor for a quick surrender and negotiating a return to rule by the Crown."

I feel my panic rise. "But won't that make all of you—of us, I mean—guilty of treason?"

"Yes. Washington will not resign and he has shown he will not surrender. He endures insults but cannot respond, for public airing of our squabbles only serves to aid the British. Gates never thought we could win the war in the first place and I daresay, for the right price he would not hesitate to lay down his sword."

Benjamin's expression is thoughtful. "Though they are three onto one, Washington is still a formidable opponent. Could Gates, Conway, and Mifflin usurp His Excellency's position without Congress's approval?"

"No, they could not."

I can't help jumping in. "But it sounds like they could have it."

Harrison nods. "That was why I contrived with my good friend Henry Laurens, the president of Congress, to call a vote."

Now Benjamin looks impressed. "A bold gambit."

The older man chuckles and rubs his hands together. "Indeed. We were certain the Massachusetts and Pennsylvania delegates would vote to remove Washington, but others, particularly from the south, would want to keep him. We needed but seven states to vote our way, and this winter we have not seen a quorum of delegates in session."

I voice what I've already concluded. "But had the vote gone against Washington, the troops might have mutinied. If word of confusion or dissention reached Howe, the British could have launched a devastating attack on Valley Forge."

Harrison nods. "I suspected you had a head for this kind of intrigue, missus—and I mean that with the utmost respect. The vote was meant to quiet the rumblings—for should those rumblings reach the ears of the French, they could back out of the proposed alliance. Without their aid, we will have little chance to defeat the British. Should the polarized factions in Congress end up undermining the revolution, our conquerors shall have the opportunity to hang us all for our part in it." He chuckles. "If I meet my end at the gallows, I shall take comfort in one thing. For the size and weight of my body, I shall die in a few minutes, but less substantial men, like my esteemed colleague Mr. Elbridge Gerry, will dance in the air an hour or two before he is dead."

Benjamin laughs at this, but I feel a cold finger of dread run down my spine. "That's small comfort, sir."

"Ah, but the day we met, Missus Stone, I had just received word from Laurens the vote to remove Washington failed. I was exultant, believing the situation quashed for good and all. As I made my way home, I came upon you in the crowd gathered in front of The Plough."

I turn to Benjamin. "Mr. Harrison escorted me to your aunt and uncle's house."

"I had no thought of using you as a courier when we met, for there was no need—and it was no trouble to see you to Samuel and Lydia's. What transpired after I returned to my own rooms made me seek your help.

"I was on my way upstairs when several of my roommates arrived. Mark me, I was well aware they wanted Washington replaced. They, in turn, knew of my close allegiance to the general and regarded me with suspicion."

"Are those the men I saw speak to you after you left me that night?"

"The same. When they came home from session, they never would have spoken freely had they known I was within. I stood at the head of the stairs, eavesdropping, and recognized Samuel Adams's voice as he demanded, 'Now what do you suggest we do?'

"Elbridge Gerry replied, 'I shan't be the one to tell Gates. Not in front of the crowd at the tavern. We must speak to him of this in private.'"

Just then, the tavern maid appears with our supper. I'm fair jumping out of my chair, waiting for Mr. Harrison to resume the story as she sets down our plates. The moment she departs I ask, "What happened next?"

He chuckles. "At that Adams said, 'No. We must not speak to him of it at all. Washington will not go. He must be pushed. We dispatch the Board of War's delegation to Valley Forge with a letter giving them leave to remove Washington from command.'"

Benjamin sets down his glass. "But how could they maintain that charade? Surely the truth would come out."

"Ah, James Lovell of Massachusetts would agree with you. He complained that there had been trickery involved during the vote—which was true—and worried that one of Washington's allies in Congress would send word ahead of the Board of War. He read my next move.

"At that, Gerry said, 'We'll put out men to intercept any couriers or post riders traveling east tomorrow.' Adams agreed and decided the matter. 'By the time the truth reaches Washington, he'll be too humiliated to demand his commission back. Mark my words—he'll scarper with his tail between his legs before any other dispatch can reach him. Now, let's hie us back to the tavern and toast our new commander in chief.'"

Rage simmers within me at their treachery. "They seem to hate Washington so!"

Harrison pats my hand. "Ah, do you perceive the fears and prejudices of Yankee tradesmen against gentlemen sprung from good Virginia soil? No. It is not that. Replacing generals who perform poorly is not untoward. That is the way of things—but at that moment in our negotiations with France, changing generals, especially in this fashion, would have proved disastrous.

"Once I was certain they were departed, I hastened to write of what I'd heard to Washington and went in search of your assistance."

"So is the trouble over, sir?"

"Nay. I daresay it is not until we finalize the Franco-American alliance and the troops have the supplies they need."

I've not yet touched my food, and now, as we eat, the conversation dies. I let my eyes rove the room and the ever-flustered serving maid draws my attention. As she heads toward the kitchen, I blot my lips with my napkin. "If you gentlemen will excuse me for a moment."

30

Lafayette's Toast

B oth men rise as I leave the table and I hasten to follow the girl into the kitchen. "Miss? May I help you?"

She looks confused to see me. "Help how, missus?"

"I confess I'd dearly love to lay eyes on the Marquis. When I left Virginia, one of my cousins teased that I would meet him, and I cannot pass up the opportunity to carry home a detailed account of him. I can help you wait table at the general's, if you like. I'm no stranger to such work."

"All right, missus. 'Tis true, I could use an extra set of hands. Follow me." We take trays of covered dishes from the kitchen and she leads me outside and into a house adjacent to the tavern. "General Gates rents this house. He holds all his banquets upstairs."

In the large, open room on the second floor of Gates's residence, a dozen men, many in uniform, occupy the banquet table. I hasten to clear away all the empty platters and the plates and silver from the first course, while the tavern maid goes behind me setting out fresh ones before we serve the lighter fare of fruit tarts, cheeses, jellies, and creams.

The quantity of empty bottles on the sideboard and the floor indicate the men have been drinking quite a lot, though they do not behave in the rowdy manner I've witnessed in my travels. Everyone here is holding something in check, strategizing, waiting for others to reveal their intentions. I recognize both Gates and Lafayette, at opposite ends of the table. The serving girl was right. The slender young Frenchman has heavy-lidded eyes and an aristocratic profile. His high, sloping forehead and long nose would make him appear haughty even if his countenance did not reflect his displeasure.

Gates, red-faced and corpulent, has his cronies gathered around him at the foot of the table, in the host's place. Conway must have left Valley Forge before we did, for he occupies a seat near Gates. I wonder which is Mifflin and wish I could take his food and leave him hungry, as he has done to my loved ones.

Someone raises a toast to the Canadian expedition. After it is drunk, Lafayette, in the guest of honor's place, remains on his feet. He is used to commanding men much older than he is and as the room falls silent, I also pause and listen.

"Gentlemen, there is one you have forgotten. I propose a toast to our commander in chief General Washington. May he remain at the head of the army until we win independence."

The men raise their glasses, but I can tell most of them do it out of obligation. Some murmur Washington's name and take small sips. Others lower their glasses without partaking and drop their eyes to avoid Lafayette's stare, which he now directs at Gates.

"General, if I accept command of the Canadian expedition, it will be with conditions. I prefer General McDougall or the Baron de Kalb as my second in command over General Conway. I will have two million in scrip and two hundred thousand in gold and silver, plus enough to commission six French officers of my choosing."

Conway sets down his glass with a thump. Gates reaches out and lays a hand on his arm to check his response and the little man pulls away and folds his arms on his chest. Lafayette's gaze drifts across the table. "General Mifflin, I require your guarantee, as quartermaster, that ample stores, uniforms, and provisions are ready for the men before I will consider invading Canada in winter. At present, the men are underfed and inadequately dressed, even for a summer campaign."

So that one was Mifflin. I told Rhoda it was the quartermaster and the commissary's job to feed the soldiers and now I look with hatred at the man who lacked the courage to visit Valley Forge and see what his lack of care has wrought. Every wife and mother of a soldier should curse his name. He made it necessary for me to carry food hundreds of miles to sustain my family, while other soldiers without such help fared worse.

The kitchen maid pulls at my sleeve, but I do not budge. This may be my only opportunity to see a moment that will make history firsthand.

Lafayette is not finished. The men grouped around the table poise for whatever stroke comes next. "Finally, General, I will not correspond directly with the Board of War, but you may be sure I will send copies of any letters addressed to General Washington, my commander in chief."

When I do leave the room, I feel the smile spread over my face.

Back in The Plough, Benjamin greets me as I come out of the kitchen and together, we return to the table where Harrison waits. "Where have you been? I looked everywhere for you."

I smile my thanks as he holds my chair for me. "I was next door, at General Gates's dinner party."

Harrison gives a hearty laugh and slaps his thigh. "You are slippery as an eel, Madam. How did you gain entry to the feast?"

Trembling with excitement, I sound like a giddy girl. "I offered to help clear away the dishes. I actually laid eyes on the Marquis de Lafayette!"

Harrison nods his approval as he rises. "Now that you've had a look at the Frenchman, I hope you'll choose to leave intrigue behind, missus. I must take leave and finish packing. We will make an early start tomorrow, I trust. Good night to you both."

Benjamin and I linger over the rest of the Madeira. On our walk back to Uncle Samuel and Aunt Lydia's, he asks, "Will I be able to keep you at home after this? Or will you show up out of the blue while we're in the thick of the summer campaign?"

I stop on the boardwalk and take both his hands in mine. "Benjamin, I love you, our children, and our life together, but honestly, traveling and having the liberty to do as I pleased has made this one of the most exciting times in my life. I daresay it will keep you on your toes if I leave you wondering whether I'll turn up."

"I told you when I proposed I wanted coming home to mean coming home to you."

I kiss him right there, with no care for being in public. "Perhaps I won't be able to wait for you to return to me. Of everything I experienced on the road, the best moment of all was finding you at the end of my journey."

Epilogue[1]

My Father's name was Benjamin Stone. His Father's name was Thomas. His Mother's name was Mary Butler. My Mother's name was Anna Asbury. Her Father's name was George. Her Mother's name was Hannah Hardwick.

My father served two terms in the Revolutionary War.

I was born in Fauquier County Virginia on June 23, 1781. My father returned home from the war for the final time on the night previous to my birth. I joined my siblings Rhoda, Elijah, William, Hannah, and Polly, and was followed in due course by Anna, Benjamin, Thomas, Eleanor, and Rebecca.[2]

---

1. Adapted from the writings of Jeremiah Asbury Stone, Benjamin and Anna's third son, and other historical records.

2. The actual birth order of Benjamin and Anna's children is unconfirmed.

Father and Mother were true American Patriots. My Father was a Baptist preacher in high repute among the Baptists and many others. Very many were added to the church through his instrumentality.

In 1794 our family moved to Fayette County, Pennsylvania, west of Uniontown. Here a great revival took place in the church over which my Father was Pastor, which lasted two or three years and spread to other churches. The community was generally awakened and during this Revival my two older Brothers, Elijah and William, and my youngest Brother, Thomas, were brought into the Baptist faith.

My Father believed that ignorance produces more evils than any other thing, for ignorance is the mother of prejudice and bigotry. Ignorance makes bad statesmen, bad laws, bad administrators, bad schoolteachers, bad preachers, bad parents, and children who become bad citizens. Ignorance boasts of its liberty while it is a slave to itself.

— Jeremiah Asbury Stone (1781–1853)

Afterword

*A*nswering *Liberty's Call* is based on *The Story of Anna Asbury Stone.* Harriet Lura Bassett Stone, the first historian of the Anna Asbury Stone Chapter of the National Society Daughters of the American Revolution, penned the tale of Anna's ride to Valley Forge in 1923—a century and a half after the events it described transpired.

Harriet and her sister, Mary Augusta Stone, founded the chapter named for their great-great-grandmother. Orphaned as teens, they were raised by their grandfather, Benjamin Butler Stone (1812–1891), a son of Benjamin and Anna's son Jeremiah. Because Benjamin and Anna lived out their final years in Jeremiah's home, young Benjamin heard stories of his grandparents' youth directly from them and passed them down to his own grandchildren.

My genealogical and historical research revealed some discrepancies in *The Story of Anna Asbury Stone*—mostly the kind that occur when a story is handed down over time. What I learned from that research also helped to shape the story and fill in more detail. For instance, the first "fact" presented in the list below is incorrect, because George Asbury died in September 1758, nearly twenty years before Benjamin prepared to depart with the army.

According to *The Story of Anna Asbury Stone*:

- Benjamin, a young Baptist preacher, deposited Anna and their three small children at her father's house when he left to fight in the Continental Army.

- When Anna learned of the privations at Valley Forge, she packed what she could carry on her fine saddle horse, Nelly, and set out through hostile territory, leaving the children in the care of her parents.
- In York, Pennsylvania, she stopped for the night at the home of her cousin. There, Congressional delegate William Harrison asked her to carry a message to General Washington warning of a conspiracy against him.
- The next morning, as Anna continued eastward, a man on horseback barred her way, saying Harrison changed his mind and demanded she give him the letter.
- She refused and eluded him until she reached the picket line, where she delivered the letter enabling Washington to thwart his enemies' plot.
- Anna presented the commander in chief with one of her stockings she filled with salt.
- Washington assigned Benjamin to the detail leaving to fetch Lady Washington from Mount Vernon, so he could escort Anna back to Virginia.
- She and Benjamin spent the Sabbath visiting the sick before departing for Virginia.

I ran into a much larger obstacle when I was unable to substantiate Benjamin's military service.

Author Elizabeth Berg wrote that discrepancies discovered during research are the bane of the nonfiction writer and bliss for the novelist. Discrepancies leave us free to pick and choose and imagine the story, and that is how I approached the writing of this book. Before I began, I had to answer two important questions:

1. What motivated Anna to make the journey?
2. What was in the letter she carried to General Washington?

I found answers to both questions in the facts I unearthed.

What Motivated Anna to Make the Journey?

Anna's girlhood experiences undoubtedly shaped her into the kind of woman who would make that daring journey to Valley Forge.

When her father died intestate at age thirty-eight, he owned no land. The court-ordered inventory of his household goods and stock valued his estate at fifty pounds or about nine thousand dollars, adjusted for inflation.[3] Hannah Asbury and her children would have been plunged into poverty. Colonial-era widows were hobbled by laws which made it nearly impossible to support themselves and stripped them of their rights to manage their children's futures. The law declared any child whose father was dead an orphan and in need of a court-appointed male guardian to manage their inheritance, education, and in the case of females, dowry.[4] If a woman's late husband was too poor to assure she and her children were not going to become a public charge, she had no power to prevent the children from being taken away from her and bound out to strangers.[5]

Aware of the kinds of hardships Anna would have faced as a child, I portrayed her as a woman who sought both security and freedom. In the novel, she finds what she craves in her marriage to Benjamin Stone—only to have it threatened by the events of the war. I now understood Anna's motivation. She knew firsthand how difficult life could be for widows and orphans and would have moved heaven and earth to save her children from that fate.

What Was in the Letter?

In the winter of 1777–8, General George Washington and his inner circle of officers suspected a conspiracy was afoot. Disaffected officers

---

3. Eric W. Nye, *Pounds Sterling to Dollars: Historical Conversion of Currency*, accessed Wednesday, December 25, 2019, https://www.uwyo.edu/numimage/currency.htm.

4. "This Helpless Human Tide: Bastards, Abandoned Babes, and Orphans," https://www.history.org/Foundation/journal/Autumn14/orphans.cfm

5. William M. Stone, *The Chronicle of Thomas Stone of Hamilton Parish in Colonial Virginia*, Second Edition (Lenox, MA: Published by the Author, 2017), 204–5.

and disgruntled members of Congress aimed to remove Washington and make General Horatio Gates, the so-called hero of the Battle of Saratoga, commander in chief.[6]

The British General Howe, wintering in luxury in occupied Philadelphia, also exerted his influence as he rubbed elbows with Tory and Quaker businessmen at social gatherings. When the talk turned to resuming transatlantic trade, Howe suggested a general like Gates, who might be willing to negotiate a surrender and a return to Crown rule, would help get things back to business as usual.[7]

Years after the fact, a delegate to the Second Continental Congress hinted that the proceedings against Washington would never be revealed: "As the old Congress daily sat with closed doors, the public knew no more of what passed within that it was deemed expedient to disclose."[8]

But Washington, who had plenty of allies in Congress, the support of his trusted officers, and the adoration of the enlisted men, would not be easily dislodged.

Unable to make a direct run at the commander in chief, the faction built up its power base by appointing Gates, General Thomas Conway, and General Thomas Mifflin to the Board of War. Though the Board was created to support the commander in chief and the war effort, by 1777 it had become a vehicle for bureaucratic posturing and critical remarks endangering those actually engaged in the fighting.

Gates, "a man whose vanity was eclipsed only by his arrogance,"[9] formed a close alliance with Conway, Mifflin, and other officers who were "disaffected toward Washington."[10] Conway, eager to stir the pot,

---

6. Keith Krawczynski, *History in Dispute, Vol. 12: The American Revolution* (Detroit, MI: Thomson Gale, 2003), 96.

7. Ibid., 242–43.

8. Ibid.,137–38.

9. George R. Prowell, *Continental Congress at York, Pennsylvania and York County in the Revolution* (York, PA: The York Printing Co., 1914), 331.

10. Ibid.

wrote in a letter to Gates, "Heaven has determined to save your Country; or a weak General and bad Counsellors would have ruined it."[11]

The contents of Conway's letter got back to Washington, who sent the quote back to Conway without additional comment.[12]

Sir, a letter which I received last Night, contained the following paragraph. In a Letter from Genl Conway to Genl Gates he says— "Heaven has been determined to save your Country; or a weak General and bad Councellors would have ruind it." I am Sir Yr Hble Srvt.

*— George Washington
to Thomas Conway November 5, 1777*[13]

Washington's action caused a flurry of panic and squabbling between Gates and Conway. Gates backpedaled and wrote to Washington, asking for help in "tracing out the author of the infidelity which put extracts from General Conway's letters to me into your hands."[14] He denied affiliation with Conway or any "faction."[15]

Lieutenant Colonel John Laurens, Washington's aide-de-camp and son of Henry Laurens, then-president of Congress, wrote to his father and complained that Conway and Mifflin intended to remove Washington, and added, "I hope some virtuous and patriotic men will form

11. Krawczynski, *History in Dispute*, 97.

12. William Dunlap, *A History of New York, for Schools in Two Volumes. Vol. II* (New York: Collins, Keese, & Co., 1837), 154.

13. Mark Edward Lender, *Cabal! The Plot Against General Washington* (Yardley, PA: Westholme Publishing, LLC, 2019), 73.

14. Ibid.

15. Ibid.,154.

a Countermine to blow up this pernicious Junto."[16] Of those involved in the cabal, Mifflin did the most damage to the war effort that winter when he walked away from his duties as quartermaster.[17] The department disintegrated, leaving "wagons abandoned everywhere, while commissaries begged for them and the purchased food spoiled. Hospitals went without wood to keep sick men warm. Hundreds of barrels of flour [were] abandoned on the banks of the Susquehanna River."[18] Horrified, Laurens wrote, "Perhaps there was an even more sinister goal: to throw everything into confusion and bring in the ancient rule." By that, he meant George III of England.[19]

That January, Washington's opponents in Congress moved to send a committee to Valley Forge to arrest the commander in chief. The motion would have been adopted had not Washington's opponents unexpectedly lost their majority.[20]

Which Founding Fathers Were Part of the Cabal?

Author/historians Thomas Fleming and Mark Edward Lender both name John Adams, Samuel Adams, James Lovell, Benjamin Rush, Elbridge Gerry, Francis Dana, and Richard Henry Lee as those in Congress most opposed to Washington.

John Adams declared mid-1777, "things would not improve until we shoot a general."[21] After Gates's victory at Saratoga, Adams told his wife, Abigail, "Now we can allow a certain citizen to be wise, virtuous, and good, without thinking him a deity or savior."[22]

John Adams and Dr. Benjamin Rush, both of whom supported Washington's appointment to commander in chief, only to become

16. Krawczynski, *History in Dispute*, 98.
17. Lender, *Cabal!*, 84.
18. Ibid., 92.
19. Ibid., 127.
20. George Reeser Prowell, *History of York County, Pennsylvania* (Chicago, IL: J. H. Beers & Co., 1907), 140.
21. Ibid.,101.
22. Ibid.

two of his most vocal detractors, were away on committee assignment that winter and were not directly involved in the cabal.

Though Anna's story did not name the conspirators, it named William Harrison as Washington's ally in Congress. But William Henry Harrison, who would become the ninth president of the United States, was a lad of four when Anna made her ride to Valley Forge. She may have encountered William Henry Harrison's father, statesman Benjamin Harrison (1726–1791) in York. The elder Harrison, a Signer of the Declaration, a member of the House of Burgesses, and a delegate to the Second Continental Congress, was a strong ally of Washington and Henry Laurens.

Forewarned by Harrison's message, Washington and Alexander Hamilton met the Board of War's delegation—which did not include Gates—with a sixteen-thousand-word report documenting the problems at Valley Forge and outlining solutions. In the absence of Gates's influence, the Board of War's delegation was soon convinced Washington's pleas for assistance were genuine.

After the delegation returned from Valley Forge, Congress, in possession of letters of support from the majority of Washington's officers, was forced to stand by him. Gates and Conway appeared duplicitous and foolish, and the movement to unseat Washington lost its steam.[23]

Benjamin Stone: Patriot and Preacher

When my research failed to turn up records to substantiate Benjamin's military service, I set out to build a case in support of it.

Prior to the American Revolution, no British colony was more protective of its established [Anglican] church, nor more abusive of its religious dissenters, than Virginia.[24] Benjamin's close association with

23. US History online, *The Conway Cabal*. www.ushistory.org/march/other/cabal.htm

24. John A. Ragosta, *Wellspring of Liberty: How Virginia's Religious Dissenters Helped Win the American Revolution and Secured Religious Liberty* (Oxford, England: Oxford University Press, 2010), 3.

some of the better-known outlaw Baptists of the pre-Revolutionary era lends credence to him taking up arms to fight for independence from the Crown.

Histories of the area detail a Baptist revolt against paying taxes to support Anglican parishes in Fauquier and Culpeper counties, with Elijah Craig as its leader. Benjamin Stone was heavily influenced by Craig, so much so he named his first son Elijah Craig Stone.[25]

Benjamin and his brother, Thomas, signed the Ten Thousand Names Petition, sent to the Virginia Assembly in October 1776 demanding an end to compulsory tithes to the Anglican Church and religious equality so, "internal animosities may cease."[26] The Virginia Baptists realized the fight for independence could lead to the religious liberty they craved—and they agreed to encourage enlistment in exchange for religious liberty at the war's end.[27] Baptist ministers like Benjamin Stone were willing to fight for their place within Virginia's religious establishment.[28]

Why Are Revolutionary War Military Records Incomplete?
No doubt Benjamin served in his local militia. All able-bodied men between sixteen and sixty were required to do so for the defense of their communities. Family lore says he volunteered for the Culpeper Minutemen. His name does not appear on their muster rolls—but those records are known to be incomplete.

A complete listing of the individuals who served in the Continental forces and the militia cannot be achieved.[29]

In the early days of the American Revolution, there was no repository for muster rolls and other military records. Some officers kept

---

25. Stone, *The Chronicle of Thomas Stone*, 94–95.
26. Ragosta, *Wellspring of Liberty*, 56.
27. Ibid., 89.
28. Ibid., 13, 92–93.
29. Wilmer L. Kerns, *Historical Records of Old Frederick and Hampshire Counties, Virginia (Revised)* (Bowle, MD: Heritage Books, Inc. 1982), 2–5.

records in their private homes long after the war ended. Requests to have such records turned in to government agencies yielded many documents that otherwise might have been lost forever. How many were unwittingly disposed of or destroyed will never be known.

Most records in War Department custody were destroyed by fire, November 8, 1800. More were lost during the War of 1812. In 1873 Secretary of War William Belknap purchased for the federal government the papers of Timothy Pickering, who between 1777 and 1785 was a member of the Board of War, Adjutant General of the Continental Army, and Quartermaster General; the papers of Samuel Hodgdon, Commissary General of Military Stores for several years during the war; and some minor groups of records and single record items. About that time, Congress authorized the transfer to the War Department of all military records for the Revolutionary War period then in the custody of other Executive branch departments.[30]

Government efforts to compile records from the Revolutionary War coincided with the founding of the National Society Daughters of the American Revolution. The NSDAR was founded on October 11, 1890, "during a time that was marked by a revival in patriotism and intense interest in the beginnings of the United States of America."[31]

According to records on file with the National Society Daughters of the American Revolution, descendants of Benjamin and Anna's children Elijah, William, Jeremiah, Mary (Polly) and Eleanor (Nelly) have sought DAR membership with Benjamin as their patriot ancestor. Though Benjamin's military service remains unsubstantiated, evidence that he served as a juror in Fauquier County in 1782 allows him to qualify as a civil servant and patriot who supported the American government.

Want to know more about Benjamin and Anna and the Conway Cabal? Visit Tracy's website: https://tracylawsonbooks.com/

30. National Archives online, War Department Collection of Revolutionary War Records, https://www.archives.gov/research/guide-fed-records/groups/093.html
31. NSDAR online, https://www.dar.org/national-society/about-dar/dar-history

For Additional Reading

Bates, Samuel Penniman, *History of Greene County, Pennsylvania.* Chicago: Nelson, Rishforth & Co., 1888.

Berkin, Carol. *Revolutionary Mothers: Women in the Struggle for American Independence.* New York, NY: Vintage Books, 2005.

Bodle, Wayne. *The Valley Forge Winter: Civilians and Soldiers in War.* University Park, PA: Penn State University Press, 2002.

Bulcock, James. *The Duties of a Lady's Maid, With Directions for Conduct, and Numerous Receipts for the Toilette.* London: Printed by C. Smith, 1823.

Döhla, Johann Conrad, translated and edited by Bruce E. Burgoyne. *A Hessian Diary of the American Revolution.* Norman, OK: Oklahoma University Press, 1990.

Dunlap, William. *A History of New York, for Schools in Two Volumes. Vol. II.* New York: Collins, Keese, & Co., 1837.

Ellet, Elizabeth F. *The Women of the American Revolution in Three Volumes.* New York, NY: Baker and Scribner, 1849.

Fleming, Thomas. *Washington's Secret War: The Hidden History of Valley Forge.* New York, NY: Harper Collins, 2005.

Harvey, Robert. *"A Few Bloody Noses": The Realities and Mythologies of the American Revolution.* New York, NY: Overlook Press, 2003.

Hening, William Waller. *The Statutes at Large; Being a Collection of All the Laws of Virginia From the First Session of the Legislature in the Year 1619.* Volume III. Philadelphia, PA: Printed by Thomas DeSilver, 1823.

Historical Society of York County, PA. *Proceedings and Collections of the Historical Society of York County, 1902–4.* Nabu Press, 2002.

Hawke, David Freeman. *Everyday Life in Early America*. New York, NY: Harper & Row, 1988.

Journals of the American Congress 1774–1788 in Four Volumes. Washington, DC: Way and Gideon, 1823.

Krawczynski, Keith. *History in Dispute, Vol. 12: The American Revolution*. Detroit, MI: Thomson Gale, 2003.

Lender, Mark Edward. *Cabal! The Plot Against General Washington*. Yardley, PA: Westholme Publishing, LLC, 2019.

Maxwell, Hu and H. L. Swisher. *History of Hampshire County, West Virginia, From Its Earliest Settlement Through the Present*. Morgantown, WV: A. Brown Boughner, Printer, 1897.

McAllister, J. T. *Virginia Militia in the Revolutionary War*. Hot Springs, VA: McAllister Publishing Co., 1913.

Meltzer, Brad and Josh Mensch. *The First Conspiracy: The Secret Plot to Kill George Washington*. New York, NY: Flatiron Books, 2018.

Norton, Mary Beth. *Liberty's Daughters: The Revolutionary Experience of American Women, 1750–1800*. Ithaca, NY: Cornell University Press, 1996.

Peters, Joan W. *The 1785 Fauquier County, Virginia Census: 12 Lists of Whites & Dwellings in Fauquier County, Virginia, 1785*. Published by the author, 1988.

———. *The Tax Man Cometh: Land and Property in Colonial Fauquier County, Virginia 1759-1782*. Westminster, MD: Willow Bend Books, 1999.

Prowell, George Reeser. *History of York County, Pennsylvania*. Chicago, IL: J. H. Beers & Co., 1907.

———. *Continental Congress at York, Pennsylvania and York County in the Revolution.* York, PA: The York Printing Co., 1914.

Russell, T. Triplett and John K. Gott. *Fauquier County in the Revolution.* Westminster, MD: Heritage Books, 2007.

Stone, William M., *The Chronicle of Thomas Stone of Hamilton Parish in Colonial Virginia and The Histories of His Sons Thomas of Virginia, William of North Carolina, and John of South Carolina.* Second Edition. Lenox, MA: Published by the Author, 2017.

Weeden, George. *Valley Forge Orderly Book of General George Weeden of the Continental Army Under Command of Genl; George Washington, In the Campaign of 1777–8.* London: Forgotten Books, 2015.

Wood, Gordon S. *Friends Divided: John Adams and Thomas Jefferson.* New York, NY: Penguin Books, 2017.

Lossing, Benson John, LLD, editor. *Harper's Encyclopædia of United States History from 458 A.D. to 1905.* New York, NY and London: Harper & Brothers, 1906.

Ragosta, John A., *Wellspring of Liberty: How Virginia's Religious Dissenters Helped Win the American Revolution and Secured Religious Liberty.* Oxford, England: Oxford University Press, 2010.

Acknowledgements

Many thanks to:

S usan Hughes of myindependenteditor.com. After editing five of my manuscripts, Susan has become more than an editor, and is a trusted friend.

Lissa Bryan, author and historian, for her early assessment of the manuscript and her encouragement.

Anna Bennett of Historical Editorial, who helped put the puzzle pieces of the story in the right order.

Robert Krenzel, author of the Gideon Hawke novels, for agreeing it would be fun for our characters to interact at Valley Forge. Readers can find Anna galloping up to the picket line in *A Bloody Day's Work*. The same scene plays out from Anna's perspective in *Answering Liberty's Call*.

Jane Baldwin, Alexandra Pearson, and Prema Propat, beta readers who gave thoughtful feedback to help shape and refine the book.

CPSIA information can be obtained
at www.ICGtesting.com
Printed in the USA
LVHW042054190322
713896LV00006B/13/J

9 781647 045388